I0579148

Revenge
of the Beast

M. Ward Leon

© Copyright 2021 M. Ward Leon
All rights reserved.

No portion of this book may be reproduced in whole or in part, by any means whatsoever, except for pas-sages excerpted for the purposes of review, without the prior written permission of the publisher.

For information, or to order additional
copies, please contact:

Beacon Publishing Group
P.O. Box 41573 Charleston, S.C. 29423
800.817.8480| beaconpublishinggroup.com

Publisher's catalog available by request.

ISBN-13: 978-1-949472-33-2

ISBN-10: 1-949472-33-2

Published in 2021. Printed in the USA.

First Edition. New York, NY 10001

For my Joanie, Meghan & Mika "the little dude"
Special thanks to Anne Hoppe

*100 million animals hunted and killed every year,
just in the United States.*

"Freeze! Drop your weapon and get on the ground, now!"

The man looked around and saw six police officers all pointing their guns at him. He slowly threw the Glock 9mm he was holding to his right and dropped onto the ground. He was quickly set upon by five of the officers who roughly pulled his arms behind his back, handcuffing him and punching him in the head as the sixth officer walked over and pressed his size 13 boot on the man's neck so hard that the man passed out.

When he regained consciousness, he found himself handcuffed to a pole attached to a cinderblock wall. In front of him was an old beat-up gray government issued metal desk with decades of coffee and bloodstains that reminded him of a Jackson Pollock painting.

Sitting across from him were a pair of what he assumed were detectives, dressed in cheap ill-fitting suits busy looking at their cell phones and not paying any attention to him until he said, "Where the fuck am I and why am I here?"

The older of the two without looking up replied, "Shut the fuck up, *mosono waago* (asshole) before we stomp the crap out of you."

"Look, just tell me what I'm being charged with."

The older detective put his cell phone down, pushed back his chair, got up with a sigh, walked over to the prisoner and slammed his head down onto the desk, breaking the man's nose. "I told you to shut up."

The younger cop, laughing got up and picked up a filthy rag laying the corner of the interrogation room, wiped his shoes off and threw it to the bleeding man. "Here, stop bleeding on my desk, *seaka* (bitch)!"

The injured man held the rag to his face with his free hand and sat silent waiting for the beating to begin. The door opened and a small woman walked in dressed in a business suit and told the two goons to get out. She sat down on the other side of the desk and announced, "I am Branch Commander Moyo of the Botswana Police Service, Mister Janssens? That is the alias that you're using, isn't it?"

"My name is Liam Janssens, and I don't know what you're referring to about an alias."

"Okay I'll play along; you are being held for murder."

"Murder? I didn't murder anyone, who am I supposed to have murdered?"

"The Bahlakwana brothers, from the Okavango Eden Safaris. We had a tip that someone from Le Gang de la Clé de Singe was coming here to assassinate the Bahlakwanas."

"Why would I kill the Bahlakwanas, they just hired me as their bodyguard, I have a signed contract back in my hotel room, which I'm sure your goons should have found by now, my only hope is that they haven't destroyed it so they can't railroad me to the gallows."

"Mr. Janssens," she said with a grin, "I would never tolerate any police misbehavior or misconduct under my command."

"No, just a little police brutality?"

"Oh, I am sorry about that, sometimes my people can get a little overly enthusiastic. I will have the prison nurse take a look at that once you've been processed. Now would you like talk to me?"

"No thank you, I think I would like to have the Belgium Consulate informed of my arrest, if that wouldn't be too much to ask and to speak with an attorney."

"I will contact the Belgium Consulate myself, personally."

"Can you tell me where I'm to be held?"

"Mahalapye prison." She said as she got up and went to the door, she signaled for two uniformed police officers waiting outside to come in and take him to Mahalapye. Branch Commander Moyo turned as Mr. Janssens was being handcuffed behind his back and said to the two officers, "There is to be no further mistreatment of this prisoner, is that understood?"

They both nodded as they led the prisoner down the hallway and out of the building.

Mahalapye Prison is located in the Central District of Botswana, the town of Mahalapye has a bus station, a railway station, a couple of hotels and a market area with many shops and fast-food restaurants, and it also has several petrol stations open 24 hours a day. It's as boring as the Kalahari Desert it sits on.

The two-hour drive from Gaborone to Mahalapye prison in the back of the Toyota HiAce mini-van was excruciating as the air condition was blowing hotter air inside the vehicle than the 101-degree air blowing outside the vehicle. Liam figured by the time they pulled him out of the van he had lost at least six pounds of sweat, he looked as if he had taken a dip in a pool.

There were four guards waiting to receive him by the main entrance, they were wearing blue prison guard uniforms, each armed with a holstered firearm and a sap neatly tucked away in a fitted pocket in their pants leg. Liam stood as the two officers who drove him there exchanged documents transferring him from Gaborone police custody to the custody of Mahalapye prison. Once the transfer formalities were over, he was led into the ochre-colored brick administration building where he was to be processed.

They marched into entrance hall straight to the registration desk where his personal possessions were collected, and a record was written down into the computer database. Then he was made to go through a strip search and given the traditional Mahalapye prisoners black & white striped uniform, a wafer-thin pillow, two bed sheets and an old worn-out gray blanket, none of which had seen the inside of a washing machine in months.

He was assigned his prison inmate number, which he was required to learn, as that is what he will be referred to for as long as he is in their custody, inmate number 1011045. After an hour of processing, he was then taken to his cell where he was introduced to his cellmate, inmate 1007942, Baruti to his friends. As they proceeded down the corridors he was welcomed with the typical catcalls, threats and taunting at the 'new fish'.

Baruti was serving a fifteen to twenty year stretch for armed robbery. He was an imposing figure, at six feet five and weighing over 280 pounds, shaved head and the body of a weightlifter, so when Liam saw him, he knew that depending how the next ten minutes went this could either be a good situation or a living Hell.

The guards slammed the cell door shut and walked away. Baruti got up from lying on the bottom bunk when they were alone; he walked up to Liam and peered down at the five-foot ten-inch white man and said, "What ya in for, *mkunda*?"

Liam knew that this was either where he would get some respect or end up getting beaten to a pulp and made this guy's bitch, he stared up at the giant and said matter of factly, "Murder. You?"

"Bullshit, you ain't no fucking murderer."

"Murder."

"Who did you kill?"

"Three brothers named Bahlakwana." Liam said, then looked around and said half smiling, "Of course, I'm innocent."

That brought a big grin to the big man's face, "Yeah, you and everyone else in here. Me too."

"They think I'm a member of Le Gang de la Clé de Singe."

"Who the fuck are they?"

"They're a group of badass assassins who go around killing poachers and folks who have anything to do with big game hunting."

"And you're one of these baddass assassins?"

"Alleged badass."

"Right."

"So, what are you in here for?"

"Armed robbery. I'm halfway thru a fifteen to twenty. What did you get, life?"

"Nothing yet. They sent me here to await my trail."

"Where you from, you're not from here. Where you from?"

"Belgium. My name is Liam, and you are?"

"Baruti. Say, what happened to your face?"

"Les flics. The police."

"Fucking *mosono waagos*. They're all pigs.

"They said they'd get me to a nurse."

"Yeah, that ain't gonna happen. Unless you pay, you got money?"

"They took everything when they processed me in here, my money, watch, everything.

"Well my friend you can kiss all that good bye. Your watch is being worn by one of the guards right now."

"Fuck that shit, I should be seeing the Belgium consul tomorrow, hopefully he can help."

The Honorary Belgium Consul Simon Van Den Broeck arrived at Mahalapye Prison at 10a.m., upon his arrival he was shown into a private visitation room where Liam Janssens was waiting. Liam sat on one side of a large wooden desk and Consul Simon Van Den Broeck took the chair opposite him. There was a guard present in the room and left as soon as Consul Simon Van Den Broeck asked to be alone with Mr. Janssens.

"Thank you for coming."

"Good morning, I am Consul Simon Van Den Broeck. Mr. Janssens, I sorry to tell you there isn't a whole lot that I can do for you at this point." He said as he removed a pencil and legal pad from his brown leather attaché case.

"Well, can you help secure me a lawyer? I want the best criminal attorney in the country, money is no object."

"Yes, of course. That would be Mr. Hilton Tebogo. He is considered to be the Clarence Darrow of Botswana. He's the best. He has a Bachelor's of Laws Degree from the University of Botswana and advanced Certificate in International Human Rights Law from Oxford University, United Kingdom."

"Great. Thank you."

"Are you being treated all right? What happened to your face?"

"Yeah, I'm doing okay, as far as my face is concerned, some goon at the Gaborone Police Station smashed my head onto a desktop for laughs."

"I will be sure to lodge a complaint with the Gaborone authorities."

"Forget it, but I would like my possessions back that they stole from me when I was checked in last night."

"I'll speak with the Warden before I leave, but it is understood that personal possessions such as jewelry, credit cards, and cell phones are not permitted, however I'll see to it that you get your money back. I'm sure that it will be of some use to you in here. I do think you should have the nurse take a look your nose."

"Thank you no, it's actually a kind of badge of honor in here, if you know what I mean."

"Of course. However, I must tell you Mr. Janssens that the whole world is watching this case with great interest, as you are allegedly connected with an infamous eco-terrorist group. I've got to say, unless you can somehow distance yourself from that organization, I fear your situation might be perilous. Is there anything that I can bring you?"

"I could really go for a couple of six-packs of Westvleteren 12."

The Consul smiled and said, "You and me both."

"Well then, I want to thank you for the advice and for coming."

"Sit tight while I speak to the warden about your possessions." As he passed the officer standing guard outside the door Liam heard him tell the man that he was coming back in a few minutes and that the prisoner should be allowed to stay until he returned.

Liam sat there until Consul Broeck returned with his money. The Consul handed Liam the small wad of cash and said, "Here you are, and they won't let you have your watch or cell phone, prison rules. I'll see about checking in on you in a couple of days. Goodbye Liam, good luck and stay safe."

"Thanks Consul Broeck."

Shortly after the Consul left the guard came into the room and escorted him back to his cell.

M. Ward Leon

Le Gang de la Clé de Singe took its name from the American writer Edward Abbey's novel 'The Monkey Wrench Gang', the story is a fictional account of four environmental warriors liberating parts of Utah and Arizona from evil road-builders, miners, and rednecks. Le Gang de la Clé de Singe was formed in Paris by two brothers whose father was the CEO of the French oil giant Elf, that was involved in the Great Oil Sniffer Hoax of 1979.

Jean Paul and Philippe Renault were two spoiled rich kids wanting to shake up the establishment and piss off their father all at the same time. They started out with some college friends by organizing protest marches, which grew more and more violent, as the oil scandal grew larger so did the movement. Eventually, there were clashes with riot police who would fire off tear gas and rubber bullets, then they started making arrests as the protesters fought back. Some protesters began throwing rocks and bottles and some Molotov Cocktails.

Soon the police response escalated to the use of live ammunition, resulting in the deaths of dozens of protesters, some as young as fourteen. The Renault brothers never dreamed what started out, as just a way to piss their father off would evolve into a movement of international outrage. Over time they extricated themselves out of the group as Le Gang de la Clé de Singe became more and more militant and violent. They unwittingly achieved their goals beyond their wildest dreams.

Liam was walking the general population yard feeling relatively safe, unlike most other prisons in Africa; Botswana prides itself on limited gang violence. Their prison's largest fault is overcrowding, Liam was lucky because, being a foreign national and still awaiting trial he was not subjected to a cell with multiple cellmates. Baruti spotted him walking by the group of men he was hanging out with and called him over, "Hey *Brayaka*! Over here."

Liam stopped and looked behind himself to see whom Baruti was calling out to and then back at Baruti who was now gesturing for him to come, which he did.

"I'm sorry, I wasn't sure who you were speaking to. What did you call me?"

Baruti smiled and said, "*Brayaka*, it means my brother. I want to meet some friends of mine."

The men were all seated at a wooden picnic style table smoking and joking and they all stopped as Liam approached. Baruti stood and put his arm around the little white man, "That's Seth, Gaone, Kym and Kabo. This is the fella I was telling you all about. He's the one who killed the Bahlakwana brothers."

Liam held up his hands, "Allegedly killed."

The man named Seth who's sporting a large Afro straight out of the1960's stared at Liam and asked, "What's that mean, allegedly?"

"I'm not admitting to anything, all I need is for someone to hear me admit that I killed these Bahlakwana boys am I'm fucked."

"Are you saying we'd grass you out to the police?"

"Now you heard everything I just said, and I never said that you would grass me out to the police, did I? All I said was I'm not admitting to anything."

The man stood up defiantly and took a step towards Liam. Liam stood his ground; he knew that at some point he would have to prove himself, he was ready. Baruti trying to calm things down stepped in between the two and said, "Hey, Seth did you ever hear of a terrorist group called Le Gang de la Clé de Singe?"

"No, I never did." Seth replied still eyeballing the new fish.

"Well, they be a group of real bad motherfuckers, ain't that right Liam?"

"Oh yeah, Le Gang de la Clé de Singe, The Monkey Wrench Gang were originally formed to combat large corporations that go around fucking up the environment, but recently they have decided to go after poachers, big game hunters and safari outfits like the Bahlakwanas, they'll kill anyone who they find to be guilty."

"Well my brother Dineo Wengazi is a big time poacher, he kill many a beast and no one better mess with him." Seth had a great big smile on his face and was beaming with pride when he realized that he may have screwed up,

"What a minute are you a member of this gang that kills poachers? Because if anything happen to Dineo you are a dead man."

"Did I say I was a member, I never said that I was a member of anything. I was just telling you about this gang that goes around killing poachers and hunters is all." He said appealing to the others sitting on the bench.

They all nodded and Baruti said, "That's right Seth, you got to ease up man. We're just talking."

Seth wasn't convinced, "What is it you do, man?"

"I'm a bodyguard, I was hired by the Bahlakwana brothers to protect them from this gang, but they killed him and now the police think that I did it."

"I guess you're not much of a bodyguard, cause you're in here."

Baruti jokingly said, "He's as much of a bodyguard as you are a bank robber, cause you're in here, too." Which brought the group to laughing and teasing. Even Seth lightened up, after that with that Liam seemed to be accepted into the group.

Commander Moyo was in her office talking on the phone to State Prosecutor Letsego Pule about the Bahlakwana case when her assistant handed her a note telling her that there were two Interpol inspectors waiting to see her. She covered the phone receiver with her hand and whispered to him, "Tell them to come in."

When he left the room, she said to State Prosecutor Pule, "Can I call you back Letsego. I have two Interpol inspectors here to see me; I'm assuming it's about Janssens. I'll call you back as soon as I'm finished with them. Okay, goodbye."

There was a knock on the door, "Come in."

The officer opened the door and entered the room followed by two very pasty looking gentlemen wearing identical well-fitting black suits. They could almost pass as twins with the exception that one wore black-rimmed glasses. She thought to herself, the one with the glasses is definitely a Brit. She stood and extended her hand.

"Gentlemen, please come in and have a seat. I'm Branch Commander Moyo of the Botswana Police Service, how can I be of service?"

The man with the glasses spoke, "Thank you for taking the time to see us Branch Commander, I'm Inspector Morris from London and this is Inspector Volker from South Africa. We're from Interpol and are very much interested in a man in your custody, Mr. Liam Janssens, as we believe that he very well may be a member of Le Gang de la Clé de Singe. We think he may be the high-ranking member known as Icarus."

The other man, Inspector Volker said, "A real nasty character, to be sure. We would like to have the opportunity to speak with him, if that's all right with you."

"Yes of course, as you know we've had problems with Le Gang de la Clé de Singe in the past. But it has usually been a hit and split attack on hunters and not so bizarre and blatant. Although, I must admit this was a rather gruesome offense."

"Just the sort of headline grabbing deed that they are known for." Morris said.

Branch Commander Moyo picked up the receiver of her desk phone and said, "Sergeant, call Warden Samuels over at Mahalapye Prison and tell him that Inspectors Morris and Volker from Interpol will be coming to interview Liam Janssens this afternoon and if he has any questions to call me. Thank you." She hung up the phone and asked, "Is there anything else I can do for you gentlemen?"

Volker smiled and asked, "May we review you files on the case?"

"Yes of course. Just ask the sergeant for a copy on your way out."

The man and woman from Le Gang de la Clé de Singe Rodin and Isala were traveling under the names Oscar Alberink with Anna Rooijakkers. Both are traveling in disguise, like all members of the gang, Interpol, M16, CIA, FBI, GRU, MSS, BND, and DGSE they're wanted internationally.

They had boarded the 2:15pm Botswana BR Express train leaving Bulawayo, Zimbabwe scheduled to arrive Gaborone, Botswana at 5:45p.m.

They're posing as Liam Janssens Belgium legal representatives and will be working in concert with his Batswana attorney Hilton Tebogo.

The locals call the Botswana BR Express 'Big Blue' not just because the outside of the train is painted blue, but all the seats are blue, the carpeting is blue and even the porters, conductors and engineers all wear blue uniforms.

The journey started out in the Bulawayo, the second largest city in Zimbabwe and traveled south thru the subtropical region transitioning into the hot semi-arid climate of Gaborone.

Upon their arrival in Gaborone Central Railway Station, they found Mr. Hilton Tebogo holding a sign on the platform 'Alberink & Rooijakkers.' After a short greeting, he led them to his car, a white Mercedes Benz C220 with license plates that read NTGUILTY.

Oscar nodded approvingly and said, "Mr. Tebogo, I like your style."

"Thank you, sir. He said smiling, as he held the passenger side rear door for Ms. Rooijakkers.

As Tebogo headed north on Nelson Mandela Drive then veering left onto Molepoloe Road he asked, "You folks are staying at the Peermont Walmont is that correct?"

"That is correct." Replied Oscar.

As Hilton looked back into the rearview mirror at Anna he said, "Is this your first time in Botswana, Ms. Rooijakkers?"

"Anna please and yes, it is my first time."

"Well, I want to welcome you and I am looking forward in working with you both, Anna and…"

Oscar interrupted by asking, "Mr. Hilton, as are we, looking forward in assisting you in the defense of Mr. Janssens. What are your initial thoughts of the case?"

"Oh, I feel that we have a solid case, and I was hoping to bring you up to speed when we get to your hotel if that is satisfactory with you both?"

"That would be excellent." Rodin said.

Liam Janssens was walking the perimeter of the general population yard for the eighth time when an officer approached him, "Prisoner 1011045, come with me."

"Where are we going?"

"The warden wants to see you."

They passed by the cellblocks that houses over a thousand prisoners, the mess hall / kitchen, two metal shops, and made their way to the administration building at the front of the prison complex. When they entered the Admin Building, they climbed four flights of stairs to Warden Samuels office. As they entered the guard told Liam to have a seat on the wooden bench next to the door they just came in as the guard continued to the secretary's desk and announced their presence. "Guard Mmusi and prisoner 1011045 as requested."

The secretary didn't bother to look up from the Botswana newspaper she was reading, she reached over and pressed the intercom button and announced, "Guard Mmusi and prisoner 1011045 are here to see you."

A tinny scratchy little voice emitted from the black plastic box, "Send them in."

As the secretary turned the page of the paper she said, "He'll see you now."

The guard turned to the man sitting on the bench and didn't say a word just gestured for him to get up and follow him, which Liam did. As Liam got further into the wardens' office, he noticed two white men dressed in identical black suits sitting at a small conference table with Warden Samuels. He knew them to be Interpol.

The guard led Liam over to where the three men were seated. The warden stood and gestured for Liam to have a seat and then he said, "Thank you Guard Mmusi, please wait outside, I'll call you when we're through."

Liam did as he was told; he sat down opposite the two strangers. The man who was wearing glasses without emotion and matter of factly said, "Mr. Janssens, I am Inspector Morris, and this is Inspector Volker, we're from Interpol."

Liam looked at them both for a long time, as if studying them, and then said, "I would like to see some identification, please."

That took Morris and Volker back. Most prisoners never ask for ID, they're too shit scared and intimidated, but not Janssens. He's a real cool character. Both Morris and Volker reached into their suit jackets and produced their ID's. Liam looked at each one carefully and then asked, "What does Interpol want with me?"

Morris smiled, "We're here to make you a one-time offer Mr. Janssens. It's only good for right now and once you walk out that door this offer walks out with you. Interested?"

Liam sat for the longest time, looking between the two Interpol inspectors before answering. "No."

Volker who was surprised said, "No?"

"No." Liam turned to Warden Samuels and asked, "May I go now?"

Before the warden could answer, Volker queried, "You're not in the least bit interested in hearing the offer?"

"No. Not in the least. Warden?"

The warden nodded and called out for the guard. Guard Mmusi entered the room, "Guard Mmusi take the prisoner back to his cell." Liam stood, pushed his chair in towards the conference table and walked out with Guard Mmusi close behind leaving the men from Interpol befuddled.

Manny, Moe, and Jack Bahlakwana were all born and raised in Tlokweng, a village located to the southeast of Gaborone, the capital of Botswana. Their father, Akanyang Bahlakwana owned and operated a prosperous gas station and garage located on Maratagiba Road overlooking the Ngotwane River.

Once, many years before his sons were born, an American Peace Corp volunteer named Skip Stofac limped his ten-year-old Toyota pickup into Akanyang's garage with a busted radiator hose, faulty brakes, a cracked manifold and very little money. Akanyang had seen the young man around town and had heard about some of the projects he had been working on helping the community.

The young Peace Corp volunteer pulled up to the garage, steam bellowing out from under the hood, leaned out of the driver's window and as Akanyang approached asked, "Can you help me, sir?"

"Well, that depends. Let's take a look. Pop the hood."

After examining the vehicle Akanyang estimated the cost of repairs were going to be in excess of forty two hundred Botswana Pula's. Skip asked the mechanic what he could fix for nine hundred Pula's?

"Nine hundred won't get you to the end of the block. Look kid, tell you what, I could use some help around here, maybe you could work the rest off by doing odd jobs."

"That would be great, Mister"

"No Mister, just Akanyang."

"Thanks Akanyang."

"Oh and just one more thing, I'd really like that tee shirt you're wearing there."

"This old thing, sure." Skip peeled off his old Pep Boys tee shirt with the cartoon characters of Manny, Moe and Jack.

Akanyang held it up proudly and said, "Who are these Pep Boys? Are the brothers?"

"No, I think they were three friends who started an auto parts store in America."

"I like their faces." Akanyang said as he put the tee shirt on.

For eight weeks Skip worked at the garage doing everything from fixing flats, sweeping out the bays, and on occasion simple oil changes. On his last day of servitude he presented Akanyang with a box wrapped with Christmas wrapping paper and a thank you note.

"What's this?"

"A little something I thought you might like. Go ahead and open it."

Akanyang tore open the paper and box and when he saw what was inside, he had a smile that spread from ear to ear. A half dozen brand new Pep Boys tee shirts. He's worn a Pep Boys tee shirt every day for twelve years without fail. Skip has long since completed his Peace Corp service years ago and has returned to his home in Duluth, but every Christmas Akanyang receives a gift of a half a dozen brand new Manny, Moe and Jack tee shirts.

Akanyang named his three boys after the Pep Boys, Manny, Moe and Jack much to his wife's dismay. She is a devout Catholic and wanted them to have biblical names like Matthew, Mark and Luke but Akanyang was adamant. He was not a religious man at all but if she agreed to the names for the boys, he would allow her to raise them as Catholics, even send them to Catholic school. And he agreed that he would, on certain special occasions, even attend church with her as well. She relented.

Manny, Moe and Jack grew up in a very strict religious home environment; they attended Christ the King Cathedral Catholic School, went every Sunday to Mass and to at least one Mass during the week. Saturdays always started off with the boys having to confess their sins between 08:30 and 09:00, rain or shine. At one point, Akanyang thought for sure that at least one if not all of his sons were headed for the priesthood.

All three attended St. Joseph's College, where they all moved slightly away from the Church and became a little more secular and even more capitalistic. By the time Jack graduated from St. Joe's Manny and Moe established Okavango Eden Safaris, safari tours specializing in high-end big game hunting excursions. They even provided all-inclusive hunting, trophy taxidermy services and a no questions asked shipping policy.

Akanyang was proud of his boy's success, but he was a little disappointed that none of them follow him into his auto repair and garage business. They never showed any interest or mechanical aptitude when they were young, plus all three hated getting their hands dirty. He blamed his wife for pampering them and all that religion. He would say even Christ worked with his hands as a carpenter.

The brothers inserted a bit of religion right into the middle of their safari company's name, Okavango *Eden* Safaris, Eden after the Garden of Eden. There were subtle and some not-so-subtle religious references in the brochures and on the website talking about how the Bible encourages man to hunt in the name of the Lord and that hunting in Botswana is in many ways hunting in the Garden of Earthly Delights.

And it did come to pass that a man named Icarus, who many would be seen as an angel of Lucifer, was sent to do evil and test the faith of many a believer and make martyrs of the Botswana trinity, Manny, Moe and Jack Bahlakwana.

Le Gang de la Clé de Singe let the Bahlakwana brothers know that they were aware of their goings on with the Okavango Eden Safaris and that Manny, Moe and Jack were indeed on a hit list if they continued to conduct hunting safaris and dealing in poached endangered species parts. Manny told the police and the press of the threats, which got nation-wide coverage and once the local television station heard about their story, they were all over the airwaves. They received mostly positive support with an occasional death threat, but overall positive.

That's when they heard from Liam Janssens, a professional bodyguard from Belgium who so happened to be traveling thru Botswana after having finished an assignment for a local extreme/death metal band, which he is not a liberty to disclose their name for security purposes. However, he could provide a multitude of client references upon request, which he did. A virtual meeting was arranged, and a contract signed via the internet, Liam Janssens was to begin his newest assignment in three days' time. Aside from several phone messages and a handful of text messages there was never any hard evidence of any face-to-face meeting between Liam Janssens and the brothers Bahlakwana.

Two hours outside Gaborone sits Jwana Game Park home to Impalas, Wildebeests, Giraffes, Zebras, Cheetahs and Leopards as well as numerous smaller animal species. The park was initially a fenced Mine Lease Area that surrounds the Jwanwng diamond mine, the richest diamond mine in the world. The park was developed, in part to counter the traditional cold heartless image of corporate diamond mining companies.

The park is off limits to all hunters and is regularly patrolled by armed rangers looking for poachers; photo safari tourists mostly visit the park. It was during one of those photo safaris that someone discovered the remains of what will forever be known as the Martyred Brothers of Botswana.

"Genesis 9...
And God blessed Noah and his sons and said to them,
be fruitful and multiply and fill the earth. The fear of you and
the dread of you shall be upon every beast of the earth and
upon every bird of the heavens, upon everything that creeps
on the ground and all the fish of the sea. Into your hands they
are delivered. Every moving thing that lives shall be food for

you. And as I gave you the green plants, I give you everything."

Liam Janssens aka Icarus closed the brochure cover and asked the three Bahlakwana brothers who were bound and gagged seated in the back of his Nissan 4X4 pickup, "Do you really believe all this or are you just playing to your base? Do you really believe that God gave man dominion over everything in the world. And that we are free to literary kill every living thing of earth if we wanted to?" The brothers remained silent.

"Let me tell you why I've brought you all here today, Manny, Moe and Jack you have been charged with crimes against nature for promoting and facilitating the slaughter of animals, many considered to be endangered species, and for the sale and worldwide export of endangered species parts for pure greed. How do you plea?"

Moe was making noises like he wanted to respond to the charges. Icarus removed his gag, "Moe, you have something to say?"

"We have done nothing wrong; we are not guilty of any crimes. We are doing God's work, as it says in Genesis 27:3, *"Now then, please take your gear, your quiver and your bow, and go out to the field and hunt game for me."* so sayeth the Lord."

"How about *"One should not kill a living being, nor cause it to be killed, nor should one incite another to kill. Do not injure any being, either strong or weak, in the world."*

"I am afraid that I am not familiar with that Bible verse."

"It isn't from the Bible; it is a quote from Buddha."

"So, not scripture."

"Oh, you only care for quotes from scripture, okay, how about Proverbs 12:27, *"The lazy do not roast any game, but the diligent feed on the riches of the hunt."* I read that and think men are slaughtering animals for wicked reasons. Elephants and rhinos are killed for their tusks and horns and their bodies are left to rot. Other animals are slain for just the sport of it and their heads and bodies are stuffed to hang on a wall for trophy of man's prowess, while the meat is discarded."

"Again I quote Genesis 9, *"The fear of you and the dread of you shall be upon every beast of the earth and upon every bird of the heavens, upon everything that creeps on the ground and all the fish of the sea."*

"You know I like that, but I'm going see your Genesis 9 and raise you

Ezekiel 25:17 *"The path of the righteous man is beset on all sides by the inequities of the selfish hunter and the tyranny of evil poachers. Blessed is he who, in the name of nature and good will, shepherds the weak through the valley of the darkness, for he is truly the keeper of the Kingdom Animalia."*

Now, I know I tweaked the passage to fit the occasion, but if I do say so myself it kinda works. And besides, we could spend all night swapping Biblical quotes back and forth but, the time has come for you boys to become martyrs and maybe, just maybe one day you'll be given sainthood like St. Hubertus, the patron saint of hunters, who by the way was from Belgium like me. Can I get an Amen brothers? No? Boy you guys are a tough crowd, tough crowd.”

"Oscar Alberink, Elif Rooijakkers and Hilton Tebogo, the defense team for the prisoner 1011045, Liam Janssens.” Hilton announced to the prison guards as the three of them were going thru the security checkpoint at Mahalapye Prison.

Liam was escorted to the same room where he had met with the Belgium Consul two days earlier. His defense team was waiting for him when he entered. They were all seated at the end of the conference room table, when Liam was shown in, Hilton stood up and introduced himself, "Mr. Janssens, my name is Hilton Tebogo, I will be your lead attorney, this is Mr. Oscar Alberink and Ms. Elif Rooijakkers, they are your Belgium legal representatives and will be working in concert with me. Please sit down.”

"Thank you, I really appreciate your help.”

"Are you all right, what happened to your face.” Hilton asked.

Liam touched his broken nose, "That happened when I was arrested. One of the arresting detectives was a bit overly aggressive when he smashed my face into a table.”

Hilton took out his cell phone and took several photos, "I will be lodging a formal complaint with the court, and this is clearly police brutality.”

Isala asked, "Has there been any other attacks either by the guards or the prisoners?”

"No, actually I'm surprised that there haven't been any confrontations. I have felt relatively safe here."

Rodin knew and had worked with Icarus on many assignments over the years, the most infamous one happened in the Central Asian country of Tibet.

Tibet, one of the few countries on earth where the endangered snow leopard still exists, there are less that 4000 known to still survive in the wild. Their main threats come from poachers, sheep farmers, and large-scale corporate mining companies.

Two teams were sent into Tibet. The Red Team under the command of Rodin was sent to convince two of the mine owners that were having the most impact on the leopard's mountain ecosystems to curtail their expansion plans in the area and possibly even reduce their footprint. Of course they would first be asked nicely and if they would refuse, then a more aggressive dialogue would be needed.

The second team was the Blue Team under the command of Icarus. Isala was attached to the Blue Team as a drone specialist. Their assignment was to stop the poaching and make arrangements with the sheep farmers that in lieu of killing the snow leopards, Le Gang de la Clé de Singe would reimburse them the fair market price for their lost sheep.

Dealing with the farmers was easy, they were eager to agree, for them it was a win win. But dealing with the poachers took a bit more convincing. The one thing that the teams of Le Gang de la Clé de Singe seem to always come across is the poacher's mentality that you can't catch me, maybe the other guy, but not me.

It took the Blue Team twelve weeks of employing constant day and night drone reconnaissance and trekking along the Tibetan Plateau in the Gaurishankar Conservation Area on the northern side of the Himalayas to snare eight teams of poachers. Two of the teams were all Chinese and the other six were a mix of Tibetans, Bhutanese and Nepalese.

Icarus wanted every poacher to know that if they were caught the same fate awaited them. He always made sure that he left his distinctive calling card of how the dead were found, hanging upside down and naked.

In the end nineteen poachers were found that way, upside down, naked and with the traditional yellow skull and cross monkey wrench flags draped around their necks with the following statement placed near their person:

Let it be known that Le Gang de la Clé de Singe declares a proclamation of war against all Poachers, Big Game Hunters and all Big Game Safari Outfits as well as anybody anywhere in the world that targets, kills, profits and or supports the killing of any animals that are endangered or any animals that are hunted for sport. Be forewarned, do so at your peril. You will be hunted down and pay with your lives. Be it, man or woman, there will be no exceptions and no mercy; we will show no quarter. You have been warned.

The Red team had a much easier time with their assignment, after assessing the issues and developing solutions of the two mines that would help solve the environmental problems created by the mines and locating where the decision makers resided. Both were companies whose headquarters were located in Switzerland. The

Central Asia Mining Corporation was located in Grindelwald, a small village in the Bernese Alps and BSISRO Plc was based in Escholzmatt just outside of Lucerne, Switzerland.

At first both CEO's were reluctant and unwilling to compromise although both men said that saving the snow leopard was truly a worthy cause, but to capitulate to a terrorist organization like Le Gang de la Clé de Singe would be setting a terrible precedent.

Rodin said that he sympathized with them and then placed a contract in front of each CEO and while holding a gun to each of their heads. He paraphrased a quote from one of the great American classic films, the Godfather, he said, *"Gentlemen, either your signatures will be on these contracts or your brains will be."*

Hilton Tebogo was looking through a stack of papers when he said, "Mr. Janssens, the prosecution's case seems to be mostly circumstantial, but they seem to think it's enough to move forward in going to trail. I would like you to tell us in your own words happened."

"Well, I had just finished up an assignment as head of security for a local band's tour here in Botswana, when I heard that there were these brothers who were looking for a bodyguard to protect them from death threats by Le Gang de la Clé de Singe. I contacted Manny Bahlakwana and conducted a series of phone calls and text messaging until the Bahlakwana brothers hired me. I was to actually meet them and start my position as bodyguard and head of security three or four days after they were killed. On the day they were killed and two days prior I was in Pretoria, staying at the Protea Hotel Fire & Ice."

"Is there anyone who can collaborate your story?"

"I guess some of the hotel staff would have seen me, I was there on vacation, not building an alibi. Oh wait a minute, I did play a round of golf one day at the Waterkloog Golf Club."

Isala while busy taking copious notes asked, "Did they pair you up with anyone?"

"Yeah, they did, an American from Philadelphia, a real *loemp*. What's the word in English, Oscar?"

"Idiot."

"Yeah, idiot."

Rodin smiled and said, "And did this *loemp* have a name, per chance?"

"He was real fat and not a very good golfer, he said I could just call him Joey Bagadonuts."

Rodin looked at Isala and Hilton with skepticism, "Are you sure, Bagadonuts? That sounds made up."

"I think it must be a nickname, when we finished our round, we went into the club house for some drinks. There were some other Americans and they all called him Joey Bagadounts. Now, I'm not sure but I think I heard one of the wait staff refer to him as Mr. Mineo."

Hilton asked, "Do you know where he was staying, which hotel? Do you think he might still be in Pretoria? It would be nice to get a sworn statement from him."

"It was near the University of South Africa, the Illyria House."

"Well, we'll check and see if he is still there, if not maybe we can find him before the trial. Did the police ask you any of these questions to see if you had an alibi?"

"No, after they broke my nose, I told them I wanted to see the Belgium Consul and have a lawyer present before answering any questions."

Hilton nodded approvingly, "Good. Now I think it's really important that we go and get confirmation with the hotel and see if we can locate this Mr. Mineo aka Joey Bagadonuts. Is there anything we can do for you Mr. Janssens?"

"I'm guessing bail is out of the question?"

"We can certainly ask, but I wouldn't think so. I think that's all for now, we'll probably see you again tomorrow. In the meantime if there is anything you need between now and then here's my card. You can have the warden call me anytime day or night. See you tomorrow."

With that he stood up and walked over and shook Liam's hand. Liam just stayed seated as they all left, he noticed that Rodin left his fountain pen behind and knew it was left on purpose. A few minutes past and Rodin entered the room, "Hey, man good to see you. Is everything okay?"

"Yeah, as good as can be expected. How in the Hell did they finger me?"

"Are you kidding it had all the markings of Icarus, hanging those three brothers upside down like that and on crosses. You can't be always doing that; it's becoming your trademark."

"It was quite Biblical; don't you think with a bit of Saint Peter style crucifixion and a hint of anti-religion thrown in. I'm actually quite proud of it. Is there a lot of buzz?"

"Dude, I'd say you're lucky you're in here, I think if you were out there somebody would find you and pile a whole lot of Saint Peter style crucifixion on your ass."

"So, how's the case looking?"

"Who knows, everyone is out for blood, I think the case is weak, but that doesn't mean anything. Not to worry, one way or another you'll be out soon enough. Isala and I got things well in hand. Stay frosty my friend, we'll see you tomorrow.

Oh, and by the way, Joey Bagadonuts. Really?"

"What weird is that's the part that's true. Hey, I got a line on a big time elephant poacher, Dineo Wengazi. If you got some spare time you might want to pay Dineo a little visit."

"Well, you know me. I'm always up for meeting new people."

Dineo Wengazi lived out in the Kweneng District on the edge of the small village of Mmopane across the road from the Sethugetsane Shopping Complex. Since the Mmopane has no names for any of the hundreds of crisscrossing spider web dirt streets, Rodin needed to locate Dineo's home by waiting outside of Mahalapye Prison and follow him home after he finished visiting his brother, like he did every Saturday.

Most of the homes in the village of Mmopane are built from unpainted cinderblocks, the majority of them are one-story rectangles with a minimum amount of windows and every home has either a chain-link or matching cinderblock fence surrounding it with a standard ill-tempered mixed breed junkyard guard dog in the yard. Since there aren't too many white faces seen in the village, Rodin bought a black 2008 Mitsubishi Pajero SUV with smash and grab window tinting that had an air of full-tilt gangsta, so he could ride thru the neighborhood and remain undetected.

Dineo's home was set up like a military compound. There were seven cinder block structures laid out in a U configuration, the main house sat in the middle of the U with three smaller buildings on either side. A chain link fence topped off with strands of razor wire surrounded the enclosure. Along with several junkyard dogs roaming within the fenced area, and there were half a dozen well-armed men standing guard.

Rodin tailed Dineo back from the prison undetected. Once in the village of Mmopane they made their way thru the maze of unmarked streets to Dineo's compound. When Dineo's red Mercedes-Benz E400 arrived, two armed men were waiting to open the gate. Just past the gate entrance sat three different models of Mercedes-Benz up on blocks that looked to be used as parts cars for Dineo's Mercedes. Once inside the compound Dineo drove into a garage, which was the first building on the right where there were two other vehicles inside, a British racing green Land Rover Discovery

4 and a jet black AM General Hummer 4-Door Wagon. Rodin had mounted several GoPro cameras inside the vehicle facing outward on all sides so as to capture as many different angles of the target so he could formulate a strategy and develop his plan of attack.

Having everyone in a confined area would have its advantages. Dineo and his crew think the fence's main purpose is to keep their enemies out, whereas Rodin thinks of the fence as keeping his enemies in.

After reviewing the footage of Dineo's base camp Rodin's plan could be achieved with just him and Isala. They would need to do a thorough scouting of not only the area but also the armed guards' routine.

"Good evening I'm Nigel Williams and this is the BBC World Headline News. Our top story this hour comes from Gaborone, Botswana where there is a report of an arrest of a man who is believed to be a member of the international eco-terrorist group known as Le Gang de la Clé de Singe. If this is true, then this will be only the fourth time a known member has been captured. All we know at this time is that the man's name is Liam Janssens, and he holds a Belgium passport. Authorities tell us that Mr. Janssens is being held without bail in connection of the brutal murders of three brothers, Manny, Moe and Jack Bahlakwana owners of Okavango Eden Safaris.

They were found murdered in Jwana Game Park just outside of Gaborone; they were discovered hanging upside down and positioned on a wooden cross, much like the way Saint Peter was said to have been crucified.

The Bahlakwana brothers were found with the traditional yellow flags with the skull and crossed wrenches around each their necks along with a letter proclaiming the reason for their deaths.

Le Gang de la Clé de Singe have claimed responsibility for the deaths of the Bahlakwana brothers, but they deny that Mr. Janssens is a member of their organization and say they have no knowledge of Mr. Janssens.

The Botswana Public Prosecutor Montsho Modise announced today that Mr. Janssens will likely be going on trial within the next week. Mr. Hilton Tebogo the attorney for Mr. Janssens claims is client is innocent and is confident that he will be found not guilty.

Meanwhile in other news…"

Two days after Rodin had followed Dineo, he and Isala went back to Mmopane to do some scouting. When they arrived around three in the morning, they discovered the compound was abandoned; there was only one man standing guard. The opportunity to do a quick and thorough recon seemed to be perfect; all the stars were in alignment. The area was pitch black because it was the first day of a new moon. There weren't any streetlights for miles and the house had no lights on. Rodin and Isala were wearing all black, with black face paint and black balaclavas, and they both were sporting Sightmark Ghost Hunter night vision goggles.

They made their way to the edge of the camp behind the garage building, as soon as they were approaching, they could hear the dogs coming toward them. They had prepared some meat laced with Acepromazine Maleate, a fast acting dog tranquilizer that is typically used in minor surgeries. Within minutes all the dogs were fast asleep. The drug's effects are good for twenty to thirty minutes. Once the last dog was out, they started the clock. Isala was stationed behind of the abandoned Mercedes. She was to keep track of the time and the lone guard and to keep Rodin aware of his whereabouts as he searched the other buildings.

The guard, such as he was, was sitting on a car seat that had been removed from one of the three Mercedes in the middle of the compound. He clearly wasn't expecting any trouble as was in such a deep sleep Isala could hear him snoring.

She softly spoke to Rodin over their radio sets counting down the time before the drugs would start wearing off of the dogs. With minutes to spare Rodin appeared, giving her the thumbs up and signaling for them to go. As they were making their way to the Mitsubishi Pajero, they could hear the dogs regaining consciousness and waking the sleeping guard who started yelling at them for waking him up.

"So, what did you find?" Isala asked as they were making their way back to the Peermont Walmont hotel.

"Well the five small structures are warehouses for illegal endangered animal parts and products mostly elephant tusks and rhino horns, but other species as well. They also have facilities to do taxidermy. One of the buildings has a rather large cache of weapons. The main building is primarily a barracks for the men, pretty basic layout of bedrooms and kitchen and a large area for eating and relaxing. By the looks of the barracks area there must be ten to twelve men in his crew."

"Where do think everyone is?"

"Not sure, but my guess is they're out poaching. We'll check back tomorrow night; we'll still have the new moon in our favor."

The man known as Icarus was born in Belgium thirty-two years ago as Thomas Peeters. He grew up in Bruges in northwest Belgium, which is known as the Venice of the north because of all the canals that encircle the city. The Peeters has been an important family in Bruges's history having been one of the original founding families in developing the bobbin lace business, which they helped start over four hundred years ago. Simon Peeters, Thomas' great, great, great, great grandfather worked alongside Phillip the Good, the Duke of Burgundy and who was instrumental in the capture of Joan of Arc and personally brokered the deal of her sale to England; not one of the Peeters family highlights.

Thomas was of course, expected to go into the family business, but he had no interest in the bobbin lace industry. He studied economics and business management at the prestigious Katholieke Universiteit Leuven, Belgium's highest ranked university. But after taking a philosophy class he switched majors to study philosophy and told his folks that he was going to become a philosopher much to his family's chagrin. After getting his undergraduate degree he went on to get his master's degree. Even though his parents were disappointed, as a graduation present, they gave him an all-expenses paid trip to India to help 'find his self'.

A month into his discovery trip in early December, Thomas was exploring the Jain Temple Kanch Mandir in Indore, located in west-central India, with its mirrored mosaic interior, when he heard the news of a major industrial disaster that occurred at the Union Carbide India Limited pesticide plant in Bhopal. It seems that there was a major gas leak at the plant and over a half a million people were exposed to the highly toxic methyl isocyanate gas. The estimated death toll could be anywhere from four thousand to as high as sixteen thousand.

The majority of the deaths were people who lived in the poorest part of the city. The government confirmed that the leak caused over 500,000 injuries. There were lawsuits flying all over the place, and people were pointing fingers at everybody. But in the end the people most responsible were found guilty of negligence and of course they received minimal sentences and had to pay a fine of only two thousand U.S. Dollars each. It was at the time considered to be the world's worst industrial disaster ever.

That was the day that Thomas Peeters stopped being a philosopher and became an eco-anarchist. While protesting the plant's negligence, the lack of compassion for the victims and the corporate greed, he met several members of Le Gang de la Clé de Singe and three days later he was involved in setting a series of bombs at the Union Carbide corporate office in downtown Bhopal that went off at 3am, causing hundreds of thousands of dollars of damage with no loss of life. That was the day he adopted the name Icarus.

Since the Bhopal disaster Icarus hasn't been back to Belgium. He has gone from one assignment to the next battling mostly corporations and their leaders, but when the new direction to go against people who hunted and profited from endangered species was formed, he enthusiastically volunteered for the new assignment.

His first mission was in the United States. It seems that just outside the small city of Guyon, Oklahoma lies the tiny town of Bishop Hills with a population of 213. it seems that large deposits of oil and gas have recently been discovered in the hills located behind the town.

Bishop Hills is also known for being home to several hundred colonies of extremely rare and environmentally protected species of prairie dogs, which prevent ManKraw Oil & Gas from developing the site and prevents the good people of Bishop Hills from profiting from Mother Nature's blessing. Unless somehow those pesky prairie vermin just happen to all of a sudden go bye bye.

A town meeting was held at Paul Mansfield's ranch out on Stonebridge Gate Road in his horse barn. It was the only building in Bishop Hills that could accommodate such a large crowd. The meeting was to see what if anything could be done to please everyone. At the meeting there was a representative from ManKraw Oil & Gas, a Mr. Charles Bennett, representing the Texas Eco and Wildlife Group was Ms. Caroline Schmidt and the town's mayor, Judd Humble, along with 192 of the 213 residents of Bishop Hill were also present.

The Mayor called the meeting to order, "All right, all right, let's settle down. We're all here to see if there is some sort of compromise that can be reached between us, ManKraw Oil & Gas and the Texas Eco and Wildlife Group."

The crowd started booing and jeering whenever anyone mentioned Texas Eco and Wildlife Group.

"People, we aren't going to accomplish anything if this sort of behavior continues. Now let's be civil and we'll be able to get through this a whole lot quicker," Mayor Humble said holding up his hands trying to calm the crowd. "Let's hear from Mr. Bennett first."

Mr. Bennett was a neatly dressed man sporting a three-piece Brooks Brothers blue pin-striped suit with a white button down collar oxford shirt and green and blue stripped tie. He had a full crop of gray hair with a matching moustache. He wore wire rim glasses and was on the chubby-side. He looked to be in his sixties but in fact was only fifty-two. As he stood up the crowd got quite.

"Thank you, Mayor. I first want to thank you all for coming out here tonight and I'd like to thank Ms. Schmidt as well."

More boos, with an occasional 'commie', peppered with a few 'bitch' thrown in for good measure.

"People please, Bottom line is that unless there can be some sort of resolution to the prairie dog's habitat issue, we at ManKraw Oil & Gas will be forced to look elsewhere. There is nothing more than ManKraw Oil & Gas would love to do is to develop the natural riches that lie beneath Bishop Hills but I'm sorry, the government regulations are quite clear on such matters when it comes to endangered species. So unless Ms. Schmidt can find a solution we'll just have to look elsewhere."

The Mayor quickly stood up again holding his hands in the air to calm the crowd and spoke loudly, "Please show some decorum. Now I'd like to have Ms. Schmidt address the issue. Ms. Schmidt."

Caroline Schmidt had model features. She was tall and thin with beautiful skin and wore her long blond hair in a bun, and also wore wire rim glasses. She was wearing a navy blue double-breasted blazer, a pink pin-striped shirt and blue jeans. Not exactly the Mother Earth tree-hugging stereotype everyone was expecting.

"Thank you, Mayor Humble for your courtesy. Good evening ladies and gentlemen of Bishop Hills. First let me say that I am not the enemy. I know that many of you don't understand why the Texas Eco and Wildlife Group are involved in trying to save the Gunnison's prairie dog from extinction. You see these prairie dogs play an important and vital role in the ecosystem. They provide food for predators like coyotes, so they won't attack your livestock and they afford shelter for other tunneling animals.

They also make the soil more fertile which makes it easier for seeds to germinate. So, you can see the prairie dogs do play a crucial role in your environment. And this particular prairie dog is usually found in the Four Corners region which makes them even rarer and worth studying being that there in this part of Oklahoma."

Mayor Humble asked, "Ms. Schmidt as much as we appreciate the wonderful job these rare little critters do for us, is there nothing we can do to accommodate them and still allow the oil company to drill up in the hills?"

"I'm afraid not, not unless the colonies migrate to another area, which they will eventually do."

"Great, how often do they migrate?"

"Usually, they will migrate to a new area every ten to twenty years."

Well, that brought the crowd to a near riotous fever pitch of curses and even a few death threats. Cody Hayes, a local rancher stood up and yelled, "What if I just go up there and fucking kill them all. Monte and I could go up there and smoke 'em out and when they come scurrying out, we just start a blasting. How 'bout that?"

"Let me warn you that the penalty for killing an endangered species is over three thousand dollars and that's for killing just one and there are hundreds of them, plus you'd be facing multiple years in Federal prison for everyone that is killed. Even if you did kill them all, there would be a lengthy Federal investigation and that would take years." Schmidt said.

"This is bullshit!" Cody shouted.

While the mob's attention and hatred was being aimed at Ms. Schmidt, no one noticed a stranger that had slipped into the back of the crowd and blended into the shadows of the barn. Icarus was there observing the people and making mental notes.

The crowd started to turn ugly and threatening, Sheriff Fields stood up and quickly addressed the horde, "People, people settle down. I don't want to start arresting anybody, I think this meeting is over, right Mayor?"

Mayor Humble nodded in agreement, the sheriff continued, "Everybody go home, now! Come on, let's go."

People started filing out and spilling out onto the street, getting more and more worked up. The sheriff personally escorted Ms. Schmidt to her car and made sure she wasn't being followed as she left. He then called the Porter County Sheriff's office and requested back up ASAP.

The barn was emptying out fast as people were moving their anger out into the street. Cody and Monte Collins lingered behind not wanting anyone to hear what they were plotting.

Cody pulled Monte into one of the empty horse stalls, looking around making sure no one was around before he spoke, "Okay, tomorrow night we'll get a bunch of rags and some kerosene and we'll go up into the hills and we'll smoke those motherfuckers out and once they come scurrying out, we'll blast the shit out of them. I'm not about to let a bunch of rodents keep us from getting rich. Right Monte?"

"But Cody won't people hear us shooting and come to see what the Hell's going on?"

"They won't hear jack shit. Remember when I went to that big gun show in Tulsa last year? Well, I bought two Salvo 12 silencers for my shotguns, so no one will hear nothing.

"Cool, okay count me in."

"Now don't say nothing to nobody, it's just you and me, right?"

"Right."

"Okay we'll talk more tomorrow. Now remember, not a word."

"Right."

"Okay, let's go."

As they left and the barn was now empty, Icarus made his way undetected out the side door and melted into the night. He had a lot to do before tomorrow night.

"All rise, The Court of the Second Judicial Circuit, Criminal Division, is now in session, the Honorable Chief Magistrate Kabelo presiding." Bailiff Phiri announced.

Chief Magistrate Kabelo, "Everyone but the jury may be seated. Mr. Phiri, please swear in the jury."

Bailiff Phiri walked over to the jury box, "Please raise your right hand. Do you solemnly swear that you will truly listen to this case and render a true verdict and a fair sentence as to this defendant?"

The jury members in unison relied, "I do."

"You may be seated."

Chief Magistrate Kabelo looked at the jury and said, "Members of the jury, your duty today will be to determine whether the defendant is guilty or not guilty only on facts and evidence provided in this case. The prosecution has the burden of proving the guilt of the defendant beyond a reasonable doubt. This burden remains on the prosecution through the trail. The prosecution must prove that a crime was committed, and that the defendant is the person who committed the crime. However, if you are not satisfied of the defendant's guilt to the extent, then reasonable doubt exists, and the defendant must be found not guilty. Mr. Phiri, what is today's case."

"Your Honor, today's case is the People of Botswana versus Liam Janssens in the matter of three counts of murder." The bailiff said.

Chief Magistrate Kabelo asked, "Is the prosecution ready?"

Prosecutor Montsho Modise stood and announced, "Yes, your Honor." Then sat down.

"Is the defense ready?

Hilton Tebogo stood and answered, "Yes, your Honor." He too sat down.

Prosecutor Modise then stood and walked to the podium facing the jury to make his opening statement, "Your Honor, members of the jury, my name is Prosecutor Montsho Modise, I represent the State, we intend to prove that the defendant Mr. Liam Janssens did willfully and with malice kill Manny Bahlakwana, Moe Bahlakwana and Jack Bahlakwana. After all the evidence is presented, we will have proven beyond a reasonable doubt that the defendant,

Mr. Janssens, is guilty of the crime of murder and will ask you to find him accountable for this heinous crime. Thank you."

Chief Magistrate Kabelo waited for the prosecutor to be seated, and then said, "The defense, please present you opening statements."

Hilton Tebogo slowly made his way to the podium, reached inside his coat pocket and retrieved a pair of reader glasses that he proceeded to carefully place on at the end of his nose and then he spoke, "Thank you your Honor, ladies and gentlemen of the jury my name is Hilton Tebogo and I am the lead attorney for Mr. Janssens.

My colleagues Mr. Oscar Alberink and Ms. Elif Rooijakkers and I will show that the prosecution's case is purely circumstantial. There is no DNA evidence, there are no fingerprints and there is no physical evidence at all linking my client to this terrible crime. We believe that in the end you will find our client, Mr. Janssens not guilty. Thank you." He paused to remove his glasses, returned them to his coat pocket and then walked back to the defense table and sat down.

Chief Magistrate Kabelo looked to Prosecutor Modise and said, "The prosecution, may call its first witness."

"Thank you, your Honor. I call to the stand Detective Mosweu."

From the gallery Detective Mosweu made his way to the front of the courtroom to the witness stand where he stood to be sworn in.

Bailiff Phiri walked over to the witness and said, "Please raise your right hand. Do you swear to tell the truth, the whole truth and nothing but the truth, so help you God?"

"I do."

The bailiff said, "You may be seated."

Prosecutor Modise stood at his desk and asked, "Please state your name."

"Seth Mosweu, I am a detective with the Botswana Police Service."

"Detective Mosweu, how long have you been with the Botswana Police Service?"

"Fourteen years."

"And how many years have you been in homicide?"

"Eight years."

"And you were the lead detective on the Bahlakwana case, were you not?"

"Yes sir."

"Would you please tell the court what you saw the night you were called out to Jwana Game Park."

"I got a call about a multiple homicide in Jwana Game Park. When I arrived at the scene, which was approximately 6:30pm in the evening, there were several uniformed officers already there and Doctor Solomon, the medical examiner was getting ready to start processing the crime scene. As I approached the crime scene, I noticed that there were three inverted crosses placed into the ground with an inverted body attached to each cross."

"Were there any obvious wounds, like stab wounds or gunshot wounds?"

"No sir."

"Were there any signs of physical abuse?"

"No sir."

"So, how did these men die Detective?"

"The medical examiner said that they died from a brain hemorrhage and asphyxiation from being hung upside down too long."

"Detective Mosweu, did you have any suspicions of who might have committed these murders?"

"Yes, I did, I had reason to believe that the French eco-terrorist group called Le Gang de la Clé de Singe was behind this attack and they in fact later claimed responsibility for the murders of the three Bahlakwana brothers. I received information from Interpol to be on the lookout for an assassin whose description fit that of Mr. Janssens. While searching the offices of Okavango Eden Safaris, the company that the Bahlakwana brothers owned, we found a contract between the victims and the defendant hiring Mr. Janssens as their bodyguard."

"Aside from the Interpol description why did you consider Mr. Janssens a suspect?"

"Well, when we went to interview the defendant, he was evasive, and he resisted arrest."

"Is that how he received his facial injury?"

"Yes, sir."

"No more questions at this time, your Honor."

The Chief Magistrate gestured to Hilton Tebogo, "The defense may cross-examine the witness."

"Thank you, your Honor. Now, Detective Mosweu you said that you had received a description from Interpol of the assassin, is that correct?"

"Yes, that's correct."

"How did you receive this alleged description?"

"I'm sorry?"

"Was it sent by mail, email, telegraph, phone call?"

"I think it was email."

"And do you have a copy of the email? We would like to see exactly what it said."

"Ah, now that I think about it, it wasn't an email. Oh yeah, I remember now, it was a phone call from Interpol."

"A phone call."

"Right."

"Did they call you on your cell phone or the police land line?"

"The station phone."

"So, if we checked there would be record of the call, correct?"

"I guess."

"Can you tell the court the name of the person you spoke to?"

"I don't remember his name."

"So, it was a man that you spoke to, is that correct?"

"Yeah."

"Do you recall what date that you received this so called phone call?"

"Not exactly, I think it was a couple of weeks ago."

"You think. Did you write the description of the assassin down?"

"Yes."

"And Detective Mosweu can you show the court the description of the assassin that you wrote down?"

"I don't know where it is."

"Did you show this written down description to anybody?"

"Yes, I did."

"Who did you show it to, can you write down their names? I will be more than happy to provide you with some paper and a pen."

"I can't remember specifically who."

"Well, can you at least tell the court what the description was? Can you at least remember that much Detective Mosweu?"

Mosweu was visibly getting rattled; he was starting to sweat and began to fidget in his seat. He reached over to the side of the witness box where a pitcher of water and glass sat and poured a glass of water and proceeded to drink two full glasses.

"Detective Mosweu, can you tell court the description?"

"It said the suspect was about five foot eight to six foot two, he had brown hair and brown eyes, Caucasian and medium built."

"Detective Mosweu, you've just described half the white men in the world. I contend that there wasn't any description from Interpol and that you concentrated all your efforts on Mr. Janssens because he was conveniently available. Isn't that right, Detective Mosweu?"

"No, that's not right."

"Was there any of Mr. Janssens' DNA found at the crime scene?"

"No."

"Any of his fingerprints?"

"No."

"Any physical evidence whatsoever of my client at the crime scene?"

"No."

"Did you investigate any other suspects other than Mr. Janssens?"

"We had a few others that we looked into."

"And I don't suppose that you would remember their names."

"No, not at this time."

"Detective Mosweu, you don't have a very good memory, do you?"

Detective Mosweu said nothing. He just gave the defense attorney a dirty look.

"So, Detective Mosweu, let me get this straight, you couldn't remember how you received the Interpol message. You don't know where the description that you say you wrote down is. You don't know who you showed it to. You don't know of any physical evidence linking my client to the murders. My question to you Detective Mosweu is, what do you know?"

Detective Mosweu sat in the witness chair fuming.

"Oh, one last thing Detective Mosweu, you testified that the defendant received his injuries from resisting arrest, is that correct?"

"That's right."

The defense counsel took something from a folder and walked over to the witness and handed him a photograph and then asked, "Do you recognize this photograph

Detective Mosweu? And would tell the members of the jury what it's a photograph of."

"Yeah, it's a photograph of the defendant's mug shot after he was booked."

"And does he have any facial injuries in this photograph of him after he was arrested and booked?"

"No."

"So I guess you were also mistaken when you said that the defendant received his injuries while resisting arrest, or you lied. Which is it Detective Mosweu?"

"I guess, I was mistaken." Mosweu mumbled.

"I'm sorry, Detective, I couldn't hear you."

"I was mistaken."

"Your Honor, I have no more question of this witness."

The Chief Magistrate gestured to Detective Mosweu, "You may step down. Prosecution, you may call your next witness."

"Thank you, your Honor. I call to the stand Doctor Solomon."

The Chief Magistrate announced without looking up from a stack of papers he was reviewing, "Will the witness please take the witness stand to be sworn in by the bailiff."

Doctor Solomon was the coroner for Gaborone. She was built like a fire hydrant, short and solid. She stood four foot eight inches, she's sixty-two years old, gray hair, thick coke bottled glasses and her complexion was that of rich dark chocolate. She walks with a slight limp from a broken hip that she suffered from a motorcycle accident when she was in her twenties and wild and crazy.

Doctor Solomon slowly walked to the stand and turned towards the bailiff.

And raised her hand before he had a chance to give her instructions. And said, "I do." before he was finished with his spiel.

The Prosecutor asked, "Would you please state your name."

"I'm Doctor Sarah Solomon, I am the coroner for Gaborone. I have held this position for over twenty-two years."

"Now Doctor Solomon could you please tell the court just how the victims died."

"Sure. The men were placed in an inverted position and were kept in that situation for several hours. When someone goes inversed, blood begins to rush to the head. Eventually a blood vessel could rupture or trigger a brain hemorrhage, but the major complication would be asphyxiation, which is what happened to Manny Bahlakwana. Jack and Moe Bahlakwana. They died because their hearts stopped from being forced to pump harder and harder because of all the blood flowing towards the heart from being upside down for such an extended period of time. Their hearts just couldn't stand the strain. I estimate that they were held in the inverted position for well over six hours, it would be an extremely painful death."

"Was there any signs of a struggle, Doctor?"

"I didn't find any defensive wounds, only some contusions and abrasions from struggling to free themselves from being bound to the cross."

"How were they bound to the crosses, Doctor?"

"Zip ties."

"Thank you, Doctor Solomon, no more questions."

Chief Magistrate Kabelo once again asks the defense council, "Defense you may cross-examine the witness."

"Thank you, your Honor. Just one question Doctor Solomon, do you know if any fingerprints were found at the scene of the murder?"

"Yes, only one fingerprint was found by the forensic lab."

"Was it that of my client?"

"No."

"Do you know if they identified whose fingerprint it was?"

"Yes, it belongs to Jimi Hendrix."

"The fingerprint of Jimi Hendrix, the American rock star of the 1960's was found at the scene of the crime. How is that possible, Doctor?"

"Obviously, it was placed there. It is my understanding that it is a common practice of Le Gang de la Clé de Singe to place a single fingerprint of a dead celebrity at the scene of all their murders as calling card if you will. I find it to be nothing more than a sick joke."

"Thank you, Doctor. I have no further questions, your Honor."

"You may step down, Doctor. Prosecution, you may call your next witness."

The prosecution called seven more police officers, four of them uniform officers and three detectives, all claiming that Detective Mosweu shared with them the description from Interpol. But none of them could remember if they had seen a hard copy or if Mosweu gave it to them verbally. And there seemed to be no official record of any call from Interpol, although a day watch commander stated that they have been having some problems recently with their phone systems.

Prosecutor Modise then called in three members of the forensics lab who primarily described the crime scene. One of the technicians said that had found several different tire tracks in the mud and one set of tracks matched the type of tires that were on the defendants' vehicle, but they weren't able to make a positive match.

The prosecution also called as a witness the victim's father, Akanyang who told the court what good boys his sons were, how they were good God fearing Christians and yes, they did provide big game hunting safaris, and yes on rare occasions there might have been some endangered animals killed and maybe, just maybe they would facilitate the transportation of endangered species products overseas, but all in all the boys were good Christians.

After three days of questioning over a dozen witnesses and presenting dozens of pie charts, bar graphs, and hundreds of crime scene photos the prosecution rested its case.

Icarus was led back to his prison cell after the court had adjourned for the day due to the prosecution resting its case and it being Friday afternoon so late in the day for the defense to start their case.

Baruti was waiting to hear all about the court proceedings. He was lying on his bunk reading a week old issue of The Voice, Gaborone's local newspaper. Last week's lead story was how the Bible has been translated into Ikalanga. Liam's trail only made the second page, but at least there was a nice big photograph of him being led into the courtroom.

"So, how did it go today, my friend?"

"Good really good. I think my attorney has been punching a lot of holes into their case. He really tore up that Detective Mosweu, but good."

"Yeah, I hear that Tobogo is one of the best. So, are you going to be taking the stand?"

"Don't know, I'll wait and see what Hilton thinks."

"How are those two *Kiekefretters* (chicken-eaters) working out? Are they being of any use?"

"They don't say much during the trial, but they have been doing the brunt of the research and paper shuffling."

"Yeah well, I'd like to do a little paper shuffling myself with that Elif Rooijakkers, if you know what I mean, and I think you do."

"Oh yeah. I hate waiting around for the weekend to pass. It's like I'm standing still, at least when the trial is going, I feel like there's some momentum. Now it's just sitting and waiting, I hate it. At least Oscar will be coming by tomorrow to chat. And no, Elif won't be coming to visit, sorry."

"You know you missed dinner, but I brought you back a sandwich, it's not much but it's something."

"That's very thoughtful Baruti, I brought you back a bag of crisps from lunch today. Here, I'll trade ya."

"I think I got the better deal, here's your cheese sandwich."

The next morning Liam was escorted to the conference room where Rodin sat dressed in his courtroom suit with his attaché case opened with papers spread out looking very professional.

"Good morning counselor."

"Hey, how are you holding up?"

"I'm doing as well as can be expected, did you ever find that Joey Bagadonuts?"

"You're kidding right? Those guys musta been jerking your chain."

"I just want this over, one way or the other."

"Well, that's what I wanted to go over with you in case it's the other."

"Yeah, I can't wait to see what you've got planned; I know it's going to be wild."

"Isala has devised an ingenious plan in the event you get a guilty plea to get you out of here."

"Well, don't keep me in suspense."

"Okay, It's an Ehang 184."

"And what the fuck is an Ehang 184."

"The Ehang 184 is an autonomous aerial vehicle. Basically, it's a drone that's large enough to fit a human passenger. A computer navigates it without any need for human control. Isala will pre-program it and it will fly into the prison yard and pick you up and fly you out. All you have to do is get in and buckle up and you're off. We're working out some minor details like the type of diversion and making sure you're the one getting aboard, but overall it should be easy."

"What about something malfunctioning?"

"This puppy has a built-in-fail-safe system, If anything malfunctions, let's say it gets hit by ground fire, the aircraft will immediately land in the nearest safe area. The plan is that Isala and I will each be escorting you in an armed Ehang 184. Yours won't be armed as you won't have had time to learn the weapons systems and plus, since yours will be pre-programmed you can't make any deviations to the flight plan. You will fly straight to the drop zone where you'll be met and smuggled out of the country. If there are no complications Isala and I will meet you there and we will each go our separate ways. But, if for some reason Isala or I get detained, the others will continue as planned and hopefully the one detained will have to make it out on their own; standard procedure."

"Wow, I kinda hope I am found guilty. This plan sounds way cool."

"Icarus, you're one sick puppy."

As Rodin was gathering up his notes and was making his way to the door, he turned to Icarus, "By the way Isala and I are going to take care of that pesky poaching problem tonight."

"Good hunting."

"It's 3am. Thank God I can sleep in tomorrow." Isala said to Rodin after a big yawn.

"Stay focused, you ready?" Rodin asked her as they watched the last of the guard dogs go down after devouring the meat laced with Acepromazine Maleate.

"Ready."

They jumped the wire fence and Isala took her position among the three old Mercedes cars used for parts armed with a Remington 12 gauge pump shotgun. Rodin eased up behind the lone guard sitting on a car seat that had been ripped out one of the three Mercedes. The guard had placed the seat by the front gate, and it looked to Rodin that the man was sleep, which made it easy for Rodin. In one stealth motion he covered the man's mouth with his left hand and thrust the dagger deep into the man's carotid artery killing him instantly.

"Sleep tight", Rodin whispered, then he moved towards the back entrance of the main house. As he ran by Isala he held up one finger indicating one down. He retrieved the Sig Sauer P226s 9mm, the handgun of choice of America's Navy SEALs from its holster. He attached the SR09 suppressor silencer and loaded a hollow point into the chamber from the 20 round extended magazine. He then slipped on a pair of panoramic night vision goggles and before opening the back door, he unscrewed the light bulb above the door. There was only darkness when he eased open the back door and slid in.

Rodin stood in the kitchen listening for any signs of movement but there were none. There was only the sound the kitchen clock ticking and the rhythmic sounds of men snoring. Rodin walked into the main room where he found two men sleeping, one on a sofa the other in an over-sized easy chair. Both men had shotguns lying next to them. From outside Isala saw two small flashes of light from Rodin's 9mm.

PHIFF PHIFF

She was able to track Rodin's path thru the house by the location of his muzzle flashes. The fact that there wasn't any return of gunfire meant that he hadn't woken anyone as he made his way throughout the structure. The last room he entered was that of Dineo who was sleeping on his right side on the left side of the bed. Next to the bed propped between the bed and nightstand was a shotgun, on the night stand a Colt 357 magnum handgun and lying next to the sleeping Dineo was a young lady, who looked to be in her early twenties.

As Rodin entered the room the woman opened her eyes and was about to shout when Rodin put his finger to his mouth to signal her to remain silent, which she did. He crossed the room to Dineo's side of the bed and carefully removed the two weapons and went and stood at the foot of the bed where he gave the bed a swift kick and loudly said, "Dineo, wake up!"

Dineo's natural reflex was to reach for his weapon, when he did, he found nothing there. He then sat up in bed and looked to see who had disturbed his sweet dreams. At the foot of his bed stood a figure all dressed in black from head to toe wearing what looked to him to be space goggles and pointing a pistol with a silencer at him. Still trying to shake out the cobwebs and clear his head he asked, "Who the fuck are you and what do you want and how did you get in here?"

"That's a lot of questions, Dineo, but not in any particular order. My name is Rodin and I'm with Le Gang de la Clé de Singe. We are an organization that kills assholes like you who go around killing elephants for their ivory. How I got in here, well let's just say you don't have a crew any more understand? Now, the big question of what do I want, I think that would be obvious, don't you?"

"You want money, how much; whatever you want."

"No, I don't want your blood money, Dineo."

"If you're going to kill me why didn't you just shoot me while I was sleeping, why wake me up?"

"Dineo, where's the fun in that. Ya dig?"

PHIFF PHIFF

Rodin then fired two shots hitting him in the chest. Dineo plopped back onto the bed his head landing on the pillow. Rodin walked over to his side of the bed and pulled the covers up to his chest. He placed a yellow flag with the logo of a skull and crossed monkey wrenches around his neck. He reached into the back pocket of his black jeans and took out a folded piece of paper and placed the note on the nightstand. On his way out of the bedroom he told the young woman, who seemed to be in a state of shock to get dressed. She jumped out of bed threw her clothes on, a pair of blue jeans and an oversized tee shirt and was out the bedroom in under a minute.

After fifteen minutes Isala saw him come out of the front door with a woman. Isala walked towards them as they were heading to the large building to the left of the main house. There was a large padlock on the door that Rodin shot off, inside of what appeared to be a storeroom was filled with dozens of elephant tusks, rhino horns, an assortment of animal skins from lions, zebras, cheetahs, giraffes and over twenty stuffed animal heads. There were boxes full of lion claws, teeth from all different kinds of animals and a box of elephant tails fashioned into fly swatters. Rodin grabbed one of the elephant tails and bolted out of the building saying to Isala on his way out, "Watch her, I'll be right back."

Moments later he returned and said to the girl, "I'm going to call the police now. You can either stay or go. It's up to you."

She in an almost imperceptible volume said, "I'm going, I was never here." And with that she leaped over the fence and ran off down the dirt road and never looked back.

Rodin placed multiple explosive charges around the storeroom and set the timers for five minutes. He then took out the cell phone that he had gotten off of Dieno's nightstand and called the police. He turned the phone off and put it his pocket hoping to maybe get names of other poachers.

As they headed for the SVU Rodin pulled off his balaclava and said, "Let's get the Hell out of Dodge."

"Mr. Tebogo, you may call your first witness."

"Thank you, your Honor. We chose not to call any witnesses. The defense rests. And at this time the defense believes that since the prosecution has failed to meet its burden of proof, we request that the court dismiss this case against my client."

"Request denied. Mr. Modise are you prepared for closing arguments?"

Prosecutor Modise rose and responded, "We are your Honor."

Chief Magistrate Kabelo turned to the jury and described the next phase of the trial.

"Ladies and gentlemen of the jury, both the prosecution and the defense have now rested their cases. The attorneys will now present their final arguments. Please remember, what the attorneys say is not evidence. However, do listen closely. They are intended to aid in understanding the case. Prosecution, you may begin."

Prosecutor Modise walked to the podium that was facing the witness stand and turned to face the jury. He placed his notes on the podium and smiled to the jury making sure to have eye contact with each of them and then he started.

"Thank you, your Honor. Ladies and gentlemen of the jury, thank you for your time and attention throughout this trail. After hearing all the facts, you are now faced with an important job of deciding whether the defendant, Liam Janssens is guilty of the brutal murders of Manny, Moe and Jack Bahlakwana.

Over the last week you each had to live with a case that has some of the most gruesome crimes, some of the most graphic violence, hopefully, that you'll ever see, that anyone will ever see. Quite frankly, I don't think any of us will ever be quite the same because of this case; and it's unfortunate that we have to deal with crimes of this nature, all of the horrific photographs and the descriptions from the coroner of the victims' injuries.

The defendant, Liam Janssens, is charged with three counts of capital murder and with three counts of conspiracy to commit murder. The fact that these crimes were premeditated and sanctioned by the international eco-terrorist group, Le Gang de la Clé de Singe proves a conspiracy.

You've heard from expert witnesses explaining how and why these vicious murders were committed by the defendant, who was working for Le Gang de la Clé de Singe to murder the three Bahlakwana brothers because they provided safaris that cater to big game hunters, which is perfectly legal in Botswana.

Now this case is about to go to you, the jury. It's not because of the war on eco-terrorism, but because of the overwhelming evidence presented to you proves the defendant Liam Janssens to be guilty as the principal in the first-degree murders of Manny, Moe and Jack Bahlakwana.

Ladies and gentlemen of the jury we ask you to return a verdict of guilty of three counts of capital murder and guilty of conspiracy. I thank you for your time, patience, and for your attention."

"Mr. Tebogo you may proceed with your closing argument."

Hilton Tebogo had taken off his suit jacket and had rolled up his shirt selves earlier that morning. Appearing more casual, he felt that jurors would see him not as a snooty high price attorney, but more of a man of the people. He didn't stand at the podium, he stood next to the jury box and when speaking he would walk from one end of the dock to the other making sure that when he spoke, he would look each juror in the eye.

"Your Honor, Counsel, ladies and gentlemen of the jury, good day.

Remember at the beginning of this case when the Chief Magistrate asked you whether you would follow the law. Whether you would be fair, and whether you would hold the prosecution to their burden of proving Liam Janssens guilty beyond a reasonable doubt. Chief Magistrate Kabelo also asked you whether you would presume Mr. Janssens innocent throughout the trail and your deliberations unless the prosecution proves him guilty beyond a reasonable doubt.

You heard from the police, from the coroner and from the folks from forensics, there was not one shred of evidence linking Liam Janssens to this crime, no DNA, no hair, and no fingerprints, in fact the only fingerprints found was that of a deceased rock star from the 60's. Detective Mosweu claimed that he suspected Mr. Janssens because of a so-called tip from Interpol that no one has seen. And even if the tip was real, the description was so vague that the murderer could have been my colleague here Oscar Alberink.

Now it's time for you to use your common sense and when you do, you will easily find Liam Janssens not guilty. Not guilty on all counts is the only proper verdict that's supported by the evidence you were presented with. Thank you."

The Chief Magistrate tapped his gavel to get the jurors attention. When he was satisfied, he began his instructions.

"Members of the jury, you have heard all the testimony concerning this case. It is now up to you to determine the facts. You and you alone, are the judges of the facts. Once you decide what facts the evidence proves, you must then apply the law as I give it to you.

In a moment the bailiff will take you to the jury room to consider your verdict. One of the first things you will want to do is to select a foreperson that will preside over your deliberations. It will be the foreperson's duty to sign the verdict form when you have agreed on a verdict. Whatever verdict you render must be unanimous. The bailiff will now escort you to the deliberation room."

Elise De Clercq grew up in Raeren, Belgium a small town that was once part of Germany, until after World War 1 when it became part of Belgium. It is one of several towns in the southeast Belgium that speaks predominantly German. Elise grew up speaking four languages, French, Dutch, German and English. She was an excellent student and received a full scholarship to Ghent University; she went on to get her Master of Science in Agro and Environmental Nematology.

While at the University, new cracks were found in Tihange 2, the Belgian nuclear power plant. Although the Health Minister was quoted as telling parliament that people living within a 100-kilometer radius would be provided iodine pills as protection in case of a radiation leak, the cracks sparked protests and public outcry over the aging reactors. Right up front leading the marches was Elise. Soon she was one of the leaders in Natuurpunt, Belgium's largest nature conservation organization. She was approached at one rally by a member of Le Gang de la Clé de Singe asking her if she would be interested in meeting other members who were like minded in social change.

She got more and more involved with the group, she started attending protest rallies and demonstration marches until one day she agreed to take part in a protest against an underground sale and convention of endangered species parts that was going to be held in Aachen, Germany, right across the border.

Over forty of them burst into the convention and started chanting anti-hunting slogans and harassing buyers and vendors. Things got ramped up when they started taking photographs of people and threatening to publicly expose them. People started pushing and shoving, punches were thrown, displays got overturned and the protesters began destroying items, and generally wreaking havoc. Then things got violent and totally out of hand.

Several of the vendors and buyers pulled out weapons and opened fire on the demonstrators wounding six and killing four. Elise was one of the wounded; she took a bullet in the calf of her right leg. Her friends were able to get her out before the polizei arrived; a doctor sympathetic with their cause treated her. Luckily, her wound wasn't too serious, and she was on crutches for only six weeks.

The German polizei arrested eight of the demonstrators and eleven from the convention including three people for murder. It was that event that Elise decided to join Le Gang de la Clé de Singe. She took the name Isala in honor of Isala Van Diest the first Belgian female doctor.

Icarus drove his Ford F-150 west on Tasosa Road and turned off on to a dirt road that took him straight up to the top of Bishop Hill, the sun was just starting to set, as he stood atop the summit, he could see the little town of Bishop Hills down at the bottom. Using his binoculars he was hoping he could see the Cadillac Ranch in Texas, but it turned out to be over a hundred miles away. He had read an article about it while flying over to the States in one of those airline magazines. The Cadillac Ranch is an art installation just outside of Amarillo, Texas on the old Route 66 highway. The exhibit includes ten Cadillac cars half buried nose-down in the ground in a single file. People say it gives off a Stonehenge vibe, very spiritual, very Zen.

Icarus parked his truck further down the hill and off to the side furthest away from the prairie dog colonies, he hiked back up to the top of the hill and planted himself under a forty-foot Soapberry tree and waited. It was well past midnight when Cody Hayes and Monte Collins drove up in a Chevy Silverado. They parked about a hundred feet away from where Icarus was seated under the tree. Monte turned the Chevy around away from Icarus and pointed the nose of the truck downhill so the headlights would shine down towards the prairie dog colonies. Once the truck was in position Cody and Monte started to get bunches of rags and canisters of kerosene out of the Silverado truck bed.

The plan was simple: Monte would go around and start plugging up a as many of the prairie dog colonies and Cody would stuff kerosene soaked rags into the openings and then light them. The idea was that smoke would drive them out where they would be waiting with their shotguns and blast them and. Those that couldn't get out would die from affixation.

Either way, they'd be gone, and ManKraw Oil & Gas would be back where they belong; pumping oil and gas and pumping money into the town. Who gives shit if a rat lives or dies where there's money to be had. If our government has taught us anything it's that you always take care of number one, número uno, the top dog.

While Monte was running around stuffing rags into wherever he found an opening, he accidently shoved his hand into a hole where a six-foot diamondback rattlesnake was resting. Monte hadn't felt such a searing pain in his entire life. He started to panic and ran up the hill to where Cody was supposed to be, screaming, "I've been bit by a rattler. Cody, help me."

But when he reached the truck, Cody wasn't there, instead there was a stranger holding a pistol. Monte held up his hand to the stranger and shouted, "Help me mister, I got bit by a rattler. I got go get to a hospital fast."

The stranger smiled, "Man, that's a bitch. Well, I tell you what. You better get going then."

Monte ran and got into the driver's side of the truck and reached for the keys, but they weren't there. The stranger walked over to the driver's door and said calmly, "Sorry friend, I must have misplaced those darn keys, so you might want to run for it. But I'm guessing you ain't gonna make it."

"Where's Cody?"

"Cody? Cody's hanging out under that tree up there."

As he got out of the truck, Monte could see that his hand was three times its normal size. He was starting to sweat profusely and was getting lightheaded, he started to walk up the hill to get Cody to help him, "Cody, you got to help me, I've been bit by a rattler. For the love of…" When he reached the top of the hill, he saw Cody hanging by his feet upside down from the Soapberry tree. His face was as red as a delicious apple and swollen so much that he couldn't even see his eyes. His mouth had a rag stuffed into it and was duct taped. Monte spun around to see the stranger walking towards him, "Mister, I don't understand."

"You don't? It's quite simple, Monte. You and your friend here were going to come up here and kill a bunch of worthless rodents and get rich in the process. Well, you found out that Mother Nature can be a real bitch, and as for your friend Cody, he found out that I can be one too."

"Please mister."

"You don't look so good Monte; I'd say you have about ten minutes to live. Just so you know I'll be hanging you upside down next to your friend over there with a little note letting the good people of Bishop Hills know what you boys were up to and giving them a warning of what will happen to anyone else if they try to fuck with these prairie dogs."

Monte never heard all of what Icarus said, he collapsed and died, as he was being carried to the Soapberry tree and hung up next to his friend, Cody. The next day Sheriff Fields found the bodies of Cody Hayes and Monte Collins after an anonymous person called saying that he would find their bodies up on Bishop Hill and that the people responsible for their deaths were members of Le Gang de la Clé de Singe.

Sheriff Fields found them hanging upside down with the yellow skull and cross monkey wrenches flags around their necks and notes in each of their pockets stating why they had been punished.

The next day the local newspaper, the Guymon Daily Herald front page carried the headline: TWO DEAD IN THE DOG DAYS OF AUTUMN. Beneath the headline was a photograph of the Yellow skull and crossed monkey wrenches flag and within the body copy was the verbiage found in the note on both victims from Le Gang de la Clé de Singe.

Let it be known that from this day forth that Le Gang de la Clé de Singe declares a proclamation of war against all Poachers, Big Game Hunters and all Big Game Safari Outfits as well as anybody anywhere in the world that targets, kills, profits and or supports the killing of any animals that are endangered large or small or any animals that are hunted for sport. Be forewarned, do so at your peril. You will be hunted down and pay with your lives. Be it, man or woman, there will be no exceptions and no mercy; we will show no quarter. You have been warned.

Two days after the murders Sheriff Sydney Fields received a phone call from Inspectors Morris and Volker from Interpol inquiring about the deaths of Cody Hayes and Monte Collins. He also heard back from the forensic lab letting him know that there was virtually no evidence to speak of, although they did find on Cody's front passenger door one single fingerprint of Walter Cronkite."

"Walter Cronkite, the news guy? But he's been dead forever."

"Well, as Walter used to say, And that's the way it is."

Branch Commander Moyo of the Botswana Police Service was informed of the killings in Mmopane, eight poachers shot dead and apparently Le Gang de la Clé de

Singe was claiming responsibility. The press was having a field day with it; it was being called the Mmopane Massacre.

Commander Moyo went out there personally to supervise the investigation,

Detective Mosweu was going to be handling the day-to-day stuff; she was there mostly for show. Branch Commander Moyo was going to be the face of the investigation; she would be the one interfacing with the press.

The initial assessment was that the killer or killers had knocked out the guard dogs who were now awake and really pissed off. The animal control had to come out and sedate them with tranquilizer darts. Once passed the dogs, the assailants appeared to have killed the man standing watch in the front yard. It was a very professional kill, quick and lethal. Next, they seemed to have entered the premises thru the back door after unscrewing the backdoor light so as not to be detected. The killer or killers started their killing spree on the first floor, probably using a silencer to remain undetected. They worked their way up to Dineo's room, saving the best for last. It looked like Dineo wasn't alone. It appeared he had a lady friend in bed with him. Since there isn't a female corpse maybe there is a witness out there. A reward might get results; it has worked in the past.

Dineo's death was definitely personal, everyone else had just been shot, but Dineo's body had been violated. Apparently after he was shot and killed the murderer flipped his body over and shoved an elephant's severed tail up his rectum. It reminded Branch Commander Moyo of picture flags that had been planted atop of Mount Everest signifying victory.

That detail was kept from the press, so if anybody were trying to confess to the killing, they would have to know the detail about the elephant tail, otherwise they were just a wannabe fame grabber.

Branch Commander Moyo held a press conference outside of the murder scene where she read a brief statement then decided to take a few questions. But Branch Commander Moyo of the Botswana Police Service wasn't prepared for how savage the press could be.

"Branch Commander Moyo, why is it that some eco-terrorist group could find these poachers and the Botswana Police Service couldn't?"

"Do you have any leads on who committed these murders?"

"What are you doing to protect the hunting industry?"

"What is the Botswana Police Service doing to put a stop to poaching?"

"Should hunters be frightened?"

"Is it true that there was sexual assault involved in these killings?"

"Have you spoken to Liam Janssens, the alleged murderer of the Bahlakwana brothers?"

"Do the murders of the Bahlakwana brothers and these killings have a similar MO?"

"Should hunters be frightened?"

"Do you think the Le Gang de la Clé de Singe is trying to send a warning about the Janssens trail?

"Were you able to get any physical evidence like DNA or fingerprints?"

"What are you doing to protect the hunting industry?"

"Do you think these murders will affect tourism?"

"Have you been in contact with Interpol?"

Branch Commander Moyo of the Botswana Police Service was clearly over her head being that this was her first time in the role of PR officer, but she muddled thru it by using the tried-and-true standard nonresponsive answers: *No commit, not at this time, we have some solid leads, were looking into it, and arrests are imminent.*

"Has the jury reached a verdict?"

The jury foreman stood and faced the Chief Magistrate, "We have, your Honor."

"Please hand the verdict to the bailiff."

Bailiff Phiri walked across the courtroom, collected the verdict and handed it to the court clerk.

Chief Magistrate Kabelo instructed the clerk to read the verdict.

"We the jury, in the case of Botswana versus Liam Jassens find the defendant guilty of the three charges of capital murder and guilty of three counts of conspiracy."

"Thank you, jury for your service today. You are dismissed. Mr. Janssens you have been found guilty of capital murder; we will set the date for sentencing to be scheduled for three weeks from today. Court is adjourned."

Hilton Tebogo felt totally gutted, he put his hand on Liam's shoulder trying to reassure him saying, "I'm sorry, but don't worry, we'll file an appeal this afternoon. I'm confident that we have a strong case to overturn this verdict. This is not uncommon as many times local juries are swayed and impressed by the power of authority."

Liam stood as two bailiffs came to handcuff him and take him back to Mahalapye prison; on his way out he turned to Rodin who said, "I'll come and visit you tomorrow."

"Yeah, up, up and away."

Icarus slept the entire two-hour drive back to prison; he arrived just in time for the mid-day meal, this being Monday today's menu is a choice of chicken & mushroom pie or jacket potato & coleslaw. Neither one is worthy of eating, but they really can't screw up a baked potato too badly.

Icarus had gone through the line and was searching for a place to sit, when Baruti spotted him, "Hey Liam, over here."

Baruti was sitting across from Gaone, Kym, Kabo and next to Seth, Dineo's brother. When Icarus approached Baruti slid over to his left towards Seth. As Icarus placed his tray down Baruti said, "Sorry to hear about the guilty verdict."

"Boy, news travels fast."

"I'm assuming your solicitor will be filing an appeal?"

"Yeah, he says he thinks it's got a good chance of being reviewed."

"You better hope it will be, cause capital murder carries a life sentence with no chance of release, ever. And I can't see you spending the rest of your life in here."

"You got that right."

"I guess you didn't hear about Seth's brother, Dineo?"

"No. Did he get arrested?"

Seth leaned past Baruti and snarled, "Your fucking French friends killed him and his crew, last night. You're a dead man, Frenchy."

"Hey, I told you I'm not a member of that gang."

"Yeah, well I don't believe you." Seth said as he grabbed his tray, stood up and walked behind Icarus, he leaned down and whispered in his ear, "Better not ever let me catch you alone or I'll kill you. You're a dead man walking."

Baruti said, "I told him that you didn't have anything to do with his brother's murder, but he won't listen. So, you just be careful."

Kabo said, "Yeah man, you better watch your back."

"Thanks man, I'll stay frosty. So, how did his brother die, was he out poaching?"

"Naw, somebody killed him and his whole gang last night in his house while they was sleeping. They left a note saying it was that French group that killed them, and they said that they'd be killing more poachers, too."

Rodin was waiting in the prison conference room where he and Icarus had met on several occasions, Liam Janssens, prison number 1011045 was shown into the room by a guard who said to Rodin, "You have a half an hour."

Rodin asked Icarus, "Is there a time that you're out in the yard? And never alters?"

"I'm always in the yard between 10am to noon and 2 until 4 everyday."

"And can you wander to any part of the yard, or are there restricted areas?"

"No, we're free to wander anywhere in the yard we want, so long as we stay away from the fences."

"Okay, tomorrow you need to be in the southeast quadrant of the yard, where there is a small cluster of five trees set in a semi-circle. You be waiting in the middle of those trees and be ready. A remote controlled drone will be piloted to land within that cluster of trees at precisely 3:30, the hatch will be unlocked, so you get your ass into that drone as fast as you can.

Once you're in, buckle up and just sit back. The drone is pre-programmed to take you to the rendezvous point for evacuation out of Botswana. If for any reason there needs to be a change of the flight plan Isala will be piloting the aircraft, do not try to override the system. She has been trained extensively and is an excellent pilot. Any action on your part to interfere in her command of the drone could be catastrophic. All you have to worry about is to be sure you're there and that you're alone.

There can be no screw-ups, this is a one shot deal. Isala will be piloting your drone from the rendezvous point and I will be nearby flying a cover drone that will be watching over you. It will be armed just in case things get hairy, but if all goes well, you'll be out of there in a matter of minutes. Just be sure you're there, alone."

Inspectors Morris and Volker were called into a meeting with Branch Commander Moyo and Detective Mosweu to discuss the Dineo Wengazi and his gang murders. Moyo was anxious to see if they could provide any conclusions or parallels between the Bahlakwana brothers murders and Wengazi and his gang murders.

"Inspectors Morris and Volker come in. Please have a seat. I'd like to introduce my lead detective on both the Bahlakwana brothers and Wengazi and gang murders, Detective Mosweu."

After the traditional handshaking ritual, Inspector Volker said, "Thank you Branch Commander Moyo for inviting Inspectors Morris and me to discuss the similarities of these two cases. We have come to some preliminary conclusions even though we haven't studied this latest case in depth. However we believe that two different killers committed these murders since the MO's are very different.

We believe that the Bahlakwana brothers were killed by a man who goes by the name Icarus."

Detective Mosweu looked confused. "Icarus?"

"Yes, the people in Le Gang de la Clé de Singe choose a nom de plume, if you will. They travel under different names and dozens of different passports. We don't know their real names and that's the point, it's very difficult to do any background checks. On those rare occasions when one of them is captured, they usually won't say anything incriminating against any of their fellow members. We have yet to flip a single one of them against any of the people up the food chain. They are willing to take the maximum prison sentence instead of giving us the names or any information. Also, the structure of the organization is such that everything is compartmentalized; basically you only know a tiny bit of the operation, so even if you want to talk you can only tell so much and give us the names of others. But what can you do with a name like Icarus, see what I mean. It's really hard to do identity checks when given names like that."

Inspector Morris continued, "We will eventually identity this character Icarus since we now have his photograph and his fingerprints. It will take a little time, but we will eventually know who he is.

"By the way, Icarus was a character in Greek Mythology; he was a man who dared to fly too near the sun on wings of wax and feathers. He got too close and the wax melted and so he fell to earth into the sea where he drowned."

Detective Mosweu still looking confused asked, "But, why Icarus? It doesn't seem like a name you'd want, because of the tragedy associated with it. Maybe someone like Hercules, a name of a hero, would be better."

"But even Hercules had flaws and like all the Greek heroes. Most have tragic endings to show us mere mortals that there is no perfect person. Besides, who knows why these people chose the names they do. It must have meaning to them. But I digress, so we think this Icarus is the killer of the Bahlakwana brothers, since he has a trademark of hanging his victim upside down. We believe the killer of Dineo Wengazi and the others was the work of a man code name Rodin or a man called the Iceman. Both are skilled assassins; both are methodical, and both leave zero clues except for the single fingerprint. By the way, whose fingerprint did they leave at Dineo Wengazi murder?"

Commander Moyo held up a folder and said, "The M.E, says it a perfect match to Muammar Gaddafi, the Libyan leader."

"After the sentencing of Mr. Janssens would it be possible for Interpol take possession of him for a while?" Morris queried.

"Yes, I think that could be arranged." Commander Moyo said while handing Morris the file on the Wengazi case then stated, "We would appreciate any help you could provide."

Morris took the file, stood up and said, "We'll take a look and see if there is anything we can do. Thank you, Branch Commander Moyo, Inspector."

That was Volker's cue. He rose and nodded to Moyo and Mosweu, "We'll be in touch."

Just south of the small village of Dinokwe, where Mogoutamba Road becomes Mokgotho Road there's a small cattle ranch of Boikanyo Kelebogile. Boikanyo has been a rancher all his life in Dinokwe like his father and his father's father. His ranch is thirty acres where he has over forty head of Tswana cattle, an indigenous cattle breed of Botswana. Boikanyo's brother worked for Botswana's Department of National Parks & Wildlife in their anti-rhino poaching squad. He was killed in an ambush along with three others. Months before his death Boikanyo's brother Dipuo had joined Le Gang de la Clé de Singe and was secretly working with them giving them information on local poachers. After his death the gang contacted Boikanyo and he agreed to help in this operation.

On Boikanyo's ranch there are lots trees, which will provide plenty of cover and privacy that Isala and Rodin need to assemble the two the Ehang 184 autonomous drones. Boikanyo had an abandoned cattle feed barn that Rodin and Isala used as their workshop.

The Ehang 184 resembles the basic shape of a 'Smart Car', except instead of wheels it has skids as landing gear and no internal combustion engine. The Ehang is a quad copter, unlike most other multirotor drones. The 184 mounts its rotor arms from the four corners of the vehicle, it has eight propellers on the four arms. It runs on a 2.6 lithium battery that gives it a 30 minute flight distance of approximately 25 miles, but Rodin modified the power units to be augmented with self-recharging solar batteries that gives the 184 an unlimited flight range during the day.

Rodin and Isala completed the assembly of both drones in less than four hours, but it took Isala another three hours to program the drone to pick up Icarus. By five o'clock as the sun was to set, they were ready. It was now up to Icarus to be in the right place at the right time.

The day started like any other in Mahalapye prison, lights on at 5am followed by roll call which lasted anywhere from forty-five minutes to an hour in Cell Block B, then everyone marched in single file to the mess hall.

Breakfast consisted of powered eggs, some sort of meat type product, a soggy grain in gravy that resembled grits and a cup of Joe. After a hardy breakfast they were herded out into the exercise yard where groups and gangs gathered. Depending on the day and which gang or group you belonged to, dictated where your assigned location was. If you wandered into someone else's' turf you could pay a heavy penalty.

Not often, but occasionally disputes were settled out in the yard, and could vary from a simple fist fight to a dance on the blacktop, which is what prisoners call a stabbing. Icarus was trying to be aware of everything around him since Seth Wengazi made a death threat after finding out about his brother's murder. For a bit of protection, he sought out

Baruti and found him with Gaone, Kym and Kabo, who were hanging out behind the prison laundry building. They were seated at a wooden bench under a small cluster of sycamore fig trees, Gaone and Kabo were playing a game of Egyptian Rat Screw for cigarettes, Kabo looked to be kicking Gaone's ass.

"Hey, Liam." Baruti shouted, waving Icarus over. "You play?"

"Aw, I'm not very good at card games. But it looks like Kabo is."

"For the moment." Gaone said without looking up.

Baruti asked, "You see Seth?"

"No, you?"

"Yeah, I saw him when we got into the mess hall. He still thinks you had something to do with his brother's murder. You just keep looking over your shoulder."

"You tell him we're going to have to resolve this one way or another. If he wants to have it out with me, so be it. But you tell him to man up and let's get it on unless he's too big a pussy to go man to man."

Icarus walked away and headed over to this afternoon's landing area for the drone to scope it out. When he got there, it was just as Rodin had described it, it seemed to be perfect. Once the drone landed, the guard tower wouldn't have a good view and the trees would give some protection if there was to be any shooting. Hopefully once he was aboard, the drone would have the umph to get his ass out of there fast if the shit hit the fan, although Rodin said he would be flying nearby giving some cover. Now all he had to do was to stay low and try to avoid Seth.

He headed back towards his cell block keeping his eyes peeled for trouble, Seth might try and set him up or ambush him when he least expects it; that's how it usually done in prison. Rarely is it an open confrontation. As he rounded the corner of Cell Block E there stood Seth with three other inmates.

"Well, well, well if isn't my old friend Liam, funny running into you like this." Seth said with a wolf's grin.

Icarus stood motionless as the four men slowly encircled him. He looked around and noticed that they were isolated and completely out of view from any guard towers.

He took a position of defense, unknown to his attackers he was a master in the art of Capoeira, the Afro-Brazilian martial art that was developed by Brazilian slaves in the 16th century. It was considered such a deadly force that it was outlawed in the 1800's.

Icarus stood ready as first attacker came at him from behind him. He twirled around in a windmill motion kicking the man square in the jaw and not only breaking it, but rendering the man unconscious. Then two men rushed him, Icarus ducked as if going into a break dance. He began spinning around with such force using his left leg to knock both men down and breaking both of their ankles. Not wasting the energy he generated, he used the spinning motion to spring up and grab Seth by the shoulders, then pulling himself up with great speed, he used his head to shatter his enemy's right cheek bone and knocked four teeth out of his mouth. The whole scuffle was over in a matter of seconds and when it was over Icarus barely broke a sweat.

He left his four would be attackers where they lay, as he headed back to his cell to get cleaned up for lunch.

Icarus was sitting on his bunk when Baruti entered with a huge smile on his face. "What the hell, man. You are one major badass. Why didn't you tell me?"

"And give away the element of surprise?"

"Well old Seth and his mates aren't going to give you any grief anymore. Nor would I or expect anybody else."

"Did they rat me out?"

"Hell no, they all claimed they were attacked by some unknown assailants, they said it must have been at least a dozen or so and that it happened so fast they couldn't really see who did it. Hell, they won't ever admit that they got their ass kicked by some skinny white guy."

"I don't know but for some reason I'm hungry; you?"

Rodin climbed into the Ehang 184's cockpit, put on the wireless headset, buckled up the 5-piece safety harness and switched on the rotors via the iPad instrument control panel digital display screen. He grabbed the stick and rudder and eased the stick towards him, and the silent aircraft ascended.

When he was twenty feet in the air, he hovered above to test his radio, "Isala can you read me? Over."

"Copy, I read you loud and clear." She said standing next to the unmanned drone. She was holding the iPad that was to operate Icarus's drone, which after tapping the screen, she started the rotors and programmed the aircraft to ascend to hover next to Rodin's drone. She looked up to Rodin and gave a thumbs-up and announced, "All systems are go, ready when you are."

"Let's roll."

At 2:45 the two drones started their 35-mile journey to Mahalapye prison. They would approach from the southwest and when they had visual contact, the two drones would veer slightly east so as to give the drone a straight shot down into the prison yard. Their altitude was three thousand feet. Isala's drone would hover over the pick-up area and once Icarus was in position the drone would simply drop down to pick him up. The whole extraction should only take 40 seconds, if all went without a hitch. Rodin would slightly lag behind and be hovering off to the southeast of the guard tower waiting to pounce if needed.

At exactly 3 o'clock Icarus was standing in position. He looked up and saw the drone descending towards him, he gave a quick glance around and to his delight there didn't seem to be anyone taking notice of a 13 foot off white aircraft falling out of the sky. As soon as Isala landed the drone she remotely opened the hatch and Icarus scrambled in. Once Isala detected that the harness had been engaged, she took off. The drone took off straight up and once it reached a thousand feet, the drone headed due north until the prison was out of visual contact, and it then banked to the west swinging a large semi-circle south back to Kelebogile's ranch.

Meanwhile, Rodin had been keeping an eye on guard tower four. He was half expecting to see the guard raise an alarm and would have been prepared to open fire on any armed response, but as it turned out the guard in tower four was fast asleep during the whole escape. With Icarus rescued safely, Rodin flew back to the ranch. Halfway there he received word from Isala, "The winged man had landed."

"Good evening I'm Nigel Williams and this is the BBC World Headline News. Our top story this hour once again comes from Gaborone, Botswana where there are several twists and turns in the bizarre tale of the man convicted of the murder of three brothers, who owned a safari company that catered to big game hunters.

The brothers were targets of the eco-terrorist group Le Gang de la Clé de Singe. They were found hung upside down on crosses, a Belgian man, Liam Janssens was charged and recently convicted of their murders.

We have breaking news that the convicted murderer Liam Janssens has escaped from Meghalaya prison this very day. Authorities currently have no idea how Janssens was able to escape undetected. There weren't any cuts in the wire surrounding the facilities and no tunnels have been discovered. Prison officials say it's almost like he vanished into thin air.

In a possible related story, it has been reported that two nights ago eight suspected poachers were murdered and a large stash of illegal endangered species goods, such as ivory, rhino horns and multiple varieties of animal skins, teeth and claws were destroyed. Once again group Le Gang de la Clé de Singe has claimed responsibility for their deaths.

In other news the British Prime Minister told Parliament...."

Icarus climbed out of the drone where Isala was waiting, he smiled and gave her a big bear hug.

"Hey beautiful, thanks for the ride. It was a thing of beauty."

"Glad to be of service. How are you?"

"Great now, your timing couldn't have been better. Things in Mahalapye were starting to become dicey."

Isala looking beyond Icarus saw Rodin's drone approaching, "Ah, here's Rodin."

Rodin opened the hatch of his drone and was greeted with hugs and kisses, hugs from Icarus and kisses from Isala.

"Hey thanks brother, I owe you one." Icarus said as they were walking towards the abandoned cattle barn.

"Icarus, you know you're having been captured, photographed and fingerprinted cancels out your ability to participate in any of the on the ground campaigns. You're basically a liability, but HQ wants you to know that there's a position in any one of the home offices, but they can't afford to have you out in the field." Rodin said.

"Me in an office behind a desk? No fucking way, you might as well just shoot me now."

"That's from the top, man. You don't want to put anyone's life at risk, would you? And that's what you'd be doing, I'm sorry."

Isala joined in, "Icarus, don't think of it as a death sentence. You have a great head for logistics, planning, and you've had years of experience that would greatly benefit the organization."

"Yeah, I guess."

She continued, "There's an operation going on in Zambia that's changing almost daily, I'm sure they could use some outside thinking. You know how that is, people being too close sometimes can't see things others can at a distance."

"Hey, when you're right, you're right. Tell me more about this Zambia thing."

That night the three of them had a meager dinner courtesy of Boikanyo: beef stew with a side of sadza, a stiff maize porridge and a bowl of nhedzi, wild mushroom soup. After dinner Boikanyo treated everyone to several glasses of whawha, his own special home brewed maize beer. Which for the uninitiated tends to kick their ass if they're not careful, and since they were celebrating, their asses got kicked royally.

The next morning when Rodin and Isala were awaked by cattle bellowing they discovered that Icarus and one of the Ehang drones was gone, left behind was a short note.

Please forgive me for swiping one of your drones. Think I'll head on over to Kafue and see if there's anything

I can do to help. I promise I won't bollocks anything up. Tell the brass I appreciate the offer, but maybe some other time.

Love you guys.
Icarus

P.S. Thanks for the ride.

"Ladies and gentlemen, may I have your attention please. I would like to welcome all of you to the 45th Worldwide Affiliates of Safari Partners Annual Gala and Awards Dinner here at the beautiful Le Casino de Monte-Carlo. I'm your host Charles Doering president and CEO of Worldwide Affiliates of Safari Partners. We are here tonight to honor this year's winners of the coveted W.A.S.P. Hunters of the Year Awards. But, before we get started, I'd like to introduce tonight's special guest host, he's the star of stage and screen, the one and only Pete 'Petey' Peterson. Come on let's give it up for the one and only Petey Peterson!"

Pete 'Petey' Peterson was not now or ever was an "A" list celebrity; it was true that he had been in several motion pictures and plays, mostly in character roles, the loveable sidekick or the wacky neighbor type.

He was known more for his standup comedy and his guest appearances on the late night TV show circuit. He didn't appeal to the younger crowd; he never could transition from the Baby Boomers to the Gen X, Gen Y, Millennial's and definitely not the iGen crowd. Petey knew he was on the other side of his career heading down hill fast, with the end staring him right in the face; he was reduced to playing these corporate gigs. At least it was something and he made a decision that if it came down to doing gigs at mall openings, he'd get personal with the wrong end of his Colt revolver, so help him God.

Petey slowly walked out onto the stage amongst rousing applause and cheering, and waved triumphantly to the three hundred plus attendees as he made his way to the podium.

"Thank you. Thank you. Thank you. It's my pleasure to be here in Monte Carlo amongst so many venators. Venators, that's Latin for hunters. I'm a bit of a hunter, if I do say so myself. Why just this year I went hunting with two Canadian hunters and we were driving through the country to do a little bear hunting, when all of a sudden, we came upon a fork in the road. There was a sign that read, 'BEAR LEFT'. So they turned the car around and went home."

Applause. Applause. Applause.

"I went elk hunting with my brother-in-law this year, when we came across a beautiful blonde sunbathing naked on a rock. I was feeling a little frisky, so I winked at her and said, "Are you game?" She winked back and said, "I sure am!" So my stupid brother-in-law shot her."

Applause. Applause. Applause.

"You know, I always eat what I kill, so last week I was preparing a meal for my kids, I thought I'd surprise them and not tell them I was cooking deer meat. When my youngest son Timmy asked what it was, I said I'll give you a

clue; it's what your mother calls me. Timmy goes screaming thru the house yelling it's a fucking asshole don't eat it!"

Applause. Applause. Applause.

"Hey, what's the cheapest type of meat? Deer Balls. They're always under a Buck."

Silence.

"Hello, is this mic on, I know you're out there I hear you breathing…"

Petey went on with those cornball jokes for over forty-five minutes and according to him, he killed them dead. And for some of them sitting in the audience, they would have liked to return the favor.

The Iceman, Odin and Isala were all seated together at a large table for nine near the front, close to the podium in the Salon Rose Restaurant with other members of the Worldwide Affiliates of Safari Partners. W.A.S.P. had rented out the entire facility for the evening's festivities. The boys from Le Gang de la Clé de Singe were traveling under the names of Roger Stone, Eddie Ward and Bobby Zhao all hailing from the great state of Utah, the Salt Lake City chapter. They were seated with members from Montana, USA, Budapest, Hungry and Naples, Italy. Their dinner companions were all members in long standing in W.A.S.P some having been members for over thirty years.

At their table sat a total of six hunters who were each up for major hunting awards of the year in different categories. The W.A.S.P. Awards were the Oscars, Tony, and Grammys all rolled into one of the hunting world. The annual W.A.S.P awards had some of the biggest names in hunting, honoring some of the most accomplished hunters in the world. Seated at every guest table were several nominees all vying not only the statuettes, but also each award is accompanied with a twenty-five-thousand dollar cash prize.

From Naples, Italy came sixteen-year-old Luigi Bianchi and his father Salvador. Young Luigi is nominated for the Young Hunter of the Year Award. Luigi scored high marks for his downing of a 12,000-pound bull elephant sporting five-foot tusks, making him one of the odds on favorites.

Seated next to the Bianchi's were the Puskas, Gergo and Csilla from Budapest, Hungary. A husband-and-wife hunting team whose most recent adventure was hunting cheetahs in Namibia, where they bagged eleven of the big cats in thirteen days.

And rounding out the table were the boys from Montana, U.S.A. Mason Campbell and his good friend and guide Zane Hanson. Mason is up for Survivor of the Year Award. The award is given to the hunter who survives from a hunt that goes terribly wrong and yet they live to tell the tale.

It seems that Mason, Zane and and a friend, Billy Phillips were hunting out in a remote area of Montana on the US and Canadian border, not far from Sweet Grass, Montana. Billy had hit and wounded an elk the day before with a bow and arrow, they were able to find it the next day and were taking each other's picture with the elk to post on

YouTube when they were attacked by a 1,600 pound grizzly bear.

Unfortunately, for them, they were several yards from their gear and weapons when the bear attacked. The Ursus arctos charged Mason and Zane knocking them both down, the beast then grabbed mason's foot and started to drag him away when Billy ran to their gear packs and pulled out a Colt 9mm handgun and fired two shots one of them hitting the bear. Once wounded the bear turned and attacked Zane who was still on the ground struggling to get up. Zane received multiple bites to the back of his head, face and neck. Billy fired off another couple of rounds, two of which hit its target. The grizzly spun around and lunged at Billy crashing into him and hammering him to the ground, ripping and tearing mid-section. All the commotion and screams from the attack attracted another grizzly bear, realizing that they were going to be unable to save Billy and had to defend themselves. Mason and Zane ran from the scene to go get help.

Mason's calf muscle had been torn out resulting in multiple surgeries and his having to walk with a cane. Zane's head and neck injuries required over two hundred stitches, plastic surgery and dozens of skin grafts. Billy's remains were later found near their gear packs and no sign of either of the grizzly bears. One man was killed, and two men will be haunted for the rest of their lives wondering if only I…

Mason and Zane told the folks at the table that if they won, they were going to dedicate the award money to Billy's family.

The others at the table all gave their sympathies and spoke of how brave Mason and Zane were having had to deal with such a tragedy.

The Iceman listened to the story, and all the people's comments, then asked them, "That's a very sad tale indeed my friend. I have a question for you two, do you think that elk suffered very much after been wounded with an arrow and having taken so long to die. Do you think it would have been an agonizing and tortuous death? It just seems to me that it would have been an excruciating slow and agonizing way to die don't you think?"

Mason looked at the man sitting across from him and asked, "Excuse me, Mister?"

"Stone. Roger Stone."

"Well Mister Stone, you seem to be more sympathetic towards the elk than to Billy or Zane or me."

"Oh, I am sorry is that why you're here, looking for sympathy? You brought all this misery and death on yourselves. First, hunting with a bow and arrow usually results in the animal suffering a long lingering death, which I take it you or your guide here don't really give a shit about, and secondly you had to know you were in grizzly bear county, so why were you so woefully ill prepared? Maybe if you weren't so into taking selfies and congratulating each other, Billy Phillips would probably be alive. So yes, Mister Campbell, I am more sympathetic to the elk."

The folks at the table just stared down at their laps in silence, until Charles Doering president and CEO of Worldwide Affiliates of Safari Partners got to the podium and said, "All right, let's give it up for Pete 'Petey' Peterson, ladies and gentlemen, thank you Petey, that was great fun. I hope everyone is enjoying their dinner, we're going to get started with the awards portion of the evening in just a few moments, but first I'd like to touch upon a subject that is on a lot of people's minds tonight, Le Gang de la Clé de Singe. As you all know there have been several attacks against hunters, safari outfits and companies that specialize in buying and selling animal parts, even taxidermists.

"Well, I have a special surprise for everyone, I'd like to introduce a true American hero and a longtime member of Worldwide Affiliates of Safari Partners. Please give a warm welcome to retired SEAL Team Commander William T. "Wooch" Brown."

The crowd erupted with thunderous applause and cheers culminating in a five-minute standing ovation. A chant of *"Wooch. Wooch. Wooch."* started in the back of the room and soon engulfed the entire dining room.

SEAL Team Commander William T. "Wooch" Brown walked out from behind the curtain waving to the enthusiastic crowd. At age sixty six "Wooch" still cuts a dashing figure, at just over six feet tall, solid physique, full crop of silver hair with a matching walrus moustache, and piercing blue eyes highlighted by wire-rimmed glasses. He meets Charles Doering at the podium and signals the audience to settle down as he takes his notes from inside his sports coat pocket.

"Thank you, you're too kind. I'd just like to thank Charles Doering and everyone at Worldwide Affiliates of Safari Partners. It's wonderful to be here at the 45th Worldwide Affiliates of Safari Partners Annual Gala and

Awards Dinner, and where better to celebrate than in Monte-Carlo. I have been a member of W.A.S.P. since the very beginning of this fine institution forty-five years ago.

"The world has changed a lot in all those years, some things for the better, some not so good.

"Today we face an enemy so evil, so ruthless that we are being threatened, not only of losing our hunting heritage, but some are also even being deprived of their livelihood. Ladies and gentlemen, there is a cancer among us, a bunch of cold-blooded killers.

I'm talking about Le Gang de la Clé de Singe, the so-called eco-terrorist group that proclaims to be the protector of nature, of animals, and wildlife. They have decided that they and they alone will act as judge, jury and executioner. They pass judgment over men, women, young and old, all in the name of wildlife conservation.

This organization of thugs and outlaws are well funded and well organized. They use tried and true guerilla war tactics, they use a run and gun style of combat that's very effective, very hard to counter, because most times they deploy small groups that aren't easy to track.

As you know very few have been captured and those that have been aren't able to give much information because the way the organization is structured. For all the evil they do, I must say I applaud their effort to stop poaching, I just wish they would concentrate their efforts there instead of their war on everyday citizens, that's what I find most egregious.

I want everyone here to know that we are not going to take it anymore, unlike the fiasco that befell David

Leeway's attempt to stop this eco-terrorist group. I knew David Leeway, he was a close personal friend of mine, in fact he came to me with his plan to try and draw out the people who attacked and killed his three children that were on a hunting safari. I tried to warn him and even provided some assistance in planning his safari. So, in some small way I feel a sense of responsibility in his death. That's one reason I decided to work with Charles here and other entities like the NRA, Glock, and Remington among others, even some world governments, to all work together to put an end to this Le Gang de la Clé de Singe. I'm hoping that these murders will receive a powerful sting from W.A.S.P.

Now, enough talking shop, let's get down to the festivities and have some fun. But before we do, I do want to say how impressed I am with those amazing dioramas out in the lobby, that one with the 15-foot tree that has those eight terrified-looking baboons with a lunging African lion, in mid-flight, wow. And don't get me started on that one of the ten hyenas hunting down a wounded wildebeest, fan-damn-tastic.

Well, I'm done yammering, I'm going to hand the mic back over to Charles Doering to present this evening's awards. Charles."

Wooch. Wooch. Wooch.

The Iceman was sitting out on the terrace overlooking the Mediterranean enjoying a glass of Chateau

Rasque when Commander Brown sauntered in and sat down across from him.

"Wooch, how ya doing? That was a heck of a speech you gave last night."

"Glad you liked it, Ice. By the way what name are you using these days?"

"Roger Stone. You like it?"

Wooch gave him the once over and said, "Yeah, it suits you. You look like a Roger Stone, although it's not as good as the Iceman."

"Thanks, can I get you something to drink?"

"Sure, I'll have what you're having."

The Iceman held up his hand and waved at the waiter, "Garcon. Un verre de Château Rasque pour mon ami. Je vous remercie."

"Oui, monsieur."

Moments later the waiter returned placing the wine in front of the Commander, "Vous voila."

Commander Brown held his glass up and said, "Cheers."

"Cheers. So, Commander what can we do for you. Oh, by the way before you go on, do you know who won the Survivor of the Year Award? We left after dinner."

"I think it was some woman who spent six months on a desert island after having fallen overboard on a pleasure cruise, why?"

"Oh, just curious."

"Yes well, since you and the boys left early, you probably missed the big news."

"Big news?"

"You're familiar with the story of Robin Hood, I presume?"

"The rob from the rich, guy?"

"Exactly. Well in the middle of the story there is the part of an arrow contest where the evil Prince John holds an archery contest in order to temp Robin out of hiding in hopes of capturing him, remember?"

"I do, and if I remember correctly Robin was captured and almost hung."

"Yes, but that was because Robin was blinded by the love for Maid Marian and was a bit fool hardy."

"Wooch, I must tell you I'm not much of an archer."

"Good to know, thankfully you won't be called upon to use a bow and arrow. W.A.S.P. has decided to sponsor a worldwide hunting contest to be held in Zambia, it's a competition to see who can kill the finest big five trophies, all are to be killed within a week, the African elephant, Black rhinoceros, Cape buffalo, African Lion and African leopard.

The competitors will be the five top winners from last night's awards show. The Hunting Network is planning on covering the hunts and making a reality TV show out of it, it'll be called the Big 5. The network has already lined up sponsors and are thinking of making it a yearly competition."

"Whose idea was this?"

"You're looking at him."

"What does the winner receive?"

"A million dollars and all kinds of swag from the sponsors. Of course if all goes well, there won't be any winner."

"Do they realize what they're in for, how dangerous this going to be for them?"

"I have explained all the deadly implications to everyone involved from the hunters, to the network execs and the sponsors. They all know the risks and they all want in. Now, just so you know, the Zimbabwean Army will be providing an armed escort with every hunter, so that will make your assignment a little harder."

"No worries, we'll work around that. What inside information can you provide?"

"I will have access to schedules and locations that I will forward on to you."

"I'm thinking that we'll let them try to do their hunts and give the show a top rating ending. Wooch, do they have any idea that you're with the dark side?"

"Not a clue, I've been a member of W.A.S.P. from the start, forty-five years. You saw last night how they feel about me."

"Wooch. Wooch. Wooch."

"You got it."

"So, when does this competition begin?"

"Six weeks."

"Okay, I'll start assembling the Red Team."

"Excellent. And by the way, nice wine."

Jason Rowe was the winner of the Outstanding Hunting Achievement Award, not given necessarily every year. Only when W.A.S.P. feels a hunter has demonstrated outstanding achievements in the finite area of big game hunting.

Jason is fifty-seven years old, an American born professional big game hunter, specializing in hunting lions. Rowe always hunts alone, never trusting his native help, and his favorite rifle for hunting lions is the Mauser M98 Magnum. He served four tours as a Captain in Iraq and Afghanistan. After the war he started his own safari business and in just five years he was considered the best and most expensive safari operator in the Democratic Republic of the Congo.

Rowe is regularly hired by Hollywood when filming in Africa; he is rumored to have had several love affairs with many a leading lady.

Charles "Butch" Anderson was born in New Jersey, he's forty-four years old, worked on Wall Street as an analyst for seven years, then wrote a New York Times best-selling spy novel called Nitro Express, now spends all his time signing books and hunting elephants.

He was this year's winner of the Apogee Achievement Award, the award that honors excellence in the field and the hunter who has demonstrated well-defined hunting achievements. Butch Anderson has claimed to have shot between 60 and 70 elephants; his weapons of choice are the .256 Mannlicher and the .280 Ross. In between slaughtering pachyderms, Butch is writing a sequel to his run-away hit, he's using the working title of Nitro Express Two.

Sir William Cornwallis Smythe is a sixty-eight year old English military engineer, artist, naturalist and hunter of big game. He made hunting history a year ago when Sir William shot an elephant, a quagga, a giraffe, a hippopotamus, a hartebeest, an Impala, a rhinoceros and a waterbuck all in one day.

This year due to a series of events he was awarded the Trailblazer Award, which is awarded to the individual who has faced with enormous challenges and displayed courage, determination and that "never quit" attitude in overcoming adversity.

Sir William Smythe recently had a string of mishaps while on safari that really tested his metal. He was gored in the chest by a rhino, mauled by a wounded lion when he crawled into a cave after the beast, and he was tusked through the leg by a bull elephant when his rifle misfired. Since then he has acquired moniker "Wild Bill".

Wendy Sutherland was born and raised in India, her father was attached to the German Embassy, she is forty-three years old, stands a mere five foot one. Wendy was the recipient of this year's Global Hunting Award that is awarded to the hunter who has hunted in the most countries, has the most total number of hunts, and the quality of game collected.

Over the course of the year Wendy shot tiger, lion, snow leopard, bear, elephant, hippopotamus, ibex, moose, gaur, chamois, nilgai, water buffalo, and numerous small game and bird species throughout Europe, India, Asia, North America, Africa and China.

Ms. Sutherland is an avid horsewoman and was very keen on pig sticking; she had been known to have speared a leopard, a cheetah, and swamp deer from horseback.

Haruto Nakamura from Tokyo, Japan is a fifty-eight and an ex-computer software developer whose family was Matagi, traditional winter hunters of the Tohoku region of northern Japan. After making his first trip to Africa, Haruto became a professional hunter and game ranger in Angola.

He won the International Professional Hunter of the year award, an award that is given to the hunter who has made the greatest contributions to hunting worldwide and has displayed unparalleled service to the global hunting community.

Haruto is an avid photographer and has published several tabletop books on the animals of Africa; he always says that when he's not shooting big game, he's shooting big game.

The Iceman, Odin and LuWei all took separate flights to Lusaka, Zambia from the Nice Cote d'Azur International Airport; they all left on different flights but arrived within two hours of each other. The other members of the Red Team would arrive the following day. They were all traveling under the passports that they used in Monte Carlo. Odin got into Kenneth Kaunda Airport first, so he was tasked with obtaining the rental car. He opted for the Renault Duster DCI, an SUV with all-wheel drive. Odin parked the rental car in the airport parking lot and waited for the others to arrive and would have them meet him at the Nsonge Walala Restaurant next to the Emirates terminal.

LuWei's flight on Air Zimbabwe was next to land; Odin sent texts to him and the Iceman as to where they should head to after they got thru customs. The Iceman showed up an hour after LuWei; Odin asked if he wanted anything to eat or drink.

"No thanks, I'll grab something when we get to the hotel. I'm ready to get going."

Odin headed out of the airport parking lot towards town. The airport boulevard fed onto the Great E/T4 highway which he took for 6 miles, then he hung a left onto the Kamloops Road heading south where he made a hard right on Alick Nkhata Road for 3 miles where it T-boned into Haile Selassie Ave and arrived at the InterContinental Lusaka in under 30 minutes.

The InterContinental Hotel is located in the heart of downtown in what has been dubbed as embassy circle, just minutes away from the Nigerian Embassy, the Indian Embassy, the Chinese Embassy, the Japanese Embassy, and the German Embassy, as well as the major international corporation offices of Barclays Bank, KPMG, DHL and MRI Syngenta.

Before arriving at the hotel the Iceman asked if LuWei was able to get the positions of any CCTV in and around the hotel grounds so as to be sure to be aware to hide their identities by either avoiding them or making sure to wear a ball cap, dark glasses and, whenever possible try and look in another direction, away from the camera. LuWei said that he had and that they should check their texts, as everyone should have received a copy of the map.

It was late in the afternoon when the Renault pulled into the driveway, the valet came running to greet them. "Good evening gentlemen. Can I get someone to help with your luggage?"

Lu Wei opening the back hatch said, "No thanks, we're traveling pretty light."

"Very good sir. Check-in is to your right in the lobby."

As they approached the registration counter, there was one associate working the front desk, "Good evening, gentlemen and welcome to the InterContinental Lusaka. Checking in?"

Odin took the lead, "Yes, we have a reservation for Stone, Ward and Zhao."

"Yes sir, I have reservations for three classic rooms for five nights, is that correct?"

"That's correct."

"Would you gentlemen like rooms on the same floor?"

"No, that won't be necessary. Absence makes the heart grow fonder." Lu Wei said.

"Very good, I have Mr. Stone in room 333, Mr. Ward in room 248 and Mr. Zhao in 425. Here are your keys. The elevators are to your right. Is there anything else that I can do you?"

"No. I think we're good." The Iceman answered.

"Gentlemen, I hope you enjoy your stay and if there is anything that you might need, please don't hesitate to call. Thank you."

As they were headed to the elevator the Iceman said, "Let's plan on meeting down in lobby in an hour. That should give everyone some time to relax and get settled in."

Both Odin and LuWei agreed as the elevator doors closed.

"Charles Doering president and CEO of Worldwide Affiliates of Safari Partners, I have a reservation for four."

"Of course, monsieur. You're the first to arrive; please right this way." Responded Gaspard, the maitre'd of Le Louis VX – Alain Ducasse a l'Hotel de Paris.

"Merci beaucoup."

Gaspard led Charles Doering president and CEO of Worldwide Affiliates of Safari Partners, as he referred to himself, to a table overlooking the Place du Casino. As he handed him the menu he asked, "Would monsieur like me to call the head Sommelier to the table?"

"That would be très magnifique."

Gaspard gave a short bow and went to find Jacque, the Sommelier, thinking what a beautiful language French is and how these rich American fucks butcher it.

Commander Wooch wandered into the restaurant and spied Doering sitting alone looking at his cell phone.

"Charles."

"Ah, Wooch. Please have a seat."

"I'm just waiting for the Sommelier; what kind of wine do you think you'd like?"

"Surprise me."

Jacque, the Sommelier strode over to the table and asked, "Good day messieurs, may I help you?"

"Jacque, we're celebrating a major event and I would like a fabulous bottle of wine to commemorate this occasion. Price is not an object, my man. So, what do you recommend, mon amie?"

"For you and your friends monsieur, I think to celebrate a momentous occasion, only something fabuleux will do, I recommend a modest 1990 Petrus Red Bordeaux, from the world famous Chateau Lafleur-Petrus from Pomerol, France."

"Sounds great, Jacque. We'll have two bottles."

"Tres bon, I shall return monsieur."

As Jacque was about to leave, Commander Brown asked, "Excuse me Jacque, I'm just curious, how much are those modest bottles of wine?"

"In US Dollars, approximately $14,500."

Charles jumped in, "Now Wooch, you let me worry about that. Jacques, you go on."

"Oui monsieur." Jacques said with a big grin.

"Wooch, W.A.S.P. is potentially going to make a gazillion dollars off this enterprise, so let's just sit back and enjoy the ride."

Gaspard the maitre'd was arriving to their table with two men dressed in suits in tow, Jack Bonem, president of the Hunting Network and Joseph Havelka president and CEO of Remington Firearms.

"Merci Gaspard, Gentlemen please be seated. I've just ordered a modest couple of bottles of wine; I think you'll enjoy."

Bonem smiled and said, "Chuck baby, I can't wait."

"Jack, Joe I'd like to introduce you to Commander William T. "Wooch" Brown US Navy, retired."

Joe Havelka seated across from Wooch, held up his hand in a greeting gesture. "Hey."

Bonem sitting next to Brown shook the Commanders hand and said, "Woochie, great nickname."

"It's Wooch, Mr. Bonem." Brown said with a serious almost deadly tone.

"Ew, touchy." Bonem said in snarky way to no one in particular.

Charles Doering tried to defuse the tension by changing the subject and said, "Oh, did I mention that it was Commander Brown's idea for Big 5?"

Havelka said, "Well Commander, we at Remington think it's a fabulous idea and we're looking forward to being a part it."

Bonem nodding agreed, "Brilliant concept. This is going to be Yuge!"

"You know gentlemen, this is not without some peril, there is an element of danger and I'm not talking about the wildlife. There will be the threat of attacks from Le Gang de la Clé de Singe. People's lives could be in danger, I just want to be perfectly clear and you understand," emphasized Commander Brown.

"But what about the Zimbabwean Army, they'll be there to protect the contestants and crew, won't they?" asked Joe Bonem.

"A couple things, first, we don't know much about the Zimbabwean Army capabilities. For all we know they might not be sending us their most elite troops, and even if they do, I don't know how top-notch they are. Second, it's hard to detect and prevent a squad of snipers or worse a single sniper. I just want to put all this on the table. I'm not saying not to go ahead with the project. I just want everyone to go in with his or her eyes wide open. Have the hunters been fully briefed?"

Jack sat up straight in his chair and became very serious, "All the hunters have been given a comprehensive briefing and have been fully made aware of the potential dangers involved in the show. Besides that's what is going to make this show a blockbuster. People will be tuning in by the millions, maybe the billions to see if someone gets killed. Its why auto racing is so popular, the possibility of someone getting killed.

"Commander Brown, if you stop and think about it, humans have basically just climbed down from living in trees or crawled out of living in caves. We humans haven't evolved all that much; look at the Roman's and the carnage that took place in the Coliseum. Unfortunately, it's human nature and fortunately for us we're going to clean up because of it. Hey, that's show biz."

Jacque, the Sommelier arrived with the two bottles of wine, he gave Charles one of the bottles to examine. Charles read the label and nodded his approval. The

Sommelier smiled and proceeded to open the wine and poured a small amount in Charles' glass and waited. The look on Charles' face was orgasmic, "Oh my God. More please."

After everyone's glass was filled, Charles raised his glass and said, "Gentlemen, here's to the Big 5. Cheers."

"Cheers."

SEAL Team Commander William T. "Wooch" Brown, is best known for spearheading several successful SEAL kill missions against ISIS that the American public will never hear of, at least not in their lifetimes.

William Brown was born into a military family going back four generations, starting with Captain Robert Archer Brown who fought with the 7th Ohio Cavalry, nicknamed the "River Regiment" because its men came from nine counties along the Ohio River. He fought with distinction in the Battle of Cynthiana, the Battle of Cumberland Gap and fought alongside General William E. "Grumble" Jones during the Franklin-Nashville Campaign where he was killed leading a counter charge that helped turn the tide for the Union when all looked to be lost.

During the Spanish-American War his great, great grandfather Lieutenant Leonard Archer Brown fought with Teddy Roosevelt's Rough Riders in the Battle of San Juan Hill. He was assigned to the Gatling Gun Detachment that was credited by Colonel Roosevelt for the success of the charge. After the war he taught classes in cavalry tactics and the art of artillery at West Point.

During the Battle of Belleau Wood in World War One, Wooch's great grandfather, Captain Julius A. Brown commanded the 3rd Battalion, 5th Marines. After suffering heavy casualties on Hill 204 east of Vaux, the French repeatedly urged them to turn back, Captain Brown replied "Retreat? Hell, we don't go backwards, only forwards".

Captain Brown, while advancing on the Germans discovered that they had been advancing in the wrong direction, rather than admitting failure he pushed ahead across the wood's narrow waist, smashing thru the enemy's southern defensive lines, often reduced to using only their bayonets or fists in hand-to-hand combat, resulting in finally clearing the forest of Germans. It was considered one of the bloodiest and most ferocious battles U.S. troops would fight in the war.

In 1941 prior to America's entering World War Two a group of American pilots volunteered to help the Chinese fight the Japanese. They formed a fighter squadron called the Flying Tigers. Under the command of General Chennault, ninety-nine discharged pilots from the Navy, Marines and Army signed up as mercenaries under a private military contractor, the Central Aircraft Manufacturing Company.

A. William Brown was one of six squadron leaders who flew in the 3rd Squadron Hell's Angels, Flying Tigers. Their primary mission was to protect the Burma Road from Japanese bombing, keeping this vital line of communication open. They were so effective that the Japanese discontinued their raids on the city of Kunming while the Tigers were patrolling the area.

The Curtiss P-40 Warhawk was the aircraft of the Tigers. It was a nimble workhorse and could take a beating and usually would get its pilots home safely. Squadron leader Brown flew 26 missions and racked up 12 victories. After the US entered the war, he was assigned to the Eighth Air Force, stationed in England, flying P-51 Mustangs as escorts to B-17 bombing raids over Germany. He was shot down twice, the second time he was captured and sent to Stalag Luft III where he took part in the so-called great escape. He made it as far as Amsterdam where he was shot and killed.

William T. Brown joined the Navy SEALs in the fall of 1967, after the grueling training program he was sent to Da Nang, Vietnam initially to train the South Vietnamese in combat diving, demolitions, and guerrilla / anti-guerrilla tactics. In 1968 the North Vietnamese launched the Tet Offensive in hopes of breaking America's will to continue with the war, but for Brown and the SEALs their missions became personal. He and his team were sent north to disrupt the enemy supply and troop movements. He was the teams' sniper and earned the nickname "Wooch" when his spotter said that wooch was the sound it's victims made every time he claimed a headshot. By the end of his tour of duty in Vietnam, William T. "Wooch" Brown had racked up a Navy Cross, 2 Silver Stars, 4 Bronze Stars, and 5 Commendation Medals as well as the rank of Captain.

Captain William T. "Wooch" Brown went on to serve on the ground in Desert Storm, Operation Gothic

Serpent, and Operation Red Wings. After 9/11 he was kicked upstairs and was promoted to Commander and sent to work in the Pentagon in planning and operations. He and his team were responsible for dozens of strikes against al Qaeda, resulting in the deaths of more than eighty-seven top al Qaeda leaders killed. In 2014 in response to the rapid territorial gains made by ISIL, Wooch and his team developed over twenty Quick Reaction Force operations helping to halt their ISIL's advancement.

After 48 years of service SEAL Team Commander William T. "Wooch" Brown retired quietly and without ceremony, just a quite dinner at the White House with the President, Vice President and several of the military's top brass.

His involvement with Le Gang de la Clé de Singe came as a result of seeing the cruelty and cavalier attitude towards animals while in the military. The mindless killing of animals from boredom or sport always repulsed him, so after making a speech at UC Berkeley on the subject of "War and its Effect on Animals" he was approached by several members of Le Gang de la Clé de Singe who persuaded him to work with them within the shadows, working with others like himself, ex-military, corporate leaders, government officials and private individuals throughout the world, all operating behind the scenes.

"Lady and Gentlemen, welcome to the Hotel de Paris in beautiful Monte Carlo, Worldwide Affiliates of Safari Partners and I want to thank you all for coming and agreeing to participate in the first ever Big 5 television show. I'd like to introduce you to the people who've made all this possible. First, I'd like to introduce Mr. Jack Bonem, president of the Hunting Network, and next I'd like to introduce the major sponsors of the Big Five television show, Mr. Joe Havelka of Remington Firearms, Ms. Sally Johnson from the NRA, Mr. Helmut Schmidt from Glock Incorporated and Mr. Lawrence Lewis from American Hunter Ammunition and, of course I'm Charles Doering from Worldwide Affiliates of Safari Partners.

"Now hunters, you all have been instructed of the rules and you've signed the contracts and just to be clear, you all have acknowledged and have accepted the risks and dangers by releasing the Hunting Network and all the signatories from all liability. As you know we will be providing each of you with an armed platoon from the Zimbabwean Army for your protection day and night.

The competition begins next week on Monday. You will have seven days to reach the quota of collecting each of the five trophies; your score will be judged on the finest and largest quality of each specimen. The decision of the judges will be final, and the winner will receive a grand prize of one million dollars along with a host of other spectacular gifts. The runners-up will also receive fabulous prizes, but unfortunately no cash rewards. Are there any questions?"

"I understand that we will be filmed while hunting, but will they be filming during our down time as well?" asked Wendy Sutherland.

Charles turned to Jack Bonem and said, "Jack, I think this one's for you."

Jack leaned forward and smiled, "Yes, Wendy everyone will be filmed at all times, except during such times as needed for personal hygiene, like going to the bathroom, showering and getting dressed. Things like that." But other than that, expect to be on camera, after a couple of hours you'll forget the camera is even there."

"Jack Rowe here, do I understand correctly that all our weapons, ammo and all our gear are being comped?"

"That is correct, you will have your choice of weapons that you need supplied free from Remington Firearms, and that goes for all of your gear. Just fill out the forms that're in you packets and whatever you need, will be provided." Charles answered.

Butch Anderson shouted out, "No thank you, when it comes to weapons, I'll keep with my .256 Mannlicher and my .280 Ross, but I will take you up on the rest of my gear, thank you very much."

Sir William Cornwallis Smythe raised his hand and was called upon from Charles, "Sir William you have a question?"

"I say, must we use your guides, or can we provide our own?"

"You may provide your own guide as long as he or she has been approved by the judges." Bonem from the Hunting Network replied.

"Jolly good."

Doering noticed that Haruto Nakamura was sitting quietly in the back of the room, "Mr. Nakamura, do you have any questions you'd like to ask?

"Īe, kekkōdesu. Genjitende wa arimasen."

"No, thank you. Not at this time." Mr. Yamada, his translator said.

Charles Doering looked at everyone in the room and asked," Are there any more questions? No, good. So we'll see everyone Sunday night at the Radisson Blu Hotel, in Lusaka, Zambia. If you have any questions or problems, please don't hesitate to call me. You should have everyone's contact numbers and an agenda in your packets. Goodnight and see you Sunday. Safe travels."

The Iceman had arranged for the Red Team to meet as tourists wandering the grounds at the Cathedral of Miracles Church, which was about a half an hour north of their hotels. Along with the Iceman, Odin and LuWei the rest of the team would be made up with an African-American from Birmingham, Alabama named Vulcan, a former veterinarian from Paris, France called Sassoon, Jimmy the Chew from Trelingua, Texas, Tommy G from Chinatown, San Francisco, Venus a young Cher look-a-like from the Ukraine, T-Bone from Chicago, and Gianfranco out of Lima, Peru. All were combat hardened in the wars against poachers and hunters.

"Just got a text from Wooch, we're on for next week." The Iceman told the team who were all gathered around him holding church pamphlets, giving anyone who happened to notice them the impression that they were on a tour of the church. "We know that they will be hunting in Kafue National Park starting Monday. Unfortunately, Kafue is one of the largest national parks in all of Africa, but as luck would have it, we have a local guide and tracker who grew up in Lusaka and who knows Kafue like the back of his hand. And speak of the devil, here he comes now."

Beenzu Sitibikeso looked like was he was hundred if he was day. He walked stooped over, wore thick eyeglasses that looked like the bottom of two coke bottles, he had very little hair and what he had was gray, and he appeared to weigh maybe eighty pounds; a good breeze could probably blow him away.

But as they say, looks can be deceiving. Beenzu was in his early fifties. He was a marathon runner who had won several international races. He grew up in Mwongo, a small mining village on the edge of Kafue. If you grew up in Mwongo; you had two choices either work in the mines or work in the safari industry. Beenzu chose safari work; he started out as a porter and after forty plus years, he worked his way up to guide.

Over the years the more time working with big game hunters, the more he discovered that, as a whole they were a bunch of wealthy self-centered narcissistic entitled white middle-aged assholes. Although he had to admit that there were some nice folks, but overall not so much. While acting as a guide on a photo safari for a retired SEAL Commander, he was introduced to the philosophy and beliefs of Le Gang de la Clé de Singe.

The Iceman extended his hand and said, "Beenzu, welcome. It's a pleasure to meet you. I'm the Iceman."

"It is my great pleasure to meet you all."

"Let me introduce you to the team. Beenzu this is Odin, LuWei, Vulcan, Tommy G, Sassoon, Jimmy the Chew, Venus, T-Bone, and Gianfranco. Everyone this is Beenzu, our guide and tracker."

After a short period of individual handshakes and pleasant greetings Iceman continued, "We will get together again Saturday to go over the plan and strategy. Not knowing where each of the Big 5 hunters will be, looks like it's going to be a run and gun type of operation, we're going to have to be pretty nimble.

"We're going to have LuWei and Venus operating a couple of drones, one for scouting and one for surveillance. So, we'll meet up again Saturday around six o'clock at the Lusaka Inter-City Bus Terminus on Dedan Kimathi Road, be waiting outside and not as one big group, in fact try and stagger your arrival times. If you see each other, you can stay together but keep it down to no more than two.

"Odin and I will be driving Renault Dusters; we'll continue to circle the station so don't panic if you don't see us right away. Once we've collected everyone, we'll head out to Kafue to set up camp. You have two days to yourselves, so enjoy the city. Again, just pairs, we don't want any suspicion or attention drawn. Everyone can go with the exception of Odin, LuWei and Beenzu. Please stay for a minute.”

“Welcome to Wawindaji Safari Lodge, do you have a reservation?” asked the blond young woman dressed in a safari jacket, khaki shorts, and hiking boots who was manning the reservation desk.

“I do indeed, the name Brown, William Brown.”

“Oh, yes Mr. Brown, I see that you’re with the Big 5 party. You’re booked in for ten nights is that correct?”

“I believe that is correct.”

“Well, Mr. Brown it looks like that you’re the last one to check in. We have you staying in one of our Luxury Safari Tents, it’s my favorite.”

“Excellent. Could you have someone take my bags to my tent? And would you know where the Big 5 group might be?

“I believe that everyone from Big 5 is at the Boma restaurant. Straight out this door and just follow the signs.”

Brown leaned close to the young girl to read her nametag, “Thank you Irene, you’ve been most helpful.”

“You’re quite welcome, Mr. Brown, I hope you have a wonderful stay with us.”

“Oh, I’m sure it will most memorable.”

Commander Brown made his way down several interior halls all decorated with native art and crafts to outside and across an open patio area to the Boma where he found cast and crew sitting at several tables laughing and joking and really enjoying themselves. Off to one side sat the executives and sponsors locked in what looked like a very serious discussion. Wooch approached the table and indicated to Charles that he shouldn't make a big deal about his arrival.

Wooch walked up and sat down in the empty chair and quietly said, "Good evening gentlemen, please go on, don't let me interrupt your conversation."

"Good evening, Commander. We were just discussing the likelihood of some sort of disruption to the program by Le Gang de la Clé de Singe and what could we do to prevent such a thing and what would we do after, if an attack did occur," said Jack Bonem.

"Well, that's definitely a discussion that we need to have, but first I'd appreciate it if someone introduced me to the Major."

Charles apologetically said, "Oh, I am sorry, Wooch. Commander Brown, I'd like to meet Major Hikeezi of the Zambian Defense Force, Major Hikeezi, Commander Brown retired. Major Hikeezi will be in command of the Zambian troops guarding our production company."

"Major Hikeezi, it's a privilege to meet you."

"Commander Brown, it is an honor. I am very aware of your amazing career."

"You're too kind Major. Thank you."

Charles Doering turned to Jack Bonem and asked, "Jack, why don't you bring the Commander up to speed?"

"Well, the Major was thinking that each of the hunting parties would have a squad of fifteen men assigned to with them at all times and additionally three advance scouts. He is also proposing a daily fly over at random times by one of their Air Force's Hermes 450 drones, so as not to be too predictable. What do you think Commander?"

"Very impressive, Major. Well thought-out and precise, I have nothing to add, except to caution everyone who is going to be in the bush, take nothing for granted and keep your eyes and ears open; these people are ruthless. Nice job Major. Now if you gentlemen don't mind, can we order? I'm starving."

Beenzu was sitting next to the Icemen in the backseat giving directions to Odin, who was driving the Renault SUV thru the outskirts of Lusaka towards the industrial part of town. Once they turned off of Sheki-Sheki Road and onto Mukwa Road, they were out past the houses of the suburbs and in amongst the warehouses and distribution centers of the city.

Down the street from the Brunelli Construction yard and across from MRI Seed Syngenta was a small unassuming storehouse. The sign on the plate glass window read Z&Z Logistics. Next to the building there was a small driveway with a modest parking lot in the back, surrounded by a ten-foot wooden fence enclosure. Parked in the lot was a white Renault Master panel van with the Z&Z Logistics logo painted to both sides and sitting next to it was black Citroen, Belingo L2 van also adorned with logos.

"What about those big logos on the side of the truck?" Odin asked.

As Beenzu got out of the car, he walked over to the vans and said, "Of course these logos can be peeled right off."

"Great." Iceman replied.

Beenzu led everyone into the back of the building where there were several large chain-linked cages filled with weapons and equipment for the upcoming campaign.

"I think you'll find everything you'll need, if there is anything missing or something you want, just let me know and I'll find it."

Odin, LuWei and the Iceman took over five hours going thru and separating everything from weapons, ammo, ghillie suits, uniforms, special gear and even several drones.

"Looks like you got it all, Beenzu", said the Iceman. "So, we're going to have the team meet here Saturday, gear up and we'll move out to Kafue Park and start making our way to where the Lufupa and Ntemwa Rivers intersect, that's where we'll make our initial camp."

LuWei asked, "Would it be all right if Venus and I take the Ehang Falcon B drones out for some tests, so we can get familiar with them?"

The Iceman thought for a moment, "Sure, just make sure you go somewhere isolated, so you won't be noticed. Beenzu, think you might know somewhere they can go and test the drones and not be seen?"

"I know a very secluded area that will be perfect."

"Great, Venus and I will pick you up here tomorrow morning around six, if that's good for you?" said LuWei.

"I'll have the drones ready to travel and be waiting for you at six."

The next morning LuWei and Venus arrived at the storehouse precisely at 6a.m. where they found Beenzu waiting outside with the two drones. Le Wei jumped out of the SUV and helped Beenzu store the drones in the back.

Venus swapped seats with Beenzu so he could sit up front with LuWei and give directions. They headed south on the T2 for an hour and a half to where they turned off onto an unmarked dirt road traveling north for about fifteen minutes where the road dead ends at the Kafue River. On the other side of the river lies the old, deserted town of Chingala, a once thriving copper mine town that had, at one time over five thousand residents, but eventually the mine shut down. The company said that the copper had all been mined out, so they closed it down. With the mine gone and all the miners out of work, there was nothing to keep anyone here, so everybody left.

"No one ever comes up here anymore. You've got the whole place to yourselves." Beenzu said as he and LuWei took the drones out of the car.

Venus and LuWei spent the whole day putting the drones thru their paces, at one point they even had dogfights over the Kafue River that escalated into the streets of the abandoned town of Chingala, when they played back the video it looked to be something out of Star Wars.

"These Ehangs are awesome!" Venus exclaimed.

"Yeah, these are fabulous, let's take them back to the storehouse for some modification and tweaking. Beenzu, let's head back, we have a lot to do by tomorrow."

Butch was having a simple breakfast of eggs, sausage, potatoes, toast with jam, and coffee, in the Boma restaurant when Windy and Jason came in. Wendy asked, "May we join you."

"Please be seated."

Once seated the waiter quickly appeared, "Would you care for coffee?"

Jason looked at Wendy who nodded, then said to the waiter, "Yes, please. Two."

As Butch was cutting up his eggs over easy, he asked his two table guests, "So, what do you two make of these threats from Le Gang de la Clé de Singe? Think we're in any danger?"

Jason brandishing a hint of bravado answered, "Hell, no. We got the Zambian Army escorts watching over us, plus we're the five best hunters in the world. Each of us are crack shots, no I don't think these hooligans will try anything. What do you think Wendy?"

"Well, I might feel a little more secure if we had SEAL team 6 watching over us. I just don't know how much of a crack outfit these guys are; are they an outfit of super commandos or a bunch of raw recruits? I think we'll have to stay really alert at all times."

Butch agreed saying, "You must have heard about the David Leeway massacre. His whole outfit of professional mercenaries was destroyed, and they were mostly all combat hardened ex-servicemen, totally wiped out. If I could I'd like to get the whole thing over with in a single day."

"Steady on, old man." Sir William said as he pulled up a chair to join the group. "You mustn't let these villains rattle you, old chap. I for one, aren't going to let these roughens get inside my head and ruin my concentration."

The waiter arrived with Jason and Wendy's coffee, "May I get you something to drink?" The waiter asked Sir William.

"I'll have a spot of tea, my good man. And if you would bring two more cups of coffee for Mr. Nakamura and his translator, who'll be down in a minute." Sir William said.

Wendy raised her hand to the waiter, "When you get a chance would you bring some menus, thank you."

"Of course, madam."

As Haruto Nakamura walked up to the table, Sir William grabbed two chairs from another table for the last of the Big 5 hunters to come down for breakfast.

"*Ohayōgozaimasu.*"

"Good morning." Mr. Yamada, the translator said.

"*Mina wa nani o hanashite iru nodesu ka?*

"What is everyone talking about?" Yamada asked.

"Le Gang de la Clé de Singe." Wendy answered.

Jason looked around the table and asked, "The question is, what are we going to do if one of us gets murdered? I personally don't think a million dollars is worth dying for."

"How about ten million dollars, is it worth ten million dollars?" Charles Doering said as he entered the restaurant, fearing one or more might back out.

"That's if I win, but what if I get shot on day one, I get zip, right?" Jason snapped back.

"Okay, how about this. Anyone who gets killed, his or her family gets a guaranteed one million dollars and the winner will receive ten million; how's that?"

"You'll revise the contracts to reflect that." Butch asked.

"I'll call my secretary now and you'll all have revised contracts by end of day; all good?"

Jason read the room; saw nothing but nodding heads said, "All good."

The Iceman was reviewing his team as they were enhancing their ghillie suits. A ghillie suit is a type of camouflage clothing designed to resemble the surroundings they will be trying to blend into. Since the environment of Kafue Park is heavily populated with thick foliage and deep thick grasses, their suits will be augmented with loose strips of burlap, cloth and scrapes of actual twigs and leaves from the area. Once out in the bush they will also paint their faces as well as have netting over their faces to further disguise their presence.

When they have positioned themselves, they may be required to stay motionless for hours, possibly for days and endure all kinds of weather, days of oppressive heat, torrential rainstorms and cold damp nights. They'll have to endure all types of hardships like insect bites from ants, mosquitos, scorpions and ticks. Thankfully there are some preventive measures such as tick patches, mosquito repellent bracelets, and lavender scented patches to repel scorpions. This kind of combat isn't for the faint of heart.

Each team member will be equipped with a radio headset, so he or she'll be able to communicate with each other. They'll be issued night vision goggles, and a CamelBak Ambush hydration pack that will provide five days of a high energy drink and several days' supplies of PowerBars, the most popular energy bars used by Tour de France riders.

They're each issued a M40A5 sniper rifle, the sniper rifle of choice by the United States Marine Corp. Each rifle is equipped with an FA762SS sound suppressor. Every member of the Iceman's Red Team is rated sharpshooter. In addition to their rifle each team member carries a Glock 17 pistol, rated as one of the world's most accurate handguns.

"Everyone ready?" The Iceman asked the team.

They all gave a "Hoorah!" in unison.

"Then saddle up and let's move out."

The entire Red Team piled into Beenzu's Renault Master panel van and headed out for the six-hour journey to Kafue National Park. They took the M9 highway straight out from Lusaka heading west until they turned right going north on Moshi Road. They traveled for an hour and forty-five minutes on the dirt road to where the road crosses over the Kafue River, which is their point of departure.

The sun was staring to set and there wasn't a living soul around, at least human soul. The Red Team along with Beenzu started their six-mile hike to where their campsite will be, and where the Lufupa and Ntemwa Rivers intersect. Beenzu's cousin Marquis drove the panel van back to Lusaka, so as not to leave any clues behind.

The march took over five hours to get to the designated campsite and by the time they had set up camp it was well past midnight. The Iceman assigned the watch list and allowed a campfire for this night only. Once the hunt began tomorrow there would be only cold camp: no tents, no fire, no footprint; they wanted to appear as if nobody had been there.

Reveille was to be at 04:30, a half hour personal time, sending the drones up, one for security the other for scouting. The Iceman and Beenzu felt that they were in a strategic place that was centrally located to attack any one of the five hunting groups; waiting was always the hardest part.

The night was a cacophony of sounds with the creatures of the night, lions, owls, hyenas, dikkops, hippopotamuses, nightjars, aardwolf's, quails, and jaguars, that would eventually lullaby them to sleep.

The sunrise on African savannah is unlike anywhere else; the sky's canopy dissolves slowly from the deep onyx milieu sprinkled with billions of tiny brightly lit diamonds evolving thru every shade of the deepest dark spectrum of blues, from Oxford blue to Phthalo blue, with an unperceivable hint of Arylide yellow that gently awakens all the creatures of the Dark Continent to a new day.

The Iceman, who had stood the last watch, started waking up the team, "All right, people rise and shine, let's get ready to embrace the suck."

The team slowly started to come to life; they started out with the expected moaning, groaning and grumbling as they transformed from their prone positions to slowly rising into a semi erect stance, working out the kinks and cramps from sleeping on the hard ground. Each wandered off in search for a private area where they can go take a leak. Venus was given first choice and she marked her territory with a bright red bandana, everyone was reminded to bring a sidearm just to be safe.

After a hot breakfast, the last one for at least a week LuWei and Venus launched the drones on a scouting mission for their first encounter. Meanwhile, Wooch had sent a message as to the areas each of the Big 5 hunters were planning to hunt. The Iceman wanted the drones to show him which of the Big 5 would be most vulnerable. They were aware that each of the hunters was being escorted with troops from the Zambian Army, but there are troops and then there are troops.

"LuWei, Venus whenever you have something give a yell. You know what we're looking for."

"Aye, aye." LuWei sounded back.

Venus gave a "Right, chief."

It wasn't long till LuWei shouted, "Ice, think we got one."

'Whatta ya got?"

"Looks like that English snob Smythe, his two-man film crew, and his guide have lost contact with his escort, they seem to be going in opposite directions. Plus, he's close by, and in fact he's heading our way."

"Great work, stay on them and keep me posted."

"All right, looks like we've got our first one. Let's get ready to move out. Beenzu, get ready to lead the way."

"Aye, aye, captain."

"LuWei show Beenzu where Smythe is and you and Venus stay put and keep us up to date. Venus keep an eye on those troops, this maybe a trick, let me know if they change directions."

"Right, boss."

"Beenzu lead the way. Red Team, let's move out and remember, stay frosty."

Beenzu and the Iceman took the point; they were followed in single file, spaced out about ten feet apart with Odin bringing up the rear. LuWei was keeping the Iceman up to date on Smythe's progress and Venus was keeping her eye on the Zambian troops, apparently, they were still heading in opposite directions. The Red Team had gone about a mile when the Iceman stopped.

"I smell a rat," said the Iceman. "This has fugazi written all over it." He held up his hand and closed it forming a fist, the signal to stop. The team stopped and they all took a knee, each facing a different direction. He radioed back to base, "Venus, what's going on?"

"The troops are now moving parallel to Smythe."

"And the other groups; are they close by or are they going off in different directions?" The Iceman asked.

"No, they're all relatively close by."

"I'm thinking this is a trap; very clever."

"What are you going to do?" asked LuWei.

"Good evening I'm Nigel Williams and this is the BBC World Headline News. Our top story this hour comes from Zambia where the first ever-American television hunting show has started production. The reality show pits five hunters from around the world in a quest to kill what hunters refer to as 'the Big 5' hunting trophies, the African elephant, Black rhinoceros, Cape buffalo, African Lion and African leopard. The hunter who successfully kills all five animals within the span of one week and are deemed the best specimens, will win ten million dollars.

However, Le Gang de la Clé de Singe has declared that they are planning on putting a stop to, what they call is an act of pure barbarism. To try and help deter Le Gang de la Clé de Singe from such an attack the show's producers have enlisted the aid of the Zambian Army, who are supplying troops to help protect the hunters.

In a related story, there is still no news on the whereabouts of escaped convicted murderer Liam Janssens who escaped from Mahalapye prison in Botswana two weeks ago. Local officials believe that Liam is no longer in Botswana and have asked Interpol for their help.

In other news, the members of the United Nations were laughing at the President of the United States when he made boisterous calms concerning his administration's achievements...."

Sir William and his guide's attention weren't concentrating on finding game. They were too busy looking for assassins disguised behind every tree and hiding in every bush, a killer camouflaged under each shrub, assailants hidden in the tall grasses, or terrorists concealed amoungst the herds of zebras. They felt like they were the sacrificial lambs led out for slaughter and the two blokes recording them looked to be oblivious to the fact that they were all being sacrificed for ratings.

Earlier that morning there was a meeting in the Boma Room of all the hunters, sponsors and TV executives to assign each hunter which of the Big 5 prey that they would be going after that day. They also were introduced to the film crews that had been assigned to them.

Charles Doering clapped his hands to get everyone's attention, "People, may I have your attentiom, please. Thank you. Good morning and welcome to the first ever Big Five hunt and television show. As you can see the filming has begun, and starting now until we award the grand prize, it's going to be non stop adventure. Remember the film crews are there to be an impartial observer. They will not interfere or aid in any way, unless of course there is a medical emergency. So, spend the next few minutes to get aquainted.

Now, as you all know there is slight possibility that we could be the target of Le Gang de la Clé de Singe. Major Hikeezi and the executive board have devised a plan we think will flush these thugs out and dispose of them once and for all; but we need your help. The idea is that we will draw the name of one hunter to act as if they have wandered astray from his military escort, thereby being totally vulnerable to attack, but in fact he or she will be completely safe and under the protection of Major Hikeezi and his troops. It will only appear that you will be defenseless but rest assured help will be just moments away. Plus, just think of the drama and excitement for the viewing audience… fabulous.

Now, we've put the names of all five hunters on pieces of paper, folded them so as not to be able to see who's who and put them into this black bag. So, let's see who the lucky hunter will be. I'll just reach into this bag of names and pull one out. And the winner is Sir William. Let's give a Big 5 round of applause to Sir William."

Sir William Cornwallis Smythe looked as if Charles Doering had just kicked him squarely in the balls, which metaphorically he did. He was unaware that he was being filmed when Charles came up to him.

"Charles, what the bloody Hell? You're out of your fucking mind; I'm not going out there naked and get my ass shot off."

"Sorry old man, but you will if you want to stay in the competition. Apparently, you didn't read all the small print in your contract, old bean."

"Wanker."

"Yeah whatever, instead of whining I suggest that you get with the plan and talk to Major Hikeezi."

"Tosser."

"Wild Bill my ass, ya fucking Pussy."

The Iceman gave the order to 'stand down' and he turned the Red Team around to head back to base camp. As they were walking back, off to their right they could see several Zambian Army troop trucks slowly traveling south, parallel to their assigned hunter. They observed the vehicles had spotters located on perches atop the truck's cab as lookouts. The Red Team dropped to the ground and waited until the trucks were out of sight.

When they returned to camp, the Iceman gathered everyone around and laid out his plan, "They were using this poor slob as a decoy to try and sucker us in to attacking him and when we did then they would swoop in with superior forces and over run us. Very clever, but we're going to switch up our tactics.

"Starting now, each of us will shadow a different hunter, not to kill but to harass just enough to confuse them and their army escorts. Ideally, it would be awesome, if possible, to wait to interfere with their kill shot. Above all try not to give yourself away by over doing it. We can achieve maximum chaos with just a single shot; it will do a couple of things, make them think we are a larger force than we are and keep them off balance by springing up at different locations spontaneously.

Hopefully, by the end of the week, since we won't have killed any of the hunters, they'll let their guard down a little. It's hard to stay sharp when nothing is happening. Any questions?"

Vulcan asked, "Will LuWei and Venus continue to monitor the troops for us?"

"Well, since we only have two drones, they'll give each of us as much coverage as they can. My suggestion is, when you think you might be getting close to taking a shot, radio in. They will be tracking the five hunters the best they can, but if you find yourself in trouble, give everyone a heads up, don't play hero. There are things we can do to get you out of trouble. Any more questions? No, okay LuWei can you take the drone up so we can see where everyone is at the moment?" The Iceman answered.

"Sure thing." LuWei said.

As the drone traveled straight up everyone standing around LuWei's computer screen could see the five groups pretty much within a mile of each other.

"I got a text this morning letting us know the approximately what area each hunter would be." Iceman said as he was pointing to each hunting party.

"So, here's the guy we were going after this morning, Sir William Smythe, some English bloke, Tommy G you take him. Odin you tail this guy here, Butch Anderson. Sassoon, you like sushi so, you'll have the pleasure of watching over Haruto Nakamura. Gianfranco, you keep an eye on Mister Jason Rowe and I'll be dancing in the dark with Ms. Wendy Sutherland. Remember, this is just a minor skirmish; we don't want a big firefight. So run and gun it; one shot and you're outta there. Okay, let's rock."

The five of them started out together then diverged off into different directions. Within minutes they lost visual contact with each other. LuWei and Venus directed them over the radio. Tommy G was the first to make contact with Sir William, who was still acting paranoid and overreacting to every sound or movement around him.

He and his guide were so freaked out that they missed several decent shots of African lions, which was their assigned prey for that day. If they didn't get a lion today, then that particular species would be added to the next day's list and so on and so on; it was conceivable that at the end of day four you'd have to kill all five animals on the last day.

G was situated about a half a mile from Smythe, who had stopped to have a spot of tea to calm his nerves, when his guide spied a magnificent male lion resting under an enormous Baobab tree. He alerted the hunter, "Sir William, I say there's a prize winning beast lying beneath that Baobab tree."

Tommy could see that there was much excitement as the hunter jumped up and was grabbing for his weapon, Tommy quickly spotted the target of their excitement, he radioed back to LuWei and asked, "Home base this is Red Three, how am I looking, over?"

"Red Three, you are good to go, over."

Tommy kept his riflescope fixed on Sir William's Griffin & Howe, .308 Winchester caliber bolt-action rifle as he raised it and stared into its Zeiss scope.

Tommy took a deep breath then fired, hitting the front site on the end of the barrel knocking the rifle out of

Sir William's hands. The splintering of the gun's barrel made a mighty noise.

KRA-KOOM

"Yippee ki yay, motherfucker."

Since Tommy used a sound suppression silencer no one was quite sure where the shot came from. The alarm went out and the Zambian troops, who were napping in the back of the trucks started to scramble looking to see where the shot came from.

Meanwhile, LuWei was keeping the G abreast of the direction they were heading. Tommy slowly circled back away from the search and ended up lying on a small mound behind them, hidden amongst several bushes watching the Keystone Cops style of search being performed by the Zambian Army.

Sir William had had enough, between the constant looking over your shoulder and now, the near miss on his life, he was calling it a day. After an hour of searching for the would be assassins, they all packed it in, hunter, guide, film crew and troops loaded everything into the transport trucks and went back to the Wawindaji Lodge. Once they had moved out of the area Tommy meandered on back to the camp, keeping a watchful eye out for that enormous male lion that had been sleeping under that Baobab tree.

Butch Anderson had been assigned the Cape buffalo, so his hunting party headed toward the Kafue River two miles from the Mayukuyku Bush Camp and directly north of the Wawindaji Lodge. There are several small islands in the river where Cape buffalo are known to congregate. Beenzu had given Odin a short cut that would get him there hours before the hunting party would arrive. When Butch and ensemble arrived at the river and found the large herd of Cape buffalo, Odin had positioned himself well hidden in the canopy of a Mopane tree.

Butch had conversed with his guide for over twenty minutes perusing the herd, carefully taking his time to assess which of the Cape buffalo was the prized trophy. As they were preparing to get the shot off, Odin had radioed in asking Venus if he was good to go and she gave the go ahead. Milliseconds before Butch took his shot, Odin fired off three rounds into the right front tire of one of the Zambian troop trucks creating quite a stir.

BARROOOOM

Sending the troops and the hunting party into a defensive position scrambling for cover, creating such a frenzy and commotion that the herd of buffalo stampeded off. In a while, when no other bullets had been fired, and a quasi-search of the area was completed, Butche's group limped its way back to the Wawindaji Lodge as well.

Shortly after Butches group returned Charles Doering and the executive team put a halt to the hunt, calling in the other three teams back to the lodge. On day one no animals were killed, a small victory for the Iceman and Red Team. Doering brought Major Hikeezi, Jack Bonem, and Wooch into his suite for a strategic confab to figure out how best combat these attacks and how to best assess next steps.

Doering started, "We can't let this aggression stand, we have to do something and do it fast."

"As far as the Hunting Channel is concerned this makes for great TV; hunters under attack, hunters being hunted. It's fabulous stuff, man." Bonem said gleefully.

"God damnit Jack, you're not helping. Major, Wooch, any suggestions?"

Major Hikeezi appeared to be thinking when Wooch spoke up, "Gentlemen, as I see it, we have a couple of options, One, cancel the show. Two, add more troops, though I don't know if that would help deter the attacks. It might help in capturing them after an attack, but we don't know their strength. A larger group would be easier to detect, engage and eventually capture or kill. I'm sure the Major would agree with me that a lone gunman in this sort of environment is near impossible to find. Three, delay the production and do a sweep of the area, although that would seem very costly and time consuming. And who would pay for that and would the Zambian Army want to use their resources of men to track down an unknown enemy? Four, proceed with the show and roll the dice."

Major Hikeezi nodding his head in agreement said, "I agree with Commander Brown, these are your options and only you can make the decision. I cannot commit to more troops and I cannot commit more time for the troops."

Charles Doering was visibly upset, "Thank you Major and Commander. I guess this will be a decision for Jack, the sponsors, and the hunters. We'll get right on it and have a decision shortly."

As the Major and Wooch left Doering's room, the sponsors were all in the hallway standing around like a herd of stunned wildebeest. "I think you should all go in now." Wooch stated as he passed by.

LuWei radioed the team to return to base as the hunt has been called off, at least for the day. Odin and Tommy G were the first to get back to base; the Iceman was the last to return. Venus was servicing her drone while LuWei kept his in the air on look out. They were always having one drone up for scouting and policing the area.

"What's going on?" asked the Icemen.

"Well, after Odin interrupted Anderson's shot, I guess the big brass decided to call it a day and try to see if they could get their shit together or maybe cancel the gig." LuWei explained.

"Yeah, I don't see them cancelling the gig. You know the old saying; the show must go on, besides there's too much money at stake to pull the plug. So, Odin, Tommy, tell us what happened. Tommy?"

"I'm trailing the limey and his guide, see. These two are all wigged out, looking all over the place to see if they can see any bad guys, but the two dudes filming are really cool, musta been in a couple war zones, cause their just focused on filming the Brit and his guy.

Then I see that the guide has spotted this big male lion snoozing under a tree, he points to it and the limey starts getting his shit together, taking deep breaths trying to calm down. Meanwhile, I positioned myself on a small mound so as to give me a clear shot. I took a breath and as the wanker was setting up his shot, I popped one off hitting the barrel of his rifle, knocking it clean out of his hands. One Hell of a shot if I do say so myself, and I do."

"Fantastic! And nice shooting pardner." Odin said.

"Much obliged."

"Odin, can you top that?" The Iceman asked.

"Fraid not. Mine's not as heroic. I was on the trail of Mister Butch Anderson, who seemed to be looking for bagging a Cape buffalo. We end up in a group of small islands north of here in the Kafue River. I get situated up in a tree with good visibility and great coverage. I see that Butch has decided which buffalo is his and just as he's getting reading, I pop off three rounds into one of the troop trucks front tires causing a small explosion of the tire and interrupting little Butchy's kill shot. Admittedly, not as dramatic, but just as effective." Odin conceded.

"Well, let's all remember this isn't a wild West show contest; it's all about getting the job done. It doesn't have to be fancy, just effective." The Icemen declared.

"So, what now?" asked Vulcan.

"Now, we sit and wait until we get an idea what they're up to and then we'll react; so, for now, just chill out."

The drive from the farm where Icarus landed to Kafue National Park would be thirteen hours, with a short stop at the Zimbabwe / Zambia boarder. But as Icarus was flying literally as the crow flies, he made the trip in under twelve. Of course, it took two days because of the solar batteries needing sunshine to recharge during flight.

Once he crossed over into Zambian airspace, he was an international fugitive. He had traveled five hours when he received his first radio call.

"Icarus, can you read me? This is Rodin, over."

"I read you loud and clear, over."

"You know that this isn't going to end well? Why don't you return, and we'll sort everything out, over."

"Negative. I'm in too deep, in for a penny, in for a pound. Over."

"Know where you're going? Over." Rodin asked.

"Kinda. Over."

"Any idea where you should be heading?"

"Not a clue." Icarus said,

"Set the GPS to -14.5398932, 26.1542861. Over."

"Roger, over."

"I'll let mom know you're coming home, over."

"Love ya brother." Icarus said.

"Stay safe and long may you run."

The rest of the flight was silent. When the sun was starting to set Icarus found a deserted area with hardly any vegetation on a small hill that gave him a decent view in all directions. He decided to sleep in the drone not wanting to build a fire for protection and or get hassled by lions and hyenas.

The next morning, feeling a bit kinked up from sleeping inside the drone, but really none the worse for wear, he woke up when a warthog was investigating the front left propellers. A quick whirl of the right propellers seemed to more than satisfy his curiosity. Icarus gave the area a quick glance around to be sure he was alone, and he jumped outside to have a brisk whiz before heading to Kafue Park to link up with the Iceman and the Red Team.

Charles and the executive team brought the hunters, their guides, and the film crews into the Bwana Room to address how they proposed to handle the problem of Le Gang de la Clé de Singe.

Charles asked for silence, "Lady and gentlemen, after a long and thorough discussion with Major Hikeezi and the executive board, we've concluded the best way to proceed is augmenting our military approach."

"Does that mean there's going to be more troops?" Sir William inquired.

"Actually no, the Major believes that a better use of our resources should be adequate. For example, we would have an advanced scouting team preceding the hunters so as to reconnoiter the area, while also having teams flanking the hunters on either side. How does that sound?"

"I think you're off your trolley, mate. I almost got me head blown off this morning and this is your solution. I almost got killed, didn't I?" Sir William uttered.

"Now Sir William, the key word here is almost. Surely if they wanted to kill you and Butch, they would have. They're just trying to scare you."

"Well they bloody well achieved that."

"Look we know it's scary, so the sponsors and I are prepared to show our appreciation to you all by guaranteeing each of you five million dollars; win, lose or draw, just for participating. And of course the winner will still receive the ten million dollar grand prize. Now what do you all say to that?"

Rowe, Anderson, Nakamura and Sutherland all voted to continue. All eyes were on Smythe.

"Sod it all, I'm in. But I'm not going to be the sacrificial lamb anymore."

"No we're not going to try anything like that again, like I said we're going with the new strategy that the Major has proposed." Doering said trying to assure everyone.

Jack Bonem stood up and addressed the group. "Look, we at the Hunting Network want to show you and your guides how much we appreciate your being such good sports, so we would like each of you to accept these Rolex Daytona Chronographs as a way of showing you our gratitude."

Bonem walked around the room distributing a watch to each hunter and their guides; a twenty thousand dollar thank you gift. When he had returned to his seat, he plopped down sulking in his chair because he was feeling disappointed from not getting a bigger response to his generosity.

Wendy rose from the table where the hunters and their guides were seated and announced, "Well, it's been real. Thanks for the timepiece, Jack, but it's late and I'm knackered. So, I'm off to try and get a decent night's sleep. See you all in the morning."

Moments later the Bwana Room was empty.

The Iceman brought the Red Team together to give them a couple updates, "First the hunting parties will continue, but with some major changes. They're going to have Zambian troops scouting out front and flanking the hunters. Second bit of news, we're getting an unexpected addition to the team, a fella called Icarus. He was apprehended while on assignment in Zimbabwe and with the help of the organization escaped from prison a couple days ago and is now heading our way via a drone. Yes, you heard right a drone. He's expected to arrive within the hour."

"So, like what's his story? Ever hear of this guy?" asked Tommy the Chew.

"Actually, I have. He's a bit of a lone wolf, sort of a specialist. Not sure why he's coming here, I guess we'll find out when he gets here. His being here shouldn't affect our strategy."

Beenzu pointed to the eastern sky, "There. There is your drone."

Everyone turned to the east to see a drone the size of a very small automobile floating above them slowly, effortlessly and then descending in front of them. As the propellers began to stop whirling, the Red Team could see the man inside unbuckling his harness and preparing to exit.

The Iceman walked up to the craft and greeted the man as he exited the drone.

"You must be Icarus, I'm Iceman; pleased to meet you and welcome to the jungle." He said extending his hand in greeting.

Icarus took his hand and patted Iceman on the shoulder, "Hey thanks brother, I'm sorry to crash your party, but I'm on the lamb as they say in the movies."

"No worries, we can always use an extra hand. Here let me introduce you to the team, this is Beenzu our guide, Odin my number two, Vulcan, Sassoon, Jimmy G, Tommy the Chew, T-Bone, Gianfranco, and my drone operators LuWei and Venus."

"A pleasure to meet you, one and all. I guess I should explain why I'm here, if you have a minute."

"Sure, come on over to the camp. Can we offer you something to eat or drink?"

"Oh man, that would be awesome. I haven't eaten since I flew out of Zambia yesterday morning."

"We can offer you a choice of MRE's. You have your choice of Asian Beef Strips, Ratatouille, Mexican Style Chicken Stew or Spaghetti with Meatballs."

"I'll go for the ever popular Mexican Style Chicken Stew, thanks."

"G would you mind? So, tell us Icarus what brings you to our little neck of the woods?" The Iceman asked.

"Well, I was sent to take care of these three brothers who were running a safari outfit that specialized in big game and endangered species safaris. They also dealt in taxidermy and the shipping of parts, if you know what I mean. I got close to them by acting as a bodyguard after they had been tipped off that the Gang had targeted them. So after they got whacked the cops pinched me and tried to pin it on me, the bastards."

"So you were arrested and sent to jail?"

"Yeah, I even went on trial and was found guilty. I was awaiting sentencing when Rodin and Isala busted me out of the joint using this drone. Pretty cool, huh?"

"Amazing." Venus said.

"Yeah, but now I'm a man without a country, now everyone will have my photo and fingerprints, so the folks high up want me to be a pencil pusher. No fucking way man, I'm a field guy. I gotta be in the shit, you know what I mean?"

Jimmy G brought over the Mexican Style Chicken Stew, "Here ya go."

Icarus smiled and said, "Thanks brother, much obliged." After taking several spoonful's he commented, "Hey, not bad, not bad at all."

"So, any ideas what you're going to do? I mean long term?" Asked the Iceman.

"Still working it out in my head. But hey, what can I do for you guys? Got any thoughts?"

"I got a couple of things knocking around in the old noggin. Finish up your meal and then let's convene and put our heads together, I'm sure we can come up with something evil."

Robert Lester, ex-Navy SEAL sniper best known for holding the world record for the longest distance kill in military history, 3,480-meter shot. Lester, a French Canadian now known as the Iceman, because nothing ever seems to rattle him. Rumor has it ice water runs thru his veins instead of blood, is the leader of the Red Team.

The Iceman joined the Le Gang de la Clé de Singe after three tours of duty in Iraq. He was looking for something meaningful to get involved with; he first joined up with Greenpeace right after the Deepwater Horizon disaster. He was one of the first who protested big oilrigs drilling in the Arctic Circle, slowing production by jamming their equipment.

Greenpeace did not condone his actions and wasn't prepared to go to bat for him legally. He was arrested for destruction of private property and vandalizing property. He spent close to a year in Goose Creek Correctional Center in Wasilla, Alaska.

When he was released from Goose Creek, he had nothing but sixteen dollars in his pocket and the clothes on his back from when he was arrested. He headed over to the prison bus stop where he would catch a ride into Anchorage. Once there, he figured he'd stop at a bar and then figure what his options were. While standing at the bus stop, he was met by a young woman wearing a sweatshirt with the name Sarah embroidered over a Greenpeace logo.

"Hi, are you Robert Lester?"

"Maybe."

"My name is Sammy."

"Your sweater says Sarah."

"So? My jeans say Gloria Vanderbilt."

"Okayyou got me there. What? Are you with Greenpeace?"

"Not exactly. My name is Sammy, and I am with an environmental organization that you might be interested in joining."

"What organization would that be? I have to tell you, I'm a little disillusioned in the whole environmental-activism-thing at the moment."

"Have you ever heard of the Le Gang de la Clé de Singe?"

"Shit yeah—the Monkey Wrench Gang."

"Well, as you probably have heard, unlike other environmental organizations, we don't just protest; we kick ass and take names. We don't ask permission; we ask forgiveness."

"Yeah, you guys do some pretty hairy shit."

"That's us, and, as the Marines say, 'We're looking for a few good men, interested?"

"Why me, man?"

"You're kidding, right? We're looking for people who are tired of playing by the rules and getting nowhere while the other side cheats, lies, buys politicians, and basically plays by their own set of rules. If you want to make a difference—I mean a real difference—and help stop the corporations of the world from ruining the environment for their own personal profit, I have a car right over there. Otherwise, you can stand here and wait for the bus."

Lester saw the bus for Anchorage approaching the bus stop, but he looked at her and said, "Lead on."

She led him over to an old, beat up, silver Honda CR-V, where he noticed two men were seated in the front. He looked at her and asked, "And they would be?"

"My friends, my protection."

"Protection?"

"Yeah, Alaska has the highest rape rate in the country; a girl can't be too careful. Okay?

"Wow, I did not know that."

As they got into the car, Sammy introduced the Iceman to her friends, Tommy G and Jimmy the Chew. Both were veterans of many eco-war campaigns for the Gang against corporate America. They would eventually become part of the Iceman's Team. They drove down the Glenn Highway into Anchorage, to West 6th Avenue across Town Square Park, and to Humpy's Great Alaskan Alehouse, where they all ordered the halibut fish 'n' chips and a large glass of Hypothermia beer. Robert said that, after almost a year in jail, this was the best meal he had ever had. As they sat eating and drinking, Sarah explained what Lester could expect and what would be expected of him in return. After several hours and several beers, the Iceman said, "Where do I sign?"

The young lady at the reservation desk was getting ready to go thru the ritual of closing for the night, when a man dressed in a traditional safari jacket and blue jeans entered the lobby carrying a small duffel bag. He was tall, tan, and a bit scruffy.

"Welcome to Wawindaji Safari Lodge, do you have a reservation?"

"As a matter of fact, I don't, will that be a problem?"

"Well, we are rather full of all the hunters and the television crew and all but let me see what I can do."

"Television crew?"

"Oh yes, they're shooting an American TV show about big game hunting."

"No kidding, how interesting."

As the young woman was scanning thru the available rooms on the computer she said, "Yes, it is rather exciting. Ah, your in luck, I see that we have one of our luxury safari tents available, would that be satisfactory?"

"That sounds perfect. Are there any big name stars?"

"No, it's a reality show about big game hunters; it's kind of a hunting contest."

"How unusual, don't you think?"

"I guess these days they'll make a TV show about anything."

"Sounds rather sad, I remember when television shows were about something, had a story, a plot. Now, it seems that if you have a camera and a bunch of people who are willing to make fools of themselves, you have a hit show."

"You know, I believe you're right."

"Oh well."

"I see that the rate for the safari tent will be three hundred and fifty US Dollars a night, but that includes all your meals, two activities per day and the bar."

"Excellent."

"And for how many nights, Mister?"

"Hanson, William Hanson, and I think seven nights should work."

"Seven nights, very good. May I have your passport and form of payment?"

"Here you go. How long have you worked here, Irene?"

"I guess you could say all my life, my family owns the Lodge."

"And are your family big game hunters?"

"My grandfather was, he shot all of these trophies that you see in the lodge, but my dad and brother aren't. They prefer to do their shooting with a camera. They shot all the photos throughout the lodge and for the brochures, website and all the photos in the rooms, too."

"Yes, very nice. Quite beautiful and lucky."

"Lucky?"

"Oh yeah, lucky that you didn't have to hire a photographer. I hear they can be very expensive."

"Are you a hunter or photographer?"

"I guess more of a hunter."

"Okay Mr. Hanson, here's your key and a map of the lodge. We're here and your safari tent, which is called the Hyena Tent, is just down this path and if you'll just follow the signs, they will lead you right to it."

"Hyena, I like it."

"Well enjoy your stay, Mr. Hanson and if there is anything you might need, don't hesitate to let us know."

"Why thank you Irene, you're very kind. Good night."

"Good night."

Icarus took the map and key and headed out the door to the Hyena Tent.

After scoping out his accommodations, it was early enough for Icarus to go to the bar and check to see what info he could glean. The bar was jumping. There were a couple of tables that appeared to be occupied by the television crews having a good time and one table with a more somber tone that seemed to be the hunters' table.

Icarus decided to sit at the bar where there was a group of three men at the other end of the bar huddled together whispering among themselves. An elderly bartender dressed in a starched white shirt and black vest approached him, "May I take your order, sir?"

"Yes, I'll have a scotch rocks, please."

"Very good."

While he waited for his drink, he studied the hunters and their demeanors. He observed their temperaments, their personalities, and their interactions with each other. He could tell who was the alpha dog and who was the weakest among them.

"Here you are, sir. Would you care for something from the kitchen?"

"Thank you, no."

As he sipped his scotch, he had Sir William as the most fragile, next was Butch Anderson, hard shell on the outside but easily cracked, Jason Rowe and Wendy were neck and neck for second. It would all depend on the situation, but without a doubt it was the silent samurai, Haruto Nakamura who just sits and observes, he will be the most tenacious and fiercest. It was going to be an honor and a challenge to defeat him.

Icarus had spent years when he was younger studying the code of the samurai and the ways of bushido; he lived in Japan for a period of time where he became skilled in the art of using the katana, the traditional Japanese long sword. Icarus had researched Nakamura and found him to be an honorable man; a man who also was a skilled swordsman. He knew that to face such a man in combat would be epic.

The rest of the evening he sat and observed his rival, taking mental notes on his every move and gesture. Afterwards when everyone was calling it a night, Icarus got on his laptop and arranged to have a package sent express delivery to him overnight from Japan.

The revised plan that the Iceman and Icarus had devised was to lay waste to the hunters, guides and executive board. It was going to be a very busy day.

The next morning things were moving particularly slowly, there was definitely tension in the air, and nobody was in any rush to be the first team out on the hunt. All the hunters and their guides were sitting having breakfast together when Charles Doering and Jack Bonem entered the breakfast room; the show's sponsors had all returned to their homes. Charles and Jack were feeling very chipper and upbeat.

"People, may I have your attention please." Bonem announced. "I know we got off on a bit of a rocky start yesterday, but I think that we all know that we've got the makings of a great show. So, let's go out there and bring back television gold. Have fun and kill something."

Icarus thought to himself, 'I can't wait to take this asshole out.'

Wendy and her guide were the first to head out with their camera crew. According to the scheduling board posted in the lobby she was going to be hunting an African leopard today. One by one the other hunters teamed up with their designated film crews and made their ways to their jeeps and their assigned Zambian military escorts.

Icarus was finishing up his traditional English breakfast while catching up on the latest breaking news in the Zambian Observer when he overheard Doering and Bonem discussing that they were planning to slip away and do a bit of hunting themselves. Not venturing out too far, basically sitting out on their veranda and knocking off anything that would happen to have the misfortune of passing by.

As Icarus was leaving, he happened to pass by Commander Brown; they gave each other a casual nod and bid each other a good day. Icarus picked up a hint of disapproval in the look that Wooch gave as they passed.

In the breakfast room, Commander Brown disclosed to Doering and Bonem that he had to leave temporarily, to attend to some pressing matters, but assured them that he would return with a couple days. He told them that he, of course felt Major Hikeezi had the situation well in hand and that if anything urgent occurred that he would be available to them 24/7.

When he returned to his room, Icarus contacted the Iceman and the Red Team with the schedule of each of the hunters and their intended prey, then he prepared for his part. He made his way over a mile to where he had landed and hidden the Ehang drone from last night's landing. He retrieved a Beretta 92FS/M9 with a threaded silencer and Icarus' favorite killing machine, the DPMS GII Compact Hunter rifle with sound suppressor. It's lightweight, a mere 6.9 pounds with a mid-length gas system, carbon fiber free-float handguard and a B5 SOPMOD stock and best of all, the irony that ten years ago DPMS was purchased by Remington, one of the Hunting Show's major sponsors.

Icarus thought what a great advertising campaign opportunity for Remington, after Charles Doering and Jack Bonem were both killed by one of their products, Hell, everyone knows that happiness is a warm gun.

On the way back to the lodge, Icarus came across something by chance that he felt was truly ironic and inspiring. It was approximately the size of a basketball and took all of his skill and adroitness to collect the prize. Once he had collected it, he made his way undetected back to his room at the Wawindaji Safari Lodge, where he changed into military camo fatigues with matching balaclava. He casually walked down the hallway with the GII Compact Hunter slung over his shoulder to the lobby where Irene was working behind the reception desk and while holding his pistol at his side said to her, "Excuse me young lady, would you be so kind as to show me where you keep the recording devises for your CCTV, please. Don't worry I'm not going to hurt you."

She nervously opened the door to the office and led him to a closet where the recording equipment was stored. He asked her very nicely to have a seat behind the office desk and please keep her hands lying flat on the desktop and don't try anything foolish. He retrieved the last three days recordings and dismantled the recorder.

"Are you on duty alone?"

"Yes, my parents and my brother have traveled to Mumbwa to purchase some supplies, they aren't expected back till late."

"Are you telling me the truth, because I don't want to hurt any of your family or staff, understand?"

"I swear it's the truth." She said starting to cry.

"You have nothing to fear. I will be gone within the hour."

"Do you want money? We don't keep a lot of cash."

"No, this isn't a robbery. Now, where is your cell phone?"

"It's in my purse over there on the floor behind that plant.

"Okay, I'm going to take your cellphone and put it out there behind the reception desk along with this desk phone, too. I'm going to lock the door and Irene do not under any circumstances come out of this office or try to get help for at least one hour, do you understand? If you do as I say nothing bad will happen."

"I understand, I promise I won't try anything foolish."

"Good girl."

Icarus closed and locked the door with the key that was sitting in the lock on the inside of the office door. On his way leaving the reception area he picked up the package that had been overnighted to him from Japan sitting behind the reception desk in the mail bin. With the balaclava still over his face he left and made his way to Charles Doering's suite where he unlocked the door with the master key, he took unbeknownst to Irene and entered.

He could see that Doering and Jack Bonem were sitting out on the extended elevated deck attached to his balcony that rose twenty feet above the grasslands below. They sat there with their backs to the room next to the fire pit, drinking what looked to him as glasses of Bloody Mary's with their rifles leaning next to their chairs.

A small stream flowed by the lodge no more than a hundred feet from where the two of them were sitting and drinking. There was a small herd of Springbok drinking from the stream, they didn't seem skittish of the noises and laughter emanating from the two men sitting on the deck, in fact they were so use to humans that one could probably go over and pet them.

Icarus was staring out at the beauty of the landscape beyond the Springboks, way off in the distance he could see a family of elephants crossing on the horizon when he heard Jack Bonem say, "Watch this Charley, see that little one on the left with the funny antlers, that head would look great in my office."

As he reached for his rifle, so did Icarus. As he took aim, so did Icarus. As he started to pull the trigger, so did Icarus.

PHIFF

Unfortunately, for Jack Bonem, Icarus pull his trigger first. Bonem lurched forward out of his chair so fast that Charles thought that he slipped and fell from one too many Bloody Mary's until he saw the gaping hole in the back of his head.

"Your friend shouldn't have tried that." Icarus said as he approached the president and CEO of Worldwide Affiliates of Safari Partners. "And you are Jack Doering, I presume?"

"You, you killed him while he was just sitting here."

"Well, excuse me, but if I'm not mistaking, I do believe he was about to shoot one of those Springboks."

"You didn't have to kill him."

"Oh, but I did and sorry to say Mr. Doering, you too."

"Why, I haven't killed anything today."

"And you think *today* is the key word in that phrase? You know who I am, or at least you know who I represent. Now, if you would be so kind as to turn around."

"Are you going to shoot me in the back."

"No, I need to tie your hands behind you."

Doering did as he was told, Icarus tied his hands behind him and he also tied a rope around his ankles and said, "Turn around and have a seat on the railing."

Doering perched himself onto the railing facing Icarus, who walked over to where Jack Bonem lay and proceeded to tie a rope around his ankles, dragged him over next to Mr. Doering and flung his body over the rail after he placed the yellow monkey wrench flag around his neck and placed a letter in his sport coat inner pocket.

"What now?" Doering sheepishly inquired.

"How many animals do you think your organization has killed over the years, Doering?"

"I have no idea. Look I…"

"Take a guess." Icarus demanded.

"Hundreds I suppose, but…"

"Hundreds? Oh, I think you're being way too modest. Try again."

"Thousands?"

"I think you're being coy, Mr. Doering. Every year more than 100 million animals are reported killed by hunters every year in America alone, Mr. Doering. One hundred Million killed. We estimate that Worldwide Affiliates of Safari Partners or as you so quaintly refer to it W.A.S.P. has done more than its fair share of killing."

"Okay, we've probably killed a couple million animals over the years." Doering conceded.

Icarus walked over to a canvas bag that contained the object he found in the forest near the drone earlier and brought it over to his prisoner and held it up. "Know what I found this morning?"

Charles just shook his head no.

"Listen." Icarus held the bag up to Doerings right ear and gave it a jolt. The bag came alive and Doering could hear buzzing coming from within.

BUZZZZZZZZZZZZZ

"Any idea what's in here?"

"No." Doering said with eye as big as two Moon Pies.

"Wasps. Yellow jackets to be precise, I found a whole hive not far from here. Ironic, isn't it. You being the head of W.A.S.P. and me with a bag full of wasps."

Doering started to say something when Icarus opened the bag and in a blink of an eye, he flipped the bag over Charles' head and tied it off around his neck, trapping him in with over 3000 angry wasps. Charles's body was flailing so violently that he fell backwards over the side of the deck and hung upside down next to the body of Jack Bonem, his body writhing and thrashing in pain.

Icarus gathered up his gear, repelled over the side of the deck to where Bonem and Doering were hanging, removed his Beretta and fired three shots into Doering's chest, putting him out of his misery.

POP POP POP

Icarus tied the monkey wrench flag around Doering's neck and placed a note in his pocket, afterwards he walked out into the open grasslands where the herd of Springbok were grazing and headed out towards the horizon where he saw the elephant herd wandering off in the distance.

LuWei and Venus sent up the two Ehang Falcon B drones after hearing from Icarus of the hunters schedules. The Iceman gave the assignments to the Red Team, they were going to send out in teams of two. Odin would be teamed up with Vulcan and they were assigned Jason Rowe. Jimmy the Chew and Sassoon would take care of Butch Anderson. Tommy G and Gianfranco would hit Sir William and the Iceman would be teamed up with T-Bone, they'd be going after the fair Wendy Sutherland. Icarus had requested and was granted that he be allowed to challenge Haruto Nakamura alone.

"Alright teams, you have your assignments, once you've accomplisted your mission you'll probably need to take evasive action, so be sure to stay in contact with LuWei and Venus. They will be able to give you advise and assistance. They are going to be launching the French Aerospatiale C.22 drone. It's equipped with two Aster missiles in the event any of you need some special help. I would really prefer that we do not inflect any casualties to the Zambian troops, that would definitely open a large can of whoop ass on the organization, understood?" The teams all gave affirmative responses.

"Red Flyer will also be doing radio checks as you head out to your assignments. Be sure to stay in contact with him. Any questions? No. Then good luck and good hunting."

The four teams each headed out in different direction that will take them to intersect with their assigned targets. They will be fed real time corrections via Red Flyer's eye in the sky drones. LuWei will be manning the Aerospatiale C.22, while Venus will be handling the Ehang Falcon B's. As the teams are

Red Flyer would be making radio contact with each of them to occasionally check on radio contact, so far everyone was on air. Odin and Vulcan were going after Jason Rowe who had been assigned for his first kill to bag an African Lion. All indications were that he and his hunting party were heading south along the Kafue River near Mulola not far from McBride's Camp, a bare bones RV/tent campsite on the edge of the Kafue River. Odin and Vulcan decided to circumvent a long day's hike and travel down the Kafue River in an Asis inflatable 3.5M boat powered by a modified Superior X-Power 4 stroke outdoor 44CC motor.

By the time Rowe and his guide had arrived Odin and Vulcan were set up in a traditional cross shot position. They had heard lions nearby and thanks to Venus they were kept aware of their position. As the hunting party got closer, they realized that they had lucked out and found themselves to be in the perfect position to make their kill shot and escape without detection. Odin told Vulcan that Vulcan should take down Rowe while he would take care of the guide. At the count of three as the film crew was filming a discussion between Rowe and his guide, Odin gave the countdown, one, two, three, now.

PHIFF PHIFF

Two nearly silent shots and the job was over. As the cameraman shouted for the Zambian guards to come running Odin and Vulcan slipped back into the Kafue River and staying close to the near shore then they slipped back to base camp completely undetected. The Zambian police and Interpol would later review the footage of the killings and determine that there were definitely two shooters.

Jimmy the Chew and Sassoon were headed off in the opposite direction than Odin and Vulcan, they weren't as lucky to take such a leisurely boat ride down the Kafue, they like the other two teams that were leaving out of base camp had to travel by the old shoe leather express.

Their target, Butch Anderson had been giving the Black rhinoceros to take down this fine day. Black rhinos are usually found in treeless open grasslands with some bushes and shrubs making it hard to blend in, but not impossible. Jimmy was an expert in the art of camouflage; once they had taking their positions Jimmy made magic with their Ghillie suits. At one point while waiting for Butch and crew one of a Zambian scout stepped on Jimmy's arm, looked down and walked on by thinking it was just part of the terrain.

Thirty minutes had past and once the advance scouts ambled thru the area Jimmy and Sassoon got the heads up from Venus that their marks were within range and the scouts were a safe distance away. The targets were standing in a field of tall grass waist high; their film crew was over to their left filming some 'B-roll', not paying attention to their subjects. When Butch and his guide stopped to pull out their binoculars to scan the horizon in all directions looking for any sign of a rhino.

You would think something as big as a compact car would be fairly easy to spot, but they're wily creatures, they stay close to the shrubs and bushes, plus they share a symbiotic relationship with the Oxpeckers, a bird that sits on the rhino and eats ticks and warns the giant behemoth of danger.

Jimmy radioed Sassoon who was off to his right lying under a fynbos shrub approximately twenty-five yards away, "Red Three to Red Four, over."

"Red Four, over."

"Do you have a shot, over?"

"Affirmative, I have a clean shot at the guide, over."

"Excellent, I'll take the hunter. On my mark, three, two, one, fire."

PHIFF CRAASH

Jimmy's bullet hit Butch in the right lens of the binoculars while he held them up to his eyes. The bullet broke the glass, traveled thru the binoculars and lodged in the back of Butches brain, killing him instantly.

PHIFF

Sassoon's shot hit the guide just to the left of the trachea, severing the carotid artery rendering him dead within seconds.

It was twenty minutes before the film crew found their bodies, by then Jimmy the Chew and Sassoon were long gone.

Sir William was tasked with killing the Cape buffalo, commonly referred to as *Black Death*, they have been said to have killed more big game hunters than any other animal in Africa.

Sir William Cornwallis Smythe always fancied the nickname that he coined for himself, 'Wild Bill', but the nickname people actually referred to him behind his back was 'Bungling Bill' due to all the misfortunes Sir William had endured.

Today would be no better, poor Bill has been gored, mauled, crushed, clawed, stomped on, bludgeoned, bitten, pummeled, and trampled on, not exactly Mr. Lucky. But, throughout it all Sir William would always rise above adversity, triumph over pain and in the end he would stand victorious. As luck would have it, or as bad luck would have it, this would be the stuff that legends and folklore are made of.

Sir William and his guide had come across a large herd of Cape buffalo on the edge of the Kafue River, they had isolated the Bull that Wild Bill deemed to be his trophy when he unexpectedly had an uncontrollable urge to, as the British say, 'Take a Slam'.

He wandered off to find a shrub for a little privacy; his guide would stand guard at a decent and respectful distance. Tommy G and Gianfranco were lying in wait across the Kafue. hidden in a large field of tall grass with their eyes on the prize, even with the herd in between themselves and Smythe, they had a clear shot when the time came. It never did.

In Africa the Black Mamba is the most feared of all the snakes, but it isn't the one that claims the most lives. That would be the Puff Adder, and that is the one that Sir William just happened to squat over when he was taking care of business.

The Puff Adder looks rather similar to the American Rattle Snake, its markings make it hard to see, especially in tall brown grasses like the grasses Sir William was squatting in. Feeling under threat the snake catapulted up and plunged its fangs deep into his goolies, *aka his testicles*. The bite was severely painful, causing swelling, blistering, nausea, and vomiting immediately.

Sir William jumped up screaming, which generated the herd of several dozen Cape buffalo into a stampede heading in the direction of him and his guide. Sir William probably would have survived the snakebite if his screech of pain hadn't caused the buffalo's panic attack, but standing there holding his cajones and with his trousers down around his ankles, Wild Bill stood no chance and both he and his guide were literally run over, crushed, flattened, squashed, and stomped into mush having been trampled over by 84,000 pounds of grinding, crunching, pulverizing, bone-crushing Cape buffalo hooves traveling over 35 miles per hour.

Luckily their film crew was away from Sir William and guide giving him a bit of privacy, but once the Cape buffalo started the stampede, they were far enough away that they recorded the entire incident. Which was the lead footage in the documentary chronicling the Zambian disaster nicknamed 'Bungle in the Jungle'.

Tommy G and Gianfranco laid on the opposite side of the river observing the dramedy; it was both hilarious and tragic simultaneously. As the Zambian army was busy retrieving the bodies, Gianfranco and G made their way back to camp.

When the press asked, the Zambian medical examiner on Sir William's condition, he quipped, "Poor chap, he looks like a hundred and sixty pounds of ground round."

Wendy Sutherland was in hot pursuit of a 115-pound male *panthera pardus pardus*, better known as the African leopard. She missed her first shot which was totally uncharacteristic of her. Just as she squeezed the trigger a female lion challenged the male leopard for the dik-dik it had just killed and was in the process of taking up into a large fever tree.

KA-POW

The shot frightened off the lion, but the leopard wasn't about to give up on a kill.

T-Bone and the Iceman got to where Wendy was tracking the big cat just in time to see her miss. The Iceman was standing three hundred yards to the right of Wendy and about the same from him and the leopard. He was hidden behind a large and imposing whistling thorn tree, he waited until Wendy was preparing for her second shot he fired and hit the dead dik-dik scaring the leopard out of the tree and causing the big cat to run off into the brush.

PHIFF

Wendy had her eye on the scope and saw the bullet hit the dead prey; she was now acutely aware that they were being watched. She twirled around and started to yell at her guide, but the words never left her mouth.

PHIFF

T-Bone's shot entered her body just below her left kidney the bullet tumbled round, traveling upwards piercing her liver, hitting and breaking three ribs before coming to rest in the supraventricular crest of Wendy Sutherland's heart.

PHIFF

The Iceman's shot hit Wendy's guide on the sphenoid bone located on the side of his head dropping him like a sack of potatoes.

The film crew was paying so much attention trying to follow the leopard once it jumped out of the tree that T-Bone and the Iceman had left the area to return to camp before they noticed the bodies and alerted the Zambian patrol.

Haruto Nakamura and Mr. Yamada, his translator and guide had come across a couple of elephant herds, but none of them had award-winning tusks he was looking for and he wasn't willing just to settle. He, his guide along with the camera crew had been driving in their Land Rover all day thru fields and fields of Kenkiliba bushes, which is a bush that on average stands eight to ten feet tall, the local natives make it into a tea that's rumored to be good for the digestion, nourishes the liver and helps with circulation. It also makes it hard to be seen by elephants, they had come into a clearing where off in the distance where a lone man was standing holding a Katana, the traditional Japanese samurai sword. Haruto's guide was going to call out for the Zambian troops, but Haruto told him, "*Īe. Watashi wa kore o shori shimasu.*"

Tony the camera operator asked Mr. Yamada what he said. "He said that he doesn't want me to call for help, that he will handle it himself."

Haruto got out of the Land Rover, walked to the back and opened the back hatch and removed a black leather covered hard case that resembled a rifle case. He opened it to reveal two swords, the katana and a wakizashi, a smaller companion sword. He removed the larger sword, unsheathed it and as he walked past Mr. Yamada he said,

"*Daremoga koko ni iru.*"

"Everyone is to stay here." Yamada translated.

Icarus started walking to Mr. Nakamura and when they met Icarus bowed and said, "*Kon'nichiwa.*"

"*Kon'nichiwa.*" Mr. Nakamura replied as he bowed and returned the greeting. "*Anata wa nani o nozonde iru nodesu ka?*

Mr. Yamada could hear the conversation going on and as they spoke, he would translate for the camera crew while they continued to film.

"What is it that you want?"

"My name is Icarus, I'm with Le Gang de la Clé de Singe. Have you heard of us?"

"Yes, I now understand. You are here to kill my guide, and me, as you believe that we have committed a great sin against nature. Is this, not right?"

"I am afraid that it is so."

"Why do you not kill us with a gun?"

"I feel that this is the honorable way."

"Are you familiar with the art of the sword?"

"I am a student of kendo as are you."

"And you are prepared to die?"

"For me there is no more noble cause."

"Very well, then." Haruto once again bowed and held his sword high and behind him with both hands, turning his body so as not to face Icarus head on. Icarus bowed to Haruto, then assumed the same fighting position.

To the untrained eye the duel seemed slow moving and lethargic with moments of brilliance and fury. To the skilled observer the engagement seemed a beautiful, choreographed ballet that lasted over twenty minutes. The deadly encounter ended suddenly when Haruto briefly slipped and that allowed Icarus the opportunity for a deadly strike. Haruto dropped to his knees and died.

Icarus stood over the vanquished, he himself had suffered several major cuts to his arms and torso, none life threatening. He dropped his sword and turned to leave as he did, he felt a sharp pain in his back before he heard a shot.

KA-POW

The shot fired from Haruto's translator/guide.

Icarus looked down at the exit wound, blood was starting to stream out, he slowly twisted around to face his assailant. He stood motionless for a moment before collapsing to the ground staring up at the sun, the warmth of sunlight felt good and a rush of calm washed over him, then blackness.

"Good evening I'm Nigel Williams and this is BBC World Headlines, tonight our big story once again involves the eco-terrorist group Le Gang de la Clé de Singe. It is

being reported that several world-renowned big game hunters along with the CEO and president of Worldwide Affiliates of Safari Partners, Charles Doering and the president of the Hunting Network, Jack Bonem have been killed in and around Kafue National Park in Zambia.

The hunters, Sir William Cornwallis Smythe, Wendy Sutherland, Charles "Butch" Anderson, Jason Rowe and Haruto Nakamura were all killed while doing what they loved best, hunting big game.

They were all participating in an American TV reality show based on the five best big game hunters going up against the big five game in a week long contest where the winner was to be awarded a grand prize of ten million dollars.

Each hunter would have to kill one of the animals that make up the group known as the big five, an African elephant, a Cape buffalo, an African leopard, rhinoceros, and the African lion.

It has been reported that each of the hunters were under the protection of the Zambian Army troops led by a Major Hikeezi, who has stated that they were not to blame for the killings as it was the hunters' responsibility not the Army's to make sure they were in constant contact. The Zambian Army is working closely with Interpol to seek to bring those responsible to justice.

For its part Le Gang de la Clé de Singe claims responsibility for the action taken, stating that these hunters were guilty of committing grievous acts of theriocide, which the act of the mass killing of animals by humans. As for the presidents Charles Doering and Jack Bonem the French group claim they were complicit in that they promoted and encouraged theriocide therefore just as guilty and deserved the same fate.

Although there were no members of Le Gang de la Clé de Singe captured there was one killed, his identity is believed to be that of Liam Janssens, the convicted murderer of three brothers killed in Zimbabwe a couple of weeks ago, who recently escaped from Mahalapye prison. Liam Jassens is believed to be an alias.

In other news, a gang of British soccer hooligans…"

Captain Snowy White and the crew of the King Edward I set sail from the town of Qaanaaq in northwest Greenland. The Qaanaaq area was first settled around 2000 BC, a desolate and remote location, the perfect spot for Snowy and his band of assassins to take refuge and recuperate after their last encounter with the Canadian Navy.

The crew of the King Edward I had been assigned to stop the killing of baby fur seals by any means necessary. Sealers, as they're called, are men who calmly walk up to a baby fur seal lying on the ice and use a hakapikor club; a four to five-foot wooden pole with a bent metal spike affixed to the end to bash their brains in.

It's the club of choice, because it's much easier to aim a blow directly at the seal pup's head with it. One swing from a hakapik will usually kill a pup right away. They keep clubbing the seal in the forehead, though, until they know for sure that it's dead. They're supposed to 'palpate' a pup's skull after they've clubbed it to feel the caved-in bone beneath the skin and blubber, or they perform the 'blink reflex' test, which consists of touching the seal's eyeball—if it blinks, they have another excuse to club it again.

Sue-B and Fu Hao are among Le Gang de la Clé de Singe's best snipers, the two of them would lie in wait on snowdrifts for the sealers to be dropped off on to the ice flows with their hakapikor club where the seal pups were lying, they would walk up to the pups and swing the club above their heads to get the ultimate velocity to crush the pups' skull into mush.

Sue-B and Fu Hao's goal was to spatter the hunter's brains out onto the ice before the seal pups.

The campaign was successful in that it halted the killing of seal pups for at least the season. Le Gang de la Clé de Singe will have come up with a new technique for the next year, something equally innovative and unexpected.

Captain White and company are currently off to northern Alaska to the Arctic National Wildlife Refuge to harass and hopefully stop RB Exploration's seismic exploration of large tracts of tundra. Areas of tundra where polar bears give birth to their cubs.

A giant 90,000-pound "thumper trucks" and other heavy vehicles will be tramping across the tundra, repeatedly pounding the earth with the force of 30,000 pounds of pressure. Horrendous noises ripping through the silence of the arctic winter night causing the earth to shake, subjecting mother bears and cubs being constantly exposed to repeated pounding and shaking of the ground. They were also going to be sending out teams of hunters to locate and kill mother polar bears and her cubs while they are hibernating.

The drilling for oil and gas will irreparably damage the beauty of such a wild place and will disturb the environment and home of the owls, arctic foxes, caribou, and polar bears that've lived here, protected for millennia.

When the world is finally waking up to the effects of climate change and when fossil fuels are being phased out and replaced with renewable energy the only reason this is being allowed is corporate greed, corporate payouts to government officials, and corporations total disregard for the future of the planet.

The King Edward I, a forty-seven-foot Motor Lifeboat; designed to weather hurricane-force winds and heavy seas, it even self-rights in less than ten seconds with all equipment fully functional if overturned. It is armed with an M240 machine gun and is equipped with a French Aerospatiale C.22 drone that is armed with two Aster missiles for reconnaissance or if needed, attack.

They sailed north up thru Baffin Bay, threading the needle of the Qikiqtaaluk region of Canada and the uninhabited northernmost edge of Greenland, around the town of Alert, Canada the most northernmost permanently inhabited place in the world and out into the Arctic Ocean heading west to Alaska.

Captain Snowy White, a French Canadian who captained a River Patrol Boat for three tours in Vietnam back in the sixties. Snowy was wounded twice and received the Star of Military Valor, the second highest military decoration one can receive, three times. He was a war legend in Quebec and even had his own statue in Melocheville, standing next to the Canadian Vietnam Veterans Monument.

When he returned to Montreal after the war, he was offered a position as a captain of one of the LNG barges for the Canadian oil and gas giant GasTell. He was responsible for transferring liquefied natural gas (LNG) from ship-to-ship, or oil rig-to-ship-to-ship. LNG is natural gas that is cooled to minus 260 degrees Fahrenheit, which becomes a liquid that can be transported without high compression, once delivered to its destination, the LNG is warmed and regasified so that it can be used as natural gas.

Snowy was working out in the Gulf of Saint Lawrence running LNG from an oil & gas rig off the Magdalen Islands to a marine terminal on Prince Edward Island, when an explosion occurred on the oil rig *"Vue en Eaux Profondes"* when the well blew out, spewing oil and gas. The explosion cracked the seabed in seven places releasing 4,000 gallons of oil an hour.

The Prince Edward Island coastline would be devastated by 6 million gallons of crude, the largest oil spill in the nation's history. A spill that would take generations to recover from.

The manmade disaster was devastating enough, but what turned Snowy and hundreds of others to join organizations like Greenpeace, World Wildlife and Le Gang de la Clé de Singe was the massive extent of the cover up perpetrated on the public. Not just the lies and the refusal to accept culpability for the spill, but the denying of any responsibility for the thousands of cleanup workers who fell ill with an array of excruciating, bizarre, and grotesque sicknesses and ailments brought about by the use of toxic cleanup products the crews were told were safe. Many of the workers suffered the same symptoms experienced by soldiers who returned from the Persian Gulf War with Gulf War syndrome.

So, the worst environmental disaster in Canadian history was whitewashed, the true magnitude obscured, the victims forgotten, the lessons ignored, and the corporations win again.

Captain White had had enough of the corporate bullshit, the lies and the cover-ups, two weeks after he resigned; he was powering Zodiacs full of demonstrators and protesters out to Gastell oilrigs in the Gulf of Saint Lawrence. With months he was the captain of the King Edward I sailing armed eco-warriors out to the rigs to do a lot more than just protest.

Shortly after the *"Catastrophe en eau profonde'*, as it was called, Henri Gagneux, the Président and CEO of Gastell was found dead hanging upside down from the wooden ceiling beams of his eleven-million-dollar estate, his hands tied behind his back and his head submerged in a barrel of liquid petroleum hydrocarbon, more commonly known as oil spill sludge. There was a yellow flag with the skull and cross monkey wrenches around his neck and a note from Le Gang de la Clé de Singe stuffed in his pocket declaring him guilty of crimes against humanity.

Inspectors Volker and Morris sat across from Major Hikeezi in his office at the Arakan Zambian Defense Forces Base on Burma Road in the outskirts of Luska. Also in the meeting was the retired American SEAL Commander Brown, along with Mr. Roger Blumenthal the new President and CEO of the Hunting Network and Thurston Bentley Hart the third, President of W.A.S.P. and Mr. Yamada, Haruto Nakmura's translator/guide.

Hikeezi wasn't in the best of moods, as he is facing a possible court-martial for neglect of duty resulting in the deaths of eleven civilians.

"Major Hikeezi, can you tell us how it all went so wrong?" Morris asked.

"Well, it seems that all the hunters allowed themselves to be separated from their escorts, resulting in their deaths. I don't see why I should be held responsible for their negligence. Do you?"

"I'm afraid not knowing all the facts I really can't comment. Major Hikeezi, would you happen to have a copy of the medical examiners reports that we could have?"

The Major opened the middle drawer of his desk and tossed a large envelope to the inspector. "Here."

"Thank you." Morris said as he and Volker started to flip thru the report. After a quick scan Volker turned to Mr.

Yamada and asked, "Mr. Yamada, can you tell us what happened to Mr. Nakamura?"

"We were in pursuit of a small elephant herd thru an area of thick brush when we came into a clearing, there standing approximately three hundred feet in front of us was a man standing alone holding a Katana, the traditional Japanese samurai sword. He spoke Japanese, he said his name was Icarus, and he was with Le Gang de la Clé de Singe. And he asked Mr. Nakamura had he heard of them. Mr. Nakamura told him that he had. Mr. Nakamura had gotten his Katana from the boot of the vehicle.

"They proceeded to '*Shinu made tatakaimasu*', fight to the death. '*Karera wa dochira mo kenjutsu no gijutsu ni jukuren shite ita*', they were both skilled in the art of swordsmanship. Combat didn't last long; unfortunately, Mr. Nakamura lost footing, which gave this man Icarus a slight advantage, which was all he needed. During the battle Mr. Nakmura inflected several sever wounds to his opponent, but alas Mr. Nakamura's stumble was his undoing.

"The man called Icarus dealt the final deathblow and Mr. Nakamura fell dead, the man, Icarus then dropped his sword and started to walk away. I could not let this man leave, so I picked up Mr. Nakamura's rifle and shot him in the back. I know that this not the honorable thing to have done, but he had to be stopped."

Inspector Morris still reviewing the case file asked Major Hikeezi, "I understand there was camera crews assigned to each hunting party, I would like to have a copy of that footage."

"I'm sorry Inspector, but I am not in possession of that film. That is the property of Mr. Roger Blumenthal and the Hunting Network." Hikeezi said.

Morris looked at Blumenthal, "Mr. Blumenthal, I want a copy of that footage."

"I'm sorry Inspector Morris, but that footage is television gold, it's going to be the highest rated television show in history. It's worth millions, possibly billions in sponsor revenue. I can't afford to allow that footage to be leaked out before the broadcast. Sorry, no can do."

Commander Brown abruptly jumped into the conversation, "Mr. Blumenthal, you can do, and you will do because if the Inspector doesn't have a copy of all that footage in his hands by five o'clock this evening, I will personally gouge out your eyeballs and skull-fuck you, do you understand?"

Blumenthal's face suddenly was drained of all color; he turned a whiter shade of pale. He quickly tried to compose himself, but as he tried to speak, nothing can out.

Wooch walked over to him seated behind Inspector Volker, leaned down and shouted, "I can't hear you, speak up!"

Blumenthal tried to make his self get smaller in the chair, beads of sweat were forming on his forehead and upper lip, and he felt faint. No one had ever spoke to him like this, we was a high-powered national network executive, a man of managerial experience who commanded respect. He collected himself and weakly said, "You can't threaten me, and everyone here heard you threaten me. I have witnesses."

"I don't see any witnesses, Volker did I threaten Mr. Blumenthal?"

"I didn't hear anything."

"Inspector Morris, did you hear me threaten Mr. Blumenthal?"

"Negative, Commander."

"Mr. Hart?"

"I'm sorry, Commander I wasn't really paying attention."

"Mr. Yamada? Major Hikeezi?" Both just shook their heads no.

"Five o'clock, is that clear Mr. Blumenthal?"

Blumenthal knew he better comply, the look on Brown's face said he was not a man to be trifled with. "Yes Commander, five o'clock."

Inspector Volker a bit taken back by Commander Browns aggressive tenor proclaimed, "Alright Mr. Blumenthal, I believe that you, Mr. Hart and Mr. Yamada are free to leave, if we need to speak to you again, we'll be in touch. Oh, and don't plan on leaving Zambia without letting me know. Have a good day gentlemen."

Volker stood up to signal that the meeting was over, "Major, Inspector Morris, Commander Brown and I will review all the data and the footage and get back to you with our report. Hopefully there will be something that will be able to help you. We appreciate all your assistance and will definitely inform your superior of your total cooperation. Is there anything that we can do for you at the moment?"

"I thank you all for anything that you might be able to do for me. There is one thing that I found very puzzling, Inspector Volker." Major Hikeezi said.

"And what is that Major?"

"The only clear fingerprint found on Icarus' sword was that of a dead Japanese actor, Toshiro Mifune. How is that possible?"

"'Tis a conundrum, Major."

"Huh?"

Inspector Morris smiled and said, "He means we don't have a fucking clue."

Veronica Ventura and Yum Wu couldn't have been more opposite. Veronica was five-foot-eleven, had long, blonde hair, green eyes, weighed one hundred and ten pounds—just plain beautiful—and she came from Greenwich, Connecticut. Her father was a hedge-fund banker, and the Ventura's were ranked as one of the ten richest families in America. Veronica graduated from UCLA and spent three years in the Peace Corp in Nepal, where she joined Le Gang de la Clé de Singe and recruited Yum Wu.

Yum Wu stands five-foot-four, has pitch-black hair, brown eyes, and weighs one hundred and eighty pounds. Standing side-by-side, they look like the perfect odd couple, but they are actually the perfect even pair. Yum was originally from the small town of Jinchang, the People's Republic of China. Jinchang is in the center of Gansu province, bordering Inner Mongolia to the north. It's known as China's 'Nickel Capital'.

Yum Wu's father was a miner, his father's father was a miner, and so on, and so on for eight generations. Her mother had died during her childbirth, and Yum and her father lived just outside of town on the West side of Hongshan Crossing, which literally separated the city from the rural community.

The property on which they lived on was all dirt, as no plants or even trees could grow; it was a depressing existence for Yum. The only pleasure she got was from practicing target shooting for The People's Republic of China Olympic Women's 50m Rifle 3 Positions Team. The event had the athletes shoot over a distance of fifty meters in kneeling, prone, and standing positions.

In the beginning, when Yum began to try out for the team, many of the officials scoffed and laughed at her because of her physical appearance. They were all silenced when she obtained a near perfect score after only her first try.

Yum had begun hunting at an early age with her grandfather; she was an excellent shot but didn't enjoy the killing of animals. She did, however, enjoy the challenge in the precision and accuracy of hitting a target. She spent hours upon hours practicing target shooting for over twelve years, and, when she heard that the People's Republic of China Olympic trials for the Women's 50m Rifle 3 Positions Team was being held in Beijing, she and her father made the twenty-two-hour trip to Beijing by bus for the tryouts, which she aced.

While they were in Beijing, they received word that her grandfather and uncle were both killed in a major shaft collapse in the Mojiang Mine, where there had been hundreds of recent complaints from the miners of unsafe conditions. The mine owners just brushed them off as being unfounded, and the government backed the owners, bringing on no charges of neglect and stating that the miners were at fault for being careless and not heeding safe practices. When Yum stood with the miners and protested against the government, she was told to stop or she would be arrested, and she was cut from the Olympic team.

Yum and her father were arrested and spent seven months in prison. She was sent to the Provincial Women's Prison, where she was forced to work in the Jiuzhou Clothing Factory. During her time there, she was systematically beaten and raped by the prison guards.

Her father, Bohai, along with dozens of other protesters, was sent to Lanzhou Prison. It was a high-security prison that included several workshops where prisoners performed forced labor. Prisoners were deprived of food and medical care, and prisoners who did not finish their forced labor tasks were tortured. Bohai succumbed to several beatings and died after five months of imprisonment; his family was never told the truth of how he died, just that he was dead.

After Yum was released from prison, she decided to leave China. She knew that her life would be hell if she stayed, so she made her way through the twelve-hundred-mile journey, on foot, across Qinghai Province to Tibet. Qinghai was a large, sparsely populated province spread across the high-altitude Tibetan Plateau. She traveled mostly at night to avoid being seen and carried a Chinese Hanyang Arsenal Experimental Semi-Automatic Rifle that was her grandfather's—he had owned it since 1918 and kept it in excellent condition. It was the only thing she had that had any sentimental value to her. She was prepared to use it if she had to, as she had decided that she was not going to be taken alive and face prison again.

On day sixteen, she reached Amne Machin, which was a six-thousand-two-hundred-and-eighty-two-meters-high peak and part of the Kunlun Mountains, a holy site for Buddhist pilgrims. She was near death from exposure, when several Buddhist monks from the monastery Wutong found her and brought her to the monastery. There, she received medical attention and was allowed to stay under their protection for six weeks until she was fit enough to continue her journey to Katmandu. After another ten days, she finally slipped over the well-guarded border under the cover of a severe blizzard. She didn't make the journey unscathed; she suffered a severe case of frostbite—lost three toes on her left foot and two on her right foot—but she was free.

She eventually found work as a chambermaid at the Hotel Yak and Yeti, a hundred-year-old, five-star hotel in the heart of Katmandu, located on Durbar Marg Street where she learned to speak English. She worked there and, by sheer luck, met Veronica Ventura while viewing the Garden of Dreams, which, created in the 1920's, had half a dozen pavilions, several fountains, and hundreds of urns and birdhouses.

A couple of young, pre-teenage boys were teasing a dog by a small pavilion in the center of the garden. Both Veronica and Yum heard the yelping of the dog in distress and went to investigate, each approaching from opposite directions. They arrived almost at the same time, and each took actions to chase the boys away. The combination of a tall, white Anglo woman and a short, stocky Chinese woman joining forces in chasing and yelling seemed to un-nerve the lads, as they decided to run off and create mischief somewhere else. The two hit it off quickly, and, after several days, they became fast friends. After Veronica learned of Yum's talents, she recruited her into the Gang. Once the Gang found out about Yum's shooting abilities, she and Veronica were teamed up as a sniper and spotter duo. Veronica had chosen the name Sue-B in honor of her hero, Susan B. Anthony, and Yum decided to go by the name Fu Hao, an infamous Chinese female warrior from the Shang Dynasty.

Captain White took the King Edward I down from the Arctic Ocean south into the Beaufort Sea towards the northern coast of Alaska where they dropped anchor at Kaktovik a small Inupiat Eskimo village famous for becoming the 'polar bear capital of the United States in the summer. Being that winter is setting in, the bears are settling in for the winter. The Inupiats would begin hunting for caribou and whales to help sustain them thru the long harsh winter. Snowy sent Weezer, the first mate into town to gather supplies for them to have enough to get them thru till spring.

Once they had all their stores onboard, they set sail for the tiny island of Tigvariak in Foggy Island Bay, east of Prudhoe Bay where thousands of transient workers come every year to support the Prudhoe Bay oil fields.

Tigvariak Island was perfect for the King Edward I, it has a natural harbor that is not only sheltered from the open seas, but also hidden from both land and sea.

Because the time of year up along the Arctic Circle there is but only two hours of weak sunlight, ideal for the kind of work Sue-B and Fu Hao were headed out to do. Hazael the ships drone operator, a recent refuge from Syria, sent the drone up for the ships first reconnaissance flight to get an idea what opposition they would be facing.

It was always the practice of Le Gang de la Clé de Singe to give fair warning to those that they felt were committing crimes that were punishable by death, so if anyone wanted to cease and desist, their life would be spared, but if they chose to ignore the warning then Le Gang de la Clé de Singe would rain bloody hell down upon them.

After the initial recon flight's data had been analyzed by the crew, Hazael sent the drone up again, this time with warning leaflets that were dropped over Prudhoe Bay and out over all the oil fields, pumping, and flow stations. The leaflet had a picture of the flag of America with the following warning: *A declaration from Le Gang de la Clé de Singe to all those that are involved in RB Exploration's seismic exploration, cease and desist immediately or pay the ultimate price. All those involved in hunting polar bear;*

cease and desist immediately or you too will pay the ultimate price. You have been warned. There will be no further warnings, no mercy, only death.

Bobby Anderson decided to take a year off from Northwestern University and head north to Alaska to make some big money working on the pumping stations in Prudhoe Bay on the Maddux Petroleum Pipeline.

Maddux guaranteed him six thousand dollars a month plus room and board as an intern on project management, working twelve hour shifts, six days a week. He had been on the job for just three months when a piece of paper floated down from the heavens that would change his life and the lives of a lot of people in Prudhoe Bay forever.

Sitting in his dormitory style room Bobby was relaxing after a grueling twelve hours working outdoors doing general maintenance at Pump Station 4. The temperature never got above minus forty-six, it would take him a good four hours to thaw out after his shift. Having been thru several severe winters while going to school in Chicago, he thought that he would be able to handle the Alaskan winter weather, boy did he think wrong.

His supervisor, Tom Broad, a native Alaskan from Anchorage who had been with Maddux Petroleum for eighteen years, all of it working on the pipeline swung by his room to tell him that he was going to be assigned to be working on the "thumper trucks" for the next couple weeks.

"You okay with that?"

Bobby asked, "Why me, I don't know anything about those trucks."

"Aww, it seems that a couple of the regulars got freaked out about these flyers and quit. You aren't worried about those crackpots, are you?"

"Well to tell you the truth Tom, it is rather scary. They were very specific about going after anyone being involved in seismic exploration or bear hunting."

"Look the company is taking these threats very seriously, that's why with each caravan of seismic vibrator trucks there'll be armed guards. Besides, you won't be operating the seismic equipment, you'll be riding shotgun as it were, operating the GPS systems. Hey, it beats working out in the deep freeze, am I right? Plus, the company will give each of you each a bonus of a thousand bucks a week."

Bobby, trying to think of a way to refuse, but knew this wasn't really a request, more of an order. Still thawing out their shift, he relented. "Okay, Tom I'm in."

"That's the spirit, report to Pump Station 3 tomorrow morning at six o'clock."

Tom shut the door on his way out; minutes later Bobby heard him knocking on his neighbor's door trying to recruit them, too.

"I got a bad feeling about this." Bobby said to himself.

Six o'clock in the morning looks a lot like six o'clock in the evening, pitch black. Bobby caught the shuttle bus to Pump Station 3 at five forty-five and were standing outside the entrance gate where the "thumper trucks" were parked. They sent the "thumper trucks" out individually. Each truck was assigned several pre-designated stops where they would stop, lower the buggy-mounted device to be flush with the ground. The device is capable of injecting low-frequency vibrations into the earth. Above ground, it sounds like a commercial jet's engine revving up for take-off, below ground it sends shock wave disrupting hibernation of mother polar bears and their cubs.

Bobby's truck was assigned to head south, two hours out from Pump Station 3 Bobby's truck started collecting seismic data. The driver was a good old boy from Decatur, Georgia, Eddie Hayes. Eddie was a tobacco chewing, rebel rousing, moonshine-drinking son of a Johnny Reb who totally believed that the south would rise again.

"You a Yankee, boy? I don't really cotton to Yankees, where you from boy?"

"Chicago."

"Chicago! Sheet."

"But the southside."

"Oh yeah, well I guess that's okay then."

"That's a relief."

Sitting between Bobby and Eddie was Scott Johnson, their armed guard. Scott was originally hired to be a roustabout on the oil field rigs, but when the threats came, they drafted him into wearing a sidearm and toting a

Winchester pump shotgun. Once they left the camp Scott fell into a deep asleep.

Two hours into their journey Bobby exclaimed, "Hey, Eddie the GPS says our first stop is right up here."

The truck came to a stop, outside there was nothing but flat countryside covered with snow, it looked like they were in the middle of nowhere, and they were. The wind was kicking up snow into the air making it look like a sandstorm was blowing, the only light outside was from the headlights of the truck and the only light on the inside was from the dimmed blue glow illuminating the cabin came from the instrument panel and the dials on the dashboard.

Bobby's full attention was on learning the intricacies and nuances of the GPS while Eddie was gearing up the seismic equipment; Scott's snoring was so loud that it was drowning out the high whine of the seismic engines. Bobby was in the process of sending their location back to base when he heard a faint sound; a crackle sound, then there was a rush of cold air.

CRACK

He looked over at Eddie, thinking he had cracked his side window only to see Eddie slumped over onto the steering wheel with a large crater that used to be the back of his head, the contents of said crater was oozing down the back of the truck cab. Scott appeared to still be sleeping, he was still reclining in his seat, hands folded in his lap, eyes closed, but he had blood spewing out from his chest.

Bobby in shock, instinctively opened his door, jumped out and started running, he ran for about a quarter mile until he tripped and fell, lying on his back hyperventilating he saw two figures all dressed in white standing over him. One of them gestured for him to stand up; he rolled over on to all fours and slowly got to his feet. He was a good six inches taller that the person standing in front of him, the second one was standing off to his right holding a rifle aimed at him. The person closest to him handed a piece of paper to Bobby and asked, "Have you seen this?"

Bobby took the paper and opened it up; it was the flyer that was dropped days before warning not to be involved in seismic exploration. Bobby started to try and explain but was cut off when the person asked, "What does the last line of copy say?"

Bobby couldn't speak; try as he may, nothing came out.

"It says that there will be no further warnings, no mercy, only death."

It was at that moment that Bobby realized that the person standing in front of him was a woman.

PHIFF

He heard a whisp of a sound, saw a small flash of light; he felt a sharp pain in his chest and a strange sensation of weightlessness as the impact of the bullet hitting him sent him flying backwards on to the ground. He lay there looking up at the blackness of the sky with swirls of snowdrifts dancing above him; he felt a pleasantness overcoming him as he slowly began to float upward towards the stars.

Tom Broad, who headed the search party when Bobby, Eddie and Scott didn't return to camp. They found all three lying beside each other next to their vehicle with yellow ensigns around their necks and a declaration for the justification for their deaths from the terrorist group Le Gang de la Clé de Singe.

Hazael was constantly feeding updated information to Sue-B and Fu Hao on what kind of forces were being detached in retaliation for the deaths of Eddie, Scott, and Bobby.

Sue-B and Fu Hao had each built individual snow cave shelters facing in opposite directions for optimal surveillance capability. This kind of shelter is the most effective because of the insulating qualities of snow. Both Fu Hao and Sue-B were wearing the latest generation of Extended Cold Weather Clothing System developed by the U.S. Army that was designed maximum protection in weather of -60 degrees. Since they were several miles from the King Edward I they needed to be self-sufficient for a couple of weeks.

While relaxing in their shelters Fu Hao spotted two hunters trekking across the horizon in search for polar bear dens, she radioed Sue-B to come and assist her. They started to follow the hunters at a safe distance so not to be detected. It wasn't too long when the two hunters came across a suspected den, one stood ready with his weapon trained at the dens entrance while the other started to unearth the den.

Fu Hao whispered, "Now."
PHIFF PHIFF

Both men were fell down like a couple of bowling pins; they lay motionless as the two assassins cautiously approached their lifeless bodies. Fu Hao and Sue-B dragged them away from the polar bears den and proceeded to do the ritual of placing of the yellow flags around their necks and putting the letters of proclamations in the pockets. They then sat them up and placed them back-to-back resting against each other, their weapons placed on their laps. When they finished Sue-B and Fu Hao retreated back to their snow shelters.

Days later, a search party found the dead bodies of the two hunters, both had been mauled and disemboweled by a male polar bear. The bear was probably on the hunt for food when it smelled the blood from their wounds; polar bears have a very strong sense of smell that enables them to detect prey up to a kilometer away.

When word of these deaths got back to Prudhoe Bay, workers refused to venture out past the main rigs, or to travel anywhere that a facility wasn't established and was up and running. Prudhoe Bay's Borough Mayor Harry T. Stone called on the governor to bring in the National Guard. Governor Mitchell did just that, he called up five hundred troops to ferret out these murderers and bring them to justice. The National Guard troops rode along side-by-side with the "thumper trucks" and troops were stationed on every oilrig and pumping station in Prudhoe Bay.

Once the National Guard troops were deployed, Sue-B and Fu Hao made their way back to the King Edward I to wait them out. It took six months for the troops to be withdrawn from Prudhoe Bay. Two weeks later six "thumper truck" crews were killed, and four hunters were found dead all with yellow flags around their necks and the proclamations on their persons.

Maddux Petroleum decided they had had enough; they hired a private German security outfit, Geist Söldner. They were made up of mercenaries, professional soldiers, and soldiers of fortune from all over the world. Conventional laws didn't bind them, they operated by the rules of war. Maddux was tired of playing nice, if these French thugs wanted to play dirty, then Maddux would play dirtier, it would be a no holds barred, winner take all. The other oil giants were in a wait and see mode, they would let Maddux Petroleum be the guinea pig and if successful then they would hire their own private army.

Hiring a private army wasn't cheap, each member of the elite Geist Söldner was signed to a guaranteed contract of a quarter of a million dollars per year, pay or play. Maddux signed eighteen mercenaries for a cool thirty million. Hell, they figured they could recoup that sum in four hours at the pumps.

Maddux Petroleum and Geist Söldner mercenaries hadn't figured on Hazael and his French Aerospatiale C.22 drone, with Aster missiles.

The average "thumper truck" is approximately ninety feet long, weighs over forty-one tons, and produces 90,000 lbf of force that makes a whole lot of shaking going on. In the front is the three-man cab, behind the cab is mounted the ground impact system and bringing up the rear is a flatbed that has room for a cargo cabinet and space for two armed mercenaries.

On the first day under the protection of Geist Söldner, Hazael observed the route of the seismic truck and maneuvered Sue-B and Fu Hao into position. By now there wasn't any snow on the ground, the terrain was covered mostly with low-shrub tundra mainly alder savannah with patches of Arctic roseroot, perfect for two snipers to blend into.

As the massive truck approached them, Fu Hao and Sue-B were positioned on either side of the vehicle. The monster truck passed right between them, and as the truck was traveling away from them, they both took aim at the two armed mercenaries standing on the back of the truck's platform and fired. The two soldiers of fortune fell off the back of the truck and not falling off to the sides. Apparently, the occupants inside the truck's cab were focused solely on what was in front of them and weren't paying much attention to anything else.

The shooters laid there motionless until they heard a large explosion caused when Hazael fired an Aster missile reducing the 41-ton truck into 41-tons of scrape metal. Shortly after the air strike Hazael radioed them the all clear, letting them know that the truck had been destroyed, they then proceeded over to the two dead mercenaries and gave them the holy sacrament of Le Gang de la Clé de Singe, yellow flags and all. After they had finished with the formalities, they continued on to the coast and found Weezer waiting for them in the Zodiac to take them back to the King Edward I.

Back on board, once Sue-B and Fu Hao enjoyed a nice warm meal and hot shower Snowy came to their cabin.

"How are you both doing?" Captain Snowy asked.

"We're good. Nothing a good night's sleep in a soft bed won't cure." Sue-B replied.

"Well, it looks like we're in for stormy weather, so you'll be on board for the next couple days. I think we'll be okay sitting in this harbor, it shouldn't be too bad. You two take it easy and rest up."

"Thanks, Snowy."

They climbed into bed, Fu Hao went first since she was the shorter of the two and best fit the contour of the bed being next to the curving bulkhead. Sue-B turned off the light, then removed her nightgown and lay next to her lover. She unbuttoned Fu Hao's pajama bottoms then slowly slipped her hand down past her stomach, Fu Hao turned on her side and kissed Sue passionately whispering, "I love you more than anything in this world."

"Oh, I love you more than life itself."

They held onto each other clinging in a tight embrace, knowing that the life they've chosen could mean losing each other at any time. They made passionate love in the knowledge that each time might be their last, exhausted, hearts pounding, and breathless they collapsed into a deep sleep, their naked bodies intertwined as one.

Rodin and Isala were driving east on Highway 284 having just left Helena Regional Airport, heading towards Cavetown, Montana an exclusive community that sits on the shores of Canyon Ferry Lake. As they crossed Valley Boulevard Rodin pulled into the parking lot for the Ace Hunting Supplies store.

"Hi, how may I help you?" The salesmen asked.

"I'm interested in purchasing a crossbow for hunting." Rodin said.

"Well sir, for hunting I would recommend the Barnett Game Crusher Crossbow Package with Multi-Reticle Scope."

"Is it the kind the pros use?"

"Oh yes, it's made for hunting big game."

"Perfect, because that's what I'm after. Does it come with arrows, or is that extra?"

"No sir the arrows are extra. Here's a pack of Barnett Headhunter Arrows, made for this particular crossbow for only $39.99."

"I'll take the bow and three boxes of the arrows."

"Yes sir, and I must say that this was probably the easiest sale I've ever made, thank you."

"No, thank you."

"Let's see, with tax that will be $684. Will that be cash or charge?"

"Cash."

Isala was waiting in the car, listening to the news on KUHM, the local PBS station. Rodin put the crossbow and arrows in the trunk of the VW Jetta rental car. As he got into the car Rodin asked, "What's the buzz in the world?"

"Oh the usual, murder, rape, war, natural disasters, crooked politicians, and a couple of school shootings, you know the usual."

"Sorry I asked."

"That'll teach you."

They continued on past the town of Cayon Ferry and around the tip of Canyon Ferry Lake to Cavetown. They turned off 284 on to Chinaman Gulch Road and drove down the hill towards the lake past Kim's Marina & Resort on the right to the water's edge where three magnificent log cabin style homes sat nestled in among dozens of tall pine trees.

Rodin and Isala got out of the Jetta, Rodin retrieved the carrying case containing the crossbow from the trunk of the car, Isala kissed Rodin goodbye and jumped into the driver's seat then drove up hill back towards Cavetown.

Rodin made his way past the first two cabins, thru the woods to the third cabin. The cabin belonged to Montana's Wildlife & Parks Director Colin Smith, who has recently come under fire when he posted photos on social media of him while on safari in Africa of a family of chimpanzees that he killed with a crossbow. The photo shows Smith smiling while posing with four dead chimpanzees, two adults and two babies.

Smith came under a lot of calls for his resignation, saying what he did was revolting, outrageous, and immoral, but like the true hunter that he is, he just scoffed at them and refused to apologize, calling his accusers liberal wimps and crybabies. The governor suggested that Smith take a couple of days off, spend some time at his lakeside cabin until this whole megillah blows over.

Smith knows how passionate and radical the people of Montana can be, so he wasn't taking any chances, when he answered the doorbell holding a Ruger EC9 pistol behind his back, locked and loaded. When he opened the door there stood a tall clean-shaven man wearing khakis, powder blue shirt, and a blue blazer holding an oversized carrying case, smiling.

"Yes?"

"Mr. Smith?"

"Yes, I'm Colin Smith."

"My name is Roger Greene; I am the Assistant Wildlife & Parks Director for the state of Maine, and I was wondering if you might have a few moments. I just talked to the governor who told me that I might find you here, I hope I'm not disturbing you or your family."

"No, my wife and children are with my wife's mothers, we thought it best until this whole chimpanzee thing blows over that they stay somewhere else. Come on in, Mr. Greene." Smith revealed the pistol, engaged the safety and said, "Can't be too careful, lots of crazies out there. Can I get you something to drink Mr. Greene, beer, soda, water?"

"Roger, please. Beer would be great, thank you."

"Beer it is, please have a seat."

When Colin Smith entered the room carrying two beers, Rodin raised the crossbow and fired one arrow.

ZING

Hitting Smith in the lower abdomen, forcing him to drop the two bottles of beer, sending him backwards up against a wood paneled wall, where there were several mounted trophy heads. Rodin fired a second arrow that landed just inches from the first and pinned him to the wall.

ZING

"Mr. Smith, I am with Le Gang de la Clé de Singe, I'm sure you've heard of us. Colin I can see you've been quite the busy little hunter, haven't you? On just your last hunting spree you killed a giraffe, a leopard, impala, sable antelope, lion, kudu, warthog, and a hippopotamus, not to mention the chimpanzee family, which I believe you killed with a crossbow. I must say that killing that family of chimpanzees was very cruel Mr. Smith, especially the baby chimpanzees.

You know who else can be very cruel, Mr. Smith? Me, as you can see. I can be very, very cruel. My partner is at your mother-in-law's house right now, where you wife and children are. What do you say that we even up the score, Mr. Smith. A family for a family."

"Oh, God please don't do anything to my wife and children. They didn't do anything, please."

"Yeah, kinda like the chimpanzee family or the lion, the leopard, the impala, or any of the other trophy's you've killed."

Rodin took out his cellphone, dialed it and spoke, "Ready? Do it." He held up the cell phone so Smith could hear the panic on the other end, women and little girls crying and screaming and seven loud gunshots, then silence.

Smith now filled with angry and rage tried to lunge toward the man responsible for killing his family, arms outstretched, face contorted and filled with hate, grunting he said, "You fucking bastard!"

Rodin stood inches from his reach, he raised the crossbow and fired the final blow.

ZING

The arrow pierced Smith's heart, killing him instantly. Rodin placed the yellow flag around his neck and the manifesto in his shirt pocket leaving him impaled to the wall. He placed the crossbow at the feet of Montana's now ex-Wildlife & Parks Director.

He walked back to where Isala had dropped him off, she was there waiting for him. He removed his cell phone as he got into the car and called 911 to alert the police that there had been a murder down in Chinaman Gulch. He looked at Isala as she drove back to Helena, smiled and said, "Well I didn't want his wife or children to come home and find him, now did I. That would be cruel."

"So, he really thought that we had killed his family?"

"I told him I could be cruel."

Weezer was standing watch on the bridge of the King Edward I when he spotted a U.S. Coast Guard Coastal Patrol Boat approaching. He hollered out for Snowy, "Captain, patrol boat approaching off starboard bow."

Snowy wasn't worried, since they had stowed all the weapons and gear, along with the drone and all its paraphernalia below under the false deck shortly after Sue-B and Fu Hao had returned to the ship three days ago.

As the 87-foot Marine Protector class ship pulled alongside the King Edward I, an officer using a bullhorn called out, "Ahoy there, captain of the King Edward I, request permission to board."

Snowy stood on deck, cupped his hands and shouted, "Permission granted."

A lieutenant and two petty officers came aboard, as the lieutenant stepped onto the King Edward, he did not salute the Canadian flag that the King Edward was flying but he did salute Captain White, Snowy returned the salute.

"Welcome aboard the King Edward I lieutenant, I'm Captain White."

"Captain White, a pleasure. I'm Lieutenant Crenshaw of the USS Thunderbolt."

"What can I do for you lieutenant?"

"Would you be so kind as to tell me the purpose of your being in these waters?"

"Not at all lieutenant, we are with the Institut des sciences de la mer a division of Fisheries and Oceans Canada, we are conducting studies for alternative control methods for managing sea lice."

"Sounds Interesting. Who besides yourself is on board, sir."

"Mr. Weezer, would you be so kind as to invite the crew topside?"

"Aye, aye Captain." Weezer stepped inside the bridge and announced on the intercom, "Would all hands please come topside, would all hands please come topside."

Within minutes Sue-B, Fu Hao and Hazael were all standing next to Snowy.

"Is this everyone, Captain?"

"This all of us lieutenant."

"May I have your names please?"

"Julie Dockery." Replied Sue-B

"Betty Haun." Said Fu Hao

"I'm Muhammad Antar." Answered Hazael

"Lieutenant, here are our passports." Snowy said as he handed the lieutenant the documents."

The lieutenant looked at each one comparing them with the people in front of him.

"Might I ask what's going on lieutenant?"

"What makes you think there's something going on, Captain."

"Well, we've been in these water for weeks and haven't been boarded, I'm just curious."

"No, nothing going on, just a routine check."

"Well, if you'd like, you're free to inspect our vessel, lieutenant."

"No, that won't be necessary. Thank you. Captain." He said as he gave Snowy a quick salute. "I'll let you all get back to studying your sea lice."

"Good evening I'm Nigel Williams and this is the BBC World Headline News. Our top story this hour comes from America where there were two incidences involving Le Gang de la Clé de Singe. The first is that of a gruesome murder of a Montana State official who was killed with a crossbow. Colin Smith was found in his home pinned against a wall with multiple arrows fired into his body.

Le Gang de la Clé de Singe claims that they took revenge of Colin Smith for his killing of, not only several big game animals such as a lion, a giraffe and leopard while on safari in Africa, but it was the posting on social media the killing of an entire chimpanzee family, two adults as well as two baby chimpanzees that brought the ire of Le Gang de la Clé de Singe. Mr. Smith leaves behind a wife and two young children.

The other story involves the attack of oilfield workers in Alaska's Prudhoe Bay, the eco-terrorist group has declared that they are in a campaign to stop further oil exploration by the use of seismic trucks that, according to the organization harms hibernating animals including polar bears and their cubs. The group has also killed several hunters who were licsenced to hunt hibernating polar bears and their cubs sleeping in their dens. The main object of the attacks by Le Gang de la Clé de Singe has been the Maddux Petroleum Company.

A spokesperson for Maddux Petroleum has announced that they are going to temporally stop seismic exploration until further notice. However, Maddux Petroleum states that the terrorist attacks had no impact on their decision to stop exploration.

In other news, the President of the United States had world leaders laughing at him once again when he said…."

Snowy White called everyone together and revealed that Le Gang de la Clé de Singe had declared the mission a success, Maddux Petroleum announced that they were going to stop all seismic exploration, as well as the hunting of polar bears. So, congratulations to everyone for a job well done.

"Now what, Captain?" Weezer asked

"We head back to Greenland for a little well deserved rest & relaxation, and then in a couple weeks after we've decompressed, we'll be ready for our next assignment."

"China."

"China?"

"China."

"Our next assignment is in China?" Odin asked.

The Iceman just nodded.

"What the Hell's in China?"

"Farms."

"Farms. We're going after farmers?"

"These farmers."

"What the Hell are they growing on these farms?"

"Bears, tigers, and rhinos among other things."

"They're raising tigers, bears, and rhinos so people can shoot them?"

"Oh no, today's tiger farms are basically feedlots where tigers are bred like cattle to make luxury items, like tiger bone wine, tiger skin rugs, tiger teeth jewelry and shit like that. They cloak these farms as tiger parks for tourists attractions, they keep a couple well fed animals for the public to see, but behind the scenes they stuff dozens of big cats into small feeding pens, fatten them up and then slaughter them for parts.

"And, they have bear farms, where bears have catheters inserted in their stomachs so they can be "milked" for their bile that is used in a lot of traditional Chinese medicines. The Chinese Government says they're planning on farming these endangered species just like cows and pigs.

"Of course the officials from China's State Forestry Administration claims that farming will save species from extinction and reduce poaching, which of course in total bullshit."

The Red Team had just days before being air evacuated out of Zambia in the dead of night to the islands of Comoros just off the coast of Mozambique. They landed on the outskirts of the coastal town Moroni, on the western side of the island.

The Comoros Islands were once a part of the French colonial empire, but since 1975 they are an independent island nation. They were sent there for a bit of R&R.

The team was booked into the Retaj Moroni Hotel for six nights, five days of relaxation, then it's off to

Dodoma, Tanzania where they will train, develop a plan, and prep for the upcoming campaign.

Rodin's real name was Todd Styles, your typical surfer boy from Southern California. He was just over six feet tall, had long blond, sun-bleached hair, an athletic body, and was who many thought could have been a true surfing champion if it wasn't for the Viet Nam War.

In 1969, while attending classes at US Berkley, Todd attended an anti-war protest that turned violent, and he was arrested for the first time. After that, he started breaking into government buildings, setting files on fire, regularly scrapping with police, burning draft cards, and, in general, being a real pain in the government's ass. Finally, he made the FBI's hit list, and they issued arrest warrants, so Todd did what any patriotic antiwar protester would do: he ran away to Canada. He was lucky he had a distant uncle living in Montreal who agreed to take him in.

He lived in Montreal with his uncle for almost seven years, doing odd jobs on ships traveling up and down the Saint Lawrence Seaway, while still working with anti-war groups protesting the Viet Nam War. Then in 1974, Todd was almost arrested; he managed to elude the police by just a couple of hours. Having learned to speak French fluently while living in Montreal, he decided to go to France and try to go underground. He made his way over to France by working on a supertanker as a merchant seaman. He worked in France for several years, doing mostly menial labor jobs; he worked as a waiter in Nice, a bouncer at a nightclub in Paris, worked on a fishing vessel out of Brest and a librarian at the Université Jean Moulin 3 in Lyon, always-just one-step ahead of Interpol.

He had thoughts of turning himself into the police; he was tired of being on the run and always looking over his shoulder. One night, while having coffee at a cafe with a friend in Lyon, his friend jokingly said, 'Dude, why don't you just join the French Foreign Legion. Hell, they don't care what you've done."

Out of desperation, he decided to go and see if, in fact, they would accept a fugitive of the law. So, in 1978 he walked up to the recruiting center, knocked on the door, and was immediately invited to see if he could pass a battery of exams to see if he could qualify. The first three days were devoted to the teaching the new recruits just what they are getting themselves into and the terms of their five-year contracts that they are required to sign. Then, for the next two weeks, they undergo psychological and personality tests, logic tests, medical exam, physical condition tests, motivation and security interviews. Then, if they pass, they sign the contract. The same week, he passed all his tests and was accepted into the Legion. No questions about his past were asked, so he took the oath and became a French citizen.

For someone who was so antiwar, he found that the difference between the US Army fighting in the Viet Nam War and what he was doing in the French Foreign Legion was somehow more just in that he played more of a peacekeeper role rather than the aggressor.

In 1982, he was part of a peacekeeping operation of a Multinational Force in Lebanon during the Lebanese Civil War along with the 31st Brigade. He spent two years there and was lucky to not have fired a shot. He did see combat in the Gulf War, as his Legion force, comprising of 27 different nationalities, was attached to the French 6th Light Armored Division, whose mission was to protect the Coalition's left flank. During the Gulf War, they operated in support of the U.S. Army's 82nd Airborne Division and provided support for the unit's bomb squad. After the cease-fire, he helped clear mines alongside a Royal Australian Navy Clearance Diver Team Unit. His war ended after a hundred hours of fighting on the ground.

After several more peacekeeping deployments to Sarajevo, Bosnia, and Herzegovina in 1993, Rwanda, Central African Republic and Congo-Brazzaville in 1997, Todd had seen enough. It just so happened that when his latest contract was coming to an end, he read an article about a French group of eco-terrorists called Le Gang de la Clé de Singe, or 'The Monkey Wrench Gang.'

The article told how an international organization had decided they had had enough with playing by the rules; many countries considered them as pirates, thugs, and gangsters. They sank whaling ships, blew up oil rigs, attacked deforestation logging camps, assaulted company headquarters, and, on occasion, kidnapped their leaders. Unlike Greenpeace and Sea Shepherd's, these guys didn't hesitate to take lives when they felt it was just. Their belief was that corporations have been destroying and killing nature for profit for generations, so now Mother Nature's declaring WAR. It's payback time!

Todd had seen the massive destruction that man is capable of doing for pure greed, and how unable or, more likely, unwilling governments have been to curtail the corporation's gluttony and selfishness. After reading more articles and doing a lot of research on the group, he started writing letters to the editors of newspapers and international magazines, all in favor of the group.

At the end of his latest contract, he walked off the base he was stationed in at Brazzaville, the Capital of the Republic of the Congo. The Legion offered him transport back to France, which he declined; after saying goodbye to his comrades, he just walked out of the base gates, carrying all his worldly possessions in the duffel bag hoisted on his shoulder. He was a quarter mile from the base, when a woman, who strongly resembled a young Meryl Streep while wearing a black beret and a camo shirt, blue jeans, and black Converse high-tops, approached him. As they met, she smiled and asked in a French accent, "Todd?"

"Oui. Et vous êtes?"

"Je suis Venus. Parles-tu Anglais?"

"Yes. Can I help you?"

"I hope so," she said, as she unbuttoned her shirt and revealed a yellow tee shirt with a black skull and crossed monkey wrench logo on it. "Where are you off to?"

"Nowhere in particular to be honest. I really haven't given it much thought. I was going to see where this road would take me. By the way, nice t-shirt. I like it."

"I thought you might. We were really impressed with your writings and articles, and we're hoping that you would be interested in joining our little group."

"As a writer?"

"Well, if that's how you feel you best can contribute to the cause, we always need good writers to help tell the outside of the story, but we thought you might want to take, let's say, a more active role."

"That sounds more my speed."

"Great. There are some folks I'd like you to meet, if you're interested."

"Lead on."

She waved her arm and gave a whistle that would make anyone hailing a cab in New York City jealous. An old beat-up red Toyota 4 Runner pulled up, with two guys sitting in the front and one guy in the back. She opened the rear driver side door and indicated for him to get in first. He walked to the back of the vehicle, opened the back hatch, and threw his duffel bag in, slammed it shut, then slowly walked back to her. She watched him and was impressed at his deliberate movements and nonchalant attitude. As he passed her and climbed in, she joined him and shut the door. She half turned to him and said, "Todd, I'd like you to meet Connie, B-Reel, and Sassoon."

The driver looked to be in his late fifties, long gray hair pulled back into a ponytail, wearing tattered blue jeans and a black Converse t-shirt. He glanced in the rearview, smiled, and said, "Hey man, I'm Connie."

The man sitting in the front passenger seat was a twenty-something black man with dreadlocks, wearing sunglasses and JVC headphones that were hooked up to his Sony Walkman. He had on a Hawaiian shirt with khakis and was sitting half turned in his seat. He held up two fingers, showing a peace sign, "Yo, welcome to the dance."

Sitting next to Rodin in the back seat was a small fat man wearing a French beret, black, plastic, round-rim glasses, and sporting a rather large mustache. He was wearing an off-white linen suit that was extremely wrinkled and looked like it hadn't been cleaned in several weeks. He smiled and nodded, "Bonjour, mon ami. Je suis Sassoon."

The SUV pulled away and headed west towards the port of Pointe-Noire, the second largest city following the capital, Brazzaville. It was a seven-hour drive over dirt roads and through mostly plantation fields of cassava, a starchy tuberous root that was a major source of carbohydrates in the Republic of the Congo.

Over the next seven hours, they got to know each other, and they discussed many things, but mostly they were vetting each other to see if they were a right fit together. Todd liked the fact that four totally different individuals were united by different reasons but for the same cause. He was curious about their reasons for joining such a militant group.

"So, guys, why did you decide to join, Connie, where you from?"

Connie never looked into the rearview; he just kept his eyes on the road as he spoke, "Bozeman, Montana. I worked as a ranch hand for several cattle ranches in and around Bozeman pretty much my whole life. Well, for me, it was when I was working on the Flying B Bison Ranch that the government had approved the construction of an oil pipeline to transverse the whole ranch. The building of the damn thing was bad enough, but then, because of shoddy workmanship, of course, there was a massive oil spill, which killed several dozen bison and a large portion of the ranch was rendered useless. The oil company received a slap on the wrist, and, when a bunch of us protested, we all got thrown into the hoosegow."

"You got arrested just for protesting?"

"Well, that and maybe all the damage we'd done to their pipeline and equipment might have something to do with it too," he said, laughing. "So, after I made bail, I hightailed it out of there, headed up to Saskatoon, and joined up with some like-minded fellas who don't like big oil as much as me. Hey, I've been over whole the world fucking with these bastards and enjoying every minute of it. I met up with my main man B-Reel about two years ago when we were messing with Exxon on one of their offshore drill rigs in the Gulf of Mexico. Right, man?"

"Right on, right on, my brother." B-Reel patted the gray-haired hippie on the shoulder; he turned down his Walkman slightly and picked up the story. "Ya see, me and my man, Connie, and four other brothers were paddling out in the dead of night to do a little sumpin' sumpin' to try and slow down production, ya know, a little sabotage. Right after we planted some C-4 plastic on two of the rig's legs, all of a sudden, out of nowhere, came six Zodiacs filled with oil company goons; they came guns-a-blazing. A bunch of our brothers were shot, and panic ensued. As we were making our get-away, we capsized; two of our mates didn't make it, and I would have been a goner if it hadn't been for my main man, Connie. He kept his cool and helped me and two other brothers back to the mother ship."

Connie kept looking straight ahead and said sheepishly, "It wasn't no big deal, man. We all helped each other."

"Sheet man, you the man! And just as we was bushwhacked, Connie even had the moxie to set the timers. As we made it to safety, *Ka-Boom*" B-Reel threw his arms out in an exaggerated gesture. "And that mother came a-tumbling down. It was a thing of beauty."

Todd looked at the two men sitting up front, shook his head, and said, "Wow, that's the kind of commitment and dedication I'm used to from my time in the Legion, very impressive."

Venus sat forward, leaned toward Sassoon, and touched his leg, "Tell Todd about the Parc Forestier et Zoologique de Hann affair."

The diminutive man blushed and smiled as if he was asked to reveal an embarrassing secret. He fidgeted in his seat and looked out the window.

She tapped his leg again, prodding him, saying, "Go on, and don't be shy."

He turned his head to her and nodded okay. He looked at Todd and spoke softly, "Well, Monsieur, I was working at a private Clinique Vétérinaire in Dakar as one of three veterinarians. We handled everything from domestic animals, to farm, and the occasional wild animals. You see, the Senegal zoo was too poor to have a veterinarian on staff, so, on occasion; we would be called upon to attend to the animals. I was the newest member of the staff, as I had just graduated from veterinary school in Paris and wanted to start my career with some adventure and not just attend to cats and dogs. So, when I heard about a position in Dakar, Senegal, I took it. Then, one day, I was called upon with great urgency to come to the Parc Forestier et Zoologique de Hann, as one of the male lions had been injured. This was to be my first experience working at the Zoo, but, when I got there, I could see that the cat had been badly beaten. His attendant claimed that the lion had attacked him while he was feeding him, and that he feared for his life. I talked to several witnesses, who said that he was teasing the lion and that the man was the aggressor.

After attending to the lion, I went around and noticed that many of the animals had been abused. I went to the proper authorities and lodged a formal complaint. All I received was, as you say, the runaround.

It turned out that we at the clinique would get calls to come out to the Zoo once or twice a month for an injured animal. My fellow doctors and I continued to complain to the officials as well writing letters to the newspaper, but to no avail. It wasn't until one day I was visited by a man from Le Gang de la Clé de Singe, who said that he had read some of my letters and articles and said that he could help. I had, of course, heard about the organization and was weary because of all the wild stories that I had read about them. I told him that I didn't think I wanted or needed their help. He said for me to think it over, and he would, on occasion, stop by to see if I had changed my mind.

Several weeks passed, when I received a call from the Zoo saying that one of the chimpanzees had died. I was prepping for surgery on a farmer's ox, so one of my colleagues went there and brought back the body to do an autopsy on the poor thing. We found that the young chimp had been beaten and strangled to death. Two days later, the man from the Gang came by again, and I finally decided to ask for their help.

One week passed with no calls from the Zoo, then two weeks, a month, and six months—nothing. I had heard from people at the Zoo that several of the attendants had quit suddenly, and they were replaced with more caring and responsible people. It seems that the people who left had been relatives and friends of the Zoo's officials and that was the reason that they were protected. But it was months later that the story of what persuaded them to leave was revealed.

It seems that, late one night, the three men who were responsible for the mistreatment of the animals were abducted at gunpoint and taken to one of the lion enclosures at the Zoo. One of the men who were responsible for the teasing and torturing of the lions was stripped naked, bound and gagged, restrained to a chair with his legs spread open and had honey poured on his genitals. A female lion was released into the cage. The lioness, I'm told, went directly to the man and proceeded to maul and nearly castrate him, before she retreated back into her enclosure. The other two men observed this and were told that if there were any more abuse of any kind to any of the animals, they too would face a similar punishment. The next day, all three men resigned, and the man who was mauled was taken to the hospital and soon died of an infection. The case is still unsolved.

I was later contacted by the man from Le Gang de la Clé de Singe, asking me if I would be interested in joining the group, as they are always wanting to have people from the medical field, both doctors and veterinarians. I was, at first, uncertain, but the more I thought about how best that I could serve abused, injured and even endangered animals, I decided to join the noble cause. So here I sit, mon ami."

"Wow, that's quite a story, my friend, I can honestly say that I'll never eat honey again without thinking of you."

Todd sat quietly, just absorbing his fellow passenger's stories while staring out the front window. For the next two hours, with the combination of the monotonous scenery of vast fields of farmland, meager roadside villages and small patches of undeveloped forests, and the warm air of the open windows had him nodding off into a sound sleep. When he woke up, still in the fog of dreams and reality, he was discovering that he had, at some point, rested his head on Venus' shoulder. Once he emerged into total conscious, he bolted upright. He apologized, "I'm sorry. I hope I didn't discommode you."

Venus smiled. "Not at all. Sleep well?"

"I did, I guess I really needed it." He leaned forward and said to Connie, "I don't know about anybody else, but I sure could use a pit stop."

Connie peered in the rearview mirror. "There is a petrol station about ten minutes ahead, can you wait?"

"No worries, I appreciate it."

Cruising on the N1 heading west, they were skirting the suburbs of Loubomo, the third largest city in the Republic of the Congo. As they approached the intersection of the N1 and N3, there was a Total petrol station. As they pulled up to the pump, Todd noticed a café.

"Hey guys, let's get something to eat; I'm buying.

Connie said, as he got out of the vehicle, "You guys head on in. I'm meet you all inside."

Everyone piled out and headed over to the La Croissanterie Café, stretching and shaking out the road trip aches and stiffness. The place smelled of greasy hamburgers and fries, and they grabbed a booth by the front window. The waitress sauntered over, handed them menus, and asked for their drink orders. When she left, Connie came in and decided that squeezing six people into a four-person booth was a little too cozy, so he decided to drag a chair over. Todd noticed that in the corner sat an old-time jukebox, so he reached into his jacket, plopped down a hand full of change, and asked Connie to go and surprise everyone with his choices. As Connie stood up, he said, "I'll have a cheeseburger, fries, and a Coke. Be back."

The waitress brought the drinks and took everyone's order, as Connie was dropping what seemed to be a ton of coinage into the juke. As he walked his way back to the booth, Steppenwolf's 'Born to be wild' filled the room. They spent the next hour listening to classic rock from the sixties and seventies—Hendrix, Janis, the Doors, and Jefferson Airplane. At one point, Todd said, "Far out man, I'm like tripping on an old LSD flashback. I got a buddy in Jamaica, Buzz, who is still stuck in the '60's, living the hippie life."

Once they were back on the road, all were feeling content, and they sat in silence until Todd turned to Venus and asked, "So, what brought you here?"

She smiled and looked out the window for several minutes, and then she started to speak softly. "I come from a small town just outside of Odessa, Ukraine called Yuzhne; it's a port city on the Black Sea. My grandfather owned a small fleet of fishing boats; my grandfather's grandfather had handed it down to him. About eight years ago, the government declared private fishing fleets would become part of a state-owned commercial venture. You had no choice, those that refused were harassed, damage to equipment would occur, so called 'accidents' happened to crewmembers, and a few even were killed—my grandfather was one.

"To fight back, a small group of resisters started to publicly protest by marching in the streets, clashing with the police. We tried to bring world attention to our cause, but there was very little outcry worldwide. It seemed our cause was so small, compared with all the other injustices in the world, that ours was a lost cause. Until some of us started to fight back using tactics that the State had used against us: we sabotaged their equipment, harassed their crewmembers. We were called thugs and terrorists, and we had to go deep underground. Then, one day, a man simply called Mars, you know, like the Roman God of War, came to us and offered us assistance in our struggle against the State.

"For several months, we wreaked havoc against the state-run fleet, but soon the Ukrainian government sought help from the Russians. We had to disband, so me and several others from Yuzhne left and joined the Gang, and here I am."

By the time they reached the port, Todd was convinced he found a cause he could believe in and one where he could use the skills he had learned in the Legion. One thing that was required was that he had to change his name, so as to keep their real identity a secret. The main reason was to protect their family members from being harassed and hassled by law enforcement.

Venus said, "Have you given any thought to your new identity?"

Todd thought for a few minutes. "Rodin."

Connie looked in the rearview mirror. "The sculptor?"

"Yeah."

Venus held out her hand and said, "Welcome to the cause, Auguste Rodin."

He took her hand. "Just Rodin, you know, like Cher or Madonna."

She smiled and said, "Gentlemen, I'd like you all to meet Rodin."

"Hello, Ghost Hunter Ranch, my name is Roy, can I help you?" The man on the phone said.

"Yes, I hope so Roy. It's my wife's and my anniversary and we'd like to celebrate it by killing something exotic, can you help us?"

"As long as it's not each other." Roy chortled.

"Good one, Roy. I've been looking at your website and I must say I am quite impressed with your selection of big game."

"Well, we at Ghost Hunter Ranch take pride in being rated the number one world class native and exotic hunting ranch in the US of A by the Worldwide Affiliates of Safari Partners."

"That is high praise indeed."

"We're not one of those 'canned hunt' ranches were the animals are just standing around waiting to get shot, no siree bob. We have more than twenty-thousand acres of the best Texas hill country hunting you'll find anywhere."

"Especially in Texas, right Roy?"

"Right. I'm sorry, who am I speaking with?"

"Oh sorry, my name is Wilson, Pete Wilson."

"Well, it surely is a pleasure speaking with you Mr. Wilson, what sort of hunting package are you and your wife looking for?"

"I think I'd like to bag a zebra and my wife was hoping to bring down a giraffe."

"No problem with the zebra, we currently have a herd of over a dozen, however we don't have any giraffes at the moment. How soon were you thinking of coming to celebrate at the Ghost Hunter Ranch?"

"You tell me Roy, when do you think you could get one?"

"I'd say we could have one down here in four to six weeks."

"That sounds perfect Roy. Let's book it."

"Okay Mr. Wilson, I'll just need a deposit for the giraffe."

"No problem Roy. Do you accept American Express?"

"We do indeed, the deposit of three-thousand dollars will be charged to your American Express card. Whenever you're ready."

Rodin gave his Amex card info as a deposit for the giraffe and he booked one of the log cabins that are supposed to be isolated in a wooded area of the park that had been relocated all the way from Tennessee and rebuilt, log-by-log, plus the addition of all the modern amenities. Before he hung up Roy asked Rodin a question.

"Mr. Wilson, just between you and me, would you have any interest in hunting something more challenging?"

"Maybe, what did you have in mind?"

"How does the prospect of hunting an African lion, you know a big ole male lion?" Roy asked.

"Roy, I could be wrong, but isn't that against the law."

"Technically, yes."

"What does technically mean, Roy?"

"It's only illegal if you get caught." Roy said laughing.

"Have you done this sort of thing before, Roy?"

"Oh, all the time without any repercussions. You ain't from around these parts are you Mr. Wilson?"

"No Roy, I'm not."

"So, here in Texas we have a saying, "Don't Mess With Texas." And that basically means we don't stick our noses in where they don't belong, everybody just minds their own damn business."

"A lion, huh?"

"If you another type of big cat, leopard, jaguar, cheetah, whatever you want, we can make it happen."

"And you do this all the time?"

"All the time. Why we got a guy hunting a leopard right now."

"Where do you get these cats, Roy?"

"Sorry, that's privileged information."

"How much?"

"Lion?'

"Yeah, lion."

"Fifty."

"Grand?"

"Grand."

"Male, Black Mane."

"Yes sir, if that's what you want."

"This isn't some old senior citizen of a cat, discarded from one of those third world country zoo's is it?"

"No sir, Mr. Wilson, we get these baby's right off the Serengeti, money back guarantee. In fact, we will even show it to you prior to the hunt. Do we have a deal?"

"Deal." Rodin hung up, hit the stop record button on his cellphone, and thought to his self, "Deal, motherfucker."

The flight from the Comoros Islands to Dodoma, Tanzania was a fourteen-and-a-half-hour flight on Ethiopian Airlines that included a stop in Dar es Salaam, the largest city in Tanzania and a change onto Air Tanzania.

Needless to say, that when the Red Team arrived in Dodoma they were wasted. Once they passed thru customs, they were met by Ambokile Werema, a local gamekeeper at the Mkomazi National Park and long-standing member of Le Gang de la Clé de Singe. They all packed into his 1994 Toyota Hiace minivan, it was a tight squeeze, luckily, he had a roof rack so they could store all their backpacks up top.

Every one of them fell into a deep sleep from fatigue before Ambokile ever got the van out of the airport parking lot. Ambokile drove straight up on Highway A104 to the abandoned Bantu Tribal village of Meia Meia, 43 kilometers north of Dodoma. Ambokile had set up camp for the team the day before their arrival with tents, food, and water; the only thing he hadn't provided was weaponry because Iceman hadn't requested any.

Upon arriving at the camp Ambokile left the van's engine running with the air conditioning on so as not to disturb the team's sleeping. The Iceman was the first to emerge from the van two hours later and found Ambokile preparing the evening meal.

"What's for dinner?"

"Nyama Choma, Ndizi Nyama and Chapatti Bread."

"I don't know what that is, but it smells amazing."

"Nyama Choma is grilled goat, Ndizi Nyama is a stew with green bananas, carrots, sweet peppers and fish, and the Chapatti Bread is similar to Indian flatbread."

"Can't wait. I'm going to roust the team out of their beauty sleep, be right back."

Iceman got inside the van on the driver's side and turned on the radio, Ambokile had the radio set to FM104.3, an African Hip Hop and Rap station that was very effective in bringing the team out of their self-induced comas.

"Wakey. Wakey, kids, dinner is served and let's remember to be gracious, Ambokile has gone to a lot of effort in making us dinner."

Everyone complimented Ambokile for an amazing meal, and it was. Several of the team went back for seconds. After dinner the team sat around a large bonfire relaxing, Iceman emerged from his tent with seven thick envelopes and distributed one to each of the team.

"These are files of our next assignment and dossiers of our targets, study them, analysis them, get to know each of them inside and out. You have two days before we travel to China don't waste them. There isn't any room for error, so stay sharp at all times.

"Ambokile and I will be going to Dar es Salaam to get our new passports from our contact and then to the Chinese Embassy to get our visas. We will be traveling under educational and cultural credentials. The drive to Dar es Salaam is over eight hours, so Ambokile and I will be returning day after tomorrow, Odin will be in charge while I'm away.

"If I don't see you in the morning, I'll see you in two days. Usiku mwema."

"And a good night to you, too." Ambokile said.

M. Ward Leon

Two hours west of San Antonio in the beautiful Texas hill country, lies the small community of Rio Frio, which has the notoriety of having the third largest Live Oak in the state of Texas and that's pretty much it, except that two miles north of Rio Frio is the 20,000 acre Ghost Hunter Ranch.

The Ghost Hunter Ranch is world renowned for its native and exotic hunting. They provide over sixty species available to hunt and if they don't have it and you want it, they'll get it so you can kill it. Hunters will see thousands of a variety of wildlife roaming free over 20,000 acres. They'll will encounter herds of zebras, elk, red stag, wildebeest, gazelle, impala, ten different species of sheep, buffalos, kangaroos, and occasionally, upon requests giraffes, just to name a few.

GHR offers over forty live game hunting cameras that allowed the hunter the ability to locate and choose their fantasy-hunting trophy, it's just like picking your lobster at a fancy restaurant. And in some cases, if the hunter can't actually travel to the ranch, or doesn't want to get off his fat ass, all the camera binds are equipped with remote control rifles so you can, let's say kill a wildebeest from the comfort of your own couch. The camera blinds are located across from the feeding stations, so the hunter doesn't have to go looking for the prize if they don't want to; the prize will come right to him. It's the new convenient way of hunting.

The animals are penned into manageable spaces with fences that are hidden away from the hunters so they have the impression that all the animals are roaming free, but with twenty-thousand acres it could takes days to find a specific animal, and as the saying goes, time is money. The Ghost Hunter likes to greet 'em, meet 'em, shoot 'em, loot 'em, then boot 'em.

"Hello?"

"Hello, may I speak with Mr. Wilson?"

"Speaking."

"Hi Mr. Wilson, this is Roy from Ghost Hunter Ranch."

"Yes Roy, how are you?"

"Just fine sir, the reason I'm calling is we've just received the package that you ordered."

"That's great news, Roy."

"I thought you would be pleased."

"So, I'm going to send you my deposit via PayPal, if that works for you."

"That will be fine. Any thoughts on when you'd like to make arrangements to come and celebrate your anniversary?"

"Is one of the cabins available in two weeks, Roy?"

"Let's see. Two weeks would be perfect, I'll put you down for the 21st, if that's good?"

"The 21st it is. We'll see you then."

"Thank you, Mr. Wilson."

CLICK

Rutherford Remington Murdochski the third, a.k.a. Buzz Murdoch, was at one time the executive producer at one of the preeminent recording studios in the world of rock and roll, Bitchin Studios located in Montego Bay, Jamaica.

Buzz was born into a very well to do family. The Philadelphia Murdochskis were one of Philadelphia's nouveau riche, made scads of money in the post war-banking boom of the forties and fifties.

Buzz was born with a silver spoon in his mouth in 1945. Went to the finest prep schools and even was accepted to Harvard but decided to attend the University of California Berkeley. He was a major activist against the Viet Nam war, a member of the SDS and multiple other anti-establishment organizations; during that time, he met Todd Styles and became best friends. Buzz was arrested on numerous occasions, mostly for petty infractions like disturbing the peace, with the odd misdemeanors for the destruction of public property, unlawful gathers, disturbing the peace, and vandalizing public property, etc.

At one point Todd was being sought after by the police and the FBI, he had an Uncle in Canada but didn't have the funds to leave the country, Buzz gave him several thousand dollars, not as a loan, he just gave his friend the money to avoid arrest. They have occasionally kept in sporadic touch over the years; Buzz is the only person Todd has ever confided in as to his new identity, Rodin.

After the war was over and his activist days ancient history, he did a stint as a roadie for several big rock bands, The Rolling Stones, The Grateful Dead and even Jimi Hendrix when he appeared at Woodstock. Then in 1776 he took the advice of one Timothy Leary by tuning in, turning on and dropping out." he literally hitchhiked around the world. On his way back to the United States he stopped off in Montego Bay where he got a gig in a recording studio as a gofer. Over the years he worked his way up the food chain to become the executive producer.

Buzz bought and lives on a 43½-foot Spindrift Sunrise sailboat he named The Sweet Mary Jane. In his spare time he sails all around Jamaica, over time he got to know every inch of the coastline of Jamaica, from Montego Bay to Alligator Pond, from Port Royale to Salt Spring Junction and all points in-between. Not only had he become an accomplished sailor, but he was also an avid SCUBA diver.

Many years ago, while diving in Luminous Lagoon, a lagoon that stretches along the marshlands of Trelawney from the small community of Rock to the town of Falmouth, Buzz encountered Bumbley Bee, an *Epinephelus Lanceolatus*, also known as a Bumble Bee Grouper. The fish get its name from the Bumble Bee like markings they have as juveniles, but as they mature the yellow patches turn to more ornate patches and their body eventually becomes green and grey or grayish brown.

Buzz met the 1600-pound monster when it had gotten entangled by a large piece of fishing net and would have died had Buzz not come along and set the behemoth free.

The giant grouper and Buzz soon became fast friends; Buzz would bring it fish that he had speared and on occasion delicacies like pork roasts, baby back ribs, and a whole rack of lamb. He named his colossus friend Bumbley Bee, even though the bumblebee stripes were long gone.

Bumbley was the only one of his kind in the tropical Jamaican waters, his natural habitat would normally be anywhere in the Pacific Ocean from Japan to the Hawaiian Islands, but as luck would have it and through a series of mishaps, he was dumped off the coast of Jamaica and it made his way to Luminous Lagoon where he met Buzz.

At twenty years old, Bumbley was approximately 1600-pounds and over twelve feet long, he now looked more like a camo colored 1963 rusted out Volkswagen Beetle meandering along the ocean floor.

Bumbley spent most of his day cruising around the coral reefs of Luminous Lagoon looking for small sharks, skates, stingrays and pretty much anything that looks eatable. To look at him you wouldn't think that something that big could be very agile, but you'd be wrong. One minute there could be a four-foot Lemon Shark casually swimming nearby and, in less time, that it took for you to read this sentence, no shark.

There came a time when Bumbley was under threat of being caught and sold to a rich Arab sheik for his private aquarium, the agents of the sheik had captured gargantuan grouper and was preparing to set sail for other ports of call to gather other exotic marine life when Buzz contacted his old friend Rodin for help.

Rodin and Le Gang de la Clé de Singe sent several teams and a ship to retrieve not only Bumbley, but also all the illegally captured sea life so they could return to their natural habitat.

Bumbley was released off the small island of Hon Lon, less than a mile off the coast of South Vietnam in the Vinh Van Phong Sea, six months later a 43½-foot Spindrift Sunrise sailboat named The Sweet Mary Jane, captained by Buzz Murdoch sailed into the harbor and dropped anchor between the islands of Hon Lon and Hòn Sāng.

Harold Costello and the rest of the Worcester Polytechnic Institute's Educational and Cultural delegation arrived at 10:37 AM into the Beijing Capital International Airport sixteen and a half hours after taking off from Julius Nyerere International Airport, Dar es Salaam with a change of aircraft in Hamad International Airport in Qatar's capital, Doha.

Jianguo Zhi Ruo waited outside the airport's customs exit, holding a sign 'Worcester Polytechnic Institute', she had been there since 8:30 AM. The Iceman was the first to exit customs and he waved to Zhi Ruo as he approached her and asked, "Nǐ huì shuō yīngyǔ ma?"

She smiled and nodded, "Yes I do. I learned English at Tsinfhua University; I have a PhD in Opto-electronic Engineering. Welcome to China I am Jianguo Zhi Ruo."

"It is a pleasure to meet you, I am Harold Costello, and I am the head of the delegation as it were. The rest of the team should be straggling out any minute."

"I have obtained a Dongfeng twelve passenger van, I believe that it should be sufficient for your needs."

"I'm sure it will be. Ah, here comes the rest of the team, I suggest we save the introductions once we're on the road."

"I agree, Mr. Costello."

"Harold, please." The Iceman said.

"And I am Zhi Ruo. Please, everyone follow me."

Zhi Ruo led the Red Team thru the maze the Chinese call a parking lot to the passenger van, again thank goodness there was a roof rack on top or the ride would have been very unbearable.

"Everyone this is Zhi Ruo, she will be our main source for everything that we need to complete our assignment. She is familiar with all the locations and our primary and secondary targets."

Iceman then proceeded to introduce Zhi Ruo to the Red Team members by their current alias. Odin is Richard Walker, Vulcan is Noah Taylor, Sassoon is Mason Barnes, Jimmy the Chew is Jacob Ramirez, Tommy G is Colin Wong, Venus is Emma Mitchell, T-Bone is Leigh Clarke, and Gianfranco is now James Torres.

As Zhi Ruo was trying to navigate thru the jungle and congestion of the streets surrounding BCI Airport, Iceman was finding out what she knew of the mission and did she know she was being asked to do.

"It is my understanding that you and your team are going to pay retribution against the proprietors of the animal and to all those persons who do harm to the animals. My job is to assist you in providing and procuring whatever you might need, is this not correct?"

"Yes, you're are correct. However, I want to make sure you understand that this will be very dangerous and at any point that you feel that you would like to stop or that you feel in danger, you are free to leave and there will be no punishment or resentment towards you, do you understand?"

"I do, yes. I am committed to this mission. Now it's a long drive to Harbin and the Siberia Tiger Park. We will make our first stop in Chifeng for petrol and something to eat. I will try and make the drive more enjoyable by pointing out interesting notables as we travel. Our journey will take us by our Great Wall in the city of Jinshan; I recommend that we stop for rejuvenation, refreshments and so as you all may revel in the beauty and majesty of such a thing."

Iceman looked back to the team who were all nodding and said to Zhi Ruo, "We would be honored, thank you."

They arrived in Harbin just after midnight; Zhi Ruo had made reservations at the Shangri-La Hotel located on the banks of the Songhua River. Zhi Ruo had arranged so everyone should have river views. She secured five rooms and decided to let the them choose their own roommates, while she and Venus would share a room.

The next day, the president of Heilongjiang University greeted the delegation from Worcester Polytechnic Institute with open arms and proudly showed off his university and its faculty to these honored guests, after a tour of the campus they were invited to a lunch in their honor with the heads of the liberal arts, science, and language colleges. The Iceman had a spirited discussion with the dean of the college of environmental and animalia sciences, it was rather disheartening to hear how little he cared about the sanctity of animal life, unless it would somehow benefit the State.

Overall, the Iceman felt that they had successfully accomplished establishing their cover story and could proceed with their real mission, the Siberia Tiger Park.

The next day was a day of tourism, they would go on a sightseeing tour that had been arranged by the university, it would include Saint Sophia Cathedral, the Dragon Tower, Harbin Stalin Park, Unit 731 Museum, a germ warfare base where the Chinese people were tortured by the Japanese during World War Two, and if that wasn't depressing enough, they would end the tour by visiting the Siberia Tiger Park.

Zhi Ruo was able to pull some strings and grease some palms and got Iceman and Odin a behind the scenes tour, they were able to see what the public weren't allowed to see. Dozens of cages crammed with emaciated tigers waiting to be slaughtered for their skins, claws and teeth, their meat sold in the black market to wealthy oligarchs, and the bones to be used in tiger wine.

After the 'special' tour Iceman had Zhi Ruo ask Zhang Wei, the park manager, and a friend of the cause, what it would take to be invited to a "Tiger Feast". Zhang Wei was skeptical that he could arrange such a thing with the owners and a couple of foreigners, but after several minutes of discussion and a bribe of two thousand US Dollars they were on the guest list for that night's tiger feast.

Isala was weeping while watching a video on her iPad when Rodin came into the room.

"What's the matter, babe. Why are you crying?"

"I can't believe this, watch this video. It's a hunter and his guide hunting elephants in Namibia, just look how it all goes wrong and they laugh and joke while this poor beast suffers."

The guide apparently took the video; it shows a herd of elephants off in the distance crossing an open field. The herd is being led by a large bull followed by cows, calves and a couple of babies. There is another bull flanking the herd, as the lead bull moves ahead away from the herd the hunter takes aim and fires, hitting the bull in the front right shoulder knocking it down headfirst into the dirt, it struggles to get up and when it does the hunter fires again, this time hitting the giant in the rear quarter shattering its pelvis. The bull goes down and can't get up, it continues to struggle but to no avail, it is in agony. The second bull see's the hunter and guide and starts to charge them, as does the herd. The guide and hunter run back to their Jeep and as they drive off the guide can be heard to say, "We'll come back in an hour to finish it off."

The camera stops recording and restarts when they're standing next to the bull that's still writhing in pain, the guide films the hunter smiling at the camera and fires the deathblow to the elephant. The hunter then poses with his foot resting on the body. The video ends with the guide proudly posting it on Facebook with their names, Nils Gustafsson and Trevor Lubbe.

Rodin kissed Isala passionately, gets up from the sofa and says, "I'll be back."

Lufthansa flight 9558 landed in Windhoek, Namibia at 5:25am, Rodin glided thru customs and was met by Ajayi Kwedhi, a game ranger at the local wildlife sanctuary.

"I have everything you asked for in the Land Rover, it's parked in space 47 and the GPS is all set. When you're finished, please just return the vehicle to the same space, place the keys under the front seat and lock it."

"Thanks for all your help, I hope this wasn't too much trouble?"

"Not at all, Etosha National Park is about fours due north on the B1, once you're in the park the GPS should direct you right to them."

"Kalei po nawa, my friend." Rodin said shaking Ajayi's hand.

"Goodbye and good luck, to you too."

The four-hour drive was uneventful, and the arid landscape was a bit monotonous. When he reached Etosha National Park the park was pure desert with very little vegetation or trees, the elephants are referred to as Desert-dwelling elephants, they tend to migrate from one waterhole to another.

Once inside the park Rodin stopped the Land Rover and changed into a park ranger uniform, attached his false moustache, dark sunglasses and wore a floppy ripstop boonie hat, he turned on the GPS and the GoPro camera mounted on the front window facing outward, then he started to follow the GPS reading. When the guidance system indicated that he was within visual distance he got out of the vehicle and scanned the horizon with his binoculars. That's when he spotted a medium sized herd of elephants heading towards him; he looked to his left and spotted the Jeep with two men preparing to take down another bull.

Rodin jumped into his Rover and hauled ass towards Nils Gustafsson and his guide, Trevor Lubbe. He was traveling at over 80 miles an hour honking his horn and kicking up quite the dust storm as he zigzagged his way in route to intercept them, all the while scaring off the elephant herd.

Rodin brought the Rover to a screeching halt just feet away from Gustafsson and Lubbe who were livid, "Are you crazy, what the fuck are you doing? You fucked my shot, asshole." Gustafsson screamed.

Lubbe approached Rodin and noticed the park ranger uniform asked, "What's the problem ranger, we have the proper licenses and permits."

Rodin got out of the car and pulled his Glock 19, pointed it at Lubbe, "The problem Mr. Lubbe is you. You allowed this dipshit, who is totally unqualified to handle a rifle much less use it to hunt. I saw that video that you posted of you and him killing that elephant, what a major cluster fuck, it was nothing less than a criminal act and you're responsible for that atrocity."

Rodin aimed and fired one shot that hit Lubbe squarely between the eyes.

KA-POW

He turned to Gustafsson, who dropped his rifle and was standing there with his hands in the air, looking as white as the desert sand he was standing on.

"Pick up your rifle and start running, asshole."

"What?"

"I said to pick up your rifle and start running, I have to take care of your friend here, so get your ass in gear. Oh, before you go, would you mind tying this yellow flag around your neck and stick this note in your pocket? It will save me the effort later on."

Gustafsson looked at the yellow flag and knew instantly what he was up against, he didn't want anything to do with that flag so he grabbed his rifle and bolted, he started running as fast as he could.

Rodin watched him sprint away for a moment then walked over to Lubbe, pick him up, dragged him over to the Jeep and placed his body in the driver's seat. Once he was seated in the vehicle Rodin placed the Yellow flag around his neck and note in his pocket. As he was walking back to the Rover, he noticed Lubbe's iPhone on the ground and saw that he had been filming Rodin driving towards them; he turned off the phone and placed it back into Lubbe's pants pocket.

He walked back to the Land Rover and positioned the GoPro to film Gustafsson running away. He reached in the back seat and pulled out a soft leather rifle case and unsheathed his Mk13 Mod 7 Sniper Rifle, as he was adjusting the scope, he noticed that Nils Gustafsson had stopped and was preparing to take a shot at him. Rodin took two steps two the right of the Rover to give Gustafsson a clear target and waited.

POP

Gustafsson fired, missing Rodin and his Land Rover, but he did hit and shattered the Jeep's windshield.

Seeing that he missed he dropped the rifle and started running again, as Rodin was preparing his shot, he noticed that Gustafsson was running in a zigzag pattern, unfortunately he wasn't mixing it up, he would run a juke twice to the left, then once to the right, twice to the left, then once to the right.

Rodin followed his target, twice to the left, then once to the right, so as he juked left Rodin fired.

BLAM

Hitting Nils Gustafsson in the left shoulder knocking him down face first into the dust, he struggled to get up, as he stumbled and struggled to run again, he made his move to the right. That's when Rodin fired his second shot.

BLAM

Blasting Gustafsson in the right hip, shattering his pelvis. This time Gustafsson didn't get up, he just lay there in the dirt writhing in pain.

Rodin picked up after himself, making sure that he left no physical evidence behind, he got into the Rover and slowly drove to where Gustafsson was lying.

Rodin walked up to Gustafsson, who was staring up at the sky whimpering and said, "Look familiar? Getting a little déjà vu?"

"Please help me, I swear I'll never hunt again, I promise, please."

"Just thought you'd like to know I'm taping this. You're going to be famous, a big YouTube star, just like the video of you killing that elephant, Karma's a bitch, ain't it Nils?"

When the authorities found the bodies of Nils Gustafsson and his guide Trevor Lubbe, they both had the yellow flags of the skull and crossed monkey wrenches around their necks and notes of their particular crime, plus the video tape of Nils Gustafsson botched elephant hunt along with the tape of their demise courtesy of Le Gang de la Clé de Singe. The police and Interpol never found any forensic clues at the scene with the exception of a single fingerprint belonging to Swedish film director Ingmar Bergman.

Isala was waiting as Rodin exited the customs area at LAX, she hugged him and gave him a long lingering kiss and whispered softly, "Ingmar Bergman, nice touch."

Every Wednesday Buzz would take the skiff over to the fishing village of Ninh Thủy located across from Hon Lon Island in the Vinh Van Phong Sea. He would beach the dinghy on the pure white sand at Doc Let Beach, then make his way two blocks to Bao's Grocery and stock up of a week's worth of foodstuffs, fruits and veggies, and of course beer. Over the years he became fast friends with the couple who owns the market, Bao and Cam Dinh.

On those occasions whenever he caught more fish than he thinks he can use; he would stop by Bao's Grocery store and see if he could sell or barter a trade for some provisions.

On his last trip into the market, Bao was repairing a broken window in the front of his store; he told Buzz that there was gang of thugs shaking down the all the local merchants and fishermen for extortion and protection. At first Bao refused to pay, so the next morning he and Cam arrived at the store to find a brick had been thrown thru their window. The same thing had happened to other merchants. Buzz asked if anyone had gone to the police? Bao said that everyone was too scared of retaliation, so they just paid.

"How much are you paying?"

"467,132.00 Vietnamese Dong a week."

Buzz stood there calculating the exchange rate in his head, "That's twenty dollars a week! That's bullshit, Bao."

"I know, but what can we do? Buzz, please don't go to the police, it will only cause more trouble."

"Alright, but something has to be done. You and Cam be careful, I'll see you next week."

On the way back to the skiff, he was met by a couple of pocket novel desperadoes, who looked like they had been watching way too many MTV rap and hip-hop videos. The two of them were dressed right out of the 1980's, one was dressed like MC Hammer and other had a big clock hanging around his neck ala Flavor Flav and the only thing he would say was, "True Dat."

"So, listen old dude if you be selling any fish in dis town, you's going to need a license, right Lil Steez?"

"True Dat."

"Who are you guys?" Buzz asked.

"I be Jiggy Janks and this here my main man Lil Steez."

"Yeah, but who are you guys?"

"We be the fellas that be selling the license."

"Shouldn't I be buying the license at the State offices?"

"Yo yo yo, this is a very special license and besides we don't want to bother the nice people down at the State, they have too much to do already. That's why K Dawg be offering these special licenses. Ya dig?

"And who the fuck is K Dawg?"

"K Dawg, he be running the show, old dude."

"How much is this special license, Jinky?"

"It's Jiggy and for you only twenty US Dollars, dawg."

"Twenty Dollars a year, that's not too bad, man."

"Naw old dude, it be twenty dollars, a week."

"Twenty bucks a week, this better be one special license. What makes it so special, Janky"

"It's Jiggy old man, and what makes it special is that if you have one then we don't break your legs, ya dig? Ain't that right Lil Steez?"

"True Dat."

"Well, it's a funny thing Joggy, I just retired as a fishmonger this very second."

"Yo, pops the name is Jiggy, and if I catch ya trying to sell even a seashell, ya ass is going to be cruising 'round in a wheelbarrow, ain't that right Steez?"

"True Dat."

"I think you mean wheelchair, but I catch your drift, man."

"We be keeping our eyes out for you, ya old coot."

"True Dat."

"Far out man, see you boys."

Buzz went back to his boat unpacked the groceries, feed his two ferrets Bosco and Groucho, and then suited up in his SCUBA gear and took Bumbley Bee a rare treat, an eight-pound rump roast.

"Welcome to the Harbin Moon Island International Golf Course and Resort, may I see your invitation, please sir?" Translated Zhi Ruo.

The Iceman, now adorning a full beard and horn-rimmed glasses, reached into his sports coat pocket and presented the invitation to the maître d' standing at the clubhouse entrance. As he and Zhi Ruo entered, they were guided to a receiving stand where patrons were asked to pay in advance for tonight's performance and feast. Once the guest paid the bill, they were handed a menu and program of the night's festivities. The price of the "show" and dinner was a mere twenty-five hundred US dollars per person and that included a souvenir your choice, either a tiger's tooth or claw.

There were thirteen tables arranged into a 'U' shape around a large wooden platform, that was set slightly lower than the dinner tables, so everyone had an excellent view for the slaughtering of the tiger.

The Iceman and Zhi Ruo looked at the menu; the meal would start with a ginger-infused tiger penis soup, followed by tiger steaks with a side of Bok Choy stir-fry with crispy Tofu.

Twelve of the tables were set for two guests; the other table was set for four. The table for four would be for the two owners and their guests. Odin and the Red Team was stationed outside, ready to enter when called.

As people were being seated the wait staff started taking people's drink orders, the majority of the guests ordered bottles of tiger bone wine, costing 100,000 RMB or about $16,000 US dollars. One patron sitting at the table next to the Iceman and Zhi Ruo, held up his glass after taking a big drink smiled and said laughingly, "Tastes grrreat."

When asked what they would like to drink, Iceman ordered a bottle of Maotai. It looks like vodka, but that's where the similarities end, at 80-120% proof, it has a paint stripping quality, definitely not for the faint of heart.

Once all the drink orders were filled, the two owners of the Tiger Park made the rounds, laughing and joking and greeting their guests. They greeted all the Chinese guests first and then came to greet the Iceman and Zhi Ruo. The owners were both middle-aged, neither in good physical shape, one wore glasses and was almost bald and the other had a full head of jet-black hair and sported a David Niven moustache.

"*Wènhòu hé huānyíng*" Said the man with the glasses.

"Greetings and welcome." Translated Zhi Ruo.

"Thank you." Iceman responded.

"*Xièxiè*" Zhi Ruo said.

"Is this your first tiger feast?" Inquired the bespectacled man.

"It is."

"Well then, you're in for a real treat. It's a night you'll never forget."

"I'm sure none of us will."

The owners smiled and headed to their table, the mustached man clapped his hands and a man dressed in a chef's uniform walked out onto the platform, he was greeted by thunderous applause. The chef took a slight bow and gestured to have the tiger brought in. He asked for the lights to be dimmed and a spotlight was concentrated on the platform. Two men dressed in all white wheeled onto the platform a cage containing a young male Siberian Tiger; weighing about three hundred pounds that had definitely been drugged. As the chef was preparing to slit it's throat, Iceman sent a one-word text to Odin, "*now*".

Tommy G having grown up in San Francisco's Chinatown spoke fluent Cantonese shouted as the Red Team burst into the dining room, "Nobody move, this is a raid!"

The owners and patrons did as they were told; the wait staff were herded off to a closet and locked in with instructions to stay quiet. The Red Team forced every one of the guests as well as the Chef to line up against a wall facing their captors as the Iceman and Zhi Ruo took the two owners thru the kitchen to the door leading to the basement.

In the dining room Tommy G held up the yellow flag and informed them, "We are Le Gang de la Clé de Singe, and you are all guilty of crimes against nature."

One of the dinner guests stated defiantly, "We have done nothing wrong, see the tiger is still alive."

Tommy G walked over to one of the tables and held up a bottle of tiger bone wine and said sarcastically, "Care for another drink?"

The team proceeded to place the flags around their necks and the declarations of allegations on their persons. Odin gave the nod, and the deed was done.

Sassoon having been a veterinarian examined the young tiger, as best he could tell, the big cat was in good health with the exception of being overly drugged.

The Iceman and Zhi Ruo took the two owners down into the basement below the clubhouse where the tiger bone wine was brewed. The room looked to be a combination slaughterhouse and wine making room, over in a corner was a ten-foot stainless steel wine tank.

Iceman asked Zhi Ruo if she would please go upstairs and have Tommy G / Colin Wong come down. She did as she was asked, and Tommy G came down to the basement.

"Tommy, tell these two to strip."

"Tuō diào nǐ suǒyǒu de yīfú"

As they were disrobing, Iceman asked Tommy to tell them who they were."

"Wǒmen shì hóuzi bānshǒu, nǐ fànle wéihài zìrán de zuì." Tommy said as he held up the yellow skull and crossed monkey wrench flag.

Then Iceman and Tommy G each opened the lids to each of the ten-foot stainless steel wine tanks.

When the Iceman and Tommy G finally appeared from the basement, the Red Team had neatly arranged the dinner guests and had done a clean sweep of the dining area making sure that there wasn't any forensic clues left behind. Sassoon and T-Bone had transferred the tiger to the Tiger Park truck that it had been transported in.

The Iceman asked Odin, "Is everything good up here?"

"All good, and you?"

"Couldn't be better, but I wouldn't recommend the tiger bone wine. Let's roll."

The drive from San Antonio to the Ghost Hunter Ranch was very scenic, it was the time of year when the Texas Bluebonnets painted the hill country landscape.

Rodin and Isala, having checked in were settling into their log cabin that sat on the edge of the Frio's River. The cabins interior was decorated to the nines, over-stuffed leather sofa, two wing leather chairs with exotic animal skin rugs scattered throughout on the solid oak floors. And adorning the walls in every room was at least one mounted animal head or skull. And the pièce de résistance mounted over the living room fireplace was a majestic American Buffalo head.

They had no sooner finished unpacking when the phone in the living room rang. Rodin picked up the receiver, "Hello."

"Mr. Wilson, this is Roy."

"Hello, Roy."

"Mr. Wilson, I'm just checking to see if everything okay with your cabin."

"Everything is fine. Very nice, thank you."

"There's no rush, but I just wanted to let you know that whenever you're ready for your and Mrs. Wilson hunt, please just give us a day's notice so we arrange the best hunting experience for you both."

"Why thank you Roy, I will certainly do that."

"Well, have a blessed day."

"You too, Roy. Goodbye."

Isala asked, "Roy?"

"Roy. He wishes us a blessed day."

"Well, isn't that special. What do you want to do now?"

Rodin said with a smirk and a bogus yawn, "I sure go use a nap."

"I know you; you're not interested in a nap; you're interested in sex."

"Yeah, but then a nap."

She crossed the living room, took his hand and led him into the bedroom.

The bedroom phone woke them both from a deep sleep, Isala being closet to the phone answered it, "Hello?"

"Mrs. Wilson, this is Roy at the front desk. I'm sorry to disturb you, but I just wanted to let you know that dinner is now being served in the main lodge."

"Thank you, Roy. We'll be there shortly. Goodbye."

She hung up the phone and said to Rodin as she hopped out of bed, "Dinner."

"Boy, am I hungry, after having worked up a voracious appetite."

"I'm glad at least one of us worked up an appetite."

"Ouch. That hurts."

"That'll teach you."

The menu features the vast majority of the ingredients sourced from the Ghost Hunter Ranch, wild game, organic garden vegetables, free range chickens, fruit orchards and local beehives. On tonight's menu you had a choice of a plump and juicy Scimitar Horned Oryx burger with a side of fries, or the peppercorn crusted duck breast with a roasted corn pudding, and finally you could have the rack of venison, pan roasted with gravy and roasted asparagus.

After dinner Rodin and Isala took a walk along the Frio's River where they encountered a small herd of Impalas coming down to the river for a drink. There weren't any lights around, which allowed them to view a canopy of millions of stars above. The tranquility was ruined as the natural sounds of the evening were shattered by the sporadic sounds of gunfire off in the distance from night hunting.

Over the next couple of days Isala and Rodin spent time taking advantage of GHR's other activities, lounging about the pool, skeet shooting, spelunking, bird watching, archery, hiking and taking the photo safari, which was more about obtaining information about the GHR's resources, camera surveillance equipment and camera positions as well as getting a sense of the geographic characteristics of the area.

By day four Isala and Rodin had developed their game plan and were ready to start their mission. Rodin left their cabin on foot early before sunrise dressed in his ghillie suit and armed with his M-24 Sniper Weapon System including silencer and scope.

Isala made her way on foot to the first of three big hunting blinds, each perched atop a hill that provided a 360-degree view for miles. Each blind can accommodate up to eight guests, each blind is air-conditioned with a fully stocked bar with ice maker, there are eight comfortable swivel chairs, twelve tinted windows that looked out onto strategically placed game feeders, well within rifle range so the "hunter" can kill its trophy in complete comfort.

As she approached the blind, she saw two dead Kudu's lying by one of the game feeders not two hundred yards from the blind. As she looked back at the blind she noticed a couple of the hunters looking at her and waving, she waved back. They were gesturing for her to climb the stairs and come in. Below the blind was parked a GHR Chevy Suburban. She climbed the stairs and knocked on the door, a moment later the guide opened the door and welcomed her in. There were five hunters and the guide, it looked to her that had just arrived, as none of them had set up their weapons.

One of the hunters stepped forward and greeted her saying, "Well, welcome little lady, what brings you all the way out here?"

The man was dressed in a loud Hawaiian shirt, khaki pants, snakeskin cowboy boots and a Stetson ten-gallon cowboy hat. The others were more suitably dressed for hunting, wearing camo shirts, khaki pants, hiking shoes and baseball caps.

"Oh, I thought I'd wander over here and get a birds eye view of the park, if that's okay with you all."

They were all affable and very congenial, another man asked her he could make her a drink.

"No, that's very kind of you but 8am is a bit early for me, thank you."

The man in the Hawaiian shirt said while holding up a glass of scotch and water, "Hell, it's five o'clock somewhere. Am I right?" Which got a round of laughter from the group.

Isala asked the group, "Do you all mind if I ask you something?"

"Why hell no. What's on your mind, darling?" The Hawaiian shirt said with a big grin on his face.

She pulled out a yellow piece of canvas with a skull and crossed monkey wrenches embroidered on it and inquired, "Do you know what this is?"

The laughing in the room stopped, the mood turned deadly serious, the guide asked her, "Where did you find that?"

"Do you know what it is?" She asked.

"It's the flag of a bunch of fucking terrorists that goes around killing innocent hunters. Where did you find it?" The guide asked again.

"Oh, I didn't find it, I brought it." Isala said as she produced a Walther PPK 7.65 mm. "Gentlemen, if you all would sit down and place your hands in your pockets and turn your chairs facing outwards. And please no sudden movements."

While there backs were turned to her, she stealthfully attached a Gemtech GM-22 silencer to her weapon.

The guide asked her, "What is it you want?"

"I want to know who killed those two Kudu's by the game feeder."

"You can go fuck yourself, bitch!" The man in the Hawaiian shirt snorted.

"You know I think I will, darling." With that she fired six times.

POP POP POP POP POP POP

She placed the ensigns around each of their necks and inserted the statements of reason in their pockets.

She holstered her pistol and she said outloud, "You know what, I think I will have a drink."

She walked over to the bar and pour herself a vodka tonic and watched a herd of impalas feed for over an hour.

As she left, she made sure to tidy after herself and as she started to climb down from the blind she left behind a single fingerprint, Clyde Barrow, one half of the infamous Bonnie and Clyde.

By the time the sun started to crest over the hills Rodin had positioned his self near a waterhole where the majority of the big game would come for a morning drink. There was a small herd of Thomson's Gazelles and a pretty good size herd of zebras standing around leisurely drinking. Now it was just a matter of playing the waiting game. He didn't have to wait long he heard the sound of an ATV approaching. It stopped, as best as he could tell about three yards away, he heard the guide and hunters talking, there wasn't any real danger of scaring any of the animals away, since they have spent most if not all of their lives around people and machines.

PHIFF

Rodin's first shot was to take out the guide, leaving the hunter stammering around in a panic and shock.

PHIFF PHIFF

Two quick shots and it was done. He placed them both sitting next to the ATV and then proceeded to perform the ritual of the flag and communiqué.

He walked to the top of a hill overlooking the watering hole, he spied an open bed truck through his scope, there two middle-aged hunters standing up in back right behind the cab, one was thin and the other rather heavy set and inside he could see the guide driving with an older hunter riding shotgun. There were two lifeless bodies strapped down in the bed of the truck, one was a Black Wildebeest and the other a Markhor. The vehicle was approaching at a pretty good clip, heading towards the waterhole from the opposite direction than the ATV had.

PHIFF

Rodin took out the guide driving the truck causing it to crash into a grove of Mesquite trees, forcing the hunter inside the truck, who apparently wasn't wearing his seatbelt to hit his head on the dashboard, rendering him unconscious, while the men that were standing in the truck bed were both thrown out of the vehicle landing hard on the ground, they seemed to be dazed and confused.

Rodin walked down to the where they were, by the time he reached them they seemed to be coherent and not too badly hurt. They were dressed in hunting outfits, bright orange shirts and camo cargo pants.

"What the hell happened?" the thin one asked and seeing Rodin dressed in his ghillie suit said, "And what in the Sam Hill are you dressed like that for?"

The other man asked his friend, "What's going on, bro?"

Rodin pulled out the yellow banner and asked, "Have either of you guys ever heard of Le Gang de la Clé de Singe?"

"Dude, like who hasn't." The man replied.

"Then you know that the penalty for hunting is death."

"You're not going to kill us are you, bro?" The heavy-set fellow asked as he started to sob.

"Fraid so, bro."

With that he fired off two quick shots in quick succession.

PHIFF PHIFF

Once again, Rodin performed the ritual of the flag after positioning the two men against the rear tire of the truck, he then went to look in the cab at the unconscious man. Rodin felt for a pulse and found none, it seems that the elderly man broke his neck when he hit the dash. Rodin thought to himself, I guess it's true, seatbelts do save lives. He completed the flag ceremony with the driver and old man and left behind the fingerprint of the other half of that famous bank robbing murdering duo, Miss Bonnie Parker.

It was getting to be early afternoon and he was heading back in the general direction of the area of the cabins when he heard a shot off to his right. He carefully made his way to where he suspected shot came from, he was making his way through a thick patch of Mountain Cedar, Desert Spoon and Honey Locusts, when he came across a women in her thirties posing with a Texas Dall Ram, that she had just killed. Kneeling behind it, holding up its head by the corkscrew shaped horns and smiling, believing that she is going to be posting this photo on social media.

Her guide had just taken the photograph with her phone when he suddenly fell backwards dropping the device. He lay motionless, the woman slowly approached him, thinking he might have had a heart attack or a stroke, but then she saw that he was in a pool of blood. She spun around looking to see if see could tell where the shot came from, she thought it had to be a hunting accident. As she was trying to make sense of it all, she noticed something odd moving towards her, a large mass of vegetation appearing to get closer.

It was a man dressed in some kind of camouflage suit made up of twigs, and branches with leaves, with grass interwoven into netting. Yards away it raised its hand and pulled off a head piece revealing a man with camouflage paint on his face, he was carrying a large rifle that was also covered with leaves and grass and things.

"Did you shoot Wayne?" She asked.

"I did indeed."

"Why?"

Once again, he revealed the yellow symbol of death. He said in a low whisper, "Le Gang de la Clé de Singe."

Seeing the flag, she realized the fate that awaited her, she quickly tried to calculate the odds of her reaching her gun leaning against the Ram, before he could raise his and fire. Still, there was no other choice, she knew that these killers never show any mercy to man or woman. There was one thing that she kept racking her brain to remember, had she dropped another round in the chamber or not.

Rodin saw her contemplating the situation and her trying to work out how the scenario would work out, he knew the question she was trying to sort out, did she put a round in the chamber. He decided to let play out, so he waited for her to make her move.

"Go ahead." He said in a non-threating way. "Go for it."

She looked hard at him, staring deep into his eyes to see if there was any tell, to see if he was just fucking with her.

"Look, I could have killed you a long time ago. I'm giving you a chance. You and I know there's only two ways this is going to end."

She took a deep breath to calm and steady herself; then she lunged.

Buzz stopped by Bao's Grocery to pick up his usual Wednesday groceries and to see Bao and Cam. The store was dark, it looked unusually empty, and there were hardly any customers and the produce looked old and wilted.

"Bao, what's going on?"

"It's those two thugs, Jiggy and Lil Steez they say everyone must pay more for protection. I say I cannot pay more. So, they hang around my store and scare off my customers."

"How long has this been going on?"

"All week. It not good."

"Bao, maybe it's time to go see the police?"

"I don't know Buzz."

"What if I went to see them, now I wouldn't mention any names, but I'd just let them know that there's a racketeer extorting all the merchants. What do you think?"

"You no mention me?"

"I promise I won't name any merchant's names."

Buzz walked back towards the beach stopping every few blocks to make sure he wasn't being followed by either of those two gangsta wannabes. When he was sure it was safe, he hailed a cab and told the cabbie, "Công an phường Ninh Diêm."

Ten minutes later he was standing outside the Police of Ninh Diem Ward Station. He walked in and the whole place got quit, he approached the desk officer and asked is there anyone who might speak English. The officer picked up the phone receiver and had a five-minute conversation, hung up the phone and said, "You Wait."

A disheveled middle-aged detective came out to the lobby, spotted Buzz, and walked over to him, held out his hand and said, "I am Detective Sinh Nguyen, How may I assist you."

Buzz stood and shook the detective's hand then said, "Very nice to meet you, my name is Buzz Murdock. Is there somewhere we came speak, privately?"

Buzz had been in a lot of police stations in his hippie-dippy anti-war life and this one was similar to all the others, the sergeant's desk in the front with civilians standing waiting to speak with someone, police officers walking in with people who were in handcuffs under arrest, in the back were the cops workspace, interrogation rooms, and the area where they fingerprint and take mug shots.

Detective Nguyen took Buzz into an interrogation rooms, there was the standard metal desk with two wooden chairs on either side of the table. Buzz sat in the chair farthest from the door and the detective sat opposite him. He removed a small pad and ballpoint pen from his suit jacket and started taking notes.

"So, Mr. Murdock what seems to be the trouble?"

"There are a group of criminals extorting the merchants in the thôn Đông Cát part of town, forcing them to pay for protection, scaring them and brutalizing them if they don't receive their money. The shopkeepers there are too scared to come forward, that's why I'm here."

"I see, and are you a merchant as well, Mr. Murdock?"

"No, just a friend."

"Do you know who these men are?"

"I only know their street names, one is called Jiggy Janks and the other is Lil Steez. They are the muscle for the big man called K Dawg, who I haven't seen. I don't know if there are any others."

"We are aware of this K Dawg and his gang; it would help if you could describe these men to me?"

"They both dress very flamboyantly, I would best describe them as wearing 1980's hip-hop clothes, they go around trying to act and speak like American gangsta rappers, does that makes any sense?"

"Yes, it does actually. Is there anything else that you think that you might be able to tell me that is relevant?"

"No sir."

"Well, Mr. Murdock I want to thank you for coming in and informing us about these men. Can you tell me the names of any of the merchants that are being extorted?"

"I'm sorry, I promised I wouldn't."

"That makes it a lot harder, but I promise that I will personally look into the matter. Thank you for coming in Mr. Murdock."

"Thank you, detective, I appreciate your taking the time."

By the time the Iceman, Zhi Ruo, and the Red Team reached the Siberian Tiger Park with the tiger that they rescued from the dinner party, Jimmy the Chew with the help of Zhang Wei, the park manager and some his friends had loaded up all the tigers in the park onto four trucks ready to transport them up north to the undeveloped area in the Heilongjiang province. It's the northern most province in China butting up to Siberian Russia, being separated by the Amur River. The tigers will be released in an area where they will thrive, it's an area where very few people live due to the harsh environment.

Iceman had Zhi Ruo ask Zhang Wei if he and the others will be okay. He smiled and nodded, they shook hands and Zhang Wei led the small caravan of trucks onto highway G1111 heading north to the tiny village of Sunwu.

The Iceman and team headed back to the hotel for a good night's sleep before starting their two-day journey to Xishuangbanna near the Laos, Myanmar boarders, where they were going to visit some bear farm owners and make them an offer, they can't refuse to release their bears.

Rodin returned to the cabin wearing faded jeans and an old tattered Van Halen tee shirt. He carried a duffel bag and a rifle case; his face was clean from any face paint having had a quick wash downstream on the Frio River. Isala was waiting for him with some good news, because of his agreed upon illegal lion hunt that had been set for the next day, the four owners wanted to know if they could meet this afternoon to go over a few things."

"Say, that is good news. It will make things a lot easier. How did you hear, Roy?"

"Roy."

"How did everything go at the blind?"

"Six, and you?"

"Eight, the last one was a particularly rough one. They're never easy, but occasionally you get one that's really tough, you know?"

Isala walked across the living room and tightly hugged him, "I know, babe. I know."

"Well, I better go take a quick shower and then we'll go meet the boys."

A hot shower always feels good after spending ten hours in a full dressed ghillie suit. He wanted to stay in the shower longer, but Roy and the gang were waiting. Rodin dressed in a sports coat, powder blue button down shirt and khaki's. Isala wore a pale green pantsuit with a navy blue scooped neck top.

"Mr. Wilson, I'd like to introduce you to my partners in crime, as it were. This is Dan Reeves, William Simpson and Doctor Harold Bloom, gentlemen Mr. Wilson."

"Pete, please and it's a pleasure to meet you all. Now Roy mentioned that you all would like to shadow me on my lion adventure, well I think that would be fun, the more the merrier, am I right hon?"

Isala smiled and said, "Yes, of course. Roy, do you think it might be possible for us to view Pete's lion and my giraffe?"

"I think that's a great idea, since we haven't released them into the park yet, whata say fellas let's all jump into my Suburban and check 'em out."

The six of them climbed into Roy's camo decaled Chevy Suburban and rode to the part of the park where guests were never taken, the part where the machinery is stored, the veterinarian's office, food for the animals, and the special pens where animals are brought to be quarantined before being released into the general population of other animals.

As they approached, they could see the giraffe's head rising above the barn and they could hear the muffled roar of the lion being held in the barn. There wasn't anyone around. People were tending to the various herds, which would take days since they oversaw twenty thousand acres.

They walked past the corral where the giraffe was nervously chewing on the leaves of a Texas Oak tree, it seemed to be unsettled by the roar of the lion being so near.

They didn't stop to exam the twenty-foot tall even-toed ungulate mammal, they walked past it and proceeded into the barn. Rodin was surprised that there were three other big cats in cages off to the side, a female lion, a jaguar and a cheetah. But it was the male lion that took center stage, the Simba was pacing back and forth in a thirty-foot cage, when they entered the barn it stopped and stared, smelled the air and gave a roar that made everyone take an involuntarily a step backwards. This Black Mane Lion tipped the scales at five hundred and ten pounds, one look at him and you knew why he had the title of "King of the Jungle".

Roy slowly approached the lion's cage, the beast never took its eye off of him, when Roy was within five feet he stopped and said, more to his self than to anyone else, "Thank God for those bars. This one's a monster."

Isala asked, "What's with all the cats?"

Roy replied, "You see my dear these are for hunters like your husband who have discriminating taste who want only the best, but for one reason or another can't travel all the way to Africa. So, we bring Africa to them."

"I noticed that you gentlemen had hunted lions in African." Rodin said.

"Yes, as a matter of fact that will be two years ago next week." Roy stated.

"I saw the photo of the four of you posing with your trophies, three females and a young male. You all look so happy and proud of yourselves. Four lions, that's quite an accomplishment, did you happen upon the pride on the hunt?"

Roy looked at the others and was about to respond when Rodin held up his hand, "Don't bother. I've seen the video taken by your guide of the four of you coming across the pride of lions sleeping in an open field, when you shot them. You didn't even attempt to wake them, you just shot them while they were sleeping. The male tried to get up, he was struggling as you approached him and you didn't even put out of his misery, the four of you stood around laughing and joking as the poor thing slowly died. For that you must pay the price."

"What the fuck are you talking about?" demanded Roy.

Rodin and Isala nonchalantly moved backwards a couple of steps, Rodin leaned into Isala and whispered, "Watch the door." He reached behind his back and drew the Walther PPK from beneath his sports coat, and announced, "Gentlemen, may I have your attention please."

The Ghost Hunter Ranch owners all turned around to see Mr. Wilson holding a gun with silencer pointing at them.

Doctor Bloom raised his hands as if he were under arrest, and asked, "Cop?"

"You wish."

"Then what's going on?" queried the good doctor.

"Gentlemen, my name isn't Pete Wilson, that young lady standing by the door isn't my wife, and we didn't come here to kill animals, we came to kill hunters.

"Roy, I'm sure you've heard of Le Gang de la Clé de Singe, am I right?"

"Holy shit, you're one of those freaks who goes around killing innocent people."

"And you're one of those freaks who goes around killing innocent animals."

"We love the animals, and that's why we kill them," Dr. Bloom said.

"And we love hunters, and that's why we kill them, Doc."

Doctor Bloom just stood there bewildered staring at Rodin with his mouth open.

"Actually no, I'm just fucking with ya. By the way what kind of medicine do you practice, Doctor?"

"Oh, I'm not a medical doctor, I'm a Doctor of Metaphysical Humanistic Science."

"Wow, no shit, I was thinking of majoring in that when I was in college."

"Really?"

"No, I'm just fucking with you again, sorry."

"So, are you going to shoot us now?" Roy asked.

"Fellas, on you last encounter with the *Panthera leo* you seemed to relish of having the advantage of it being asleep, well he's not asleep now."

"You're not seriously considering putting me in with that lion, are you?" Challenged Doctor Bloom.

"Heavens no Doctor, that wouldn't be fair, no all four of you are going into the lion's den. That seems to much more equitable, don't you think?"

"Why you're mad, I'm not going in there with that monster, you'll have to kill me first." Doctor Bloom declared crossing his arms over his chest in defiance.

"Okay." Rodin raised the gun and shot the good doctor between the eyes.

POP

Roy and the others moved quickly towards the cage, not taking their eyes off of the madman with the gun. When they reached the cage door Rodin handed the three of them a yellow standard, having them place it around their necks and gave each of them a note to put in their pocket.

The lion was sitting at the opposite end of the cage appearing to be bored, so much so he laid down seeming to be dozing, even when the three men entered the cage where they all huddled in a corner as Rodin locked the cage door. Rodin whispered to them, "Maybe, just maybe if you're real still and quite you just might make thru this ordeal."

Rodin stopped by Doctor Bloom's corpse and placed the yellow flag and note on his body, he also placed a copy of the video showing the four men killing the pride of sleeping lions in Bloom's pocket, as well as the taped phone conversations he had with Roy discussing that fact that they regularly import illegally big game cats to the Ranch for hunts.

Isala looked around outside to see if anyone was in the area and it appeared that the coast was clear. "All clear." she said.

Rodin was halfway out the barn door when he stopped and looked back to see how the men in the cage were doing, the lion seemed to be observing them. Having taking the silencer off the Walther PPK earlier, Rodin aimed and fired one shot up into the rafters of the barn, scaring Roy and his companions enough to make them scream, which startled the lion.

The last thing Rodin saw as he closed the barn door was the beast slowly approaching his dinner.

Texas Ranger Tom Conway and his partner Ranger Peter Brown arrived at the Ghost Hunters Ranch after the Rangers had received an anonymous call about multiple murders by Le Gang de la Clé de Singe at the Ghost Hunters.

An anonymous call was also placed to the Real County's Sheriff's Department of Texas as well as the London office of Interpol, informing them both that Le Gang de la Clé de Singe had recently killed several people on the Ghost Hunters Ranch in Texas. The Sheriff's Department sent officers and the Medical Examiner.

Interpol sent Inspectors Morris and Volker to the scene. By the time the Inspectors arrived most of the forensics had been completed by Real County's M.E. The Texas Rangers also brought in their forensic experts just as a safety backup. Interpol took the reports from both forensic units and compared them.

Afterwards the three entities sat down to analyze the findings. The Texas Rangers, because they are the Texas Rangers decided that they should take the lead being that they are after all they are the Texas Rangers.

Just as Texas Ranger Tom Conway was about to take command of the meeting Inspector Morris raised his hand and said, "Ranger Conway, if I may, my partner Inspector Volker and myself have been investigating dozens of Le Gang de la Clé de Singe murders over the years, and without even reviewing the excellent work that your forensic teams have done, I think I can sum up the findings that both of your exemplary forensic experts have come up with. And let me just say I am not belittling any of the hard work your folks have done, but they have got nothing, no DNA, no hair samples, no matching ballistics, no fibers, no surveillance videos, no biological samples and no fingerprints with the exception of one. One clear, perfect, beautiful fingerprint that when your forensic team found it, everyone thought, gotch ya. But then you sent it off and lo and behold it's bogus, but because everything is bigger in Texas this time you discovered not one but two fingerprints belonging to Texas outlaws Bonnie and Clyde. Does that pretty much sum up the evidence that we have Ranger Conway?"

"Not quite, Inspector Morris. The killer or killers left a CD and a voice recording of evidence that they left behind justifying their actions. We're analyzing those pieces now."

"Ah yes, do let us know the results of those findings, we'll be most interested in what you come up with."

"Listen, Inspector I don't like your cavalier attitude, you come strolling in here like you're some kind of Sherlock fucking Holmes. I don't know what kind of operation you boys run in Interpol, but we're the Texas Rangers and by God we get 'er done."

"I say, good show old man, a real rousing speech as it were. Now tell me Mr. Get 'er done, when we can expect results from you boys of the by God Texas Rangers?"

"We'll have some promising leads inside a week, guaranteed."

"Well, I think we have all that we need, Inspector Volker and I would like to thank you all for everything. And

Ranger Conway, I can't wait to hear from you in a week's time. Until then, we bid you a good day."

"This is Josh Colman, CNN News, coming to you live from the Ghost Hunters Ranch two hours outside San Antonio, Texas where Le Gang de la Clé de Singe was struck in the heart of America.

Local authorities are telling CNN that at least sixteen people have been killed, we believe that thirteen of the dead were shot and three of the owners were mauled to death by a male lion.

Le Gang de la Clé de Singe, the international eco-terrorist group known to have committed murderous acts all over the world has once again struck here in the United States. Their proclamation states that they are at war with all poachers, big game hunters, all big game safari outfits, as well as anybody anywhere in the world that targets, kills, profits, and/or supports the killing of any animals that are endangered or any animals that are hunted for sport.

The Ghost Hunters Ranch was advertised as a big game hunting ranch, where hunters pay a large fee to hunt exotic big game, they were however not licensed to allow big cat hunts.

We at CNN have been told by authorities, that they have proof in the form of audio recordings that the owners were secretly allowing lions and other big cats to be hunted on the ranch.

It is said that a video exists showing the four owners, while on a hunting safari in Africa killed a pride of lions that were asleep. If proven to be true is quite shameful.

Not only are the local sheriff's department on the case, but also the Texas Rangers was well as inspectors from Interpol have flown in to aid in the investigation.

I had the opportunity to speak with Texas Ranger Tom Conway earlier and this what he had to say."

"We at the Texas Rangers find these acts of murder as heinous and abominable, but we feel that these murderous thugs will be quickly brought to justice."

"Why do you think that you will be able to bring these people to justice when other police and law enforcement agencies, including Interpol haven't?"

"Because we're the Texas Rangers."

"Well, there you have it, for now this is Josh Colman reporting from the Ghost Hunters Ranch in Texas."

Bao was turning off the lights in the store, "Are you about ready Cam?"

"Yes dear, I'm ready."

As they were walking out the front door, Bao closes the front door, and locks it. They walk to the corner, turn right and walk the ten blocks to their apartment unaware that they were being watched.

Jiggy and Lil Steez were lurking in a doorway at the other end of the block. Once Bao and Cam turned the corner

Jiggy and Steez walked towards the grocery store, Jiggy looks at his watch to check the time, "It's only 1am, Lil Steez. We got time, whatda say we easy up and light up a Bong Son Bomber"

"True dat."

Jiggy reaches into his jacket and pulls out a joint, lights up, takes a drag and passes it over to Lil Steez, "Dude, That's the sheet, man!"

Lil Steez takes a long deep drag and holds it deep into his lungs, "True dat!"

They're sitting in the alley across the street from the grocery until 2 o'clock when they headed over to the store, as they approach the front door, they keep looking in every direction. Lil Steez was looking around so much he stepped on a plastic water bottle someone had thrown onto the sidewalk, which got a dog barking, "Shhhhhh. Man, keep it on the down low!" Whispered Jiggy.

"True, dat."

Jiggy tripped the front door lock, jiggled the door, and in an instance, they were in. They stand there in the darkness for a couple minutes with just the sound of their own breathing. Finally, Jiggy feeling satisfied no one saw them turned to Lil Steez, "Okay, brother, let's start thieving."

"True, dat."

Bao had a sneaking suspicion that something bad was going to happen at the store, and after being pushed and taunted for so long he didn't get scared, he got angry.

Jiggy and Steez headed to the office in the back of the store and stared to ransack the office, going thru files, overturning furniture, and breaking things. Occasionally, putting things in their pockets they think might have some value. They slowly start to make their way back towards the front when the overhead lights pop on, they freeze in their tracks.

A deep booming voice announces, "Can I help you two?" Bao was heading towards them carrying a Louisville Slugger baseball bat, the Reggie Jackson model that Buzz gave him for a little New York Yankee style protection.

Jiggy holding out his hands speaking softly, "Hold up, brother. Be cool."

"What the fuck do you think you're doing?"

"Easy, B. Everything's cool, we're just doing a little jacking, we don't want no tussle, my man."

Bao slowly lifted the baseball ball and rested it on his shoulder, "There isn't gonna any tussle. I'm just going to pound your ass!"

Bao starts to approach Jiggy and Lil Steez when he hears a voice from behind him, "Drop the bat, nigga."

Bao turned around, he looked K Dawg up and down and smiles. K Dawg was dressed all in black, he wore a black fedora, a black tee shirt with eight gold chains around his neck, black pants, black Nikes and black thick rim sunglasses.

"What the fuck you supposed to be?"

K Dawg held up a Sig Sauer P226 9mm pistol and coldly smiled, "I'm the last thing you're ever gonna see, muddafucka." K Dawg stares into Bao's eyes and fires.

BOOM

Bao looks down at his stomach and back to the gunman then drops to the ground.

K Dawg steps over the body and walks to where Jiggy is staring down at Bao with eyes as big as saucers, "Jiggy, ya need to be making this look like a robbery gone bad."

"You, you, you...killed, em!"

K Dawg looks back at Bao lying in an ever-growing pool of blood, he grins, and says, "No shit!"

Lil Steez points to Bao, "What about him?"

"Just leave 'em. Now get ya ass in gear. Oh, and Jiggy, ya just peed your pants. You're both are just a couple a fuckin pussies."

Jiggy looks down and to his surprise he had wet himself, "Aw, shit!"

Lil Steez was going to make a joke until he saw he had pissed his pants, too, "True dat!"

K Dawg steps over Bao pointing the gun at him, he gives him a kick in the side to see if he moves, but Bao doesn't move. When he reaches the front door, he stops and turns to Jiggy, tosses him the gun and says, "And don't do anything stupid, like running to the cops, I used your gun Jiggy." He turned and walked out the door.

As a boy, Thao Pham grew up in the farming village of Cao Bằng, North Vietnam during the war, his father was a highly decorated Sergeant Major in the Vietnam People's

Army. He was wounded in the battle of the Tet Offensive and during the Seige of Plei Me, he won the Bravery Order, the Feat Order, and the Ho Chi Minh Order for great meritorious service.

During the war his father encouraged his son to join the army, Pham did manual labor, digging trenches, carrying supplies and ammunition to the front lines, he himself was wounded. When the war was over Pham's father was awarded a district councilman position for his service to country. The war had changed his father, he never would have admitted it, but he showed all the signs of Post-traumatic stress disorder, it got so bad that he and Pham would get into terrible arguments. It reached the point that it could become physical, so Phem said goodbye to his mother and father and went south to seek his fortune.

He landed in Ho Chi Minh City where he fell in with a gang of black marketers, selling cigarettes, running liquor, and drugs. Many on the police force were on the take, as were many of the judges. Pham was a quick learner, he took his knowledge and decided to open up shop for his self, so he left the gang in Ho Chi Minh City and moved to Ninh Hoa with Jiggy and Lil Steez where they started their own gang. He went from Thao Pham to K Dawg, he and his crew were heavily influenced by the MTV music videos of the American gangsta rappers, Ice Cube, Ice Tea, Fitty Cent, and NWA.

Over time he built up quite the colorful band of thugs, there was Chedda, Lil Steez, MZee Bugsy, Chuck-Bizz, J Squared, Mack E. D., and Jiggy Janks. They all had been with other outfits and were either asked to leave or read the writing on the wall and split A-sap.

The K Dawg Gang were known to the local police as kind of a joke, oh they did some bad shit, but 9 times out of 10, they somehow managed to screw the pooch. They were mostly known for minor league stuff, small time extortion, loan sharking, blackmail, drugs, fencing of stolen goods, robbery, and protection racket.

Detective Nguyen and two uniformed officers were called to the Bao Grocery to investigate the shooting of the storeowner. When they arrived, they found his wife Cam and the American hippie Buzz consoling her. At first the crime scene looked like a robbery gone bad, but it was too staged. Fortunately, the victim, who was still in a coma appeared would survive, but the doctors said they believed that he would be paralyzed and confined to a wheelchair. Detective Nguyen had placed an officer stationed outside his hospital room.

The inside of K Dawg's office was dark as a bat cave, the walls were covered from floor to ceiling with photos of Rap, Hip-Hop, and criminal royalty. One of his lackeys, Mack E. D. knocked on the heavy oak door and poked his head in and saw the boss sitting behind a massive desk with what seemed to be a small dog on his lap. As his eyes got used to the darkness it wasn't a dog but head of a woman bobbing up and down. K Dawg looked at Mack E.D. and said, "S'up, dawg." The woman stopped moving and looked up, "No need to stop darling."

Mack E. D. took a couple steps towards the desk, "We have to talk."

"Okay, girl, we'll finish this later."

"Aw, do I havta?"

"Listen, baby, the K Dawg will make it up to ya later." He whispers in her ear they both and laugh.

The girl stands up and gives him a big kiss, then leaves the office. Mack E. D. closes the door behind her.

"S'up, my man?" K Dawg asks.

"Word on the street is that the grocery guy that got shot isn't dead."

"Well, ain't dat a bitch." K Dawg picks up his phone and dials. "Yo, Jiggy I need to see you, now!"

He hangs the phone up. Mack E. D. walks over and sits in an over-stuffed chair opposite K Dawg and waits. Twenty minutes later there's a knock on the door, and Jiggy and Lil Steez come in.

Jiggy sheepishly says, "Whas'up, boss?"

"My man, Mack E. D. here, tells me that the grocery bill hasn't been pain in full. So, ya'll need to go and make sure that the garbage is taken out, ya dig?"

Jiggy looking at the floor, at the ceiling anywhere but at K Dawg, whose eyes are burning a hole in his head, "Yo, uh, I mean, uh,uh"

K Dawg motions for Jiggy to come closer to him, he pulls out a gun from his desk drawer and points at Jiggy.

"Listen, ya little shit, either you're part of the solution or you're part of the problem. It's that simple, either you take care of this, or I take care of you. Dig?"

"No worries, we'll take care of it. Right, Steez?"

"True, dat!"

"Jiggy. Don't fuck this up. Now get the fuck out of my office."

Jiggy and Lil Steez leave, and close the door. K Dawg sits down and looks at Mack E. D. "You watch. They're gonna fuck it up."

The Ninh Diem Hospital is located two miles from the Bao Grocery store, on Highway DT1A. It is a two-story, 400-bed multidisciplinary institution. The Ninh Diem Hospital provides specialist services and is the only hospital outside of Ho Chi Minh City that has a renowned trauma center known for its "gunshot" team. From the outside, the hospital has an institutional feel; zero style, no frills all function.

Buzz had checked in with the admission desk and alerted them that he was there for Bao Dinh. He had been sitting in the corner of the waiting room with his headphones on listening to his 1980's Sony Walkman, grooving to Cat Stevens singing Peace Train when a doctor approaches.

Buzz looks up at the doctor, "Hey, Doc. How's Bao doing, man?"

"It's not good Buzz. He lost a lot of blood, and the bullet is lodged very close to his spine. We haven't gone in and taken it out yet, right now it's just too dicey. I wouldn't want to have to put him through that trauma at the moment. It's still too early to tell."

"How long before you like, have a sense of what's what, man."

"The next forty-eight hours will be critical; right now, he's stable and resting. If he can make it through the night without any incidences, I think it will be a very good sign. But, Buzz, even if he does make it, he will be paralyzed."

"Can I see him, Doc?"

"No visitors while he's in ICU, okay."

"Okay, well, I'm just gonna sit here for a while, man."

"As soon as I know anything, I'll let you know, promise, you should go back to the Sweet Mary Jane and get some rest."

"Maybe you're right Doc."

As Buzz is about to leave, he notices Jiggy and Lil Steez walking into the waiting area. He goes and sits down; he turns off his Walkman keeping the headphones on and holds up a newspaper that somebody left on the seat next to him. He sits there acting like he's reading the paper and listening to music. Jiggy and Lil Steez sit down in the row of seats in front of Buzz with their backs to him. Jiggy jumps up and gets the attention of a passing nurse. "Excuse me, my brother was brought here with a GS, where'd he be?"

"Most likely in the intensive care unit, you can inquire about him at the receptionist in the lobby."

"Can I see him?"

"I'm sorry, no visitors in the ICU. Sorry."

The nurse walks away. Jiggy sits back down next to Lil Steez.

"Shit. She's saying we got to ask the receptionist. What the fuck was that's dude's name?"

Buzz leans forward and taps Jiggy on the shoulder, "That dude's name is Bao Dinh, man."

Jiggy and Lil Steez look at each other, then turn around and look at Buzz.

"Say what?" Jiggy said.

"The name of the guy you shot, was Bao Dinh, man."

"What da fuck ya talkin 'bout? We didn't shoot nobody, muthafucka!"

"True dat!"

"So you're here to visit your brother, but you don't know his name, I take it you guys weren't close?"

"Let's get da fuck outta here, Steez."

"True dat."

Jiggy and Lil Steez leave the waiting room and walk out of the hospital. Jiggy pulls out his cell phone and dials. "K Dawg listen up. We got troubles."

Buzz had to get away from this madness and lose himself in nothingness. He just wanted to get away from everyone and everything. He was heading to where he could go primeval and rejuvenate his soul. He needed some Bumbley time. It was 2 o'clock on a beautiful sunny afternoon when The Sweet Mary Jane set sail out of the Vịnh Vân Phong Harbor heading southeast.

The moment the salty air hit Buzz's face out on the open sea, he broke down and cried like he hadn't done since his parents died when their KLM flight 4905 crashed during takeoff from Tenerife in the Canary Islands on the 27th of March 1977 in what has become known as the Tenerife airport disaster, the worst aviation disaster in history. The ground collision was caused by a number of factors, including weather conditions, pilot error, and technical limitations. A total of 583 people aboard both aircraft died.

There were a couple of divers already in the water when Buzz weighed anchor. He decided to wait until everyone left, he knew Bumbley would hide and avoid the interlopers, besides he wanted some quality alone time with the Bee.

It was almost 5 o'clock when the last diver left NHA Phu Bay. Buzz was already geared up and putting on his air tank when he first noticed what appeared to be a slow moving squall off to the northwest moving in his direction. Buzz had seen hundreds of these; most would blow thru and be over in an hour. This one looked like he and a couple hours before it would hit the bay. Over the side he went, within minutes he spotted Bumbley and swam towards him bringing with him his snack, a couple dozen sides of pork ribs. They say animals can sense human emotions, whether they're happy, angry or even sad. It seemed to Buzz that Bumbley was extra affectionate, he seem to be sensitive to Buzz by staying close by and rubbing up against him. Buzz wasn't sure if he was sensing his depression or maybe it was the pork ribs, he wanted it to the former and he convinced himself that he and Bumbley had developed a close psychic bond.

When Buzz reached the surface, the wind was picking up and the swells were starting to show white caps. He got underway still wearing his wetsuit and headed for port, feeling a lot better and able to cope with the human race. Seeing Bumbley always cleared his head, and on the way home he lit up a 'fattie' and now life was good, at least for the moment.

K Dawg was smoking a Cuban Montecristo and drinking Johnnie Walker Black, just kicking back enjoying the good life siting in the main salon of his new 48' Torres Sportsfish Yacht named 'Buoys in the Hood'.

Jiggy and Lil Steez stood on the dock in awe and started laughing when they heard an all too familiar voice. "So, whata think, is this bitch kickin' or what?"

Jiggy looks at Lil Steez and says, "Dawg, this is phat!"

"True dat!"

"Glad you like 'er boyz. Let's be taking this mutha out. Jiggy, you and Lil Steez throw off the lines, and let's see what this skeezer can do."

"We be going out to sea? S'up wit dat?"

"We got business to discuss, and we need our privacy."

Jiggy started to untie the stern line while Lil Steez went to the bow and untied the rope. K Dawg cranked up the twin Detroit Diesel engines, for a moment the back of the boat was engulfed in a fog of diesel exhaust. K Dawg broke out laughing as Jiggy and Steez were coughing and gasping for air. Once the yacht started picking up speed, the cool ocean breeze blew all the smoke away. K Dawg took the yacht about three miles out to the open sea and cuts the engines. "Can I get you boys something to drink?"

Jiggy feeling a little queasy, but doesn't want anyone to know says, "I'll have what you're having, boss."

"Lil Steez?"

"Tru dat."

K Dawg points to the bar, "Well help yourself."

Jiggy pours his self a large glass of scotch, "K Dawg, your da man. I got to tell ya, you are one mad baller."

Lil Steez hold up his glass up in a salute, "True dat!"

"Why, thank ya boys."

"Now, Dawg, what are we gonna do 'bout Bao Dinh?" Jiggy said after taking a drink.

K Dawg got up walked over to the back of the boat with his back to Jiggy and Lil Steez. "Ya know, this reminds me of an old Chinese Proverb. Do you like Chinese Proverbs, Jiggy?"

"I don't know, are they kinda like the fortunes we get in the cookies at that Chinese joint, Momma Wongs?"

K Dawg turned around to face Jiggy and Lil Steez and smiles, "Not exactly. You're thinking about fortune cookies. No, this is more like a Rap tune. It goes like this, *That the birds of worry and care fly over your head, this you cannot change, but that they build nests in your hair, this you can prevent.*"

"That's beautiful, boss. What da fuck's it mean, Dawg?"

K Dawg held up a 9mm pistol, "It means, how long can you and Lil Steez tread water. Over the side you go, you too Lil Steez."

"Now, listen, Dawg, this shit ain't funny, man. Quit, fuckin with us."

"True dat." Lil Steez said.

"Either you jump overboard, or I'll blow ya head off, ya dig."

"But I cant's swim, I'll drown." Lil Steez pleaded.

"No, ya won't." K Dawg walks over to Lil Steez, puts the gun to his head and shoots.

KA-BOOM

There's a cloud of red mist that fills the air and then Lil Steez falls backwards overboard. He turns towards Jiggy, who jumps into the water.

K Dawg throws the gun into the water and pulls up a director chair, as Jiggy is flaying in the water trying to keep his head above water, K Dawg casually sits down to watch as the sharks start to attack the body of Lil Steez.

"Dawg, you're one cold hearted muthafuckin bastard!"

K Dawg smiles as he raised his glass and said, "True dat."

Manis is the genus of pangolins. Pangolins are scaly anteaters; they have large protective keratin scales covering their body. They are the most trafficked mammals in the world for their meat and scales. One of the largest markets, outside of China is Vietnam.

Rodin contacted his old college friend from the 1960's, Buzz Murdock when he found out that his next assignment would be in Vietnam. Buzz had been living there for over two years and had a good feel of the people, the culture, plus he spoke the language.

Qantas flight 5152 from Singapore touched down in Tan Son Nhat International Airport at 9:1pm, by the time Rodin and Isala made their way thru customs it was almost 10. As they exited the customs area stood his old friend, the self-proclaimed Ayatollah of Rock&Rolla, Buzz.

Rodin held out his hand, but Buzz went in for a giant bear hug.

"Hey man, it's good to see you."
"You too Buzz, you too. Buzz I'd like you to meet Isala. Isala, this is my old friend Buzz Murdock."

"Buzz, it is a pleasure to finally meet you, Rodin has told me so much about you."

"It's very nice to meet you too, you can just call me Buzz. Hey man, is she like your special lady friend?"

"Yes Buzz, she's my special lady friend."

"Far out man, that's very cool. Hey, so follow me, I have my van outside, what hotel are you guys staying at?"

"We're staying at the Rex Hotel; do you know it?"

"Oh yeah, it's a real classy place, man."

"Well, I booked you a room as well, since you're going to be chauffeuring us around, is that okay?" Rodin said.

"Oh yeah, man, that's far out. We'll be there in no time; traffic shouldn't be too bad at this time of night. If my memory serves me right, it's on Nguyen Hue Boulevard."

Rodin was in the front with Buzz and Isala was seated in the backseat. Rodin was afraid to ask, "So, how's…"

Buzz interrupted, "He's doing fine, I really think he's much happier here than he was in Jamaica. I think he even has a girlfriend. I don't see him like I use to, which in some respects makes me sad, but I am happy for him.'"

Isala leaned forward and asked, "Who are you taking about?"

Buzz looked at Rodin in disbelief, "You've never told her about Bumbley Bee? And she's your special lady."

"Well, Buzz I thought it best come from you."

"Who's Bumbley Bee?" the tone in her voice made it clear that Isala wanted answers.

Buzz regaled her with the amazing tale of Bumbley Bee, of how they first met, of their decades long friendship, and how a couple years ago a group of fish thieves tried to fishnap the behemoth grouper for an Arab sheiks private aquarium, but thanks to Rodin and Le Gang de la Clé de Singe, Bumbley was saved and relocated into these waters, where he's not alone.

"Wow, I would love to meet Bumbley Bee, think we might be able to swing it dear?"

"What do you think Buzz?" Rodin inquired.

"For sure man, no problemo. So, what brings you guys to my neck of the world?"

"Pangolins."

"Hey, I've heard of those man, they're those cute scaly little buggers. People eat them, I've seen them on the menu, and they go for over three hundred dollars each. It's a big smuggling operation here."

"Well, I'm here to try and stop it, or at least slow it down."

"Well if there's anything you need, just let me know, I'd love to help."

"Thanks Buzz, I appreciate it."

They pulled up to the valet parking station, left the van and checked in; then rode up on the elevator where Buzz was on the third floor and Rodin and Isala were on four. As Buzz got off the elevator Rodin said, "Hey Buzz, how about we meet down in the lobby at eight o'clock?"

"Far out, man. See you kids in the AM, good night."

"Night, buddy."

After breakfast, Isala said that she had some work to do up in the room, so she said good-bye to Rodin and Buzz. As they went to get the van from the valet, Rodin went by the concierge desk and asked the young lady, "Do you have a package for Mr. Thompson, room 404?"

"Let me see sir." She went into the mailroom and came out with a small package and handed it to him, "Yes sir, here it is."

"Thank you." He said as he handed her a tip.

They headed out to the parking lot and the valet handed Buzz the keys. As they were driving away Buzz asked, "Where to man?"

"Look Buzz, the less you know the better about what's going on, okay?"

"Whatever you say, man."

"Good, take me to the Vin Tower Office Complex, 33 Quách Văn Tuấn."

As it turned out the office building was only twenty minutes away from the hotel. Buzz dropped Rodin in front of the building and told him that he would wait for him at the G-Café at the end of the block.

Rodin got out of the van and entered the building. He looked on the lobby directory and found TPF Nhập khẩu xuất khẩu, next to it was the English translation TPF Import Export, fifteenth floor. He pressed the elevator up button, when the doors opened, he got in and selected the top floor. He rode alone to the fifteenth floor, the doors opened and as he exited the elevator, he walked down a long hallway to where two men were standing guard outside the end office.

As he approached one of the men held up his hand for him to stop. "Bạn muốn gì?"

"I'm sorry I do not speak Vietnamese; I am here to see Bùi Xuân."

"What is your name?"

"Thompson. Lynn Thompson."

"You wait here."

The man entered the office while the other man stood with his arms crossed staring at Rodin, there was no expression whatsoever on the man's face. The man came out into the hall and said, "Okay." He gestured that Rodin raise his hands so as to be searched for weapons; he did as he was told. They found no weapons. The two men followed him into the office, they were right behind him, one on each side.

The office was one large room, at the far end of the room was a middle-aged man sitting behind a large wooden desk, in front of the desk were two guest chairs and off to the left was a wooden cadenza. Behind Bùi Xuân was a large painting of a flower field with two women walking in a field of bright yellow flowers, it was signed by one of Vietnams most celebrated artist Le Thanh Son, Rodin was impressed.

As Rodin started to approach the man behind the desk, he took one step and did a quick pivot to his right and slammed his heel into the man's rights instep arch causing the man to keel over in pain, Rodin then brought his knee up and smashed it into the man's face, knocking him backwards unconscious. Seing the other man reaching for his holstered gun, Rodin quickly punched the man in the face breaking his jaw. He leaned down and took the man's pistol and pointed it Bùi Xuân who sat at his desk calmly. He smiled and said,

"Very good Mr. Thompson, they were two of my best. I am surprised that you knocked Ngo Diem out so easily."

Rodin opened his right hand and let the roll of quarters drop into his left. "We call that a sucker punch in the Chicago."

"What is it you want Mr. Thompson?"

Rodin sat down in one of the chairs facing Bùi Xuân, leaned back and said, "I want two things, first all trafficking in pangolins must stop and secondly you will wire-transfer seven hundred thousand US dollars into the account of Save the Pangolins Foundation by the end of today."

"That's not going to happen Mr. Thompson. I cannot authorize either of those demands. You see, we are just one part of a multinational conglomerate who was many corporate board members, a decision this big would take months of discussions."

"I see. In all organizations there are dozens of men like yourself who can say no, but there is always one man who can say yes. Who is that man?"

"You're very wise Mr. Thompson, but I cannot give you his name."

"Then I'm afraid you're no further use to me, Mr. Bùi Xuân." Rodin aimed the gun at the man sitting across from him.

"Wait, I will try." He dialed the number on the office phone and pushed the button for speaker phone."

The voice sounded mature with a British accent, "Yes, what is it."

"I'm sorry to bother you Mr. Morgan, but we have a situation here, there is a man sitting across from me holding a gun demanding that we stop all trading in pangolins and in addition we must wire-transfer seven hundred thousand US dollars into the account of Save the Pangolins Foundation by the end of day."

"Just who the fuck does he think he is?"

"His name is Mr. Thompson, and he is threating to shoot me if we don't meet his demands."

"Are you on speaker?"

"Yes sir."

"Thompson, you're fucking crazy if you think we're going to stop anything or pay you one red cent. Do you understand."

"Mr. Morgan, have you ever heard of Le Gang de la Clé de Singe?"

"Oh, so you're from some fucking French terrorist group threating me and my organization and I'm supposed to shit myself, well you can go and fuck yourself Thompson. You understand me ?"

Rodin, still pointing the gun at Bùi Xuân fired and killed the man sitting opposite him.

POP

"Mr. Morgan, you're going to need to fill a position in this office. Morgan, it won't be in today, he won't be tomorrow or next week. As for you I'll coming with a vengeance. Oh, and Mr. Morgan you better hope to God that none of your family members are in anyway involved, do you understand me?"

Rodin hung up the phone and proceeded to place the calling card of Le Gang de la Clé de Singe on the three dead in the room, he also placed two pangolin scales, one on each of Bùi Xuân's eyes. As he was leaving, he noticed an address book on Bùi Xuân's desk that was filled with names, numbers and address of hundreds of contacts that he put in his coat pocket.

When he entered the G-Café, Buzz was chatting up the woman behind the counter, "Hey Buzz, what's good here?" Rodin asked.

"You gotta try the Bánh patê sô, it's to die for."

"Yeah, there's a lot of that going around."

Detective Nguyen interviewed Bao Dinh and got a positive IDs on the two men who robbed him, Pham Van Duc, aka Jiggy Janks and Nguyen Van Lu, aka Lil Steez. Bao identified the shooter as and the man who shot him as Thao Pham, aka K Dawg.

There had been rumors that Pham Van Duc, aka Jiggy Janks and Nguyen Van Lu, aka Lil Steez have gone missing, either that or they've run away to escape the police. Detective Nguyen was on his way to pick up and arrest the man accused of shooting Bao Dinh, Thao Pham, aka K Dawg.

The police were sent to his last known address, but he wasn't there. Detective Nguyen arrived at the Vin Ninh Marina only to find Thao Pham's boat was missing, the harbormaster informed the detective that his records show that Thao Pham had slipped out of the harbor six hours ago.

Detective Nguyen contacted the Vietnamese Coast Guard, *Cảnh sát biển Việt Nam*, which literally means "Sea police of Vietnam, to be on the lookout for a boat named, "Buoys in the Hood" and Thao Pham, who they should consider to be armed and dangerous.

Buzz's forty-three-and-a-half foot Spindrift Sunrise; the Sweet Mary Jane sat at the end of the Vin Ninh Marina with its engine idling. Rodin and Isala made their way down the length of the dock passing mostly small fishing boats and a few Chinese junks until at docks end floated a small bluish cloud of diesel. Rodin was waving his arms wildly like a madman trying to disperse the cloud of choking fumes. Rodin yelled, "Hey Buzz, you're killing us!"

As they approached the SMJ the cloud of fumes started to lift, and they could see Buzz casting off the bowline and as he turned around, he waved with a big grin. "Welcome, aboard, guys."

Isala and Rodin climbed over the port railing. "Wow Buzz, what a great boat." Isala said as she was receiving a big bear hug.

"Thanks, I'm like a hermit crab, man. I take my home wherever I go, man. So, you guys ready to go out?"

"How long have been you sailing?" she asked.

"Oh, wow man; I guess it's been over thirty years. It was the early seventies, when Crosby, Still, Nash and Young were recording their Deja Vu album, man. One day when they had some down time David Crosby took me out sailing, and I was like hooked. Hey, could you unhook that line?" Buzz said pointing to the aft. "And, we'll be off." Rodin obliged and gave a thumbs up.

Buzz took the helm and slowly started to steer toward starboard taking the SMJ away from the dock and into the channel leading out of the marina. Vịnh Vân Phong Bay was like glass as they started to head east. When they were about a mile out of the marina Buzz cut the engine and started to drop the sails. He first dropped the Mainsail and the jib and because the wind was light, he dropped the Halfwinder. He left the Genoa and the Yankee sails rolled as they weren't needed, he only ever unfurled them in case he needed extra oomph or stability.

The Mainsail had a ten-foot graphic of a peace sign and the jib was one enormous, tie-dyed canvas that could be seen for miles. Buzz slowly made his way aft to take the wheel where Rodin and Isala were sitting on either side of the cockpit. Buzz looked right at home standing at the wheel wearing an old pair of Levi's cutoffs, a Rolling Stones Steel Wheels t-shirt, a pair of John Lennon round sunglasses and worn-out Topsiders as he was leaning into the wind.

Rodin looked at Isala and smiled, he enjoyed looking at Buzz in his element as Master and Commander: on the far side of the world. Not exactly Russell Crowe, but then again Russell Crowe was no Buzz Murdoch.

Isala asked, "So, Buzz tell us about your boat."

"Yacht."

"Right, yacht. Tell us something about your yacht."

"What would you like to know?"

She thought for a minute, "Tell me about the engines."

Buzz looked at her, "Really? Okay. The engine is a Ford Lehman, its diesel, and is a direct drive with a propeller shaft transmission. She holds about 900 liters and burns an average of 4 liters an hour. How's that? What else would you like to know?

"Wow." Isala said. "How big is she?"

"She's forty-three and a half feet long, with a S-shaped hull, she has three cabins, one head, that's bathrooms for you land lubbers, a full galley and a saloon. As you can see, she has teak side decks and a teak cockpit, down below you'll find that there is teak throughout, and just to ease your mind, we have the latest Furuno GPS, a Danforth compass, Autohelm 7000 hydraulisch autopilot, and a Navtex weather fax receiver." Buzz gave them both a bit of a playful look. "Satisfied that I know my shit, man?"

Isala was impressed, "I never doubted you for a minute. She's beautiful, Buzz."

"Yeah, I love her. There's nothing better being out here, away from everything. It really keeps me centered man."

"Have you ever sailed to any other countries in Asia?"

"No, I'm happy right here and besides I don't like to leave Bumbley for too long."

Buzz started to slow the Sweet Mary Jane by making a long sweeping arc so as to start maneuvering around the tip of Hon Lon Island. He jumped out of the cockpit and dropped the Mainsail, just relying on the jib to bring her into the lagoon. He shouted to Rodin, "Rodin, pull back on the lever with the grey knob, it releases the anchor!"

"Aye, aye, captain!" Rodin yelled. The 45-pound anchor dropped creating a loud splash at the bow.

Buzz was walking back to Isala and Rodin after he collapsed the jib, "You kids hungry? You want some munchies, some vino, beer or maybe do a doobie, man?"

Rodin nodded, "I'm a little hungry."

Isala took off her bathing suit cover up to reveal blue and white one-piece said, "Me too, I'll go, which way is the kitchen?"

"It's ah, called the galley, and it's down below, want I should show you?"

"No, you guys stay here, if I need help, I'll holler."

"That's cool; I got all kinds of stuff, man. Just take anything you want. Me casa, su casa, man."

Isala took the five steps down the semi curved teak steps into the saloon. She was taken back on how beautiful and spacious it was, it was all teak. There was a booth on the left with navy blue cushions surrounding a teak chart table with a lip all around so in rough seas any tableware wouldn't slip off. To the right were two unfixed captain chairs in the same navy blue fabric. Just beyond the saloon was a step down to the galley. She stepped down into the galley, it was very compact, but she didn't feel cramped, everything was right at her fingertips. She started to investigate; she opened the small refrigerator door and found some cold cuts, mustard and pickles. There was a small bucket on the counter filled with beer on ice next to one of the open cabinets she spied a loaf of bread and with an open bag of cookies.

Moments later, Isala came running from below deck in a panic. "Buzz, I saw a couple giant rats! In your kitchen, they were huge! One ran across my foot!" she said with a shudder.

"It's the galley, and they weren't rats. Was one chocolate brown and the other cinnamon colored?"

"I think so, it happened so fast."

"It was Bosco and Groucho, they're my ferrets, man. I keep 'em around cause their good mousers, man. I'll show you, Groucho, Bosco come!"

Two ferrets come running scurrying across the teak deck, stopping at Buzz's feet. Buzz picks them up and shows them off.

"See, Bosco is that yummy chocolate brown color and Groucho has a little dark patch under his nose, which looks like a little moustache."

"Aw, they're so cute."

Rodin laughed saying, "Sure, now they're cute, a minute ago they were evil and disgusting rats."

"Shut up. It was quite a start." She said.

Buzz took the two ferrets and set them in the cockpit, "You guys stay in here until I call you." The ferrets looked at him and laid down and snuggled up intertwined where you could hardly tell where one began and the other ended.

Isala headed back to the galley, "I'm heading down to the 'galley' to bring back lunch, everyone want beer?"

"Yeah, a beer would be cool, and a chunk of cheese, man." Buzz replied.

Isala comes out from below with a tray with three ham and cheese sandwiches, a bowl of Cheetos, three beers and a hunk of cheddar cheese. Buzz takes the hunk and takes a bite then breaks the remaining cheese in half, calls out to his furry friends, who come scampering out of the cockpit and sit at Buzz's feet. Buzz leans down, giving one half to Bosco and the other to Groucho. They each take their piece of cheese and bounce back down to the cockpit.

Isala hands Rodin a sandwich and a beer, then presented a plate and beer to Buzz. Buzz waved off the sandwich but took the beer.

"Not hungry right now, maybe after I have a beer, and if no one objects, a little doobie." Buzz pulls out a joint from his shirt pocket and lights up. He reaches over flips a switch, and the boats stereo kicks on. It plays the Grateful Dead's "Truckin". "Ah, the pause that refreshes, right, boys." The two ferrets pop their heads up and make a couple of squeaks and squeals, then drop back down.

Rodin holds up is beer as a salute, "Buzz, this is awesome. I guess the sixties still live."

"Tell you the truth, I don't remember too much of the sixties. I don't think I remember much of the seventies either, man. I do remember the eighties; I remember that they really sucked, man. Disco, what a bummer, man. Talk about the day the music died, and It's been pretty much downhill since, man."

Isala got up and put her plate back on the tray, she sat next to Buzz. "Buzz, you've must have a great time living here."

"It's been really a gas, man. That is, until recently, man. A friend of mine was shot by a couple of thugs trying to shake him down for protection. I was talking to a detective yesterday, he said they can't find the guys who shot him anywhere. But hey, you know what, fuck it, man. Let's not have those creeps bum us out. I think I'll introduce you to my special buddy, Bumbley."

He walked towards the aft and just before heading down to the galley he turned to Rodin and Isala and said, "You guys wait here I'm going to get him his treat. Be right back." Buzz made his way down past the galley to the first cabin where a opened the drawer under the bed and pulled out a canvas bag about the size of a microwave oven, then headed up to the deck. When he got topside, he opened the drawstring on the canvas bag and pulled out a 26-pound brisket of beef. He pulled a 12-foot piece of cord from the a cabinet and tied a bowline sailors knot around the hunk of beef, he slowly lowered it and out of the water. "It won't be long now."

Isala was visibly excited looking overboard. "Wow, I can't wait to see the Bee."

The water was clear with about 15-feet visibility; the yacht sat at around 50 feet above the bottom. They saw a school of barracudas cruising under the boat that must have gotten scent of the brisket, when all of a sudden, they darted away in a hurry. Slowly from below an image of something that kind of looked like small two-man immersible began to rise to the surface. Buzz lowered the brisket into the water, "Here he comes."

Isala said in astonishment, "Oh my God!" Her eyes got as big as saucers.

Buzz pulled the knot and the brisket fell loose and in a blink of an eye the meat was gone. Buzz walked to the back of the yacht, Rodin and Isala followed him as he stepped onto the teak boat swim platform and waited. The behemoth surfaced next to the platform where Buzz sat down and started to rub the back of the beast. It turned on its side, its head sticking slightly out of the water so Buzz could rub around its great mouth, his eyes looked like they were rolling back into its head.

After a few minutes Buzz patted the fish on the head and said, "Okay big guy I'll come down and see you a little later." The fish turned and headed down to the bottom to wait for his friend. Buzz stood up and climbed back onto the deck, "So what do you think?"

"That was fucking awesome Buzz." Rodin said as he just plopped down on the port side cushion opposite the cockpit.

"Yeah, he's pretty cool." Buzz passed the cockpit and dropped the cord from the brisket on the deck and headed towards the hatch leading to the galley, "Think I'll grab another beer. You guys want anything?"

Isala was standing by the hatch and said, "I'll go Buzz. I know where the kitchen, err galley is. Be right back."

Isala heads down to the galley, as she's grabbing a couple of bottles of beer, she catches a glimpse of movement to her right. She thought it might be the ferrets, but when she turns, she is surprised to see a man dressed in outrageous outfit is pointing a gun at her with a big shit eating grin on his face.

She screamed.

"I guess Isala must have run into Bosco again." Buzz said. Then he notices both ferrets are still asleep in the cockpit. He was ready to say something snarky to Isala when she emerged from below, then he saw her with what looks like an Asian Snoop Dog walking behind her coming out from below deck. K Dawg and Isala step out from the darkness of the saloon onto the deck, the man is holding a gun.

He pushes Isala in Rodin's direction, "Well Scooby Doo! S'up, dawgs."

Rodin catches Isala as she is stumbling towards him and swings her down next to him. "Who the Hell are you?" Rodin asked.

"It's time we break it down, boys and girls." He points the gun toward Buzz, "Hey, geezer sit your ass down there or I'll blow your fucking head off, ya dig?"

Buzz's high came crashing down as he inched his way towards the cockpit. He sat down to the right of his friends behind the helm, his face was getting red and he shouted, "Hey, man. Did you have anything to do with shooting Bao Dinh, man?"

Rodin grabbed Buzz's arm, "Buzz! Chill."

"No, man. If he's going to kill me, at least I want to know, man." Buzz said.

K Dawg with a big grin on his face said, "Dats cool, man. The hippies right, I'm gonna clock ya'll, so if you got questions, let's hear them."

"So, you shot Bao, man?" Buzz demanded.

"Yeah, man, I shot little fuck."

Rodin was holding Isala tightly to him, he was thinking what are his options, could he get to the gun before this crazy lunatic starts shooting, could he at least get Isala safely overboard and more importantly what's Buzz thinking. Rodin thought maybe they could talk their way out of this. As long as the gunman is talking, he's not shooting and that's a good thing.

"What's this really about?" Rodin asked

"He knows, dawg!" pointing at Buzz.

Buzz said, "Yeah, you needed to make an example of Bao so the other merchants would fall in line, right? So, when Bao wouldn't play ball with you, you shot him. But you botched it, you didn't kill him, and he identified you and those two goons of yours. You know the police are looking everywhere for you, so you figured kill me and steal my boat."

Isala said, "Yacht."

Buzz looked at her and smiled, "Right, yacht."

"Right on, old man. I popped that little fuck cause he gave me no respect, also I wasted those bumbling fools, Jiggy and that stupid moron sidekick of his, Lil Steez, they're sleeping with the fishes. Like ya'll be. Now everyone move to the very back or we end it all right here." K Dawg motioned everyone aft waving the pistol.

As K Dawg was following his three captives aft, he inadvertently bumped into the helm, waking the sleeping ferrets. A startled Groucho jumps up on the gangsta's leg, who instinctively spins around and fires his gun, freaking out Bosco, causing him to leap to up onto the gunman's stomach, throwing him off balance, as he's spinning around, he gets his feet tangled up in the cord Buzz dropped on the deck from feeding Bumbley, forcing him to lose his balance and he goes overboard.

Bosco and Groucho both fall into the water with him. As the three of them hit the water the two ferrets let go and instinctively start swimming towards the teak swim platform and scamper up onto the platform and hop back into the safety of the cockpit.

Buzz grabbed an orange ring lifesaver as Rodin and Isala scramble to the starboard side. K Dawg was flailing in the water trying to swim while still holding onto the gun. Buzz yells, "Here, grab this!" as he tossed the orange ring. As he was trying to grab hold of the lifesaver something quickly emerges from down below, it's Bumbley. He was drawn to the surface to investigate all the commotion. As the drowning man is thrashing about in the water, he inadvertently kicks Bumbley. K Dawg thought that he kicked a shark that was coming to attack him, he fired several shots into the water.

POP POP POP POP

Buzz kept shouting out to the drowning man, "Grab the lifesaver, man it's right next to you. That's just a fish not a shark!" Rodin was getting ready to dive in when Bumbley who had been shot twice had had enough of this aggression, he dropped down below the surface, got a running start upwards with his mammoth mouth wide open and swallowed K Dawg, whole.

Isala starting to sob, "Oh, God, oh, my God, what a horrible way to go."

Buzz looked at Rodin, "That fucking asshole shot Bumbley. I'm going to suit up and check on him."

Buzz went below and quickly changed into his SCUBA gear, grabbed a spear gun, then leaped into the water. He was down for close to an hour. When he emerged from the dive, both Rodin and Isala could tell it was bad.

Rodin asked, "How's Bumbley?"

"He's dead. That creep killed him. I had to come up, I just couldn't stay down there and watch the sharks devour him."

Isala gave him a hug, "Oh, Buzz I'm so sorry."

"Well, we did have eighteen years together, aside from Rodin, he was my best friend. He died saving my life."

Buzz got out of his diving gear and went below to change into something dry. When he came up, he went to the bow and weighed anchor, then set sail back to Vin Ninh Marina without saying a word.

"I guess I should go to the cops and tell Detective Nguyen what happened, how that crazy fuck tried to kill me, and got into a fight with the ferrets, fell overboard, and a big shark ate him. Cause nobody's going to believe what really happened. I'll be sure to leave you guys out of it. Well, that's going to be my story and I'm sticking to it. Now let's get the fuck outta here, man." Buzz said trying to man up and be stoic.

"Hey man, Isala and I can't tell you how sorry we are. We feel it's partially our fault, if we hadn't wanted to go sailing this might not have happened."

"Who knows what would have happened if we did things differently. Maybe that crazy fuck would have killed us all. No man, it happened like it was supposed to happen. I've got no regrets; me and the Bee had a great run, you know. Sometimes you just got to say, what the fuck."

It took less than an hour to return to the marina, everyone was silent, Buzz was deep in thought, as he sailed into the harbor, and looked around he thought, what a long, strange trip it's been, man.

Buzz met Detective Nguyen at Bao's Grocery store, Bao had just been released from the hospital, he was in a wheelchair looking weak, but grateful to be alive. Cam had brought her mother in from Tuy Hòa to help out at the store until Bao was feeling well enough to return to work. The store was back to being prosperous, now that K Dawg's street gang was no longer harassing people.

"What is it you wanted to tell me, Mr. Murdock? And why here?" Detective Nguyen asked.

"Well detective, this afternoon while I was out on my yacht, I was briefly held hostage by K Dawg. Unbeknownst to me he stowed away on my yacht and when I was anchored off of Hon Lon Island, he revealed himself to me, he had a weapon and threatened to kill me. We struggled and at one point his feet got tangled up in some rope and he was knocked overboard. Before I could save him, he drowned and was attacked by sharks. As he threatened me, he revealed to me that he had killed his two gang members Junky Janks and Little Skeez."

"I think they were called Jiggy Janks and Lil Steez." Detective Nguyen corrected Buzz.

"Right."

"Well, Mr. Murdock that is quite a tale. Is there anyone who can corroborate your story?"

"I'm afraid not, detective."

"All right Mr. Murdock, if you would be so kind as to come down to the police station tomorrow and make an official statement, I would appreciate it. If there is nothing else, I shall see you tomorrow; good day."

When Detective Nguyen had gone, Bao asked him, "So, Buzz you can tell us what really happened."

"That is what happened, honest. Bao, how are you feeling?"

"I am still very weak, but everyday I'm getting my strength back, soon I'll be able to take over the store again."

"Listen, you're lucky to be alive, right Cam?"

"We are so blessed that he is still with us."

"Listen, I wanted you to know that I have decided to go back to America. I'll probably take sail in a couple of days. So, I'm going to need plenty of supplies from you guys."

"What about Bumbley?" Bao asked.

"Bumbley passed away a couple days ago."

Cam put her arm on Buzz's shoulder, "Oh Buzz, we are so very sorry for your loss."

"Thank you both for the kindness you've shown me; I will miss you both. But I'll see you a lot before I go."

Buzz gave them both a hug and he was off back to the Sweet Mary Jane.

The two-day journey to the Xishuangbanna in the southwestern Yunnan province was uneventful. The team kept a watchful eye on the state-run news media about the Tiger Farm incident. In the newspapers, there was a brief one column and a small blurp on television. But they knew playing down of the killings was just for public consumption. Behind the scenes, the government wasn't going to allow this massacre to go unanswered, so the Red Team had to stay inconspicuous and act fast.

Outside Xishuangbanna to the west in the foothills of the Tea Mountains on the Luisha River is the village of Menghai. It is reported to have two bear farms that are purportedly owned by the same man, a Zhang Changpu. It is said that he is a man of great wealth and political connections.

Zhang Changpu, 66 years old lives on a large six-acre estate, with a five thousand square foot mansion, swimming pool, and private dock with a forty-foot yacht on the Lancang River. He is married to Zhang Qiaolian, 63 who, by all accounts is the driving force behind these bear bile farms. It's just the two of them, they have no children, they raise Shar Pei show dogs, which they have had several best in show award winners.

Fearing that such a large group of foreigners would attract undo suspicion Zhi Ruo had made arrangements with a trusted sympathizer Qin Ehuang whose father owns a natural rubber plantation, which has several dormitories that are currently vacant due to the seasonal nature of the collecting and processing.

Once reaching the outskirts of Xishuangbanna traveling on the G214 heading into the town center they split off the main highway onto a feeder road, the X179 that eventually turned into Lantsangjiang Road. Staying on that road for eight miles they turned off onto 093 Country Road, which is not a road for the faint of heart. It has more twist and turns than a cheap garden hose.

Since turning off onto the country road it took three hours to reach the plantation, where they found Qin Ehuang sitting on the veranda, waiting for them. Qin Ehuang was in her mid-thirties, tall and quite striking, well-educated and thankfully could speak English.

Zhi Ruo and Qin Ehuang greeted each other as old friends do, big hugs and kisses. Zhi Ruo introduced Qin Ehuang to the team and gave her a brief and sketchy overview of why they're there. Iceman told her that by her aiding them that she was placing herself and family at risk, he wanted her to consider that before she agreed to help them.

"Thank you for your consideration. I have discussed this with my father, and we are in agreement that this is the right thing to do." Qin Ehuang said.

The Iceman told her, "We will do everything we can to not implicate you, so please no questions; the less you know the better."

"I understand."

They settled into their dorm rooms; they were going to have the next day off so they could get rejuvenated after spending two days of bone jarring roads. The Iceman, Tommy G, and Zhi Ruo would take a ride to scope out the two bear bile farms in the village of Menghai and the estate of Zhang Changpu.

The initial plan was to have several local Le Gang de la Clé de Singe members rendezvous with half of the Red Team to seize control of the farms and rescue all the bears and then transport them 420 kilometers to a bear sanctuary outside Hoang Lien National Park, Vietnam. While Iceman, Sassoon aka Mason Barnes, and Zhi Ruo would visit the home of Mr. and Mrs. Zhang Changpu to give them a little taste of their own medicine.

The Red Team started out from the plantation three hours before sunrise. They made it to the first bear farm just as the sun was rising. They were all wearing black uniforms, black gloves, black balaclavas, and tinted goggles so no one would be able to tell their race. They were all carrying Glock 19's equipped with silencers.

Odin, Jimmy the Chew, Vulcan, and Tommy G were dropped off at farm number one, while T-Bone, Venus, and Gianfranco would take possession of farm two until the rest of the team could join them.

As Odin and his team approached the warehouse where the bears were kept, they realized that the word farm was just a picturesque term to paint an idyllic image of the reality and horror they were about to discover when they entered.

Outside the "farm" they could hear the sounds of the bears suffering and crying. When they entered, the stench was unbearable. They found a handful of attendants preparing the bears for the milking of their gallbladders.

Odin had seen all sorts of animal cruelty, but this was indescribable. Bears in cages so small that they couldn't stand on all fours; a couple cages were so confining that the bears couldn't even turn over. All the adult bears had metal catheters inserted into the stomachs draining the bile. In one corner there were four bear cubs in a single cage crying for their mothers.

A man in a lab coat came rushing towards the group yelling at them in anger, gesturing for them to leave. Odin raised his gun and shot him dead.

PHIFF

He then walked throughout the rest of the "farm" disposing of the rest of the cruel heartless offenders of nature.

Le Gang de la Clé de Singe local members arrived with four veterinarians who went and started treating the most seriously endangered animals. The rescue team had all five hundred bears ready for transport in six hours. They left the farm with the bears in an eight-truck caravan. While the bears were being rescued Odin and his team prepped the scene with the Le Gang de la Clé de Singe signature flags and declarations.

It was early afternoon when Odin and the rest of the Red Team arrived at the second farm, it was identical as the first farm. By the time Odin and crew entered the building the rescue team had almost evacuated all four hundred bears. The team had already prepped the deceased and were ready to move out, after Odin gave it a quick once over, and placed the signature fingerprint that would drive the authorities nuts, it was that of Chiang Kai-shek.

The Iceman, Sassoon, and Zhi Ruo entered the residence of Zhang Changpu as the Red Team were rescuing the bears from the "farms", pre-sunrise. They found Zhang Changpu and bride sleeping in separate bedrooms. The Iceman and Zhi Ruo gently woke them up with a slight sap to the head with a gun. Zhang Changpu and the misses were herded downstairs into the basement where two bear cages were awaiting them. Zhang Changpu struggled briefly but was quickly subdued from an injection of Pentothal, an anesthesia given to both of them that would have them sleeping until the procedure was complete. Sassoon did the procedure of implanting catheters into their stomachs.

When Zhang Changpu and his wife were brought around, they discovered that they couldn't move, the cages they were in was so confining they didn't have the room to take a deep breath. As the anesthesia was wearing off, they complained of severe discomfort.

Zho Ruo explained that was because they were having their bile was being extracted from their bodies just like the bears on their farms. She told them that the catheters that were implanted, came from the farm. Zhang Qiaolian, the wife declared that she had nothing to do with the bear farms that it was all her husband; if anyone should be punished it should be him and not her.

The more the effects of anesthesia wore off the more painful the catheters were becoming, plus the discomfort of confinement of the cages was excruciatingly unbearable.

The two captives were crying out in pain, but to no avail. Iceman, Sassoon and Zhi Ruo had gone up stairs, while they let them experience the painful treatment that they inflected on thousands of bears over dozens of years. The bears suffered for their greed.

When the Iceman and Zhi Ruo returned several hours later he revealed who they represented, and he held up the yellow banner.

When the police found Zhang Qiaolian and his wife dead in bear cages with Le Gang de la Clé de Singe flags around their necks and a proclamation that their deaths were more than justified due to the heinous acts of cruelty.

The police officers told the Chinese authorities that photographs and videos of the horrible conditions how the bears were kept for years were being sent to multiple world news organizations as well as incriminating photos of the criminal acts that had been conducted at the Tiger Farm.

The Iceman and Red Team had one more stop; Yunnan Wild Animal Park in Kunming, the park that China has started importing rhinos for potential "farming".

The Chinese believe that rhino horn can help treat everything from cancer to gout when consumed in powder form. Even if their intentions are good, the relocation of these gentle giants are proving to be difficult and they are having a hard time surviving in a rainforest-type environment. In addition, there's concern about nutrition and their overall ability to cope. The rhinos need to have supplementary food, or they'll starve.

It appears that the government looks to be on the verge of legalizing the consumption of farmed rhino horn for "medicinal use" which would increase poaching.

While making their way to the Yunnan Wild Animal Park, the Iceman received a coded text from Wooch saying that the rhino mission has been terminated, and the Red Team are ordered to make their way to Phonsavan, Laos and await further instructions. They were to drop Zhi Ruo and the weapons at a safe house in Xishuangbanna, then proceed on to Laos. The explanation that was given for the change in plans was that the Chinese had deployed hundreds of troops to secure the state sanctioned "farms" from what they were calling, foreign aggression.

"Good evening I'm Nigel Williams and this is the BBC World Headline News. Our top story this hour is once again news of the eco-terrorist group Le Gang de la Clé de Singe. The radical organization has attacked a so-called tiger farm that was raising tiger to slaughter for their meat, skin, teeth, claws and bones to use in tiger bone wine. They also attacked a bear-bile farm that enslaved bears by housing them in cruel confining and restrictive cages hooked up to catheters for years.

The raids rescued hundreds of animals and reportedly sent them to sanctuaries in neighboring countries. They have reportedly killed 37 owners and workers in these facilities. The group has sent disturbing videos and photos of the "farms" that they sent to news organizations as well as multiple wildlife institutions around the world.

After great internal debate, we have decided that the public has a right to view these videos. But we must warn you that the images you are about to see are quite disturbing. Viewer discretion is advised; we strongly suggest that no one under the age of sixteen should view these images..."

Mr. Roger Blumenthal, the new President and CEO of the Hunting Network along with the new President of W.A.S.P. Mr. Thurston Bentley Hart the third, and retired Commander William "Wooch" Brown were meeting at the Hunting Network's headquarters in New York City for the first time since that terrible tragedy happened in Africa.

"Gentlemen, I want to thank you both for taking this meeting. Since the airing of our documentary "The Big Five" last week, which by the way was the most highly viewed television show ever in the history of television, thank you very much. People have been clamoring for more, so I know that if we put our heads together, we could come up with something as big." Blumenthal proclaimed.

"Roger, people were killed, murdered and all you care about is ratings? That's disgusting!" Thurston blasted.

"Listen Thurston, I know that since that incident, W.A.S.P. was seen an increase in membership like never before. You're enrollment is skyrocketing thru the roof, so don't play that holier than thou routine with me, pal."

Wooch stepped in to try and calm things down, "Gentlemen please, let's try and be civil. What exactly are you wanting, Roger? Are you wanting to try and do another hunting reality challenge show, because I think you might have a hard time finding contestants, since the last ones were all killed. And why did you happen to invite me? I was just an acting consultant for the last show."

"I know Wooch, if I may call you that, I just thought that with your military expertise you might bring some insights. I have an idea, now just hear me out. What if we can get, let's say, six volunteers from W.A.S.P. and six members from Le Gang de la Clé de Singe to challenge each other for a winner take all prize. Come on now Thurston, just listen; what if we drop each team of six on opposite sides of a deserted island and the first team, or team member that reaches the other side wins."

Thurston was getting excited, "No, no, not who gets to the other side of the island, that's like playing flag football. No, Roger, it's go big or go home time. Its which team members are still alive; it's literally winner take all. Our best six hunters against those French bastards best six. They've always had the advantage in the past because they were always on the offensive, but now they won't have that advantage."

"Whoa, wait a minute. You're talking about a TV show where the object of the show is for people to kill each other, for real and the winners get money? That's insane, no government will allow that to be broadcast on the air." Argued Wooch.

"So, we'll stream it on the Web, and sell it as pay-per-view event subscription; it'll run 24/7 as long as the fighting continues. And you know we can get sponsors to put up the prize money. Thurston, this is going to be, as a certain friend of mine says, this is going to be yuge!"

"Okay, okay, let's bring this back down to earth. First of all you have to find six people who are willing to risk their lives for what, money. And second of all what makes you think Le Gang de la Clé de Singe will even consider it?" Wooch argued.

Thurston was sitting with his eyes closed contemplating the possibilities when he said, "What if we promise Le Gang de la Clé de Singe 100 million dollars to be donated to the wildlife charity of their choice if they win? That way we won't be accused of financing terrorism, in addition, all W.A.S.P. members will stop all hunting of the big five. But if W.A.S.P. wins, Le Gang de la Clé de Singe will stop hunting big game hunters, but the hunting of poachers and all illegal traders would still be far game, as it were."

Roger's face lit up, "That's gold, Thurston, pure gold. Wooch?"

"You're both fucking nuts. Just the logistics and working out all the details, negotiations between sides, then you have to find an island whose country would allow such a thing to happen. It would be almost impossible and could take months and months, if it could be accomplished at all."

"Wooch, I can think of no one more qualified to take this on; you will be the impartial negotiator to try and make this happen, please? We will pay you whatever fee you want, please." pleaded Roger.

After much pleading and begging to take on the role of arbitrator and if this project were to go forward also the adjudicator, Wooch finally agreed.

When he was able to get to his private secure line, he made a phone call, "Wooch here, oh you're not going to believe this."

"Kanacea Island is a volcanic island with seven peaks in Fiji's Lau archipelago. It's eight square miles, with a maximum elevation of 850 feet. Currently there is a coconut and sugarcane plantation, which would have to be evacuated, of course. The island features many fresh water streams, and even has a deep-water port if needed. And best of all it's for sale for a mere twelve million." Wooch said as he passed around photos of the island along with the breakdown for the installation of video cameras, transportation costs, crew costs, medical unit costs, equipment costs, the list went on and on.

"Wooch, all this looks great, you've done an outstanding job, have you been in contact with Le Gang de la Clé de Singe?" Blumenthal asked.

"I have and they tell me that they are definitely interested, of course there's lots to be negotiated like is each team responsible for their own equipment, gear, and weapons, is it only firearms they're allowed to bring or are explosives allowed? Things like that."

"Yes, I see what you mean, well that's beyond my purview. I suggest you have someone from each organization, and you meet on neutral ground and iron these details out. As far as the island, go ahead and buy it. After this is all over, we can use it for other shows or maybe I'll just use it for myself, what the hell."

As Buzz driving Rodin and Isala to the airport he said, "Are you sure you and Isala can't stay longer, I sure could use the company now that Bumbley is gone, man."

"I know Buzz, but I have some pressing business in England I have to take care of. Maybe when it's done, we can plan to meet up somewhere and hang out. We sure could use a break, right babe?"

"That's for sure, but Buzz it's been a delight meeting you and I promise we'll get together soon.

"Okay. Well, here we are at Tan Son Nhat airport. You guys have a safe fight and I'll keep you posted. I think I might head back towards the good old USA, man. It's been a while."

Rodin and Isala grabbed their luggage out of the van and gave Buzz a bunch of hugs and kisses, then they were gone. Once they were gone and he was driving back to Vịnh Vân Phong Harbor, it really hit him that he was, for the first time in in a longtime he was all alone.

He felt better once he was back on the Sweet Mary Jane preparing for the journey home to America. His first stop would be sailing south to Jakarta, Indonesia, then head east thru the Java Sea on to Thursday Island off the northern most tip of Australia, and that's as far as he's planned.

He made one last trip to Bao's Grocery Store to say goodbye to his dear friends and to see how Boa was coping being confined to a wheelchair.

"How's it going, man? You're looking good."

"It is hard learning to adjust to only being half as tall as I used to be."

"True, but you scored a really cool set of wheels, man. I think all you need is to have some flames painted on the side, man."

"Buzz, it was very kind and generous of you to buy me this expensive wheelchair, you are too kind my friend."

"What are you talking about? I found that piece of junk when I was diving one day. I was going to use it as an anchor, man, but then you go and get shot. Hey, I'm glad you like it."

Cam having finished with some customers came by to say goodbye, "Buzz, you were so kind to buy Bao this special wheelchair. We're so sorry to see you go, please stay in touch."

"You know I will; I'll email you whenever I'm in port and you guys can email too. Let's not grow apart." Buzz gave each a big hug and took a couple of selfies before he left.

On the way back to the Sweet Mary Jane from the harbor on his skiff, he suddenly shut down the engine. In total astonishment, sitting in the harbor was the Tynan Institute of Oceanography's ship the Ogygia. He just sat there in the dinghy gob smacked, bobbing up and down like a cork in the water. The Ogygia was the ship that stole Bumbley from his lagoon in Jamaica all those many years ago, that set in motion Buzz contacting Rodin to come to the behemoth's rescue and was the reason that he and Bumbley ended up in Vịnh Vân Phong Harbor in Vietnam. He wondered if she was still on board, working, collecting rare and unusual species for rich Arab sheiks.

As he passed the 240-foot ship, he kept his head down until he was well clear of it. As he got closer to his yacht, he saw a Zodiac raft tied off onto its aft, and as he got closer, he saw her, Doctor Laura Runnel, she was every bit as beautiful as he remembered her to be.

"Hello Buzz, it's been a long time." She said. Her voice was just as sexy, and her smile was to die for.

"Hey Doc. What brings you to a không có thị trấn like this?"

"As you know, it's the không có thị trấn like this that some of the biggest finds are."

"So, what are you looking for here?"

"I have to confess that when I heard rumors about an old American hippe living on a yacht in the bay, I thought I'd swing by and look in on my friend. So, how are you doing, old friend?"

"Well, Doc to tell you the truth I'm actually planning on setting sail tomorrow and heading back to L.A."

"With Bumbley?"

"No, he was killed five days ago."

"Sharks?"

"No, some asshole shot him; thought he was a shark."

"What happened to the asshole who shot him?"

"Well that's the only good thing to come of this whole tragedy. Bumbley swallowed him whole and took him down to the bottom, where by the time I got suited up and got down there, my old friend, Bumbley was fading fast. I stayed with him until the end, I couldn't stand to wait around to see the sharks attack him, so I said my goodbyes and well left him, so nature would do her thing."

"Oh Buzz, I'm so sorry. How about we get out of these dinghies and have a drink, if I remember correctly, you make a hell of a Bloody Mary. What do ya say?"

"Sounds like a plan, Doc."

The hack stopped in front of a four-story brown brick apartment building at number twenty Aubrey Road. The sign on the brick fence stated that this was the Aubrey Lodge. The couple climbed the six stairs that led to the front door and pressed the doorbell marked "Manager".

A buzzer buzzed and the front door unlocked and opened slightly, an elderly woman, short, white curly hair, no makeup, smoking a Dunhill opened the door and asked, "Yeah?"

"Good day I'm Thomas Hamilton and this is my wife, Margaret. We've come about the furnished apartment on the top floor."

"Right you are. Here's the key, all the way up and to the right, number 44. There ain't no lift, so if that's a problem?"

Hamilton took the key, "It's no problem. We'll bring the key back down after we take a look. What apartment would you be in?"

"The one that says Manager, dearie. Don't bother knocking, door's open, just come on in."

Up four flights of stairs they climbed, once they pasted the second floor Isala challenged Rodin to a race to the top. He won by a step, "I'll get you next time." She said.

They opened the door and went in; the window blinds were up and, since they were facing west, the sun was shining in at this time in the afternoon. Isala handed Rodin the pair of Nikon 8X42 Monarch 7 binoculars she was carrying in her bag.

The Aubrey Lodge sits atop of a hill, which overlooks a small sliver of the Holland Park where the green belt dead ends into Holland Park Avenue. Now, it just so happens that on the other side of that small green belt of the Holland Park that separates middle-class Aubrey Road from snooty Holland Park Road is number 36 Holland Park, the white, four story, 5000 square residence of Sir Nigel Morgan.

"Can you see him?"

"Yep, he's sitting at his desk on his laptop facing us and the street, looks like he's talking, must have his phone on speaker. This is perfect, let's go see that lovely landlord."

They found their way to the manager's apartment, the front door was partially open, when they walked in and found her watching an old episode of 'Ab Fab', drinking a can of Bank's Bitter, and eating a bag of Walkers Prawn Cocktail crisps. Without turning her head from the telly she asked, "So, you Yanks want it or not?"

Rodin holding the key out to her said, "We'll take it. How soon can we move in?"

"You can move in right now, lovey. Just sign those bits 'n bobs on the table there and of course the first and lasts, and I don't take no checks."

"That's no problem, Mrs.?"

"Martin."

"How about I just pay cash, how would that be, Mrs. Martin?"

 "That would be brilliant, dearie."

Rodin had made a note of Mr. Morgan's residence after he discovered it in the address book that he found on Mr. Bùi Xuân's desk in Ho Chi Minh City. He copied the addresses of everyone in the book before sending it on to Wooch in Washington DC.

"Hello."

"May I speak with Mr. Jeffery Morgan, please."

"Speaking."

"Mr. Morgan, this is Mr. Thompson, we spoke several days ago when I was visiting Mr. Bùi Xuân. We had a brief discussion about the exporting of Pangolins and the transfer of seven hundred thousand US dollars into the account of Save the Pangolins Foundation, do you happen to remember that?"

"Yes, and I told you to fuck yourself."

"Ah, so you do remember, how nice. You know Mr. Morgan, I've done a bit of research on you and your family, and it seems that your wife Melinda is an avid big game hunter who likes to post photos of herself posing next to her trophy kills, like the one hanging on the wall behind you, of her with a giraffe. She's quite beautiful." Rodin was peering through his B-10, 1.8-10X42 sniper scope that was sitting atop his Mk-12 rifle.

Morgan didn't bother looking behind him, he stared straight-ahead and said, "Give me the account number of the Save the Pangolins Foundation and I will transfer the money while you're still on the phone."

"Excellent."

Rodin had Morgan in his sites when Isala whispered in his ear that the money transfer was confirmed.

"I see that the transfer has been completed, I thank you for your contribution. Now, there's the matter of the exportation of Pangolin's and Pangolin parts, Mr. Morgan."

"I will send an email to all my contacts to cease all collecting, all poaching, all killing of Pangolins immediately, how's that?"

"That would be wonderful, just one thing Mr. Morgan I want to be blind copied on that email."

"I can't do that; you would have the names and emails of all my contacts."

"Exactly."

"I'm sorry, I can't do that."

PHIFF

Rodin squeezed the trigger and put a hole in the photo of Melinda with the giraffe, except that now there is a hole where her head use to be.

"Mr. Morgan would you please turn around."

Morgan saw the marksmanship he was dealing with, he replied, "Okay, okay, what's the damn email address?"

"Thompson@kp.com. Don't bother trying to follow the link, you'll just be wasting your time. You have two days to have all Pangolin trafficking stopped or next time the hole won't be in a photo, you got it?"

"Got it."

Melinda Morgan had just posted a photo of her standing next to her latest trophy, a five-thousand-pound female forest elephant of the Lokomo Forest in Cameroon, Africa. All of her social media platforms included this photo. Then she texted her husband to share the good news.

"Just landed the trophy of a lifetime. Will be home in two days; make room over the mantle. Love M."

"Oh Shit." uttered Morgan under his breath.

He texted her, *"URGENT! Do not return to London, go to Palm Beach home. Will explain later. Matter of life and death. Jeffery."*

Morgan knew that even with his direct orders to stop all trafficking of Pangolins, the odds were pretty good that his edict would be ignored. The man on the phone gave him two days, which he was going to put to good use. He started to sell off and liquidate as much of his assets as he could. He planned to transfer as much money into his Monte Carlo bank account, then skip town, and meet up with Melinda in Florida and then they tried to stay off the grid and go underground, eventually living in Monaco. He was ready to go "underground", but not underground "underground", more like one floor below the penthouse underground.

Before flying off to meet up with the wife, Morgan sent off a short email to Thompson@kp.com, "Go fuck yourself, asshole."

Six weeks later, the Monacoian Police found Mr. and Mrs. Jeffery Morgan dead in their luxury condo located on the 21st floor of the 22nd story building over-looking Port Hercules. The Morgan's were found with the traditional Le Gang de la

Clé de Singe flags around their necks with a note stating the reasons why each of them had to die.

It was discovered that Mr. Morgan died from choking on a Pangolin scale that was lodged in his throat, Mrs. Morgan died from an overdose of an injection of ground up elephant ivory, believed to give one's skin a luminous glow. It didn't.

The police found a single fingerprint in he room, that of Princess Grace Kelly, Princess of Monaco, who had passed away in 1982.

Buzz conjured up two of his special Bloody Mary's and brought them on to the main deck to where Doctor Runnel was sitting on the aft bench petting Bosco and Groucho, who were vying for her attention.

"Hey, you guys, you two go lay down. If she going to be petting anyone around here, it's going to be me. Now scram." He said as he handed her a drink.

"Why Buzz, you always did know how to sweet talk a girl."

Buzz held up his glass to the doctor and took a sip, "Cheers." Then he sat next to her.

"So, Doc what are you really doing these days, still poaching specimens for the rich and famous?"

She took a long slow drink and said, "No, those days are gone, after that incident two years ago. The institute is now concentrating on research. So, we've been studying the *Neophocaena phocaenoides* in Ha Long Bay."

"The finless porpoise, yeah, I've seen a few of those around, man."

"Very good, Buzz. You always did amaze me with your knowledge of nature."

"Yeah, not bad for a burned out old hippie, huh Doc?"

"Not bad at all."

"So, what about the little buggers?"

"Well, because of the uptick in the fishing industry in Vietnam, the populations of these smiling little sea-pigs are on the brink of being wiped out."

"And now you're one of the good guys."

"Like I said, after the incident with Le Gang de la Clé de Singe and the disappearance of Jack Williams, the institute figured it wasn't worth the risk and hassle of ever having to go up against those French radicals again."

"How long is your research here on the porpoises going to last?"

"Could go on for months; we've just gotten started."

Buzz finished off his Bloody Mary and was chewing on the stalk of celery when he said with a wolfish grin, "Hey, Doc. wanna see my etchings?"

"Oh Buzz, you're such a romantic, I thought you'd never ask."

She handed her glass to him and he placed it on the teak table next to his, took her by the hand and led her below deck to the master cabin where they undressed each other, laid down on to the cool sheets and made love. After, they lay exhausted, close together, legs entangled, arms entwined, back to front, as one. They fell into a deep sleep and were only awakened when two frisky marmots scampered over the bed in a high-speed game of chase.

"What time is it?" she asked still drowsy.

Buzz trying to get his eyes to focus, "Ah, it looks like four o'clock."

"Mmm, feel up to seconds, old man?" she purred.

He nuzzled in her ear, "I'm old, not dead, Doc."

"Hello, this is Inspector Morris Interpol calling for either Ranger Tom Conway or Ranger Peter Brown."

"One moment please, I'll see if they're available."

"Yellow, this is Texas Ranger Tom Conway, I am unable to come to the phone, if ya'll like to leave a message, I'll get back to ya as soon as I can. Thanks for calling....

…Beep."

"Good day, Texas Ranger Tom Conway, this is Inspector Morris from Interpol, or as you so quaintly called me "Sherlock fucking Holmes". It's been over two weeks since you said you'd have a suspect in custody for the Ghost Hunters Ranch murders, so I'm just calling to see if I had somehow inadvertently missed your call. I look forward to hearing from you really soon. Cheers."

Ranger Conway put his cellphone on speaker so Peter Brown could listen in on the message.

"Fucking limey." Brown snickered.

"Where are we with Mr. and Mrs. Wilson? I'm sure they're the killers. Let's send the forensic team in again; maybe we've missed something. I'd love to stick that smug Brit's nose in it."

"I'll call Marshall in forensics and get them over there tomorrow."

"That stupid tea slurping, crumpet munching, royalty fucking, beer guzzling wanker. I'll show him what the Texas Rangers are all about!"

Whenever anyone mentions Casablanca the first thing that comes to mind is Humphrey Bogart, Ingrid Bergman, Rick's Café American, and play it again Sam.

Wooch liked the city of Casablanca because of the general chaos of the city. People can easily blend in or lose themselves within the teaming masses and it's hard to track anyone.

It was like an old homecoming reunion of the Red Team elites: Rodin, Odin, Isala, Iceman, Sue B, and Fu Hao. Most of them had been split up on different assignments. But now they were brought back together as Le Gang de la Clé de Singe's all-star team. Wooch had arranged to meet at the Novotel Casablanca City Center Hotel, at 9am in the LYS BLANC meeting room.

"Ladies and Gentlemen, we have been giving an amazing opportunity to take giant leap in stopping a large portion of trophy hunters in their tracks so to speak."

Wooch laid out the proposition for a shootout between W.A.S.P. and Le Gang de la Clé de Singe, which was to be a winner take all death match; literally a fight to the finish where the last man or woman standing wins for their organization.

"The location will be the desert island of Kanacea. It's a volcanic island with seven peaks. It's located in Fiji's Lau Archipelago, it's about 8 square miles, and the highest peak is almost 850 feet. There is a working coconut plantation and of course all the residences will be evacuated off the island for the duration of the game.

On the northeastern side of the island there is a boat opening and a large lagoon and the island has several freshwater streams.

This is not by any means an order. There will be no ill will or repercussions if any of you decide not to participate. I want you all to take a couple days if you feel you need time to think it thru. Any questions?"

Sue B asked, "Do we know who any of the opposition is?"

"No, we agreed that since we won't give any of your names, that they didn't have to divulge any of their team members."

"What about equipment and weapons?" Rodin inquired.

"Each team can bring pretty much anything they deem necessary, with the exception of bombs, grenades, or any type of explosive devices."

"How soon?" asked Sue B.

"Three weeks."

"How will we be deployed?" she followed up.

"Each team will arrive on Kanacea Island at the same time on opposite sides of the island by helicopters."

"Who decides which side of the island we land on? Because I say we want the east side, right Rodin?" the Iceman inquired as he was looking at the map.

"Definitely, the east side." Rodin concurred.

"Okay, I'll make it happen, east side it is." Wooch said.

"Also, I would like to know the location of all the cameras." Isala asked.

"I don't think that should be too difficult, Isala."

"Is there any restrictions when it comes to taking advantage of the ocean?" Rodin asked.

"Everything must happen on the island, so using the water is unacceptable."

"What happens if we do anyway. What are they going to do, kill us?"

"The offender or offenders will be removed, and that team will be down a man, or woman. Anything else?"

"Well, I'm in." Rodin announced.

Within seconds all six had volunteered to be a player of the most death-defying reality game show in the world, where one false move or mistake could cost them their lives.

Wooch smiled and said, "Great, I knew I picked six of the best. Now, I have some thoughts and some information that I can relay now, because once the game starts there can be no outside communication with any members of Le Gang de la Clé de Singe and of course the other team won't be able to contact their support system either.

Just so you know I am to be the impartial umpire, so all requests, questions and rulings come thru me, and I will make all the rulings, understand?"

They all smiled and nodded affirmative. Rodin said, "Well Wooch, it's like that old adage, "All's fair in love and war."

"Right you are boy, right you are. Now, let's go over some ideas I had."

"I'm starving, how about you Doc?"

"I am and I bet you are, you must have worked up quite an appetite, mister."

"What are you in the mood for?"

"Surprise me."

"Okay, you set the table and grab me a beer, if you would be so kind."

Buzz prided himself as a bit of a gourmet cook. He spent less than an hour rattling around in the galley whipping up an authentic Vietnamese favorite. Runnel sat at the dinette bench wearing one of Buzz's chambray shirts and her blue-stripped panties watching Buzz, who was wearing nothing but an apron that read "I don't need no stinking recipe" cooking it and booking it in the galley.

"Here you go." He said as he placed several bowls on the table in front of her.

"Wow, that smells and looks fabulous. What special dishes have you conjured up?"

"I call it Bun Cha ala Buzz, its grilled pork and meatballs, with herbs, rice noodles and my own secret dipping sauce."

"Oh my God! This is to die for, Buzz."

"Well, don't go dying on me, Doc.

"You keep cooking like this, and I can't guarantee it."

Buzz brought in a couple of bowls for him, placed them on the dinette and slid into the bench seat next to her. Bosco and Groucho jumped on the bench seat reared up on their hind legs and begged.

Buzz tossed each of them a meatball, which they caught in their mouths and skedaddled up the stairs topside. "Hey, you two moochers just one meatball each. Here you go, now beat it."

"Are you really leaving today?"

"Why?"

"I don't want you to."

"You don't?"

"No, I don't. Stay here Buzz, we just might have something special, but we'll never know if you leave now."

"Why don't you come with me, Doc. We'll sail around the world; we'll turn the Sweet Mary Jane into the Love Boat."

"Oh, wish I could Buzz. But I'm under contract with the Tynan Institute for another year."

"So, what happens if you just quit?"

"Well, they could sue me, I guess."

"Hey, fuck em, man. It's not like you're going to be working for the competition, besides they'd have to find you first. Come on Doc, sometimes you just gotta say, what the fuck."

"And what happens if we find this isn't working, I've just blown my career."

"Hell, we'll just tell them that I Shanghaied you. Come on Doc, let's blow this popsicle stand, what do say?"

Mr. Thurston Bentley Hart the third called the emergency meeting of W.A.S.P. to order, "Ladies and Gentlemen, may I have your attention please. As you all are aware of the tragedy that befell five of our fallen heroes, as well as our beloved President and CEO Charles Doering of Worldwide Affiliates of Safari Partners, who were all killed by that terrorist group Le Gang de la Clé de Singe. A bunch of cowardly murderers, who should all be caught and stand trial and then hung."

A crowd of twelve hundred hunters from all over the world that had come to assemble together at the Miami Beach Convention Center for some sort of revenge against the perpetrators of these egregious crimes went nuts, applauding, cheering and chanting "String them up. String them up."

T. B. Hart the third brought the crowd under control, "I know we all want justice."

Someone deep in the crowd shouted, "We want blood!"

"And you shall have it, I have negotiated a deal that will give us revenge, satisfaction, and blood."

The audience erupted in more chants, yelling and screaming approval.

"We have challenged these French thugs to a winner take all battle royale, pitting our six best against six of theirs; a titanic battle of champions as it were.

"We will have six of our bravest volunteers do battle against six from their goon squad. If we win, we will no longer have to worry about these criminals lurking in the bushes and weeds ambushing our hunters. They have agreed that they will concentrate all their energies to capturing and killing poachers and leave decent God-fearing hunters alone.

Ideally, we would like the volunteers to have had military experience, as well being excellent hunters. The six will be helicoptered on to Kanacea Island in the Pacific; it's basically a deserted island near Fiji. You will have three weeks to prepare, and in that time, you will be given a complete download of the terrain, special training and any equipment that you feel that you will need to accomplish your mission."

A voice from the rear of the convention center a man stood up and shouted out, "Are you telling us that these six W.A.S.P. hunters are going to this island in order to kill six human beings so we will continue to have the privilege of hunting animals? What happens if they get killed? Are we then not allowed to hunt ever again, is that the wager?"

"Yes sir, that is the wager, we can refuse this challenge and go on hunting in fear or we can take up the gauntlet, seize the day and vanquish these murderers and continue our hunting way of life free of fear.

I have enlisted retired SEAL Commander William T. "Wooch" Brown, who will be the referee slash umpire during the conflict to come and give military advice to our team before the exercise commences. Also, we have Mr. Roger Blumenthal, the new President and CEO of the Hunting Network who has committed to place over six hundred cameras thru out the island to make sure there will be no cheating."

A woman seated near the front raised her hand and was called on by the W.A.S.P. president, "So is this going to be broadcast on TV like a deadly game show?"

"I wouldn't categorize it like that. To accomplish our objective, we needed to be entrepreneurial in our thinking, think out of the box, as it were. That's why we're asking for volunteers. If you're interested, please come by the table just outside the hall here and sign up, and someone will contact you shortly. Remember that this is dangerous, deadly and requires the taking a human life."

The rest of the day was broken down into workshops, exhibits, courses and speaker seminars. Outside the hall standing in line to volunteer for "Operation Payback" were sixty-six men and four women, waiting patiently to write their names on the signup sheet. Seated at the table was President Thurston Bentley Hart the third and Commander "Wooch" Brown greeting the volunteers and answering any questions they might have.

"Is there any remuneration for the winners?"

"Is there any compensation if they get killed in action?"

"How long will this go on?"

"What happens if you want out?"

"Do you get extra if you kill more than one of the enemy?"

"Will this be a 24/7 operation?"

"Do you get weekends off?"

"Are there makeup people?"

"What happens if you get wounded?"

"Do we have to supply our own ammo?"

"Will it be catered?"

"Is this like that survivor show where you have to eat bugs and grubs?"

"Are there porta potties on the island?"

"Can I bring my girlfriend?"

"Will the game be called if there's bad weather?"

And those were the lest crazy and silly questions, Hart and Wooch finally narrowed it down to seven potential candidates:

Matt Jones
Christopher Garcia
Glenn Anderson
Richard "Dickie" Davis
Jennifer Martinez
Steve Taylor
Felipe Lopez

Matt Jones is an ex-Army, served four tours in Iraq, and is the recipient of the Bronze Star and a Purple Heart. Been a member of W.A.S.P. for ten years. Matt joined the 101st Airborne Division and was in the thick of it during the Battle of Mosul, the second Battle of Fallujah, the Battle of Tal Afar and the Battle of Ramadi.

As a big game hunter, Matt has killed four of the big five, he's missing the Cape Buffalo. He is only interested in hunting only rare and exotic game, Saltwater Crocodiles, Addax, Barasingha, Reeves Muntjac, Pere David Deer and the elusive Sitatunga. There has to be a challenge to it, or he's not interested.

Christopher Garcia an ex-Marine, a veteran of the Vietnam War, fought in the Tet Offensive. His outfit was pinned down and under fire for 26 days in house to house, hand to hand combat. Chris revealed to Wooch that he still suffers from post-traumatic stress disorder but assures Commander Brown that's he's combat fit.

Glenn Anderson wasn't a veteran; he's been a safari scout and guide for over thirty-four years in Africa and Asia.

He's South African, born and raised and comes from six generations of guides and trackers. He likes to say that "An army of lions commanded by a deer will never beat an army of lions." When Wooch asked him who said it, Glenn said, "My old man." Wooch shook his head no, "Napoleon, but it's still a great line."

Richard "Dickie" Davis, a retired Major in the first battalion of the Royal Regiment of Fusiliers, fought with honors in Bosnia, Iraq and Afghanistan. Dickie has been a member of W.A.S.P. for fourteen years. While being interviewed by Wooch, Dickie confessed that he has a bit of a gammy leg from an IED that killed eleven of his squad while fighting in Kandahar. But he assures them that he too, is combat ready.

Jennifer Martinez is a celebrity of sorts. She sparked public outcry after she posted pictures of herself on social media with a black giraffe that she killed in Botswana. Recently, while on safari she tried to take down an elephant using a bow and arrow. After twenty arrows her guide finally had had enough and put the suffering beast down with his rifle. He was later overheard to tell someone that it looked like she used the poor thing for target practice.

Jennifer is known for her exploits in hunting and killing rare species and then professing how she is doing God's will and if God didn't want her killing these 'gifts' he wouldn't have made her such a great marksman.

Steve Taylor is one of today's most prominent writers for Hunter World magazine. He isn't just a great writer; he is a world-renowned big game hunter. Best known for his skill as a big cat hunter, Taylor has killed at least one of the big cats in every continent. He is only the third man ever to do so. Through his writings he has inspired generations of new hunters to take to the sport.

Finally, *Felipe Lopez* who was inducted into the Bowhunters Hall of Fame two years ago. Since Felipe grew up bowhunting, it became a way of life as his father owned an archery shop. He learned not only how to hunt, but he designed and made his own bows and arrows. He received a full scholarship at the University of New Mexico and won a silver medal at the 2008 Summer Olympics held in China. Felipe has harvested over 200 North American big game animals and 45 different species of African animals.

President Thurston Bentley Hart the third and Commander "Wooch" Brown decided that they needed a combination of military experience and hunting/tracking know-how. They're ultimate roster was Felipe Lopez, Steve Taylor, Jennifer Martinez, Richard "Dickie" Davis, Matt Jones, and Christopher Garcia.

"So, what did they say? Are they going to bring the heavy hand of the "Man" down on you?" Buzz asked as he was helping the Doc stow her bags on board the Sweet Mary Jane.

"No, they were very understanding, I just told them I was pregnant."

"You're what?"

"Relax, I'm not pregnant. Oh, you should've seen the look on your face, it was priceless."

"Not funny, Doc."

"It was a little funny."

"No."

"A little."

"Yeah, okay it was a little funny."

"Hey, Buzz I'm hungry, you know now that I'm eating for two."

"Okay, now you've gone too far." Buzz dropped her canvas duffel bag and started chasing her around the deck, she ran down below and Buzz followed her as she ran into the main cabin where he tackled her on the bed. He pinned her down and started taking off his shirt, "Just what do you think you're doing Mr. Murdock?"

"You want pregnant? I'll give you pregnant, Doc." he said as he leans down and give her a kiss, she wraps her legs around his waist and brings him down on top of her.

She whispers in his ear romantically, "I don't think you have it in you, you old hippie."

He slipped off her shorts and panties as she unbuttoned her blouse, she then took off his board shorts and said, "Mmm, looks like I'm wrong Buzz, you look like you're more than ready for action."

As he began to make love to her, he caresses her face with his hands and begins to kiss her, he softly says, "You know Doc, this looks like the beginning of a beautiful friendship."

The sun was setting when the two ferrets starting to nuzzle Buzz from a deep sleep for their dinner. He was sleeping on his left side when he finally gained total conscienceless. He rolled over to find he was alone in bed.

He made his way topside to find the Doc drinking a cup of coffee watching the sunset, her back was to him when he approached her.

"Hey Doc, can I get you anything?"

"Nope, I'm good, babe, just watching the sunset. What a pretty red sky."

"Red sky at night, sailors delight. Red sky in the morning, sailor take warning."

"Old wives' tale?"

"Actually, it's pretty accurate." He held her shoulders and bent to kiss the back of her neck, "So, Doc is there any place in particular you want to go first, or shall we just let the wind take us?"

"You know Buzz, I've been on a strict schedule for the last six years, so let's let the wind take us where it will."

"Doc, I like your style. Come first light we'll weigh anchor and begin our adventure."

Dmitriy always had the feeling that the Orca in pen number 44 was always watching him whenever he would attend to the enclosures. None of the other sixteen Orcas or the ninety-eight Beluga wild whales that were being held in sea cages off the coast of Srednyaya Bay, near Nakhodka, Russia seemed to ever take notice of him, but #44 was watching, always watching.

Russian traders had captured these unfortunate Cetaceans with the intention of selling them to marine parks, dolphinariums, and swim-with-the dolphin water parks in China.

The poor creatures were trapped in a network of small sea cages that where all they could do in swim in circles, basically they were in 'whale prison'. Multiple dolphin and wildlife organizations have lodged complaints internationally and protested, but so far, the Russian government has done little to nothing to ban the sale of these leviathans or impose a ban on their capture.

That's the difference between Le Gang de la Clé de Singe and other wildlife watchdog organizations. While others protest and demonstrate, Le Gang de la Clé de Singe confronts and kicks ass.

Le Gang de la Clé de Singe decided to send in a three-man team to try and dissuade other traders from also getting into the business of selling endangered species, by setting an example.

Rooster, Mad Jack and Nacho, all Russian members of Le Gang de la Clé de Singe arrived in Nakhodka and checked into three separate hotels so as not draw suspicion; the arrival of a group of three strangers could get tongues wagging.

Nakhodka is a port city located on the Trudny Peninsula that juts into the Sea of Japan, approximately two hundred miles from the North Korean border. South, on the very tip of Trudny Peninsula is the abandoned army base МБОУ СШ № 2 that the traders have transformed into their headquarters. Directly adjacent to what used to be the mess hall is a pier that protrudes five hundred yards out into Srednyaya Bay where the sea cages are attached.

Rooster drove up to the entrance gate and was met by an armed sentry who asked, "What is your business?"

"I represent a client who might be interested in purchasing several Orcas."

"Orcas? We don't have Orcas; you must be misinformed."

"My mistake, I guess my clients will just have to go elsewhere to spend their dollars."

"Dollars? American Dollars?"

"American Dollars. Sorry to have bothered you."

"No wait here." The sentry turned away and dialed a number on his cell phone; he briefly spoke in a whisper, and then gestured for Rooster to enter.

When he reached the first building marked as Building Number One, there was someone standing out front waving for him to park his car. Rooster did as he was told and was greeted by a man who identified himself as Dmitriy, "Greetings my friend, my name is Dmitriy Sokolov, and you would be?"

"Yaroslav, Yaroslav Kurnetsov. Like I told the man at the gate I represent a client who is interested in the possible purchase of several Orcas. Do you have Orcas? The man at the gate said no."

"Yaroslav, we have to take precautions, you understand."

"Yes, of course. So, you do have Orcas."

"We currently have sixteen, but we can get you more if needed."

"I am interested in obtaining six, three males and three females."

"Come this way." Dmitriy said as he guided Rooster towards the sea cages. They met Sergei, who was in the process of feeding the Belugas. The Orcas were kept in the furthest pens away so not to disturb the Belugas. Rooster was surprised to see how many animals were crammed into each pen, the Orcas, however, were kept in individual pens.

"They are all beautiful specimens, are they not?"

"That they are. How soon can you deliver?"

"As soon as we receive payment. Where would you like them delivered to?"

"Jiangsu, China."

"Ah China, that shouldn't be a problem, Yaroslav. Shall we go into the office and make arrangements?"

"Of course."

The two men walked back to the building where Rooster had parked and went into the office. The so-called office consisted of three metal desks with matching chairs and a beat-up sofa with a large bulletin board standing in a corner with the pen numbers and feeding schedules. There were two other men sitting at desks talking on phones trying to make deals.

Dmitriy said to the two men to the phones, "Sasha, Artyon this is Yaroslav, he is here to purchase Orcas."

The two men barley acknowledged him, as they were both in heated discussions on their cell phones.

"Pay no attention to them, they're socially inept. Now for six Orcas that will be four hundred thousand US Dollars, of course that includes delivery. So, Yaroslav when do you think you can have the dollars?"

"After I have my experts inspect the Orcas to be sure they are of the proper sexual specimens and appear to be in good health. Would tomorrow be too soon?"

"Not at all, here's my number. Call me when you're coming."

"Of course, until tomorrow."

"Until tomorrow, proshchay."

From what Rooster had seen there seemed to be a total of eight men that they would have to contend with, three in the office, one sentry and four men maintaining the sea-cages and they were all armed. As he was driving towards the main gate, he noticed that there looked to be living quarters for the maintenance workers behind Building Number One.

On the morning as the Sweet Mary Jane set sail, Buzz received a text, *"Six weeks • -17.079902, -179.234945 • R"*

"Good evening ladies and gentlemen and welcome to the world's first ever pay-per-view reality show, "Winner Take All.". I'm your host Buck St. John. You're in for a treat, Winner Take All is the first 24/7-television show that is brought to you live. You will see in real time the unscripted, unedited and unrehearsed no holds barred, a battle royale combat between two opposing teams for the future of big game hunting. There are over a two thousand cameras

strategically placed throughout the island, so you won't miss a single minute of action.

Let me remind you that this is real, so if you're squeamish this show is not, I repeat not for you. We have two teams of six warriors each, they will be landed on opposite sides of an island in the Pacific Ocean and the object is to reach the other side of the island and leave no one from the opposing team alive. You heard right, this is real combat warfare, the action is live and so is the ammunition; when someone is shot, they're really shot.

Let me introduce the two teams, first, Team W.A.S.P. representing the Worldwide Affiliates of Safari Partners, there is Felipe Lopez, Steve Taylor, Jennifer Martinez, Richard "Dickie" Davis, Matt Jones, and Christopher Garcia. We will have more on each contestant's background and qualifications in upcoming episodes.

The second team represents the notorious French eco-terrorist group Le Gang de la Clé de Singe. Because these individuals are wanted by the law, we do not know their true identities. What we do know is that there are four men and two women, if and when any of them are killed then their identities shall be revealed.

Before the action starts, I want to reminder our viewers that I will only intercede with commentary when appropriate, so you'll truly experience the actual sights and sounds of the island and the action. As a subscriber, remember you have multiple viewing options such as, following the W.A.S.P. team or the Le Gang de la Clé de Singe team. Viewing multiple screens at once is available or you can watch the general broadcast. We also provide instant replays and a recap and a highlight option as well.

For just twenty-five dollars a day extra we will send you texts of all impending clashes. And be sure to tell your all of your friends and family to subscribe to this incredible once in a lifetime live pay-per-view event, it's quite a bargain for only $99.99 a day. Call now; operators are standing by.

As you can see the two teams are being choppered in, for those who haven't subscribed, we return you back to today's regular programming."

Team W.A.S.P. landed a few minutes before the other team. They were all dressed in jungle camo fatigues and wearing camo face paint. Once the helicopter sat down on the west side of the island, they unloaded all their gear onto the beach in one neat pile.

On the east side of the island, Rodin and the Red Team were wearing their ghillie suits designed with the island's specific vegetation specially interwoven on to their suits. They were wearing camo balaclavas as well as having their faces painted. When they unloaded their gear, they moved everything into the brushes and shrubs. Just before the chopper was preparing to leave, Rodin gave a whistle and Rodin's dog Buster jumped out and stood by his master.

Buster is a pure breed American Leopard Hound, who Rodin has used on several previous missions. Buster would accompany him out into the fields and lay by his side, waiting any number of commands—he could attack either human or beast, he could be called upon to do tracking, and he was an overall team morale booster.

When Thurston Bentley Hart the third, watching the broadcast saw that Le Gang de la Clé de Singe had brought a dog, he called Wooch, "Wooch, did you know that Le Gang de la Clé de Singe was bringing a dog?"

"I did."

"Well, that's not legal!"

"No, Thurston it is legal. If you remember it was agreed that each team can bring anything, they deem necessary, with the exception of bombs, grenades, or any type of explosive devices. There wasn't any mention of excluding dogs, so it's legal."

"It doesn't seem fair."

"Fair? This is real combat, people are going to die, Thruston. There is no fair, there's only surviving."

"Still, I'm sure we'll get tons of letters and tweets protesting."

"Fuck 'em. This is war, they're not playing by the Marquess of Queensberry Rules, its kill or be killed."

It had been decided before they landed on the beach that Matt Jones was to be the commander of the W.A.S.P. team since he had the most combat experience. His first order of business was to get a scout up on the first peak to keep lookout for any movement heading their way while the rest of the team would set camp. Christopher Garcia the ex-Vietnam vet volunteered to be the scout.

Matt's strategy was to hunker three men down at base camp and send out a three man team every morning to do recon and try and engage the enemy, calling in back up if needed. Play offense, don't sit and wait for something to happen, go and make something happen.

Rodin had a more of a come and get it strategy, like a spider that waits for its prey to enter the web, then it's death to the intruder. He would let the enemy do the work of hiking the island. His plan was to have five people lying in wait, leaving Isala back in base camp with Buster; Isala would be operating a series of drones. As soon as they landed Isala put an Ehang Ghostdrone 2.0 up high in the sky to keep track of the enemy.

"Wooch, did you know that Le Gang de la Clé de Singe was bringing a drone?"

"I did."

"Well, isn't that illegal?"

"No, Thurston, once again, it is legal. There wasn't any mention of excluding drones, so it's legal."

"I fear a slaughter coming."

"I had a meeting with both teams to answer any questions they had about the rules of engagement and any and all gear that they could and couldn't bring. The W.A.S.P. team asked mostly questions of things they could bring, and Le Gang de la Clé de Singe asked mostly questions of things that they couldn't bring. It wasn't my job to tell either team what they should bring, only what wasn't allowed, I am just the umpire."

Rodin had everyone take all the gear out of the bags and containers and either hide them in the surrounding vegetation, bury some things on the beach, and some things were hidden within the shallow water reefs just offshore.

While the team set up camp, he and Sue B ventured out to set up some booby traps. They first went deep into the jungle and built several bamboo whips. In the Vietnam War the whip consisted of bamboo spikes tied on a long bamboo pole. The pole was pulled back into an arc using a tripwire, once the tripwire is triggered the spiked pole whips around and strikes the person's chest at over a hundred miles an hour. But Rodin used a tightly woven mat instead of spikes, since the object was to stun the enemy not kill them.

While Sue B was finishing off the bamboo whips, Rodin was rigging some aerial snare traps. As someone stepped on and tripped the wire, their foot would become caught and they would be flipped upside down hanging from a tree several feet above the ground. The idea was that if one person got caught, others would come to help and then you would have several targets located together.

Finally, they set up some sound grenade booby traps, which they bought several dozen of on the internet. Once the sound grenades' pins are pulled. They emits an ear piercing 130dB siren, causing panic, fear, and confusion while alerting the Red Team to their presence.

Rodin put on his ghillie suit and took the first watch as his team finished setting up the camps. One camp which was a decoy camp looked to be a traditional camp with tents, a large working fire pit and common camping objects lying around such as cooking gear near the fire. The second camp was the real camp. It was a cold camp with no fire and only camouflaged sleeping bags. After the camps were set up the

Iceman radioed Rodin and asked if they should suit up and move out.

"Affirmative. Have Red Flyer put up the bugs, over."

"Roger that."

The Iceman looked at Odin and gave a thumbs up signal letting him know to send up the insect drones.

The Red Team would be dispatching Bugbot Nano Drones to the enemy's camp when sunset began. Bugbot Nano Drones are insect drones measuring no more than three inches long and resembled black beetles; they would send in swarms of eight. The insect drones would look like a small swarm, and then, when they were a few dozen yards away, they would land on the ground and crawl towards the campsite. Odin would monitor and control them remotely, they all were equipped with cameras and microphones, perfect for eavesdropping on the other team.

The team started to slip into their ghillie suits and wrapping their rifles in tactical sniper veils. The Iceman checked with everyone to see if they were ready. Once they left camp, they would have to stay in position for at least twenty-four hours, maybe longer so they had to make sure they were equipped with enough liquids and high energy snacks. Each team member had a Camelback Ambush One Hundred Oz. Antidote Pack filled with a special concoction for anti-dehydration.

"Everyone remember to put on the Rid-A-Tick patches; those bites can kill you if left untreated. Okay, and are everyone's radio headsets working?" The Iceman asked.

Each team member was equipped with an M2010 Enhanced Sniper Rifle, a rifle the U.S. Army had developed to give extra range. It had a computerized scope that could mark a selected target and uses a special trigger that doesn't pull until it's sure the bullet will land where intended. The effective range is over one thousand two hundred and fifty yards.

Once everyone was ready the Iceman gave the order, "Move out."

For the first day the Sweet Mary Jane sailed south along the coast of Vietnam until she was parallel to Nha Trang, then they headed out into the South China Sea towards Banggi Island that sits on the northern most tip of Malaysia.

There on the eastern side of the island is Kg. Maliyu, a small grocery market where Buzz and the Doc stopped and stocked up on fresh water and fruit. From there they would sail thru the Celebes Sea, threading the islands of the Philippines and Indonesia to Thursday Island on the tip of Queensland, Australia for a couple day's rest and relaxation.

All was going according to plan until late on afternoon as the SMJ was between Bacan Island and Bisa Island, Buzz noticed off in the distance three Zodiac rafts heading towards them at high speed, pirates.

"Doc we got trouble come topside, now!" Buzz yelled.

Doc Runnel ran up from below, "What's happening Buzz?"

"Pirates, come take the helm."

She didn't have time to ask him what the plan was. Buzz sprinted down below deck and returned carrying a M1918 Browning Automatic Rifle and an ammo box full of loaded magazines. He quickly set it up on its stand and returned back down below deck and returned with a rocket-propelled grenade launcher and a dozen grenades.

He looked at his love and said calmly, "Gifts from a friend. Now just stay the course."

Buzz's plan, as it were, was to try and scare them off with a couple salvos of grenades, hopefully knock one out of action, then if they persisted, go to the BAR.

They could hear some gunshots in the distance, for now they were too far out of range, but that wouldn't last long. Buzz loaded up the RGB launcher, aimed and fired.

BAWHOOOOOOM

Buzz wasn't sure if he was a great shot or just plain lucky, but he hit the lead Zodiac and blew the shit out of it, sending six or eight men flying. The explosion was so massive he couldn't be sure how many men were thrown off. That left two Zodiacs still in pursuit. They split up, one coming in from the port side the other from the starboard side fast and guns a-blazing.

ACAK ACAK ACAK ACAK ACAK ACAK

Buzz had the Doc set the autopilot and had her get behind the BAR. "Have you ever used one of these?"

"You're kidding right?"

"Okay, just aim the barrel towards that Zodiac and squeeze this trigger lightly, fire short bursts. If you run out of ammo just shout and I'll reload for you, okay. Just stay calm, it will be okay, I promise, love you."

"I love you, too."

Buzz reloaded the grenade launcher and fired at the Zodiac off the port side.

BAWHOOOOOOM

The driver zigged at the last second and Buzz missed by inches. The bullets from the pirates were starting to whiz by.

WHISSSH WHISSSSH WHISSSSH

Some of them tearing holes in the mainsail. Meanwhile the Doc was really getting into a groove with the BAR.

BLAM BLAM BLAM BLAM BLAM BLAM

She hit two of the pirates throwing them out of the craft leaving four men firing and hitting the stern.

Buzz loaded the grenade launcher, then feigned being wounded, yelling to the Doc he's just faking hoping the Zodiac will stop shooting and try and get close to board the SMJ, which is what happened. The moment they stopped shooting and concentrating on boarding, Buzz jumped up and fired the grenade into the Zodiac, hitting the engine and starting a fire that caused all the men to abandon the raft.

Buzz then reloaded and came over to help the Doc. He reloaded the BAR and together they peppered the remaining pirates with thirty-aught-six shells and RPG grenades, as they soon realized they were beat and dropped back to try and save their partners in crime.

The Sweet Mary Jane took some hits, nothing too serious, it looked worse that it was. Buzz looked around to make sure all was clear, then he went down below and came back topside holding a yellow hunk of canvas. He went over to the mainsail and hoisted a yellow flag with a black skull and two crossed monkey wrenches. "That'll teach 'em, nobody fucks with the Sweet Mary Jane and Le Gang de la Clé de Singe, man. Right babe?"

"Right, Buzz."

"Hey Doc, you were fucking amazing with that BAR. Nobody be messing with my lady, you go girl."

"You were prettying amazing yourself old man."

"Couldn't have done it without you, Doc. I think now that were past this strait, we should be good, we're too far out from land for these bands of pirates to venture out into the open sea. But we'll sail on thru the night with minimal running lights just to be safe.

We're going into the Ceram Sea, heading for the Arafura Sea towards Australia, should be smooth sailing from here on out to the land down under."

Rooster pulled up to the guard's station at 5:30 as the whale prison looked to be closing for the night, "Can I help you? We're closing for the evening."

"Is Dmitriy still here? I am ready to close the deal."

"Hold on, let me call."

The guard went into the small guardhouse, made a phone call, nodded and returned to the red Lada Samara that

Rooster was sitting in and said, "Dmitriy is waiting for you at Building Number One."

As Rooster was about to put the car into drive he said, "Oh, I almost forgot, I have something for you."

The guard perked up, "Really, what?"

Rooster held up a Makarov .380 handgun equipped with a Spetsnaz silencer and fired two shots hitting him in the chest forcing him to fall back into the guardhouse, collapsing on the floor, dead.

PHIFF PHIFF

Once inside the gate he turned to the back seat and announced, "All clear."

The trunk popped open from the inside and Mad Jack and Nacho jumped out each carrying an AK-47 with Wolverine PBS-1 DeadAirSilencers. Mad Jack and Nacho scurried to the building where the maintenance workers were believed to reside as Rooster drove to Building Number One.

Dmitriy was once again standing outside to greet him. "Greetings my friend, I didn't expect you back until tomorrow."

"My clients are most anxious to proceed with the acquiring of the Orcas." Rooster told him as he grabbed a briefcase from the passenger side of the car.

"Do you have the American Dollars?"

Rooster said nothing, he just held up the briefcase.

When they entered the office, it seemed time had stood still, Sasha and Artyon were still in heated discussions on their cell phones oblivious to anything. Dmitriy invited Rooster to have a seat across from his desk. As the two men sat down, Dmitriy smiled and opened a folder that was sitting on his desk with the name Yaroslav Kurnetsov scribbled on it.

"So you are interested in six Orcas, three males and three females, correct?"

"Correct."

"I haven't had time for my men to separate out your order, I wasn't expecting you until tomorrow, sorry."

"That is not a problem."

"So, you do have the dollars with you?"

"Yes, I believe that you quoted a price of four hundred thousand dollars."

"Four hundred thousand dollars is correct. I have the contract here." Dmitriy said as he pulled out an official looking document from the folder.

Rooster had the briefcase resting on his lap, he snapped open the case and removed the Makarov .380 pistol, aimed it at Dmitriy and said, "Dmitriy, have you ever heard of Le Gang de la Clé de Singe?"

While Rooster has busy negotiating a deal with Dmitriy and friends, Mad Jack and Nacho had burst into the suspected dormitory and found not only the workers, but also their spouses and children. It was decided that Nacho would hold everyone captive while Mad Jack went to get Rooster.

By the time Mad Jack had arrived at Building Number One he found that Rooster had disposed of Sasha and Artyon, they were lying on the ground next to each other with monkey wrench flags hanging from around their necks and their cell phones stuffed in their mouths. Rooster and Dmitriy were getting ready to head down to the pens and start releasing all sixteen Orcas and ninety-eight Beluga whales back into the wild.

"Rooster, we have a problem."

"And that would be what?"

"There are wives and families."

Rooster thought for a minute, "Leave them alone, they are just workers trying to make a living. Just tell them who we are and what we stand for. Collect all the cell phones and then meet me at the car, I will be there soon."

He and Dmitriy continued down to the pens and they released all the creatures, even the Orca in pen number 44, who, even after being released remained nearby to watch his captor take his place in pen 44.

The Russian Ministry of Internal Affairs police officers discovered the bodies of the four murdered Russian nationals floating in the sea cages that had been used for holding the captured whales. The police found all four men with the flags of Le Gang de la Clé de Singe around each man's neck with the letter of explanation for their deaths. They were surprised to find a single fingerprint, that turned out to be that of Grigori Rasputin, President Putin was not amused.

When asked by Inspector Morris of Interpol if they had found any fingerprints, the official response was "Net!"

"Good evening ladies and gentlemen, this Buck St. John, with a recap of the very first day of "Winner Take All."

I'm here tonight with my special guest retired Green Beret Three-Star General Rex O'Brian.

"Welcome General."

"Thank for having me, Buck."

"General, you've been watching both teams today, how would you categorize each team's strategies?"

"Well Buck, today was primarily a day where both teams settled in, unpacked and started planning. The W.A.S.P. team seems to be more of the aggressor, whereas the Le Gang de la Clé de Singe team looks to be playing defense.

We saw them setting up a series of booby traps that tell me that they plan on letting the W.A.S.P. team do the heavy lifting, by letting the enemy come to them. Le Gang de la Clé de Singe look to me to be the more polished of the two teams, Buck."

"In what way General?"

"It's apparent to me because of the little things, they brought ghillie suits, drones, even a dog. It shows me there's a lot of combat experience and a lot of outside of the box thinking.

I think the W.A.S.P. team could be in for real surprise. But of course, one should never underestimate your opponent. The W.A.S.P. team looks to be very agile and nimble. So, this could be a real interesting matchup."

"Thanks, General, for your expertise. Folks we'll be right back with more insight from General O'Brian right after these messages from our sponsors...."

Rodin was awakened before dawn, "Red Leader, Red Leader, this is Red Flyer, Over."

"Red Leader, Go."

"I've picked up a lone target headed your way, over. Looks to be coming in at one o'clock, over."

"Roger that."

"Red Team, Red Team this is Red Leader do you copy?"

Each of the team responded affirmative, Rodin alerted them to the possible of a bogie coming their way.

Matt Jones had asked for a volunteer to do a recon to the other side of the island to see what the enemy was up to. Christopher Garcia, the ex-Vietnam Marine volunteered and left, just after the sun had set.

Wearing a pair of night vision goggles he weaved his way thru the patches of dense jungle, climbed over six of the seven peaks and reached the apex of hill number seven when he stopped dead in his tracks. A chilled shiver of death ran down his spine and he had a feeling something wasn't right. He felt that there were eyes on him; he sensed that there was death all around him. He knelt down on one knee; he held his M27 automatic rifle tight against his chest at the ready.

Rodin whispered into his radio, "Red Team, this is Red Leader. Do not, I repeat do not engage. Do you copy?"

He received four affirmatives.

After twenty minutes, Christopher stopped dead in his tracks, stood up and retraced his steps walking backwards, not wanting to turn his back to whatever was watching him.

Just before sunrise he came out on to his beach campsite. Steve Taylor, who was on watch duty announced his return. Members of the W.A.S.P. team slowly emerged from their tents to greet Chris as he returned and was anxious to hear what he had to report.

"I reached the peak of hill number seven; I could see their beach camp. They had a small fire and one man on watch. But I dared not go any further, I sensed danger, it was all around me. I'd been in a couple jungle ambushes back in Nam and after a while you get a six sense about these things, you know?"

"Did you see any evidence of someone from their team making their way over here?" Matt asked.

"None. I would travel several hundred yards, stop, and listen for any sound of movement. Nothing."

"Well, I can't believe that they aren't heading over to us. I say we take the fight to them; we'll pair up in teams of two, and we'll stagger our departures every hour, each team taking different paths."

"I say old man, do you not think one team should remain in reserve here at camp in case they manage to slip thru?" suggested Dickie Davis.

"No, this isn't a game of capture the other teams flag. You don't win by capturing the other teams' camp. We only win if we're the team that survives, it's kill or be killed. So,

I think we should team up and go. Do you guys want to pick your partners, or would you like me to pair you up?"

"I'd be interested in who your picks would be." Said Jennifer Martinez.

"Okay, I think Steve and Chris would be a good match, Dickie and Felipe would seem a good fit, and me and Jennifer. If you think differently, feel free to change, if not let's saddle up and head out.

"Dickie and Felipe, why don't you lean towards the left side of the island, Steve and Chris, right down the middle, since Chris you already know the way and Jennifer and I will travel down the right side.

"Remember, this is real, they're not fucking around, believe that they are out to kill each and every one of us. God willing we'll all meet up on the other side of the island."

They all shook hands and gave each other hugs. As they went to their tents to prepare for battle Jennifer noticed a large black beetle on the back of Matt's shirt. She started to shoo it away, but it quickly flew off past her head. She swatted at it as it flew by. She thought it a bit strange as its wings didn't seem to make a natural flapping sound, but more of a small motor buzzing sound. She was about to mention it to Matt when he turned to her and asked, "You okay?"

"Yeah, I'm good." She replied.

"There she Doc, Thursday Island, not to be confused with Friday Island or Wednesday Island."

"I'm not even going to ask."

"Aw come on, Doc."

"Okay, why do they call it Thursday Island?"

"Funny you should ask; Thursday Island was named by Vice-Admiral William Bligh of Mutiny on the Bounty fame back in the mid-1800's."

"Buzz my love, you're just a fountain of useless information."

"Why thank you, I knew all those years studying at the Sorbonne weren't for naught."

As the Sweet Mary Jane sailed thru the Normanby Sound Ledge and on to Thursday Island Harbor, she received plenty of attention from onlookers who couldn't help but noticed the battle scars from their run in with the Indonesian pirates, with over forty bullet holes peppering the hull and mainsail.

Once they had tied off on the dock, Buzz and the Doc made their way into town; they split up. Buzz headed to MI Marine Services to get some fiberglass repair kits to patch up the bullet holes in the hull and some canvas patch fabric kits to repair the rips in mainsail while the Doc went to IBIS Supermarket for provisions and then to T.i. Fruit Barn for some fresh fruit. They met up at See Hop Trading to do some much-needed laundry. Afterwards, before heading back to the SMJ they stopped off at the Grand Hotel overlooking the Harbor located on Upper Victoria Parade to grab a bite at the Malu Paru Restaurant.

It took Buzz the whole of a day to repair the damage, but once completed she was good as new. Buzz was down below deck when a Constable from the Thursday Island

Police Station came to inquire about the bullet holes, he had heard so much about.

"Hey, Buzz come on up, there's a Constable Aubrey here who wants to talk to us."

Buzz popped his head out from below and said, "Be right with you, just changing my clothes."

"No worries." The Constable replied.

"Constable Aubrey, I'm Doctor Laura Runnel, can I offer you something to drink?"

"No thank you Doctor."

Buzz then appeared wearing a Grateful Dead tee shirt and Levi's cut-offs. "Hi, I'm Buzz Murdock. What can we do for you Constable?"

"I'm inquiring about those bullet holes, how did that happen, if I might ask?"

"Well Constable, we were sailing thru the straits between Bacan Island and Bisa Island, when I noticed off in the distance three Zodiac rafts heading our way, they were firing weapons at us, so I took evasive action, you know a combination of zigzagging, jibing, and hard tacking. We were very lucky, man."

"I'm curious Mr. Murdock, did you return fire?"

"Buzz, please. As a matter of fact, we did. I was lucky to have hit their auxiliary gas tanks and one of the rafts exploded and the Doc here is no slouch with a firearm. She wounded a couple of those scallywags herself. Yes, sir she quite the deadeye, Constable."

"What sort of weapons did you use, if I might ask, Mr. Murdock?"

"Buzz. I have a licensed Winchester Model 92 lever action and a Winchester Super X Pump shotgun. I can go get them if you'd like to see them Constable."

"No that won't be necessary Mr. Mur, I mean Buzz. I would say that you and the good Doctor here were very lucky. I understand those pirates are ruthless."

"We were very fortunate, Constable. I think it was a combination of luck and Buzz's excellent sailing skills that got us thru." The Doc said putting her arm around Buzz's shoulder.

"Aw shucks mam, twernt nothing."

"Are you sure Constable you wouldn't care for a beer?"

"Oh no Doctor, I'm still on duty. Well, I'll be making my report of the incident and send it off to the proper authorities. Well, I believe that's all, how long will you be staying on here Buzz?"

"We'll probably be off sometime tomorrow."

"Well if I don't happen to see you before you go, I wish you smooth sailing."

"Thank you, Constable."

Odin called Rodin and the team together to alert them to the latest information he had picked up from the insect drones.

"They're breaking up into three two-man teams, one pair will be advancing from the left, one from the right and one will be coming straight down the middle."

"Did they sound authentic, or do you think they might know we're tapping into their camp?" Rodin asked.

"I've been checking their movements with the Ghostdrone and they've definitely broken off into three teams. Now, they may at some point rendezvous back together, but I'll be watching from above and will keep everyone apprised of any deviations."

"Okay then, Fu Hao, you and Sue B go up the middle, Odin and Ice you go right, and I'll head left. Let's all stay in radio contact with each other and with Isala. Once the mission has been accomplished, we'll all meet back here to commence our evac plan. Isala is everything ready?"

"Ready to rock & roll."

"Good. Okay everyone good luck and stay frosty. Let's move out and kill some wasp's."

The President of Interpol summoned Inspectors Morris and Volker down to Interpol Headquarters in Lyon, France. Interpol Headquarters is at 200 Quai Charles de Gaulle, which sits on the Rhône River next to the beautiful Musée d'art contemporain de Lyon, Morris always found this amusing having crime and art side-by-side because at times he thought it was hard to tell one from the other.

President Kasbidi invited the inspectors into his office, "Please do sit down. I want to thank you both for responding so quickly to my request. I understand that you are the lead inspectors heading up the investigation of Le Gang de la Clé de Singe.

"There is a development, that I'm sure you are aware of, it's this Winner Take All reality television program that involves six members of Le Gang de la Clé de Singe. It seems that several countries are planning an attack on the island within the next couple of days, in an effort to capture these outlaws and arrest them under international law as terrorists and hopefully interrogate them to get them to reveal other members of Le Gang de la Clé de Singe.

"The raid will be led by the United States FBI in conjunction with a twenty-member multinational coalition of law enforcement agencies. Since you both have been working on many of these Le Gang de la Clé de Singe attacks, I thought it only fair that you both should be involved."

"Thank you, sir, we both appreciate it. It will be very rewarding to be able to hopefully capture so many of these terrorists. Usually, we may apprehend one or two and unfortunately most of the time they're there usually dead, like that fellow in Africa, a chap by the name Icarus. I'm sure you remember, sir." Inspector Morris said.

"Yes of course."

"Where and when do we meet up with the Americans, sir?" Volker asked.

"You are to travel to Andersen Air Force Base on the island of Guam. There you will rendezvous with the FBI and once everything has been arranged, you will fly to the island of Fiji before participating in the raid on Kanacea Island. Here are your orders and the files you'll need to review. Are there any questions?"

"No sir." Morris said.

"I wish you both good luck then."

"Thank you, sir." Volker said.

"Good morning ladies and gentlemen, this Buck St. John, with breaking new. It looks like both the members of Le Gang de la Clé de Singe and the members of W.A.S.P. have set off to do battle.

I'm here with retired Green Beret Three-Star General Rex O'Brian and the President of W.A.S.P. Mr. Thurston Bentley Hart the third. Welcome to you both, I'll start with Mr. Hart, how do you see your team doing stacked up against the ruthless members of Le Gang de la Clé de Singe?"

"Well Buck, we at Worldwide Affiliates of Safari Partners feel that our team is more than capable of handling these thugs in a fair fight. Sure, these terrorists are excellent when they have the home field advantage but were playing on an even playing field. My team are experts in tracking and hunting. I really think out team will prevail."

"General, your thoughts?"

"Well Buck, I feel there's a big difference between hunting big game and the killing of humans, I'll give the

W.A.S.P. team the edge if this were hunting game, but it remains to be seen how they do confronted with killing a human being."

"Well, it looks like we'll know soon enough, as you can see from our spy cams the teams are getting closer to engaging each other very shortly.

"We'll be right back with all the action right after this quick commercial break..."

Fu Hao and Sue B headed up into the jungle. If given the opportunity they always preferred to lay for the enemy in a tree instead of hiding on the ground. So, they found a good sized small-leaved fig tree.

Sue B climbed almost to the very top and positioned herself so as to have an excellent field of vision for anyone approaching from the other end of the island. Fu Hao positioned herself halfway up the tree where she felt the separation of the branches gave her the possible opportunity for a clear shot. They blended in so well that they had a hard time spotting each other within the tree. Now, it was just a matter of waiting.

Christopher Garcia and Steve Taylor were almost at the spot where Chris had stopped the night before turning around. They were cautiously moving forward, for every few steps they took forward they would stop and scan the horizon 360 degrees, it never occurred to them to look up into the trees.

Chris being an ex-Vietnam vet had had experience with Viet Cong booby traps and as they were making thru the jungle like vegetation, he spotted one of the bamboo whips.

"Hey Steve, see that, that's called a bamboo whip. You tripped that and a bamboo arm comes swinging out like a bat out of Hell, that mother will kill ya for sure. We got to be extra careful as we move forward." Chris whispered.

"Fuck me, this shit just got..." Steve never got to finish his sentence, Fu Hao had spotted Chris and Steve a couple yards before they reached the bamboo whip. She had waited to see if either of them would trip it. When neither of them did, she took Chris out, one shot to the head. Prior to firing she told Sue B what she planned on doing, "Sue, do you see the targets at 300 yards at one o'clock?"

"Roger that."

"I'm on the one wearing the Boonie Hat, you take the one with the square garden cap."

"Roger, got him."

PHIFF

The red mist from Fu Hao's shot panicked Steve. He started running erratically and firing his M16 blindly into the jungle.

SPROOONNNNGGG

He tripped one of the snare traps and caught his foot in the noose resulting in his hanging upside down, making an easy target for Sue B.

PHIFF

It seemed ironic that Steve Taylor, one of the most prominent writers for Hunter World magazine and big game hunter, who used to brag about how easy it was to catch unsuspecting prey in snare traps because animals aren't as smart as hunters, ended up seeing the world from their point of view, but only for a second.

Fu Hao and Sue B made their way down from their perch in the fig tree to dress the men where they lay with the Yellow banners. They left no notes due to the fact that the network was keeping a running commentary on both the W.A.S.P.'s and Le Gang de la Clé de Singe ideology and convictions for participating in such an event.

"Red Four and Five reporting, over." Sue B radioed in.

"Red Leader, go."
"Two down, Red Leader, over."
"Red Four and Five, nice work. Go home, over."
"Roger that."

"Wooch here."
"Wooch this is Morris, don't have much time. You were right, it's hammer time. Ciao."

"Good Afternoon ladies and gentlemen, this Buck St. John, with breaking news. You've just witnessed the first blood drawn by Le Gang de la Clé de Singe in what can only

be described as an ambush of two members of W.A.S.P. I believe them to be Christopher Garcia and ex-Marine Vietnam Vet and Steve Taylor, a big game hunter and well respected author. General O'Brian your thoughts, please?"

"Well played by the two Le Gang de la Clé de Singe members, they appear to me to be two women and I must say they are a credit to women everywhere, proving like I've always said, a woman is every bit as good a combat fighter as a man, and these ladies, I believe have proven my point."

"Mr. Thurston Bentley Hart the third, you thoughts?"

"Well Buck, sadly I have to agree with the General, but I just wonder how these women would stack up in face-to-face combat with men rather than bushwhacking them from a tree."

"Mr. Hart, I don't know if you've ever been in combat, but as a combat soldier you take any and every advantage given to you. In war there is only kill or be killed. This antediluvian, antiquated thinking and archaic glorification of war over the millenniums by ignorant people who have a heroic and grandiose vision of war and have never experienced the shock and tragedy of holding a dying friend in your arms is what keep perpetuating war.

I only hope that seeing the naked, authentic, raw images, and not the sanitized, sterilized, and Hollywood make believe version of war, will shake people to the core.

These people aren't playing dead when they get shot, they won't get up and go home after the cameras stop rolling. A large portion of Chris Garcia's head really did get blown off and Steve Taylor really is dead after being shot in the chest while hanging upside down in terror. So, I really hope the people who paid to watch this show and to see people die feel like they're getting their money's worth."

"Wow, that was a real buzz kill General. We at the Hunters Network want you folks to know that the opinions expressed by our guests aren't necessarily those of this station and our sponsors. Hey, speaking of sponsors, here's a word from Flagship Ammo..."

The Sweet Mary Jane sailed down along the coast of Queensland until they reached the port city of Mackay to stock up for the long voyage to New Caledonia across the Coral Sea.

Two days out to sea Buzz and the Doc were leisurely sailing along, they had been taking a nap while sunbathing nude on the deck, when they were awakened by a large flock of frigate birds circling above. Buzz looked off to the port side and saw what all the commotion was. A school of mahi-mahi were in hot pursuit of a glide of flying fish.

"Hey Doc, come watch this."

They sat with their legs hanging over the side with their arms leaning on the rope guardrail, naked watching the show. With the mahi-mahi chasing them, and the frigate birds above the flying fish are literally stuck between the devil and the deep blue sea. If the flying fish fly too high, they become easy prey for the frigates, if they drop back into the water too soon, they could end up being gobbled up by a mahi-mahi. It's a hard knock life for sure.

The show lasted only fifteen minutes, a couple of the flying fish landed in the cockpit and were flopping around. Buzz threw them back into the water and said, "Too bad these guys are so boney, they're not worth the hassle, man. And on top of that they're just plan bland tasting."

Unfortunately for one of the flyers, Bosco and Groucho didn't agree with Buzz and shared a meal. The Doc stood up and was heading below deck when she noticed the dorsal fin of a great white shark following behind them.

"Hey Buzz, we've got company."

"Bummer, I was in the mood for a swim."

"I'm sure he'd appreciate it."

Buzz went below and put on a pair of cut-offs. When he reappeared, she said, "Whadda get dressed for?"

"I just feel a lot more vunerable being naked around a shark."

"That's too bad babe, cause I'm feeling a bit frisky."

Buzz was out of those cut-offs and standing at attention and giving a full salute before she could even blink an eye.

"Wow, but what about the shark, lover boy?"

"What shark?"

Inspector Morris and Volker were met at Antonio B. Won Pat International Airport, Guam by FBI Special Agent Tim Simons.

"Welcome to Guam, Inspectors. I'm FBI Special Agent Tim Simons, we'll be heading over to Andersen Air Force Base from here to join the rest of the task force."

On the ride Morris asked, "Agent Simons, would you mind stopping at that Burger King, I haven't eaten all day."

"Okay, but we'll have to get it to go, everyone is waiting, you two are the last to show."

As they were waved onto the base, Morris and Volker each polished off their Whoppers, French fries and chocolate shakes. Simons drove along Arc Light Boulevard until they turned left on Vandenberg Avenue and onto the tarmac where the Boeing C-17 Globemaster was going thru its final checks. At the bottom of the ramp was U.S. Army Captain Lewis Watts standing by with his clipboard, as Agent Simon, Volker and Morris approached he asked, "You Morris and Volker?"

Morris nodded and said, "Guilty."

"Okay climb aboard, Agent Simons will see that your gear makes it on board."

Morris and Volker climbed the stairs to the main cabin, which was configured primarily for transporting cargo, not people. This was going to be anything but traveling first class. It was going to be more like steerage.

Along each bulkhead of the aircraft were fifty-five jump seats facing the cargo space across to the other fifty-five passengers facing you, and in between them were two Humvees, each equipped with a mounted 50-caliber machinegun and several boxes and cases covered with a green canvas tarp.

Morris and Volker were seated in the last two seats at the back of the aircraft nearest the lavatories. Morris took the very last seat, leaving Volker to sit next to Agent Simons. Morris leaned across Volker as the plane was taxing to the runway and asked Simons, "Hey Agent, what time do they wheel the drink cart down the aisle?"

"First time in a Globemaster, Inspector?"

"Quite right."

"No drink cart, no served meals, no blankets or pillows, and no in-flight movies, it's no frills. There are some box lunches, sodas, coffee and tea for you Brits up front if you want. They do help to break up the flight. It's a six-hour flight, a long, long six-hour flight."

"So Agent Simon, what's the plan when we Fiji?"

"There will be four Black Hawk helicopters and two CH-47F Chinooks waiting on Fiji to transport us to Kanacea Island for Operation Hellfire."

"Operation Hellfire, catchy name, don't you think Volker?"

"I say, good show."

'Say, Agent Simons just how many countries are represented?"

"Seven, the United States, Britain, France, Japan, Zimbabwe, Botswana and China. More wanted to be involved but everyone thought would be over kill. No pun intended."

"So, who's in charge?"

"That would be Brigadier General Lance Fargo, he's the one over there standing by the Humvee, with grey hair and the handlebar moustache."

"Right, you know I'm already bored. Either one of you care for a box lunch or something to drink?" Morris asked.

Simons refused but Volker said, "I'm bored too, I'll go with you."

"You sure?" Morris asked Simons.

Agent Simons raised his hand in refusal. He closed his eyes, folded his arms and slouched in his seat and proceeded to fall asleep.

Morris looked at Simons and then to Volker and said, "Crikey, I've never seen anyone drop off so deep, so fast."

The two of them made their way up to the front of the aircraft where the box lunches were stacked ten high, ten deep and thirty long. They each took three box lunches, grabbed two cans of Coke and worked their way back to their seats.

When they were in sight of Noumea, the capital of New Caledonia, Buzz headed straight for Anse Vata Bay rather than the more crowded Port Du Sud Marina.

"Why Anse Vata Bay and not Port Du Sud Marina." The Doc asked.

"I read that there's this great tapas bar called La Bodega del Mar. Thought we'd give it a try."

"Buzz, you're a nut, that's why I love ya."

"Back at ya babe."

Later that day they docked the SMJ at Ponton du Château Royal and checked into Le Méridien Noumea Resort & Spa for the night. While the Doc was in the shower, Buzz proceeded to, as it is the habit with all men, channel surf thru all the channels to see what else was on TV. When he came across the 24/7 reality show, "Winner Take All" on the Hunters Network. They were playing a compilation of the morning highlights, leading off with the slo-mo instant replay of Christopher Garcia and Steve Taylor getting killed, showing it over and over and over again.

When the Doc entered the room, her reaction was one of shock and horror. "Oh my God, what is that? Is this some sort of news program?"

"No, it's a pay-per-view reality show about one team pitted against another, and the object is to kill everyone on the other team. Can you believe that people actually pay to watch people kill each other, unbelievable man. I'm turning it off."

Just as he was hitting the off switch, he was sure he saw Todd, aka Rodin on camera. Even with his ghillie suit on, he was sure it was him. Now the cryptic text was starting to make sense.

Felipe Lopez and Dickie Davis were slinking along the shoreline until the vegetation got too thick and they had to go inland. Davis' injured leg, he suffered at Kandahar was starting to bother him, he wasn't used to trekking on such extreme terrain. So, he thought it best that he not hold up Felipe.

"You go on ahead, I won't be too far behind you, besides I feel like I'm holding you back."

"You sure?"

"Yeah. No worries."

Whereas Felipe was quite stealth making his way thru the jungle, Dickie was thrashing along, sounding like a herd of elephants on a stampede. Felipe was actually glad to be separated from Dickie, the sound machine.

Dickie's loud presence wasn't lost on the Iceman and Odin who were dressed in their ghillie suits. Odin was lying on the jungle floor, while the Iceman was up in the jungle canopy hidden high among the branches of a Yaka tree. They were so distracted by Dickie, that Filipe slid past them undetected.

Odin contacted Iceman, "Ice, I have a clear shot."

"Take the shot."

PHIFF

Felipe had made his way to be positioned slightly behind Odin and noticed the flash from his rifle as Odin killed Dickie. Felipe drew back his bow and let loose an arrow.

ZING

The arrow hit Odin in the lower left side, traveling upwards thru his body piercing his left lung and nicking the left pulmonary artery. Ice heard Odin cry out in pain and noticed a man with a bow and arrow getting ready to fire off another arrow again.

The Iceman aimed and fired one round into the top of Felipe's head.

PHIFF

The bullet travel down through his head, torso, and exited out his left thigh.

The Iceman gave a quick survey to see if there were any other targets in the area, and when he was sure there were none, he repelled down out of the tree and went to the aid of Odin, who was already dead by the time he reached him. He then went to check on the two W.A.S.P. hunters to confirm that they were both dead, and indeed they were, so he draped them with a yellow ensign.

He then radioed the rest of the Red Team, "Red Ice here, over."

"Red Leader, go." Rodin replied.

"We have a man down, Red Two is dead. Over."

"The opposition?"

"Two down, over."

"Go home, Red Ice."

The Iceman picked up the body of his fallen comrade and carried him back to base camp.

"People, may I have your attention. For those of you who don't know me, I am Brigadier General Lance Fargo. I will be leading Operation Hellfire; our objective is to capture as many members of Le Gang de la Clé de Singe alive if possible. Since there are other civilians on the island as well, we will treat everyone as a potential hostile. Do not shoot unless you have been fired upon.

Once we reach Fiji, we will transfer over to the waiting helio's for transportation to Kanacea Island. We will be landing troops on both sides of the island in two teams with Black Hawks. I cannot reiterate how important it is to try and capture these people alive. We believe some of these individuals to be high ranking members of Le Gang de la Clé de Singe and therefore have a wealth of valuable knowledge.

Are there any questions? No, then good luck men."

Minutes later, the Boeing C-17 Globemaster landed at Nadi Airport. They were directed to runway 27, then to a ramp leading to the Fiji Airways Main Hanger, where the four Black Hawk helicopters and two CH-47F Chinooks were waiting with engines running. Inspectors Morris and Volker along with Special Agent Simons were directed to one of the Black Hawks and up they went for the forty-five minute ride to Kanacea Island.

Morris turned to Volker and yelled because you couldn't even hear yourself think, "Hey Volker, you know with all this testosterone flowing around in here you'd think we were going after members of the Taliban and Bin Laden. I admit these are bad guys but, we're packing enough firepower to take down a small rogue nation. Ain't no fucking way they're going to capture anyone alive.

My guess is they'll be blasting the guys coming from the other side of the island when they meet in the middle.

I'm planning on just staying on the beach working on my tan, until this cluster-fuck is over."

"I'm with you."

"Welcome back to Winner Take All. I'm your host Buck St. John, and things are not going well for the W.A.S.P. team. Two more hunters have been killed, Richard "Dickie" Davis and Felipe Lopez, for a total of four of their team are out, leaving only Matt Jones and Jennifer Martinez. It's worth noting that Felipe Lopez was able to take one member of Le Gang de la Clé de Singe out with a spectacular shot with his bow and arrow before he, himself was killed.

"General O'Brian any thoughts?"

"Yes, unlike Le Gang de la Clé de Singe the W.A.S.P. hunters made the mistake of trying to go with teams instead of staying together as a six-man unit. There is strength in numbers, I believe that they are so used to hunting as individuals and not as a team seems to be their downfall."

"We also have in our studios Mr. Thurston Bentley Hart the third, President and CEO of Worldwide Affiliates of Safari Partners. Mr. Hart, it isn't looking good for the W.A.S.P. team, what are your thoughts?"

"Well Buck, I'm sorry to say, that I have to agree with the General. We didn't go in to this competition with the right strategy. These hunters are great hunters and trackers individually and it seems that just isn't going to be

enough to take the day. However, there have many been allegations of widespread cheating committed by Le Gang de la Clé de Singe and if that's the case, then the agreement will be null and void."

"Do you have any proof of cheating?"

"Lots of people are saying that there is cheating."

"What people?"

"Oh, there's lots of people saying it and we demand a full investigation. You know the French are notorious cheaters and colluders."

"Colluding with who?"

"I'll be calling for a full investigation of the cheating and collusion. Everyone is saying no one in the history of hunting have colluded as much as Le Gang de la Clé de Singe."

"Mr. Hart, do you have any proof of either cheating or collusion?" St. John demanded.

"Collusion!"

"Mr. Hart, if it's shown that there was no cheating or collusion and if your team loses, are you and your members still committed to cancel all big game hunting worldwide; will you still honor that agreement?"

"We'll have to wait and see about the cheating and collusion, Buck. They're cheaters."

"Okay then, let's return to all the action on Winner Take All...."

Buzz threaded the many small islands that make up Fiji and weighed anchor off the small island of Naitauba, seemingly in the middle of nowhere, but they dropped anchor at the exact coordinates that Rodin had sent to Buzz in the text: *-17.079902, -179.23494.*

To pass the time Buzz threw a fishing line over the side and plopped down with legs over the stern.

"Buzz, any idea what we're waiting for?"

"Not a clue, man. But Rodin said this is the place and the date. Hey, Doc would you mind grabbing us a couple of beers?"

Soon after the Doc went below deck Buzz saw a formation of military helicopters off in the distance heading in their direction, "Hey Doc, come here, you gotta see this." He shouted.

See reappeared with two beers and a bag of chips, closely followed by Bosco and Groucho. "What's up?"

"Look over there, helicopters." He said pointing to the west.

"Wonder if that has anything to do with us being here?"

"Oh man I hope not. Anything military is never a good thing, man."

The group of six helicopters passed over Yacata Island far to the Sweet Mary Jane's south and did a lazy sweeping arc towards the island of Kanacea.

Buzz looked at the Doc and said, "That's not good."

"Hey, it could be a rescue mission, Buzz. Keep a good thought."

"Maybe, but I didn't see any red crosses on any of those choppers."

"Wanna go see?"

"No fucking way, man. I've spent my life avoiding having anything to do with the army. Think we'll just sit tight. Hey, what kinda chips do we got?"

"Sweet Maui Onion."

"Far out man, Bosco and Groucho's favorite."

The Iceman brought the body of Odin back to camp where Isala and Buster were waiting with Sue B and Fu Hao. Iceman placed Odin's down respectfully, mumbled a few words over him and then looked to the team and said, "Ready?"

Isala handed everyone a different map of where cameras were located, "Make sure you disable them all, we don't have much time, so let's rock and roll. And stay in constant contact and keep your eyes out for the last two wasp's."

One by one all of the cameras that covered their end of the island were being knocked out of commission, driving the folks at Hunter Television crazy. They improvised and concentrated on the cameras that were following the W.A.S.P. hunters and the lone Le Gang de la Clé de Singe figure. It appeared that they would be crossing paths any minute.

Rodin spotted the two WASPS first, he laid down in a clump of Arthropteris repen, a common fern found throughout the island, very thick and excellent for cover. He was setting up his shot when he heard a slight rustling from behind, he slowly turn to see Buster slinking towards him barely making a sound.

Rodin whispered, "Good boy. Down."

Buster did as he was commanded, he lay next to his master. Rodin lined up his shot at a clearing that he knew the two hunters would head towards, it was the path of least resistance, the path you should never take in combat.

Matt Jones was very adept and astute in street and desert fighting, having fought in Iran in Mosul, Fallujah, and Ramadi, but jungle fighting is a different ball game, and this was Rodin's ballpark.

Matt Jones held a giant Balaka macrocarpa palm leaf so Jennifer could pass and wouldn't get hit in the face if he had let it go. Chivalry may not be dead, but Matt Jones is. As soon as Jennifer passed Matt, Rodin fired hitting Matt in the thorax, not a true kill shot, but good enough.

PHIFF

Matt had turned slightly to let Jennifer pass and the bullet just missed his heart by millimeters. Matt laid on the ground slowly dying, much like most of the big game he hunted.

Jennifer swung around firing her AK-15 indiscriminately in all directions until she emptied her clip. As she was fumbling to reload, Rodin gave the command to Buster, "Attack."

Buster bound thru the jungle brush zigging and zagging as he had been taught, until he was within five feet of his target, then he sprang up aiming for the victims' neck. Jennifer was trying so hard to concentrate on getting the loaded magazine into the rifle, she barley heard death racing towards her at literally breakneck speed.

By the time Rodin reached Jennifer both she and Matt were dead. Matt had succumbed to his chest wound and Jennifer from Buster hitting her at such great force that he broke her neck.

"Buster. Release." Rodin commanded.

Buster released his grip on her neck and walked along side of his master back to camp.

While the Red Team was battling it out in the South Pacific on the "Winner Take All" reality television show, Sassoon, T-Bone, Vulcan, and Gianfranco were heading off to Limpopo, South Africa where rumors of poachers poisoning five lions and then chopping off their faces and paws to sell to trophy collectors and African tribal medicine men for use in black magic spells.

Vulcan and the others flew into Pretoria and drove the two hundred miles to Limpopo where they met their local contact Nelson Khumalo, a security guard at Kruger National Park. According to Khumalo, the lion killings was the act of a small rogue sect of the Zulu tribe that have broken away from the traditional beliefs and have moved to worshiping the ways of black magic and the dogma of the dark side. They are a small roving band of forty, both men and women.

The tribal medicine man and three of his assistants are believed to be the ones who committed this killing and poaching.

One of Nelson Khumalo's informants had told him that the poachers are hiding out in the Maremani Nature Reserve, somewhere along the Limpopo River, which separates South Africa and Zimbabwe. Maremani Nature Reserve is considered a tropical savannah. It is mostly arid with scruffy vegetation and occasional patches of Baobab, Syringa and Fever trees.

After they had set up camp between the Dongola Ranch and the Klein Bolayi Game Lodge, both located off highway R572, T-Bone sent up a Ghostdrone to see if they could track down the poachers.

It only took them less than an hour to spot the campsite of the four poachers. They were camped about a quarter mile from the Border Posts - Beit Bridge along the Limpopo River.

Vulcan's plan was to make their way on the R572 heading south until they intersect Route 1 going north towards the Beit Bridge. When they are about a mile from the bridge, they would go off-roading east along the river until they come across the poacher's camp.

Khumalo figured that they would reach the poacher's camp sometime after 3am. By then they should all be either asleep, drunk, or passed out, either way there would be no real resistance. Khumalo was right, they found the four passed out, surrounded by empty bottles of Three Ships Select Whiskey. Their campfire was almost out, so Gianfranco and Sassoon piled on more and more firewood to bring the fire blazing back to life. As they added more wood to the fire the flames stretched several feet up towards the sky illuminating the camp with a bright warm glow. But it was the enormous amount of heat the fire generated that actually brought the inebriated felons to consciousness.

"Ungubani?" The Zulu medicine man asked belligerently.

"He asks who we are." Khumalo translated.

Vulcan said, "Tell him we are the avengers of lions."

"Abagibeli bezingonyama." Khumalo said.

The medicine man staggered to his feet as did the other three men. He reached into a bag that hung on his shoulder and pulled out one of the lion's paws that they had cut off. He held it out to Vulcan and started to chant "Kapilayyo!"

The three other men answered, "Jee!"

"Kapilayyo!"

"Jee!"

"Watinahaa!"

"Haa!"

Khumalo turned to Vulcan, "It's a war chat."

Vulcan held up the yellow banner of Le Gang de la Clé de Singe and said, "Ask them if they know what this is."

"Uyazi Lokhu." Asked Khumalo.

"Cha."

"No, he doesn't."

"Tell him it's the angel of death."

"Yingelosi yokufa."

The medicine man and the others stood side by side, they each held up a lion's paw defiantly gathering courage, then the medicine man yelled, "Bulala!"

As they started to charge, Vulcan, T-Bone, Sassoon and Gianfranco all raised their pistols and fired in unison.

POP POP POP POP

All four lay dead where they once stood.

The South African Police Service received an anonymous phone call stating that they will find the people responsible for the mutilation of the lions a quarter mile east of the Border Posts - Beit Bridge.

When they arrived, the SAPS found the bodies of four men with Le Gang de la Clé de Singe flags around their necks. The severed paws and mutilated faces of the lions in a bag lying beside the medicine man. They also found that the poachers were all missing their faces and hands and one single fingerprint, other than the four deceased, on one of the whiskey bottles.

Inspector Verwoerd of the South African Police Service, who headed up the investigation was informed it belonged to Louis Botha, the Boer War General who captured Winston Churchill during the Second Boer War.

Inspector Verwoerd had but one thing to say, "Fok me."

"Well, I must say Le Gang de la Clé de Singe has certainly made short order of the W.A.S.P. team. Wow, I didn't see that dog coming and I guess either did Jennifer.

"General O'Brian your thoughts?"

"Well Buck, in my thirty-five career in the U.S. Army, I have to say that was one of the cleanest operations by any unit I've seen. Le Gang de la Clé de Singe were masterful.

When compared to Le Gang de la Clé de Singe the W.A.S.P. team of hunters were so ill-matched, especially when it came to military tactics. If it had been me Buck, I would never have matched those hunters against Le Gang de la Clé de Singe fighters. I don't know what Mr. Hart and the people of the Worldwide Affiliates of Safari Partners were thinking."

"Mr. Hart would you care to comment?"

"Collusion, Buck. Everyone says there has been rampant cheating and collusion. I want to lock them up, every single one of them."

The General chuckled and said, "Yeah, good luck with that."

"We've got breaking news, this just in, it seems that there are reports of an international task force approaching Kanacea Island in an effort to arrest the members of Le Gang de la Clé de Singe. They are rumored to be armed and willing to use lethal force if necessary.

Ladies and gentlemen, this is an unexpected bonus for all you pay-per-viewers, and we do apologize for the technical difficulties that we are experiencing with some of our cameras. But this should be and could be a wild finish to the already fantastic Winner Take All.

Let's cut to a quick word from one of our sponsors before the exciting conclusion of WTA. Friends, do suffer from hemorrhoids? Then you need…"

Rodin and Buster entered the camp to find the team ready to evacuate, Rodin quickly changed into his wetsuit and slipped on his Poseidon Se7en Rebreather, fins and mask.

The Iceman gave the order for Fu Hao to ignite the pile of equipment and gear that they had brought onto the island. To make sure everything would be destroyed, they had mixed in amongst all the items thousands of metallic magnesium chips, which burns at over 2000 degrees and is almost impossible to extinguish, guaranteeing that no traceable evidence would be left.

Isala set in motion what the team hoped would give them the escape advantage they would need. She had programmed a drone swarm of ten thousand drones that when released. would emit colored smoke and produce flashing colored lights. The swarms were divided into four groups of 2500 drones each; each group had been programmed to perform individual choreographed aerial maneuvers. When viewed from below the swarms would display a magnificent light and colored cloud extravaganza, but from the air the swarms would look chaotic, disorganized, dangerous, and distracting, forcing the helicopters to alter their landing plans. Along with the smoke generated from the magnesium fire there was no way they were going to be able to land on the beach, rather they would have to land more inland or on the eastern side of the island.

As the helicopters moved in, the Red Team entered the water and swam underwater north for a mile where they recovered five of the six ROTINOR military diver propulsion vehicles, also known as underwater scooters. Since they were using rebreathers instead of diving tanks there would be no taletell air bubbles to give away their position.

They did bring the body of their fallen brother Odin, which they buried at sea. The only one they had to leave behind was Buster. Before they evacuated the island Rodin gave Buster the order to 'evade and hide', in the hope that after things cooled down, he would be able to come back and retrieve him. Rodin had researched the wildlife on the island, and it turned out that there were Birds, reptiles, insects, chickens, and goats. Buster would be well fed until he returned.

Buzz and the Doc had just finished setting up their boom tent. A boom tent is a cockpit awning that utilizes the mainsail to create a sheltered area over the companionway that extends over the cockpit. The one that sheltered the Sweet Mary Jane was a little more unique as theirs extended over the starboard side for six feet.

Completed, Buzz and the Doc were going down below to make lunch when Doc noticed the commotion happening in the sky over the island to the south of them.

"Hey Buzz, look over there towards that island, it looks like a light show."

"Oh wow man, it's like I'm tripping, man. Wish I had some weed."

The aerial show lasted for over two hours. When it was over the six helicopters that flew past them earlier in a tight formation were now flying spread out, each one going off in different directions.

One of the Black Hawks flew over the SMJ then returned and began to hover over the Sweet Mary Jane when a man in a wetsuit jumped into the water next to the hull on the port side from forty feet above and climbed aboard.

The helicopter remained hovering over the sailboat as the diver approached Buzz and the Doc.

"What are you doing in these waters?" The diver asked.

"We're on our way to Hawaii. Who the fuck are you, man?"

"Are you two the only ones on board?"

"We were until you dropped in. Who the fuck are you, man?"

"Mind if I look around?"

"Again, who the fuck are you, man?"

The man finally flashed a badge, "I'm FBI Special Agent Simons, were looking for a group of international terrorists."

"No shit, man. Sure, go ahead and look around if you want, just watch out for my two ferrets, man."

"That's an interesting boom tent, I've never seen one that extends over the side before."

Buzz smiled, "It was her idea. We like to sit in tubes and chill out sometimes, but you know too much sun is a bad thing. So, we like got it made in the shade, man. "

"Smart."

As Special Agent Simons searched below, Buzz and the Doc took pictures of the people in the helicopter taking pictures of them. After Buzz took a couple pictures he quickly turned around and dropped his cutoffs and mooned everyone.

The FBI man reappeared from below, jumped overboard, gave a hand signal to the chopper above which lowered a rescue basket that he climbed into and was raised back up to the helicopter.

As Agent Simons was being hoisted Buzz yelled, "Ya'll come back now, ya hear!"

When the swarm of ten thousand multi-colored drones suddenly shot straight up and started to gyrate unpredictably, releasing colored smoke and flashing colors the helicopters took evasive action to avoid possible collision with the drones.

They were also hampered from the enormous amount of smoke that was generated by the magnesium fire making landing and even hovering above that particular beach area impossible, so they looked for another place to set down. Morris and Volker were on the Black Hawk designated to land on the W.A.S.P. side of the island, so the swarm of drones didn't affect them, although they did get to enjoy the show from afar.

Once on the ground, while others were running around looking for members of Le Gang de la Clé de Singe and not finding any, only the bodies of W.A.S.P. hunters, the two Interpol Inspectors were chilling out on a couple beach chairs that they found.

After a couple of hours, a captain in the U.S. Army approached them, "Brigadier General Fargo would like to see you two. Follow me."

They did as they were told, they followed the captain to an open area where the bodies of the W.A.S.P. hunters were all laid out side by side and covered with army green tarps.

The captain smartly saluted the general and reported, "Here they are, sir."

"Thank you, captain, that's all."

"Yes sir."

"I understand that you two are Inspectors with Interpol is that correct?"

"It is." Morris replied.

"And that you're some kind of experts on these terrorists."

"Well, I don't know about experts, but we have been working on just about all the cases."

"What can you tell me about them?"

"Well, they're extremely professional, disciplined and they're always prepared for the unexpected. Just like today, how many outfits that you know of would have had the forethought and insight to anticipate the possibility of an air strike, I'm sure they had a contingency plan if you had decided to come in by sea or even if you had tried to attacked from both. They're the best of the best, and I'll bet you dollars to donuts that you'll find only one fingerprint that doesn't belong to any of these poor fools."

"Yeah, what's with that whole fingerprint thing, anyway?"

"Not sure, but my best guess is it's stick in the eye, a big fuck you."

Volker said, "I can tell you right now General, you're not going to catch them, they're long gone."

As they were chatting a CSI came running up, "Pardon me sir, but we just found a great fingerprint. I'll send it in asap."

"You do that son, you do that."

As everyone was evacuating the island, the General texted Morris and Volker, "*Fingerprint identified... Thurston Bentley Hart the third, President and CEO of Worldwide Affiliates of Safari Partners.*"

Morris looked at Volker and said, "Damn. Those guys are good."

An hour after Special Agent Simons boarded the SMJ, five heads popped up from below the surface of the water off the starboard side. Rodin swam to the ladder Buzz had hanging over the side, climbed on board and proceeded to remove his diving gear. He shouted out, "Ahoy there, permission to come aboard."

A voice from below shouted, "Permission granted, man."

Buzz and Rodin gave each other a huge bear hug. Buzz said smiling, "It's great to see you again, I suppose those heads bobbing off the starboard side are with you?"

"They are."

"Well stop fucking around and get everybody on board."

Rodin leaned over the side and signaled for them to come aboard. The Doc appeared from below and stood next to Buzz.

"Hey man, I want you to meet my special lady friend, Doctor Laura Runnel. Doc this is my oldest best buddy, Rodin."

"Pleased to meet you Doctor, I can't tell you how grateful me and my team are that you would endanger yourself to help us."

She shook his hand and said, "My pleasure, we're glad to help."

Once the Red Team was all on board Rodin introduced them to Buzz and Doc Runnel. Buzz thought it best that they all head down below to avoid the chance of being spotted.

Buzz and the Doc made lunch for everyone, tuna sandwiches, Cheetos and ice cold beer. Bosco and Groucho made an appearance to check out the strangers, but mostly to beg for food.

"I made the boom tent extend over the side just in case the man has a drone up above spying down on us, so I recommend you guys stay under the tent or down here until we reach where we're going. By the way, man where are we going?" Buzz asked.

Rodin took a sip of beer and said, "I must say, smart thinking with the boom tent, Buzz. I'm sure you're right about the drones, right Isala ?"

"Right, that's why I made the drone swarms extend out over the water far enough to give us cover until we got into deeper water."

"Far out man, so I'm not paranoid after all."

Rodin laughed, "Like Joseph Heller once said, "Just because you're paranoid doesn't mean they aren't after you."

Buzz looked at the Doc and said, in a I told ya so tone, "See."

"Well, that's debatable." She said, and then asked Rodin, "So where are we off to?"

"Kiribati. It's an island republic a little over 2000 miles from here, and since you told the Feds you were heading to Hawaii, this isn't out of your way, if they are tracking you."

"Why Kiribati, man?"

"They are one of the only governments that doesn't recognize Le Gang de la Clé de Singe as an outlaw organization. They provide a safe port for the ships we use to fight the Japanese whalers in the Antarctic. So, once we land there Le Gang de la Clé de Singe will send a charter flight that will take us to our next mission."

"Where's that, man?"

"Sorry Buzz can't tell you, it's more for your protection. The less you guys know the better."

Roger Blumenthal, President and CEO of the Hunting Network along with Thurston Bentley Hart III, President of W.A.S.P. and retired SEAL Commander William "Wooch" Brown were having a meeting with Brigadier General Lance Fargo at his office to discuss the complete and utter failure of Operation Hellfire.

The General sat at the head of the conference table, his hands were folded in front of him, his head was down, he seemed to be concentrating on what he was going to say.

When he raised his head, he looked at the three men and said, "Gentlemen, I've been asked by the international community to see if any of you might be able to help shed any light on how it was possible that Le Gang de la Clé de Singe had knowledge that there would be a raid on Kanacea Island.

"Mr. Hart, I understand that you've accused the Hunting Network, or Commander Brown to be in cahoots with Le Gang de la Clé de Singe, is that right Mr. Hart? Because if you have any evidence of collusion I would like to know, you see the international community and the United

States Army have spent a lot of time, effort, planning, and money in trying to capture these terrorists, so if you know something, I want to hear it."

"No, I never said it was Blumenthal or Commander Brown, I just felt that Le Gang de la Clé de Singe made such easy work of these world-class hunters that it seemed to me that the fix was in."

"Well, it's my understanding that there were only three people who knew all of the details of the where, the when and the how, isn't that right Mr. Blumenthal."

"That's right General, me and Wooch were the only two, aside from Hart who had total access to all the details. So if there were to be any cheating or collusion it would have to be one of us three."

"Wooch, your thoughts?"

"Well, General as you know war is a dirty business and unfair, but it's my opinion that when Mr. Hart pitted hunters against soldiers, he was sending them to their deaths. I'm sorry Thurston, but it was the case of the better and more experienced people winning. Maybe if you had wanted to have the show be about who were the best hunters, things might have turned out differently. Your people thought like hunters, Le Gang de la Clé de Singe's people thought like soldiers. That was the difference, they knew the opposition better than your people did."

"Unless you know of anything further Mr. Hart, I'm afraid I must agree with Commander Brown, there doesn't seem to be any proof of cheating or collusion. I had an Inspector from Interpol, who has been assigned and has investigated just about every incident pertaining to Le Gang de la Clé de Singe, and it is opinion that they're just that good. And from what I've seen, they are. Well, I want to thank you all for your time."

As the three men were leaving Wooch turned back to General Fargo and said, "Maybe next time Lance."

"Yeah, maybe. See you around Wooch, don't be a stranger."

"Ciao."

"Good evening everyone this is Josh Colman, CNN News. We have breaking news. Today an international law enforcement team led by Brigadier General Lance Fargo led a raid on the island of Kanacea, just off the main island of Fiji.

The island was where an unorthodox reality show was being filmed. The Hunting Network sponsored a pay-per-view show called Winner Take All, where the object of the show was two opposing forces engaged in mortal combat. The two so-called teams were made up from six members of the Worldwide Affiliates of Safari Partners, better known as W.A.S.P. and six members of Le Gang de la Clé de Singe, the international eco-terrorist group.

CNN has learned that the ultimate prize, if the W.A.S.P. were to win, would be that Le Gang de la Clé de Singe would not attack big game hunters and would concentrate on poachers and those who deal in illegal endangered species good. But if Le Gang de la Clé de Singe won the hunters would stop the killing of the big game and contribute one hundred million dollars to anti-poaching charities.

Well it appears that Le Gang de la Clé de Singe has won the contest, if you will, killing all six members of W.A.S.P. Shortly after the last of the W.A.S.P. member was killed, the law enforcement team led by Brigadier General Lance Fargo, who's assignment was to kill or capture the six members of Le Gang de la Clé de Singe and bring them to justice. However it has now been confirmed that all six Le Gang de la Clé de Singe members have escaped.

When asked to comment, the spokesperson for the Army had no comment. So, the search continues for these international outlaws as attacks and raids continue around the world. Why just yesterday there was a report from South Africa that four lion poachers were killed and their bodies mutilated in the manner that the poachers had done to four lions earlier in the week, and they too have escaped.

We'll be right back with our panel of experts, Lloyd Townsend, notable zoologist, Jackson Noel, Ethologist and CNN contributor and retired SEAL Commander William Brown, after this short break..."

While the Red Team were catching up on some much needed sleep after three days of deadly war games below deck, Buzz and Rodin watched the setting sun turn the western sky fire red as they sat in the cockpit drinking a beer. The Doc and Isala were laying with their backs against the forward hatch on the bow having a cup of tea enjoying the summer breeze as they sailed towards Kiribati Island.

"So Buzz, what's next?" Rodin asked.

"I don't know man, right now just getting you guys somewhere safe. How about you man?"

"Well, after my next mission, I'm going to try and get Buster, my dog off Kanacea Island. He's a tough old pooch. He'll be able to survive until I can get back to him. It's a private island, so he shouldn't have to worry about some fool thinking he's vicious or mean. He's only aggressive if I give him the command, otherwise he's a sweetheart."

"Who owns the island?"

"Actually, I hear it's up for sale. I think they're asking twenty-six million for it."

"Does it have anything on it, or is it just a deserted Island?"

"Naw, it's over three thousand acres, it has a nice coconut and sugarcane plantation, a bunch of freshwater streams, a large lagoon with a boat opening and it even has great cell phone signals across the island."

"And they're asking twenty-six million for it."

"Yeah."

"Twenty-six million, Hell, I'll buy it, man."

"Right." Rodin said sarcastically.

"You thinking I'm joking? I'm loaded, I inherited over seven billion dollars when my folks passed away."

"Billion with a B?"

"Pretty cool, huh man?"

"Buzz, you're wearing that exact same fucking Rolling Stones tee shirt that you wore in 1976, except for this boat you've got all the same shit."

"Yeah, well it pays to buy quality, man. Besides it's just stuff and I don't need more stuff."

"You're telling me for real that you're worth seven billion dollars?"

"Yeah." Buzz picks up his satellite phone and dials.

"Hello Reggie, Buzz here. Hey what's happening man? Yeah, I'm doing great, just sailing around the Pacific with my special lady friend. Say Reggie, just wondering what am I worth these days?" Buzz holds the phone out so Rodin can hear.

"Buzz, your net worth is 8.4 billion dollars as of yesterday morning."

Rodin's jaw drops. Buzz brings the phone back to his ear and says, "Listen Reggie, I want you to do me a favor, I want you to purchase the island of Kanacea. Yeah, island. It's near Fiji, I hear it's going for twenty-six mill. See what you can do by offering them cash, and call me back and let me know how it goes, okay? Hey, I love ya, man. Thanks, brother."

"Un-fucking-believable."

"Hey man, we got to get you and Buster back together, right?"

"Buzz you're a crazy, man."

The Doc and Isala were walking back to where Buzz and Rodin were, Doc was heading to go down below to the galley for another couple cups of tea, "You boys want another beer?" Isala asked.

Rodin looked at Buzz and softly asked, "Does she know?"

"Know what?" Asked the Doc.

"Hey Doc, did I ever tell you I was filthy stinking rich?"

"No, you never did."

"Well, I am."

"That's nice, so do you boys want another beer?"

Buzz nodded yes, Doc and Isala each grabbed an empty bottle of Fiji Taki Beer and went below. As the two friends sat looking up at the billions and billions of stars that were starting to shine above them, Buzz's satellite phone rang, "Buzz here, Hey Wooch, what's happening, man?"

THE END
the revolution continues in
Wounding of the Beast

M. Ward Leon – the Author

M Ward Leon is a former advertising creative director who started his career at Doyle Dane Bernbach, New York, during the Madmen era. While at DDB his writing on the Volkswagen Rabbit campaign won him inclusion into the Smithsonian Institution Advertising Archives. Recently his writings has earned him two Emmy Awards for Public Service advertising.

He is a graduate of California State University Los Angeles and an alumnus of Art Center College of Design.

Other books by M Ward Leon: _Blood of the Beast_ • _The Strange and Curious Cases of Roscoe Brown, Detective NYPD_ • _Revenge of the Beast_ •

www.ingramcontent.com/pod-product-compliance
Lightning Source LLC
Chambersburg PA
CBHW061347190726
48288CB00005B/1635